By Christy Kenneally and published by Hachette Books Ireland

Second Son
The Remnant
Tears of God

Coming Soon ...

Sons of Cain
The second book in the epic trilogy by Christy Kenneally

THE BETRAYED

CHRISTY KENNEALLY

HACHETTE
BOOKS
IRELAND

First published in 2011 by Hachette Books Ireland
First published in paperback in 2012 by Hachette Books Ireland.

1

A CIP catalogue record for this title is available from the British Library.

ISBN 978 0 340 96171 1

Typeset in Bembo by Hachette Books Ireland.
Printed and bound by CPI Group (UK) Ltd, Croydon, CR0 4YY

Hachette Books Ireland policy is to use papers that are natural, renewable and
recyclable products and made from wood grown in sustainable forests. The
logging and manufacturing processes are expected to conform to the
environmental regulations of the country of origin.

Hachette Books Ireland
8 Castlecourt Centre, Castleknock, Dublin 15, Ireland

A division of Hachette UK
338 Euston Road, London NW1 3BH

BOOK ONE

Simon Tauber wiped the blackboard clean, folded the cloth carefully, and placed it on his desk. Tiny flecks of white danced in the beam of light from the classroom window and he inhaled their smell. It was a good smell, he thought, a smell that permeated his clothes which, during the long evenings, reminded him of the classroom. He would store it in his memory, along with the smell of the fresh ink he poured into the tiny ceramic cups at the top-right corner of the desks every morning; the smell of weathered desks, pencil shavings and the ashes still warm in the stove. Every morning, he turned the key in the lock and stepped into this space. His students came at eight thirty, some dewy-eyed, fresh from sleep, smelling of carbolic soap. Others smelled of the cows they had milked earlier. Karl, the carpenter's boy, had a piny whiff of wood-shavings from his father's workshop. Even with his back turned, the teacher could identify them by their smell; his students, the boys and girls who shuffled into desks, flipped the flaps of their satchels, set their books and copybooks in neat piles and looked expectantly at him.

'Good morning,' he said.

'Good morning, sir,' they chorused.

His eyes ranged across their faces. Karl was bright-eyed and attentive as ever, his books sorted, his pens aligned; a workman standing ready with his tools for the day. What a solid student he would make, in time and with the right teacher. Elsa, the miner's daughter who sat beside him, was chaos to his calm. Already, she was digging in a shapeless bag for the things that eluded and frustrated her. He had no doubt that the brilliant and undisciplined Elsa would plough a significant academic furrow, if she could be brought to focus. And Max? Ah, Max, the policeman's son; the third member of the bright triumvirate. No, triumvirate was the wrong word – it implied three men. Trio then? Yes, accurate and gender neutral, but it didn't really do them justice. They did reign over the others, in terms of intellectual ability. Max could even qualify as their pole-star. The boy was a polymath – excelling across a range of subjects, but he was such an arrogant shit. Simon Tauber closed his eyes and asked God's forgiveness for his uncharacteristic cruelty. 'I am not myself, today, Lord,' he reminded his Maker. 'I know a good teacher would never put such a label on a child – but...?' And there, his prayer ended. He knew that a man who was truly penitent could never 'but' before God. But his rational mind insisted there was something in Max that tainted his brilliance and when Karl and Elsa conferred on a task, there was something in his face. Perhaps it was just a longing to be part of their unconscious closeness. But?

To distract himself, the teacher let his attention move among the others. Apart from Elsa, he surmised, most of the girls would leave school at the earliest possible opportunity to work on the family farm or in the village, until they married. Why not? he argued with himself; it will be a good life for them, here in Hallstatt. And yet his heart protested against the inevitability of it. His heart sank further as he assessed the boys. How they hankered after war, he despaired. Have their fathers no memories? Who could remember the Somme or Passchendaele and not bar the recruiting sergeant from the door? Why do the young insist on drawing Death's attention, like children edging to the centre of the frozen lake where the ice is thinnest? Suddenly, a burst of sunlight defied his mood, and the dusty classroom window, to flood their faces. As one, they turned to it, like sunflowers. Only he could see their shadows stretching long and black behind them. 'Carpe diem,' seize the day, his heart urged but his tongue caught and swallowed it. Small children inhabit and are possessed by the present, he knew.

These young men and women existed only in the present moment, but it was the future that occupied them. It is only the old who appreciate the preciousness of each passing moment and, by then, it is too late. He had read somewhere that if mothers truly remembered the pains of childbirth, they would never give birth to another child. Amnesia, he concluded, is the real recruiting sergeant. It dulls the agony of the man-boy blown to bits or crucified on the wire. And so, it urges us to put up monuments; huge slabs of stone to suppress the real memories. We cast the dead in heroic bronze to transform the terrible into something more palatable in the short term, and more seductive to the next generation. Let's not forget the shame, he prompted himself. What happens to those who lose a war; those who barter a generation of golden sons for the dross of defeat? Shame, he thought, is the anger that sours and eats the soul. It is such a small step from 'shame' to 'blame' and then a nation and every house within it divides against itself, and those whose words fall like sparks on that dry tinder blaze to prominence and power. And what of those whose faces do not fit – whose faith has made them, even marginally, separate and therefore suspect and …? He was surprised at the sheen of sweat on his forehead. I am afraid, he thought and let that shuddering realisation run through him. I have fallen under the shadow of the Chinese curse and have 'come to the attention of the authorities'.

The policeman had come before dawn. The teacher had asked him inside because invitation lessens the sting of intrusion and he had treated him with all the courtesy he would have extended to any neighbour. The policeman had been his neighbour before his duty brought him in another guise. They had sat across the kitchen table from each other, Tauber in his dressing gown and slippers, trying to ignore the feeling of nakedness that chilled his bare ankles. The policeman had asked for his papers in a formal language that marked and measured the distance between them. With trembling hands, he had unearthed his papers from the drawer in the kitchen table; tugging them free of the bric-a-brac that seemed to protest their leaving. The policeman's lips moved as he read and the teacher wondered if he was aware of that.

'Everything in order?'

He asked the question to relieve the tension that was becoming an ache in his belly.

'I'm afraid not, Herr Tauber. Your wife … your late wife … was a Roman Catholic, according to her papers.'

'Yes, yes, of course, she was baptised here in Hallstatt.'

The policeman nodded. 'But you, Herr Tauber ...' He paused and picked up a page as if to re-read something, but his lips did not move.

'I was born Jewish, in Vienna. It's all there; including my conversion and baptism into the Roman Catholic Church before our marriage.'

'Ah,' the policeman grunted.

Simon Tauber knew he should let the silence stretch. Even a rural schoolteacher knew how filling silences revealed more than you intended, but his fear overrode his good sense.

'This all happened some years ago, so, you see, the new laws concerning Jews converting to Christianity do not apply to me.'

The policeman brought the page a little closer to his eyes.

'Herr Steiger, the current laws apply only to those who have recently converted,' he said, as if explaining some crystal clear fact to a particularly dense student.

'And why do you think that is so, Herr Tauber?'

'Why? I suppose ... of course, I am not a legal person but, I surm— ... imagine it is to prevent Jews from evading the law in some way ... by converting, that is.'

'But, the motive, Herr Tauber,' the policeman said, placing the page on the table before him, 'the motive, then or now, could be the same.'

'If you will check with Father Kyril—'

'I have spoken to Father Kyril. He cannot, in conscience, vouch for your motives. There is room for doubt, Herr Tauber,' he concluded, tapping the side of his nose with his forefinger as if considering a complex legal problem.

For a moment, Tauber was at a loss. His papers were in order. This nit-picking over motives was ... Ah! He leaned back in his chair as he realised his error. He had forgotten the rules of the game. It was a simple game played in every walk of life. It had other names, of course, like 'observing the proprieties', but it all boiled down to the same game. According to the rules of the game, the shopper greeted the butcher, formally and respectfully, before they both proceeded to the transaction. The priest was asked if he could provide a baptism certificate, as a favour, even though it was a right and he had a duty to provide it. Herr Steiger, according to bierkeller gossip, was a man of small ability and enormous self-importance. Tauber had heard him referred to as 'the little corporal', and he idly wondered, in his teacher's way, if the reference was to Napoleon or Hitler. In his innocence, he had asked his wife and, he remembered, she'd looked at him with a mixture of exasperation and affection. 'Not Hitler,' she'd said definitively. 'Herr Steiger has Hitler at home.' When she was sure he had digested this, she had continued to warn him of the importance of 'staying out of his way'. This most Christian of women was wiser in the ways of the real world than the learned Simon Tauber. Essentially, she had cautioned him to observe the rules of the game. He leaned forward and bowed his head. When he spoke, his voice was deferential and subdued.

'Surely,' he began, 'a man in your position is empowered to exercise a degree of ... discretion in such matters?'

He watched the muscles of the policeman's jaw relax. The game had begun.

'Of course, of course,' he huffed. 'My superiors in Vienna leave many matters to my discretion, but ...'

The teacher dropped his voice to little above a whisper.

'Of course', he concurred. 'They rely on you to do what is best for the community under your protection. I'm sure this is yet another burden you carry, along with all your other duties. I hope the community appreciates that.'

The policeman pursed his lips and nodded solemnly. 'Some do,' he granted.

'I would like to consider myself among them,' Simon Tauber said. 'I am sure you and I can come to an accommodation that would satisfy the law and all parties concerned.'

The policeman nodded again, stretched his legs and stood. 'Perhaps, you're right, Herr Tauber,' he said. 'Such things are best kept local; between people who know and understand each other. Yes, leave it with me. I'm sure we can arrive at an accommodation.' He scooped the papers from the table. 'Until tonight, Herr Tauber.'

Simon Tauber broke from his reverie and looked through the schoolhouse window at the lake. He had scraped together every schilling he could find and hoped it would be enough of an accommodation for the policeman, who was coming again that evening. And perhaps some night next week, Tauber mused bitterly, as 'complications' arose. This was a game he could not win. At best, he could only hope to limit his losses.

'Herr Tauber?'

'What?'

He realised his students had been waiting.

'I'm sorry,' he said. 'I'm afraid I … I was somewhere else. No doubt you would also like to be somewhere else as well.' They smiled dutifully. 'I've been looking out over the lake and thinking how lucky I've been. I came here to Hallstatt as a substitute teacher and found my wife. She knew more about the history of Hallstatt than any historian. We walked a lot; I was younger then. Naturally, we explored the mines, as I'm sure you have.' He looked at them and added mischievously, 'We didn't need our parents' permission.'

Some of the students smiled while a few dropped their eyes self-consciously.

'And we walked in the Dachstein Mountains,' he continued, 'but our walks always ended at the lake. She told me how our Celtic ancestors threw offerings in the water because they thought God lived there. Sometimes, I allowed myself to become distracted by … by really important things like correcting essays.'

They laughed at this while he strolled to the window.

'When you're young, it's so easy to become distracted from what matters,' he said quietly. He lifted his eyes to the white crests of the mountains. 'Whatever happiness I have known since … I have known here with you and I thank you.'

He turned and looked at them.

'It is much too nice a day for you to sit here listening to me ramble. Go, go for a walk,' he said, flapping his hand at them. 'Adam and Eve did not know they lived in Paradise until it was lost to them.'

*

Simon Tauber stood in the centre of his kitchen and concluded that it was as clean as a man could make it. He padded into the bathroom and shaved, carefully, avoiding his eyes in the mirror. He dressed in his best, dark suit and tied a cravat under his stiff, white collar. When he left, he simply pulled the door behind him. The streets lay deserted as twilight blurred towards true night under the looming shadow of the mountains. A little light leaked from the window shutters of the tall houses so that he didn't have to watch his step and could look around him. Simon Tauber imprinted the topography on his mind as he walked through the silent village. His eyes travelled over the canted roofs and the stark silhouette of the church until they lifted to the houses that straggled up the slopes and vanished in the darkness. His eyes swung back to the church and to the little light that identified the priest's house sheltering in its shadow. Perhaps if I spoke to Father Kyril, he thought. He remembered knocking on the door of that house when he had gone for instruction, prior to baptism. The priest had not made any eye contact and had gone through the motions, like a man whose mind and heart were elsewhere. Tauber remembered the contorted cross behind the priest's shoulder as they had sat at the table and he had wondered if it had been strategically placed so that a penitent or, as in his case, a supplicant would reflect upon his part in that agony. His baptism had occurred before dawn in the cold and echoing church; 'to avoid scandal,' the priest had muttered. After breakfast, Clara had encouraged him to go for a walk. In her wisdom, she'd invented some excuse to stay at home so that he could have time alone with his thoughts. He'd followed the same route he took now, letting the memories of his bar mitzvah and many happy Seder meals wash over him. Three days later, a final letter from his sister informed him that his father had recited Kaddish for him – the Jewish prayer for the dead.

The road edged the lake and he followed it to a fringe of beach that jutted into the water. His boots crunched on the shingle, keeping time with the rhythmic slapping of the small waves. Their walks always ended here. All along the route, Clara would stride forward, lured by the next object of interest, while he would trail behind, slowed by his own thoughts, until she was almost out of sight. Then he would call to her, 'Wait, darling, I don't want to lose you.' She would retrace her steps and link his arm. Even in the gathering dark, he'd known she was smiling. He stepped into the lake and shuddered as the water lapped his knees and then higher until he found it hard to hold his footing. 'Wait, darling,' he gasped before the water filled his mouth.

HALLSTATT: THE BIERKELLER, THREE NIGHTS LATER

The occasional pop of wood burning in the hearth was the loudest sound in the bierkeller. Gert finished wiping the bar top and started to polish the glasses. He knew it was a futile exercise. During the night, the downdraught from the chimney would coat both bar and glasses with a fine ash. His solitary customer sat swaying on a stool, trying to stay in synch with his glass on the bar. The one-armed boatman was alone tonight, Gert noted; no Erich to shadow and steer him home when the drink inevitably took his land legs. He hoped the boatman's son was at home with his mother and sisters. No boy should see what had come up on his father's grappling hook that morning, Gert grimaced. The women would know how to handle him. The beer would dull the reality for Johann, as it had done since he'd left his arm in Ypres.

'Hard work,' he muttered sympathetically, and leaned forward to refill the glass. Johann showed no sign of having heard him and the barkeeper returned to his meaningless chores.

The carpenter came in at about nine. Gert saw him scan the room and read the boatman's back. He wasn't surprised when he took the stool beside Johann. Rudi was like that; tough as seasoned teak on the outside and soft as balsa when there was trouble. Rudi crooked a finger and watched the foam rise in his glass. They were on their third glass when Tomas, the miner, arrived. He ducked inside the door as if he had made the journey from home in a thunderstorm. The salt mines took some of them that way, Gert knew. Most miners raised their heads when coming up in the cage, like divers coming up for air. He'd see them in the village at the weekends ambling tippy-toed and looking up as if they could inhale the sky before submerging again. Not Tomas though. Tomas loved the closed spaces. His workmates said he became almost jolly as the cage went down; straightened up and became a different man; different to the man who hunkered into the inn the odd night and burrowed into whatever shadowy nook was available. Gert watched the big man pause inside the door, shake himself, like a wet dog, edge towards the shadow-side of the chimney breast and stop. His eyes found Johann and Tomas and, with slow steps, he approached the bar, hoisting himself on a stool so that the boatman was flanked by himself and Rudi. His eyes never left the bar top as Gert poured.

'Never saw him without a book,' the boatman said to no one in particular. ''Specially after his wife died.' He made an effort at crossing himself but abandoned it. 'Always a book. Sitting there with his face to the fire.'

'Wasn't too fond of company, then?' Rudi prompted gently. It was a ploy, the barkeeper knew, to keep Johann talking. They all knew it for what it was – except Johann.

'No,' he protested, backhanding the foam from his mouth, 'not like that at all. Not an ignorant bone in his body. Sat more side on, like, so you'd know he didn't mind being spoken to.'

'Did he?'

'Did he what?'

'Mind being spoken to,' Rudi said patiently.

'No, never. Someone'd always say "Evening, Herr Tauber", and he'd always answer, like he'd like to say more but didn't know how. Shy kind of a man, he was.' He took another long swallow and angled his elbows for ballast on the bar. 'Lively enough when she was alive, though.'

'The wife?'

'Yes. Always saw them walking around. Knew the pair of them from the boat. See everything from the boat. She'd be tacking over and back and him lagging back, but they always ended up together at the lake.'

'Is that where she—?'

Johann's stare froze the barkeeper before he could finish his question.

'Clara Tauber was a good Christian woman,' he growled. 'She died in her bed.'

The three men nodded at this and addressed their drinks. The barkeeper sighed and drew a glass for himself. 'Maybe it was because he was …' He angled the glass beneath the spigot and watched the foam rise.

'Was what?' Johann asked.

'Well, you know, not of the faith,' the barman said, raising the glass to the vertical and setting it to stand.

'Not of the faith,' Johann mimicked.

'It's common knowledge he converted to marry her.'

'Common knowledge,' Johann said derisively. 'Everything around here is fucking common knowledge.'

Rudi stepped into the role of peacemaker.

'I think what Gert means is—'

'I know what he means,' Johann said harshly. 'He means Tauber was a Jew. There, I've said it. Did the fucking roof fall in? What he was never mattered a damn to anyone – well to anyone who mattered around here. Live and let live was always our way. What those other bastards think is—'

'I heard tell he had a visitor,' the barkeeper said hastily.

'What?'

'You know how it is around here – someone always sees.'

'What visitor?'

'As I heard it, the little corporal.'

'What! Jesus Christ, don't say there's a law against reading books.'

'Well, as a matter of fact …'

'Ah, for pity's sake, what will they think of next? Herr Tauber was an educated man. Books to a man like that were like food to folk like us.'

'Still …'

'Still my arse. That little prick in a uniform always makes more of himself by watching his neighbours.'

'He's not a little prick.'

The others sat stunned into silence; not by what the miner had said but that he had spoken at all.

'Why not?' Johann asked cautiously.

'I was in school with him,' the miner answered. 'He was a little prick then. He's a bigger prick now.'

And then they were laughing. Johann beat his fist on the top of the bar while the others leaned back and howled. After a while, they came back to their glasses.

'No backbone in a prick,' the miner added, 'she has enough for both of them.'

A geyser of beer jetted across the bar, and Rudi beat Johann on the back. When he could get his breath back, the boatman swivelled on his stool to confront the miner.

'This fucker doesn't talk for twenty years,' he declared, 'and then says it all in the one night.'

Rudi raised four fingers and the miner smiled self-consciously as Johann pounded his shoulder.

'You're a dark one,' Johann grunted approvingly. 'Folk do say it's her, not him. Not from around these parts, of course. Somewhere in Yugoslavia, or such.'

'They have a boy,' the barkeeper said.

'She has,' Johann said, after a pause.

'Max is a fine lad,' Rudi said quietly.

'Aye,' Johann pounced, 'if she'd let him be. Poor lad has Church and state for parents what with him trying to walk like Adolf and her haunting the Church.'

'The priest …?' the barkeeper prompted.

'Off limits,' Johann said, suddenly sober. 'We don't talk about the priest. He pours the water, hitches man and wife, and buries the dead. Minds his business. Suits us fine, that way. One policeman is plenty.'

'But Tauber …'

'Dead man,' Johann said fiercely. 'Walked into the lake. Three days and he came up on the hook, where I knew he would.'

'Maybe he slipped or fell,' Rudi suggested quietly.

'Maybe Frau Steiger sleeps with her husband,' Johann snapped. He emptied his glass and set it on the bar with a thud. 'He had stones,' he muttered.

'Stones?'

'In his pockets.' The anger was gone from Johann, leaving his face creased and haggard. 'There's things can twist a man out of true,' he added. 'Rest in peace.'

'Not in our cemetery,' the barkeeper blurted, and paled as the three men glared at him.

'As I hear it,' he added weakly.

'Haggling over a corpse,' Johann shook his head wearily. 'Soon enough, they'll be burying more outside the cemetery than in it. Like the last time.'

LATER, THE POLICEMAN'S HOUSE

Something in the pattern of their conversation drew him from his book. Reluctantly, Max slotted a bookmark between the pages and closed the covers. He moved to the bookshelf, sliding noiselessly in his stockinged feet across the timbered floor of the attic bedroom. The book slotted precisely into the space where he had found it. He spun on the balls of his feet, slid back to the chair and listened. He had taught himself to listen. Most people his age, he'd concluded, merely heard. They opened their ears with their eyes, every morning, and let the torrent of competing sounds wash through their brains. Only the most strident sounds seemed to snag on their attention and then only momentarily replaced immediately by the next loud sound. He had taught himself to listen – to close his ears to a sharp focus so that he could sieve the occasional kernel from the general chaff. Over time, he had developed an ear for speech patterns; the way his mother talked to the butcher, for example. She would enquire about quality and price in a disinterested tone and make non-committal sounds as the man enthused about the joint in question. She would interrupt and ask about something else and that abrupt shift would catch him off-balance; make him hesitate, scrambling to redirect his flow. Before he could gain a new momentum, she would switch the conversation again, gradually taking control of the interaction from the flushed and gabbling man until he was reduced to silence and only one voice prevailed – hers. She never paid the asking price; never haggled in an apologetic, half-hearted tone. She declared – yes, that was the correct word – declared what she would spend and let him play the supplicant. How did she do this, he'd wondered, when other mothers moved instinctively towards compliance? Why would the only butcher in the village permit this woman to dictate when he could have refused and moved on to serve someone more willing? He knew that part of the answer lay in who she was and that led him to consider her sense of identity. Although she couched something in the language of 'ask', her tone left no doubt that she 'expected'. Of course, the other part of the answer lay in the fact that she was the policeman's wife and everyone knew that. They also knew, as Max did, that Steiger wore the uniform but it was his wife who exercised the real authority. Over time, he had mastered the range of non-verbal messages she could convey with a raised eyebrow, the twitch of her mouth or the slow turn of her head. There was still much to learn about wielding power, but his mother was the master and he was her apprentice.

Max Steiger knew that he was adored by his mother. He accepted that totally; never applying the analysis he brought to all other matters. The boy saw his perfection reflected in her gaze and had no room for doubt or need for self-reflection.

'She never touches you,' a voice whispered in his head. 'When has she ever brushed your hair out of your eyes, like Frau Hamner does with Karl? She—'

'My mother loves me,' he muttered savagely and stilled himself to listen. The buzz of his mother's voice continued unabated through the floorboards and he relaxed.

'Elsa never looks at you the way she looks at Karl,' the voice said.

He stood and began to pace the floor, shaking his head as if he had a wasp inside.

'Elsa is nothing to me,' he said fiercely. 'Bloody troll's daughter. I could have any girl. Eloïse watches me all the time and—'

'But you ignore her.'

'Of course I do,' he said. 'Mother does it to the women who try to make friends with her and the silly bitches just try harder.'

'She does the same to your father.'

'My father is nothing,' he growled.

Again, he tilted his head to the side to listen but the only voice in the Steiger household was his mother's, kneading away at the clay that was his father.

'Your father loves you.'

He clenched his teeth on the rage that boiled up like bile from his belly so that his throat swelled and the veins stood out on his neck.

'No,' he gasped, 'I don't want his stupid love. I loathe his praise. When I see him smile like a beaten dog, I want to puke.'

His eyes opened and he saw his hand hovering before his face, twisted into a claw. With a huge effort, he clasped it with his other hand and forced both into his lap as he slumped on the bed. He took deep breaths into his stomach and forced himself to relax. After a time, he rolled upright and palmed sweat from his forehead. His father, he accepted, was peripheral to his life. Herr Steiger had long ago given up the unequal contest for his son's affection and compensated for his invisibility at home by trying to expand his importance in the community.

The pattern of their conversations was usually made up of longer statements from her interspersed with shorter offerings from him. Tonight, the pattern was wrong. Their voices bounced through the wooden house, reflected on and upwards by the hard surfaces to the conical ear of the attic. Where Max sat listening. Where he heard the details of Simon Tauber's death and the subtext of his father's clumsy attempts at blackmail. It could have worked, Max reasoned. It would have worked if the policeman had presented the lure of a big bribe up front and ... Better if he had ... what? He thought it through for a few minutes, sitting immobile on his bed, his eyes open but out of focus. Abruptly, he sat forward. His father should have made an appointment with Herr Tauber and apologised for taking up his valuable time. His father ... no, he, Max, would have given the papers a cursory glance and dismissed the whole thing as bureaucratic pen-pushers being over-zealous. In Vienna, of course. He would accept a glass of schnapps as a symbol of ... of what? Friendship? No. Complicity? No. As a sign of an understanding between two professionals; men of standing within the community. He would have left the papers as a token of trust and assured the teacher that the matter was ended ... as far as he was concerned. Why? Unconsciously, he ticked off the reasons on his fingers. Tauber would have been relieved and grateful – and beholden to the policeman. Vienna would have filed the policeman's letter recommending that no further action be taken on the matter, thus avoiding crushing a very small grape in the enormous bureaucratic wine press, with nothing to show at the end of it all but a stain of juice-blood on the policeman's hands. But a drowned teacher ... the rumours that would run rife in Hallstatt. Max tuned into his mother's monologue, just long enough to hear her confirm his analysis.

So, Max mused, Tauber is dead. The man had been an adequate teacher, if a little prone to moralising and embarrassing flights of reminiscence. He hoped the replacement teacher would have more to offer. Education, his mother repeated often, was Max's passport to possibilities beyond Hallstatt. The world was changing, she said, and a young man should seize every chance to better himself. Seize the day, the teacher had liked to say, and then, under pressure from a petty official, he had simply let go. Tauber, he concluded, had been a weak man and the world didn't tolerate weakness.

He took the book from the shelf again, found his place and blanked out the world beyond the page.

THE MINER'S HOUSE

'That you, Elsa?'

'No, it's Baba Yaga, the witch, your mother.'

She hefted the basket to the table and unbuttoned her coat, reflecting on how strange it was that sometimes she opened her mouth and her mother spoke. It had been ten years now but the thought of her mother still brought her pain. She remembered her as being as broad across the shoulders as her father, but that was impossible. No one could be that broad. But her last memory of the stick woman with the huge eyes who seemed to be drowning in white pillows was crystal clear. Only her mother's sharp tongue had remained unimpaired, she remembered, smiling. She was always chivvying her husband, always prodding him with sharp remarks while he pretended to be shocked and frightened. And then she'd died. And him? He began to … shamble. He began to favour small spaces – places where he could burrow away from the pain. She worried about him. She was worried now that he hadn't responded with some witty reply.

'Are you deaf as well?' she challenged.

'Elsa,' he called, and her heart chilled. When she opened the door, he was sitting at the corpse of the fire, his stockinged feet curled like sleeping pups in the hearth.

'Sit down,' he said, 'I have something to tell you.'

She was not a girl who cried easily but the tears burned her cheeks, dripping sharp drops on her hands.

'Oh, the stupid, stupid man,' she said raggedly.

'No, Liebchen,' he said softly. Such a gentle voice from such a big man, she thought, through her tears. 'Up,' he said and she climbed into his lap as she had not done since childhood.

'Up' was sometimes for swinging her, almost as high as the rafters, while her mother shouted, 'You'll knock her brains out.'

'Couldn't happen you,' he'd say, swinging his daughter happily. 'Can you see the stars?' he'd laugh.

Other times, 'Up' was for wrapping her in his massive arms while he crooned away some fright or pain.

'He was a good man,' he whispered. 'It's only right that you should cry for him.'

He anticipated and stilled her protest with a gentle squeeze. 'You are angry at the waste of a good man,' he continued. 'Rest awhile and think of him.'

She did as he'd asked and her tears felt softer.

'What will happen in school now?' she sniffed.

'They'll find someone else,' he said practically. 'He will never be Herr Tauber but he will be a teacher and you'll respect that.'

'Yes, Papa.'

'Good. In the meantime, maybe you and Karl can study together – if it wouldn't be too much of an affliction.'

'What?'

Immediately she was on the defensive. 'You can't think I … I mean …'

'No, Liebchen,' he said seriously, 'of course not.' But she could feel the laughter rumbling in his chest.

'Karl is my friend, Papa,' she said tartly but she knew her father was a lost cause.

'And a good one,' he said. 'I am happy for you.'

She stared into his eyes for a moment. 'You know your eyebrows are like caterpillars?' she said, smiling, but her voice shook.

He closed his arms around her and she laid her face against his warmth.

'Can you see the stars?' he whispered.

'Yes, Papa,' she said, although she knew it was just the light of the lantern distorted by her tears.

THE CARPENTER'S HOUSE, THE FOLLOWING MORNING

The light woke him. Karl lay still for a minute, letting the familiarity of his bedroom dispel the weird landscape of his dream. In the dream, a small man had been hurrying through the shadows of looming houses. He had moved faster and faster and finally escaped the mazy streets that tried to confound him. Lying in the secure warmth of his bed, Karl wondered why he couldn't remember the man's identity or what he had done next or why his mother hadn't called him.

He knew, the minute he entered the kitchen, that something was amiss. His mother leaned from the stove for her morning hug, as she always did. His father sat at the table, his chair, as always, angled sideways so that he could see the forested slopes of the mountains through the kitchen window. His father cradled his coffee mug in both hands, letting the warmth ease his fingers before he went to the workshop. Karl was an only child. 'Only is lonely,' he'd heard other mothers chide his mother. Without the distraction of siblings, his attention had always been focused on his parents; like the blinding white sunspot he created with a magnifying glass when he burned his name on timber off-cuts.

'What's wrong?' he asked.

Even their surprise looked feigned and his anxiety tightened another notch.

'Sit down, Karl,' his father said, hooking the chair beside him from the table. He sat. His father looked expectantly at his mother and sighed.

'It's Herr Tauber, isn't it?' Karl blurted. He stared at his father for a moment and swung his head to his mother, who continued to prod whatever she was cooking. He knew from the set of her shoulders that she was crying.

'Where?' he asked.

'In the lake,' his father said softly.

Karl dropped his eyes to the table and concentrated on following the patterns of whorls and grain lines that rippled in the polished timber. He felt a swelling in his chest and a hot pressure behind his eyes.

'I'm sorry, son,' his father said and reached across to touch his head.

Karl wanted to lean into his father's strong, warm hand. He sensed his mother was waiting to come and wrap him in her arms but he was sixteen years old; longing for and resisting the comfort in equal measure.

'He was a good teacher,' his father offered.

'Yes,' he heard himself say, and once his tongue had shaped the single word, its companions followed in hard clumps that hurt his throat. 'Yesterday ... yesterday he talked ... he told us about walking with his wife. It was funny ... and sad. He said it was too nice a day for class and sent us away.' He was silent for a long time, even though his throat moved as if words were welling up from inside. 'Elsa and I walked to the lake. She said he'd sounded ... troubled.' The word warbled in his mouth and he turned his head away.

'She's a bright girl, Elsa.'

'Yes … yes, she is very intelligent.' He blushed. Rudi saw the colour rise from the hollow in his son's throat and climb his cheeks to the roots of his hair. He stood, took his mug to the sink and rested his hand on his wife's shoulder.

'I'm working on a table for Heinze,' he said sadly and walked out to the workshop.

'Mutti?'

'Yes, my son.'

'Why … why would a man choose to die?'

Oh my boy, she thought, wrestling to control her tears. Questions, always questions from the time when you were old enough to ask. And always the 'why' questions; the hardest ones to answer. She pressed her apron to her face and came to stand behind him, resting her palms on his shoulders. She could feel the warmth of him and measure the spread of his shoulders through his shirt.

'I don't know,' she said. 'Sometimes … sometimes I think people don't choose to die unless they feel that have no chance of living well.'

He turned his head and looked at her and she was cut by the expression of incomprehension on his face.

'But he was a teacher, Mother,' he said. 'He knew so many things and I …'

'I know, son,' she said wrapping him in her arms and resting her chin on the crown of his head so he'd know she couldn't see him cry. She hoped he wouldn't ask any more questions.

THE OFFICE OF CARDINAL TISSERANT, THE VATICAN

The cardinal squeezed his eyes shut and snagged a fistful of his beard in a white-knuckled fist. Those who knew the cardinal would have smiled at his familiar pose of intense concentration. His secretary knew him well enough to remain immobile and silent. Eugène Tisserant was a Prince of the Roman Catholic

Church – he was also a man with a volcanic temper. His white-knuckled left hand, which closed around a letter, trembled slightly.

'When?' he growled.

'Two, perhaps three weeks ago,' the secretary said softly. 'It has been in Leiber's desk-tray since then.'

The cardinal opened his eyes and held the letter more closely, as if he could stare it into denying its message.

'Roncalli,' he said, dropping his eyes to the signature.

'Cardinal Angelo Roncalli is our nuncio in Turkey and Greece,' the secretary replied promptly. 'He—'

'I know who Roncalli is,' Tisserant interrupted. 'Born near Bergamo; a little sheep-shit village in northern Italy. Big brain, big belly; a career diplomat watching his promotion like all the other Italians elbowing at the trough in this ...' He gestured with the hand holding the letter to encompass ... what? Saint Peter's Basilica, across the piazza three floors below them, was just waking to the early light. He saw a solitary pilgrim push through the great bronze door. In his more cynical moments, he thought of the basilica as a religious tourist attraction; a semi-sacred souvenir stall, joined at the hip to the Vatican Palace. Oh yes, it held out its colonnaded arms to the world but the offices of powerful men crowded its back and sides; the private power base behind the public face.

'I should have gone to war,' he said wearily, tucking the letter in his cassock pocket. 'I did, the first time. Tisserant of the French intelligence corps.' He coughed a sharp laugh. 'If ever there was an oxymoron.' He slumped in the comfortless chair, turning his face to the window. 'He refused me permission this time,' he continued, as if to himself, 'he said the Church was already at war with the Bolsheviks.'

'Surely the Holy Father meant the Nazis?'

'Don't come all snide with me, Emil,' the cardinal snorted, in mock reproof. 'You know very well that Pacelli the Pope cannot wage war against the people with whom Pacelli the Secretary of State signed a concordat. The little corporal guaranteed our schools and property, and the quid pro quo was the conscience of the Catholic Church in the Reich. And now the shepherd is silent as the lambs are led to the slaughter.' He tapped the pocket containing the letter. 'Especially when the lambs are not of our flock. Roncalli is a diplomat to the pin of his size eighteen collar,' he continued. 'As you would expect, his letter is carefully crafted. The sources of his information are not named. He presents this information without recommendation. All the more reason to believe that what he says is true.' He snagged his beard in his fist again and gave it a firm tug before continuing. 'The Jews are being culled, Emil. We have eyes and ears throughout Europe. Mon Dieu, we have people in the Reichstag. Every time Hitler farts, someone in the Vatican rushes to open a window. And what does the pope do? I advised him in 1939 to write an encyclical telling Catholics that it was their duty to resist the unjust laws of an authoritarian state. He said he didn't want advisors; he wanted people who would do what he told them. And now, he receives the Nazi Ribbentrop in the audience chamber where they have coffee and argue theology in fluent German. He sends bloodless letters to Der Führer spending hours picking and choosing his words in case they upset that lunatic. *Merde*, I'm beginning to ramble just like my father.'

'Does your father have an appointment with his Holiness in five minutes'?

'What? Oh!'

Cardinal Tisserant barrelled down a walkway, latticed by the columns of Bernini's colonnade. Saint Peter's Square yawned to his left, the Egyptian Obelisk silhouetted against a brightening sky. He glanced over his shoulder and saw the ever-present truck parked at the mouth of the Via della Concillazione, just beyond the boundary of the square, and a single black-clad figure watching the pigeons strut to and fro.

'Benito keeps a beady eye on his prisoners,' he growled, before hunching his shoulders and stepping through the bronze door. He nodded to the Swiss Guards flanking the entrance, speculating on how these sons of the cantons would fare with ceremonial lances against carbines, and pounded up the Scala Regia, Bernini's ornate staircase. Slightly out of breath, he passed through the Sala Regia, ignoring the works of Sagallo, slowing only to admire Michelangelo's *Crucifixion of Saint Peter* in the Cappella Paolina. 'That could be prophetic,' he muttered, as he braced himself to climb yet more stairs to the Sala Clementina, the anteroom to the pope's study. Even at this early hour, it was crowded. Tisserant stepped inside the door and waited.

Gradually, the hubbub died away as they became aware of the Secretary of the Congregation for the Oriental Churches. Slowly, he made his way down the aisle that appeared as the diplomats ebbed to either side of the room. Tisserant nodded sympathetically at the British ambassador to the Holy See and presented a stony face to the German, von Bergen. It was an effort to keep his face expressionless as he noticed Paveliç, the Croat fascist leader, hovering at the back, trying to hide behind the broad shoulders of men who looked uncomfortable in formal morning suits. 'Wolves in sheep's clothing' he said to himself, 'waiting for an audience with the shepherd. That's an anomaly to consider later.'

The papal secretaries rose from their desks flanking the door to the inner sanctum. Leiber and Kaas, he knew, were 'souvenirs' Pacelli had brought back from his spell in Germany. Oleaginous, he thought as they adjusted their identical, obsequious smiles. From the Latin, 'oleaginous' and the French 'oleagineux', he knew. The root word was 'oleum', meaning oil, and Tisserant could have ransacked the twelve other languages he spoke fluently and not found enough words to describe the unctuous pair.

'His Holiness has been expecting you, Eminence,' Leiber wheezed, with just a taint of reproof in his voice.

'And something from Roncalli, I imagine,' Tisserant said, and took sinful pleasure as the colour drained from the secretary's face. As if choreographed, the secretaries spun as one and preceded him through the door. When they had closed it behind him, they sank to their knees with downcast eyes.

The only other person present, apart from the Supreme Pontiff, was Cardinal Maglione, the Secretary of State. Tisserant knew the Romans liked to pun on his name which meant 'sweater' in Italian. 'When the Pope goes out without his sweater, he catches cold,' the local mantra ran. Pius XII was not close to Maglione.

Tisserant had heard Pius say, on more than one occasion, that he preferred to insult his friends rather than his enemies because his friends were more likely to forgive him. Tisserant also knew he himself didn't number among the papal friends. How much of an enemy the pope considered him to be, he didn't know.

Tisserant inclined his head to Maglione, who returned the gesture of recognition without changing his expression, and took a moment to examine the office of the Successor to Saint Peter. If 'the apparel oft proclaims the man' as Shakespeare contended, then, the cardinal concluded, this room reflected the austerity that characterised Pius XII. After the ornamental excesses of the rooms he had just come through, this one was almost studiously bare. There was nothing here of colour or warmth. The desk was as spare and functional as the man who sat behind it. The pope continued to scan the document before him, a fountain pen poised in his right hand, like a harpoon, the cardinal mused, ready to strike at the slightest error. A document containing the most innocent mistake or one that failed the rigid double-spacing rule would be returned to the writer … once. Pius was a thin man, made even more wraith-like by his blinding-white cassock and skull cap. The ensemble seemed to bleach his already pale face. Some thought it made him appear angelic. Yes, like a Bernini angel, Tisserant thought, bloodless and cold as only marble can be.

He watched the pope perform the rituals that marked the conclusion of any work he did on documents. First, there was the careful examination of the nib of his fountain pen for any foreign bodies that might impede its flow. Then, he dipped it fastidiously in the inkwell, like a heron plucking a fish from a pond. Carefully, he scraped off the excess ink on the rim of the inkwell before signing the document. Next, he wiped the nib clean with a cloth and laid the pen aside so that it was perfectly aligned with the edge of the blotter. Finally, he blotted the document and held it out before him. Leiber rose from his knees, took the document with due reverence and subsided to his knees again.

'*Procedamus in pace*,' the pope said tonelessly. 'Let us proceed in peace.'

On cue, Kaas cleared his throat and began to speak.

'Holiness, we have been informed by the nuncio in Berlin that Major General Erich Marcks has completed his plan for the invasion of the Soviet Union. Our sources in the Berchtesgaden say the Führer will authorise the operation in May to avail of the mild weather.'

The pope inclined his head fractionally in Maglione's direction.

'He will strike north to Leningrad to secure a port and south to the Baku oilfields,' Maglione said, confidently. 'But the armies at the centre will strike directly for Moscow. It is Hitler's belief that the Soviet Union will disintegrate when Moscow is taken.'

'His belief and our hope,' the pontiff murmured.

'It won't happen.'

Tisserant sensed the secretaries stiffen from their reverential crouch. In his peripheral vision, he watched Maglione fold his hands in a pious pose and bow his head. For the first time since he'd entered the room, the pope looked at him directly.

'His Eminence doesn't believe Hitler will take Moscow?'

'That's not what I said, Holiness,' Tisserant answered evenly. 'Hitler may very well take Moscow, if he can supply his forces and outrun the winter, but the Soviet Union will not fragment if he does.'

'If you cut the head from a bear, does it not die?' the pope asked dryly.

'Russia is more a hydra than a bear, Holiness. Cut a hydra's head and it grows another; perhaps two more heads. Wherever Stalin is will become the capital, and there is a lot of Russia stretching from Moscow to the Siberian border.'

'So, Stalin will run. But surely even he cannot outrun General Guderian's Tiger tanks?'

Kaas and Leiber sniggered dutifully, and Pius allowed himself the ghost of a smile. Tisserant knew the pope liked to collect esoteric information. He kept a vast library of reference books on a huge range of topics and had minions to devil for him night and day. So, he thought, the Supreme Pontiff of the Holy Roman Catholic Church wants to play at war.

'Tiger tanks have a fuel capacity of four hundred and seventy litres which allows them an operational range of just two hundred kilometres, Holiness. That fuel will have to be transported by road – a road that will become longer and longer as the blitzkrieg succeeds. They may well be running on fumes before they get to Moscow. As for Stalin running, history tells us the Russians retreated before Napoleon, whose Grand Armée was reduced to attacking their rear, but, when they were ready, the Russians turned. Half a million Frenchmen marched into Russia – just over a quarter survived to escape across the Berezina river.'

There was a long silence before the pope spoke again.

'Such matters rest in the hands of God, Eminence. It is easy to become distracted from our purpose by the affairs of nations.' He leaned back in his chair.

Cardinal Tisserant felt he might explode. In just two short sentences, Pius had summed up his papal style. Firstly, he had steered a discussion he found unpalatable into the 'God cul-de-sac'. To his supporters, it sounded like the response of a deeply spiritual man. To those inured to his platitudes, and Tisserant knew a growing number of churchmen and diplomats who were beginning to despair of this pope, it was just another example of avoidance. Among the Vatican civil service, placing something 'in God's hands' was a euphemism for sitting on your own. 'It is easy to become distracted from our purpose by the affairs of nations,' reflected the duality that split the pope. Like the Manichean heretics, he saw the world as an arena in which absolute light contended with absolute darkness. His world was bisected between the affairs of God and the affairs of men, and there was more than a mild reproof to Tisserant in the suggestion that churchmen shouldn't become immersed in or distracted by the latter.

'Your Eminence would favour us with a brief on your plan for the evangelisation of the Slavs,' the pope said.

Finally, and this is what made the French cardinal remember his doctor's mantra to 'breathe not blow', he was being asked to spell out a secret plan before a brother cardinal, who was not privy to it, and two German monsignori he did not trust.

'I would be happy to brief the Holy Father on that matter,' he said softly.

Tisserant had to admire Pius the diplomat. The mask did not

move. Perhaps the flick of his left hand was more peremptory than usual. Kaas and Leiber jerked as if on strings and stumbled upright, reversing out of the office. Maglione simply bowed as deeply as his arthritis would allow and shot Tisserant a look that was half-sympathetic and wholly cautionary when his back was turned to the pontiff. It was some moments before the pope spoke again.

'You do not trust my Secretary of State in this matter.'

It was a statement delivered without inflection.

'Cardinal Maglione has been my friend for many years, Holiness. But it is well known within these walls that his office is a war room complete with maps detailing the deployment of armies; a map which is changed each day according to reports from our nuncios. I imagine it mirrors the maps in the London war office, the Berchtesgaden and the Kremlin. Unlike theirs, his office leaks like a colander.'

'And my secretaries?'

'I have no hard evidence against either man, Holiness. But, to put it bluntly, prudence demands that we limit access to this information. What they don't know, they can't divulge, either accidentally or by design.'

'So be it. You may proceed.'

Tisserant detailed the various seminaries throughout Rome that housed priests who were preparing to enter the Soviet Union through Romania and make contact with the Latin Rite Church. The Latin Rite was loyal to Rome and the thrust of his plan was that the infiltrated priests would use the contacts made to reach out to the larger and more influential Russian Orthodox Church. Tisserant was a man who respected words and now chose them carefully and sparingly to impart the essentials. When he had stopped speaking, the pope looked at a point over the cardinal's head.

'Perhaps this is the time ordained by God when the East will return to Rome,' he said fervently.

'The East will never return to Rome, Holiness.'

Pius blinked.

'And why not?'

'There are a number of reasons. Among them, we must consider the fact that we excommunicated them. There is also the fact that they have managed quite well without us for centuries. In that time, they have developed a theology, liturgy and spirituality that is of their culture. As I understand it, our mission is to establish friendly relations with a sister church to our mutual benefit, not for them to bow to our authority.'

The pope reached for a document on his desk and picked up his pen.

'Thank you, your Eminence,' he said. 'Please keep me abreast of developments.'

Tisserant bowed stiffly and moved to the door.

'You didn't support my papacy, did you, Eminence?'

Tisserant paused with his hand on the door handle. He turned and looked at the pope, who continued to work on a document as if nothing had been said. The cardinal waited until the movement of the pen slowed and stilled and the pope looked up.

'I would like to sit,' the cardinal said.

He watched the other man's face as he wrestled with this concept, a concept so alien to him that he put his pen on the desk without any of the usual nonsense.

'I would like to sit,' Tisserant repeated. 'As a Prince of the Church, it offends my vanity to stand before your desk like a student before his headmaster. Vanity is unbecoming in a cardinal, I know, but I am not as young as I once was and so I would like to sit.'

Seemingly at a loss for words, the pope waved vaguely at a chair beside the door. Tisserant lifted the chair and paced forward to place it before the desk. He sat. 'You were saying?' he prompted.

'I ... I said you didn't support my papacy.'

'If you're asking if I voted for you in conclave, then you know I can't answer that question. We are both bound by the same oath of silence, never to divulge how we or any other voted. However, it is no great secret that I was opposed to your candidacy.'

'And do you now support and serve me as pope?'

'No, I do not. I support the gospels and serve the Church that tries to promote them. Whoever happens to be pope at this or any time should have no bearing on my primary commitment. Many have sat on the throne of Peter who were selected by the patrician families of Rome and not elected by the College of Cardinals. We have had the mad and the bad, murderers and fornicators as popes, and the Church has managed to survive them all.'

'You think I am an unworthy pope?'

'No one is worthy to be pope, Holiness. No one deserves it of right and I wouldn't wish the burden of it on an enemy. But, as a member of the College of Cardinals, I do owe you the truth, as I see it. I did not support you because I felt you had been chosen by others long before the conclave and had been groomed accordingly. I felt you would be focused on the survival of the Church and the primacy of the papacy, to the detriment of both.'

He looked at the still, frail figure opposite and paused. Inside every role, there is a man, he reminded himself. And that man was once a boy. While other boys had kicked a rag-ball on the streets of Rome, Eugenio Pacelli had been cosseted by a pious mother who had provided him with a piece of damask as a vestment and had helped him set up an altar complete with candles in tinfoil so that he could play at saying mass. While other young seminarians studied in institutions noted for their severe discipline and poor rations, Eugenio had been granted a special dispensation to live at home so that Signora Pacelli could cook the special meals demanded by his weak constitution; a condition that would have precluded any other seminarian from the priesthood. Eugenio Pacelli had never been just another boy or just any seminarian. He had been the intellectually gifted son of a lawyer in the service of the papacy; marked at an early age by his family and parish priest as suitable for priesthood. The boy Eugenio had been in training to this destiny from his earliest years, carrying the dreams of others on his frail shoulders. While other young Roman men searched for work and sought out the company of young women, his only female friendship had been with a young cousin whose father had considered it inappropriate and forbade it. Friendships among seminarians were carefully monitored to ensure they did not develop into 'special friendships', and life in the Vatican after ordination was not conducive to forming the easy relationships a man might develop with business colleagues in the world beyond the wall. For fifty-nine years, a succession of popes had opted to be prisoners of the Vatican to protest the confiscation of the Papal Territories until the concordat with Mussolini had granted autonomy to the tiny Vatican State. Pius XII, he realised, was not a political prisoner but a prisoner of the role of the papacy, a role he had been prepared for from childhood.

He wondered what it was like to be Pacelli the Pope – to be ring-fenced by powerful cabals and courtiers, who decided whom he should meet and what he should hear. Even in what passed for his private life, this inner circle was mediated by Kaas and Leiber and manipulated by Pascalina, the German nun who had been his housekeeper in Munich and who had turned up, uninvited, in Rome after his election to take control of his household. It had been Pascalina who famously had interrupted a meeting with a foreign ambassador to announce that the pope's hot milk was growing cold. It was Pascalina who choreographed his Christmas Day meetings with his family; formal, stilted affairs which ended when La Popessa, as the Romans dubbed her, decided they should end. Pius XII, he concluded, the Supreme Pontiff and Ruler of the Universal Catholic Church, had to be the loneliest man in the world.

He remembered the Hebrew proverb, 'What is spoken from the heart speaks to the heart,' and decided it would be worth the risk.

'Holiness,' he began carefully, '*Tu es Petrus* … you are Peter. You are the supreme leader of the Church and I am one of its princes. You cannot attain any higher office, and I have no wish to. At heart, I believe, we are both priests and I would like to speak to you from my heart as a brother priest. Do you understand?'

The pope nodded warily.

Cardinal Tisserant suddenly realised that he had been holding his breath and now released it in a shuddering sigh.

'I would also like to use the title one priest confers on another. Do you agree?'

He could almost hear the gears grinding as the absolute ruler of the Church contemplated his question.

'Yes.'

'Don Eugenio,' the cardinal began carefully, 'you were chosen for the Church at an early age. Your father and your brother both served the Vatican with devotion and distinction. From your ordination as a priest, you have been here. This has been your world. Yes, I know you have travelled widely as a diplomat and nuncio. You went to North America where you were received like royalty. America never really forgave the Founding Fathers for the presidency. In South America, they fired cannons on your arrival and priests pulled your carriage through the streets. I am not suggesting that you were seduced by such pomp. I am saying that you were seen in such places, not as yourself, Don Eugenio the priest, but as the voice and presence of your predecessor. And so, you met rulers and diplomats and powerful people and were housed in state cabins, palaces and mansions. A man who moves in such circles rarely sees beyond the circle. He rarely encounters those outside … the poor, the disenchanted, the unbeliever. It is part of the burden of all Vatican diplomats that they carry the Vatican like a carapace wherever they go in the world.'

He paused and took a deep breath before continuing.

'And when a crisis arose, you were sent by your predecessor to Germany. And there, for the sake of the Church you served, you signed an agreement with Adolf Hitler. It was an error, Don Eugenio. I believe a grievous one. As priests, the Church can never be our first concern. The Church is simply an institution that serves the people of God. You put Church before people.'

Tisserant realised the enormity of what he was saying and paused to anchor his trembling hands to his knees. The man across the desk had bowed his head so that his eyes were hidden behind his steel-rimmed spectacles. When he spoke, his throat contorted with the effort.

'They put a pistol to my head, Eugène,' he whispered.

Somewhere outside, a great bell rang once. The sound was muffled as if whoever was pulling the rope was reluctant to intrude on their conversation. The cardinal allowed the silence to stretch as the other man struggled with his emotions.

'Yes,' Tisserant continued, even more gently than before, 'they threatened to take our schools, appoint their own bishops and take control over the Church. They might have. But they would not have taken the faith and hope of the Catholic people ... the real church in Germany. The gospels promise us that the gates of Hell would not prevail against that Church but you, and those who sent you, didn't trust the gospels. You agreed to silence the moral voice of German Catholics in exchange for a pact with Hitler. I fear it was a pact made with the devil and now the Church and the world will pay a fearful price.'

He took the letter from his cassock pocket and slid it across the desk. The pope started from his reverie and slid his finger to the bottom of the single page.

'Roncalli,' he whispered.

'Yes, Roncalli. He is our nuncio in Istanbul; listening over the Bosphorous to East and West. We both know him as a cautious man and, yet, he sends this urgent message to the Vatican. Why? Because he hears what is happening and realises we can never say we didn't know. We do know, Don Eugenio. We could paper the Sistine Chapel ceiling with reports of pogroms, forced exile and arbitrary arrests. We even know what Hitler plans to do. He has told us himself in *Mein Kampf.* He will create a master race in Europe and nothing and no one will be allowed to stand in his way. He will sterilise and euthanase those he considers *Untermenschen* ... lesser humans. The Slavs, the Russians, the gypsies, and all who are deemed unworthy of Hitler's Reich, will be eliminated. He has said publicly that the Jews will disappear from Europe for a thousand years.'

'Propaganda,' the pope breathed. 'Rhetoric! He tells the Germans what they want to hear, to compensate for the shame of Versailles.'

'This,' Tisserant said, leaning forward to tap the letter with a forefinger, 'is not rhetoric or propaganda or anything else but fact.'

For a moment, they locked eyes over the flimsy page between them. Tisserant saw the agony of indecision bunch the muscles in the pope's face and then ripple away to be replaced by the mask.

'Where did you get this letter, Eminence?' the pope asked stonily, and Tisserant knew he had lost him.

'It has been in Monsignor Leiber's desk drawer for over two

weeks.' He sighed, leaning back in his chair.

'And why is it in your possession?'

'Because,' Tisserant replied irritably, 'if I hadn't taken it, you'd never have received it.'

'This is highly irregular,' the pope continued, as if he hadn't heard. 'There is, of course, so much correspondence. I'm sure my secretary would have placed it on my desk … at the appropriate time.'

'Who decides when is the appropriate time for the pope to receive a letter from his nuncio concerning the murder of innocents? Leiber? Kaas? The appropriate time has passed, Holiness,' Tisserant growled, rising from his chair. 'You should ask why this letter was hidden from you. Why the Nazis would fear your response. Obviously, they consider that the moral leader of half a billion Catholics possesses formidable power … if he chooses to use it.'

Tisserant bowed stiffly and turned away.

'I did not dismiss you, Eminence,' the pope snapped.

'That, Holy Father, is not within your power,' he replied and left the office. He didn't realise that he had slammed the door until he raised his eyes to a tableau of frozen faces.

VIENNA, 1940

Franz Steiner checked over his shoulder, again. The Judenplatz was as empty as the last time he'd looked … and the time before that. He raised his coat collar, even though the sun was shining. He felt as if the gaping doorways and broken windows were inhaling the warmth from his body. It had been a place bright with shops and raucous with people before the night of the broken glass … Kristallnacht.

'Six thousand Jews arrested in one night,' Klaus, the Professor of Mathematics, had confided to him over coffee.

'Where did they take them?'

Klaus had looked annoyed. 'No one knows,' he'd said irritably, draining his coffee and slamming out of the coffee shop. Franz had sipped at his *einen braunen*, a strong coffee with just a dash of milk. A mistake to drink it then, he thought, a mistake to remember it now as the bitter phantom taste of the coffee erupted at the back of his throat.

'You are looking for something?'

The voice rooted him to the pavement. He sensed it came from the doorway he had just passed but he didn't turn.

'I'm … I'm looking for Professor Eli Baruch,' he whispered. 'My name is Franz Steiner. I am a friend.'

'Step inside the next doorway and wait,' the voice commanded.

Standing in the shadows, Franz smelled the sour reek of burned timbers and damp plaster. The skeleton of the house loomed over him. Shafts of sunlight pierced through holes in the walls that had once been windows; back-lighting fractured floorboards like a giant x-ray. He clutched the large envelope tighter and tried to breathe through his mouth.

'Come.'

He followed a trail of small sounds as his invisible guide led him through a labyrinth of ruin until he stood before a door that seemed miraculously intact. The man who opened the door to his knock was a stranger. The Eli Baruch he'd known had been a liberal Jew; a patron of the opera, a member of the board charged with the upkeep of the Figarohaus, where Mozart had lived. He had also been a man who favoured tailored, dark suits and blinding white shirts. This man before him was a caricature of an Old Testament prophet. Wispy white hair haloed a gaunt face. He wore a collarless open-necked dress shirt that had faded to a weary grey. That grey extended to the trousers that had once been black. In contrast, the hand extended to him was spotless; scrubbed a shocking pink. And the eyes … the eyes hadn't changed. They were still shining with much of the intensity and humour Steiner remembered. He took the hand and held it as if he would never let it go.

Eli Baruch squinted his eyes into slits as he held the x-rays against the light of a window that was largely intact. When he finished, he slipped them carefully back in the envelope and dropped it on a chair. A chair, Franz noted, that needed three large medical textbooks to compensate for one short leg. With the ease of long practice, the professor plucked a stethoscope from a drawer and motioned Franz to remove his coat and shirt. He was tapped and prodded for what felt like a lifetime, coughing on command until the professor bade him to get dressed.

Franz Steiner shot his shirt cuffs just a fraction proud of his jacket sleeves and checked himself in the frameless mirror that leaned against the wall. Flakes of the backing silver had succumbed to age and gravity so that pieces of his reflection were erased. He was not a vain man and he looked dispassionately at the figure in the glass. A little more salt in the hair, he thought, a lot less flesh in the face. He moved his head to the side and the smudges under his eyes moved with them. The dark suit enhanced his pallor and hung from the straight rack of his shoulders. The man in the mirror smiled back at him. He remembered being fitted for his first formal suit. The tailor had tugged and tweaked and said, 'It hangs well on you, sir.' When the man had excused himself to attend to another customer, his father had laughed. 'You look as if you could spin right around and the suit wouldn't move,' he'd said.

Franz walked from behind the screen and lowered himself gingerly into an overstuffed chair. It wheezed under his weight and his nose wrinkled against the dry smell of mortar dust.

Professor Baruch was washing his hands methodically in a porcelain basin. He soaped the back of one hand, moving the other hand in a clockwise motion until he extended the motion to the tip of each finger. He then turned the hand over and carefully massaged the palm and the heel of his hand before starting on the other. The triangle of sunlight from the window turned the droplets to silver as he sluiced his hands. Franz looked around at the bare walls. He shifted his feet and heard the gritty rasp under his shoes. A small, oval carpet stretched between him and the desk. He thought it emphasised the desolation of the room. There had been a waiting room, he remembered, cluttered with antique furniture. And a receptionist, was it Rachel? Rebecca? He couldn't recall her name. Why would he? She had been a person, like so many others, whose life had glanced against that of the Herr Chancellor of the University in the interlude between one important appointment and the next. They had stuck faithfully to the script that marked the boundaries of their roles and social station.

'Good morning, Herr Chancellor.'

'Good morning.'

'The Herr Professor will see you presently. Please be seated.'

'*Danke.*'

Where was she now? How could he ask after someone who had no name? That appointment had been two years earlier. Lisl had pestered and he had capitulated. His wife had monitored every small cough and sniffle of his during their thirty years of marriage, intent on warding off the most negligible signs of mortality in her husband and growing increasingly blind to her own … until it had been too late. Too late to do anything more than hold her hand. What a small hand she'd had.

'Schnapps?'

Startled out of his reverie, Franz looked up. Somehow, Professor Baruch had managed to wheel his chair from the other side of the desk and set it beside his own. He wondered briefly how his old friend had managed to snag two glasses and a bottle on the way.

'Why not?' he smiled. 'The sun is setting somewhere in the world.'

The surgeon nodded and poured generous measures into both glasses.

'It's that bad, then,' Franz said softly.

Eli Baruch held his gaze for a moment and then tossed the cork into a waste basket.

'We are alive today,' he said, 'let us drink to life. *L'Chaim.*'

The fiery schnapps consumed the air in Franz's lungs so that he had a moment of breathlessness. He remembered childhood asthma and the terror time between one breath and the next and the recent episodes when he'd been ambushed by a shortage of air. Self-induced, this time, he thought.

When he could speak again, he looked his friend in the eye.

'How long?'

'As your doctor, I must say not long. As your friend … too soon.'

Franz nodded and dipped his eyes, moved by the sadness in the other man's face.

'There may be … periods of discomfort,' Eli Baruch continued, his long fingers cupping the glass in a cat's cradle. 'They may become prolonged.' He took an envelope from his trouser pocket and handed it to Franz. 'These will help in the short term. For later, I think it best if I refer you to a colleague who will help you. I hope this isn't too inconvenient, Franz. You have been my patient since … well, for thirty years, but things being as they are … it might be politic for you to consult someone else.'

Franz Steiner had a sudden flash of insight a moment when all the little pieces of the jigsaw clicked into place; the empty waiting room, the absent secretary, the bald spot on his friend's head that had been hidden by a skull cap for thirty years. A wave of anger rolled over him and his fingers whitened on the glass so that a tiny wave washed over the rim and freckled the carpet.

'It is no matter,' his friend said. 'A doctor's carpet is chosen for no higher aesthetic purpose than soakage. I've had it for forty years; it deserves a little schnapps.'

'I think,' Franz said, when he managed to get himself under control, 'I would prefer to continue as your patient. As one gets older, one becomes more resistant to change.'

Eli Baruch nodded thoughtfully.

'Did I ever tell you about my sister Sarah?'

'No, I don't believe you did.'

'She and her husband took a trip to America. She went in February and had become obsessed with a fear of icebergs. Well, on the third day of the voyage she went to the captain. 'What will happen if we hit an iceberg?' she asked.

'Madam,' he replied, 'the iceberg will continue as if nothing had happened.'

'You made that up.'

'The bit about my sister going to America is true. A friend of a friend said she should. He said the winter would be very harsh this year. They managed to collect the money for the tax we must pay the Reich for the privilege of leaving our country. Her whole family went and anyone she could persuade.'

'But not you.'

Eli shook his head. 'You can still pay the fare but nowadays the voyage ends somewhere else.' He drained his glass and tipped the bottle in Franz's direction. The Chancellor nodded.

'My grandfather walked out of Russia in winter,' Eli continued. 'The Cossacks thought even a Jew couldn't be that desperate. My father walked out of Poland, all the way to Vienna. Where else could the grandson of a kulak become a surgeon and call the Chancellor of the University his friend?'

Franz raised his glass in a small salute.

'I have friends in Switzerland,' he said.

Eli leaned forward and patted Franz's knee. 'You are blessed in your friends and your friends are blessed in you, Franz, but Calvinists make me nervous. No *Gemütlichkeit* … they're not comfortable in their skins. As if God had trapped an angel and clothed it in butcher's wrapping paper. Anyway, I think the walking gene skipped a generation. I was born here, Franz,' he said fiercely. 'If they want me to leave, they'll have to take me.'

As the professor sat back into his winged chair, Franz Steiner saw the shadows steal his eyes.

KARL: HALLSTATT, 1940

Karl hunched over the desk under the eaves of his attic bedroom. He'd woken with the dawn and gone down to have breakfast with his father. The talk had been of what was being fashioned in the workshop and the steady trickle of orders from people in the village and from villages beyond the valley. He noted how his mother and father finished each other's sentences and smiled, stretching his legs beneath the table and curling his toes like a cat. When his father had left for the workshop, he'd stacked the bowls, excused himself and returned to his room.

The replacement teacher hadn't come yet, but he didn't want to pass the days in idleness. He chided himself for using the word 'replacement'. Herr Tauber couldn't be replaced. He was the one who had unlocked Karl's mind to the rich hoard of history in Hallstatt and encouraged the carpenter's son to read his way over the enclosing mountains and discover the wider world beyond.

As he read, sunlight edged across his desk and finally teased him to the window. 'Adam and Eve didn't know they had lived in Paradise until they'd lost it,' Herr Tauber had said. Karl propped his elbows on the sill and let the view and the sunlight soothe his sense of loss. He could think of Herr Tauber now without feeling the sharp pain he'd felt a few months before. His mother had assured him that this would happen.

'We hurt for a time,' she'd said, 'and then we remember warmly.'

Looking out of the window, he knew he lived in Paradise. By noon, the lake would begin to steam and shroud the far shore. Now the air was limpid and the mountains lined his vision. He let his gaze dip from the white peaks, down the glistening shale, through the pale green of the upland vegetation to the dark forests that carpeted the lower reaches. His eyes dropped further to the mountains' reversed reflection in the lake, and fastened on the boat.

Johann, the boatman, and his son Erich were making their way to the far shore, anticipating the arrival of the early train. The oars dimpled the water and their wake angled out in lazy and diverging lines, rippling the reflection of the mountains. The steeple of the Lutheran church reeled his attention back to the foreshore and the houses that stood on stilts at the fringe of the lake. The bell of St Michaelskappelle, the Catholic church, tolled faintly from higher up the slope, and he watched women hurry from their homes for early mass. Men who had farms on the fringes of the village ambled to their fields, while miners hiked the road that led upwards past his house, their heads already bowed in contemplation of the earth that would swallow them. Behind him, the mountains converged to cup the valley. Up there was the worked-out salt mine he and his friends liked to visit. Higher still, the working-mines honeycombed the mountains to a depth of four hundred metres and stretched far into the massif. This was his place. These were his people. For a moment, he felt a surge of warmth in his chest as it occurred to him that he would live here forever.

It was the perfect start to the perfect day, he thought, as he moved away from the window and clattered down the stairs. Today, he would meet Elsa and Max outside the bierkeller near the Michaelskappelle, and they would ... they would share this perfect day together; just three friends enjoying a carefree day a world away from whatever was happening on the other side of the mountains. If Max would come. If his mother would let him. He shook that shadow from his thoughts, kissed his mother fleetingly on the top of the head, and hurried outside.

VIENNA

Franz could hear the blood pulse in his ears as he wove through the narrow streets of the Jewish Quarter until the hum of the city began to override the drumming in his head. Rounding a sharp corner, scored by generations of wagon wheels, he was rewarded, at last, by a thin sliver of sunlight. Ahead, he knew, was Wipplingerstrasse, and he felt such an overwhelming sense of relief that he staggered and almost fell on the sunlit pavement.

After a few steps, he felt the first sour gust of nausea rise in his throat and placed his palms on the low wall that bordered the pavement. The schnapps, he thought; I should have passed on the schnapps. When the spasm passed, he moved shakily to another section of the wall and sat. His handkerchief showed streaks of red when he wiped his mouth. He balled it and looked vainly for a rubbish bin. He thought of throwing it on the pavement, but the Chancellor of the University couldn't bring himself to do such a thing and so he folded it carefully and put it back in his pocket. The visit to Eli Baruch had been what? he mused. A journey in pursuit of hope? A quest for the definitive answer to the question he hadn't asked and the medics hadn't offered to answer? It was both these things. Eli Baruch had provided the answers to all the questions except perhaps to the most important one. The most important question, he concluded, wasn't when he would die but how he would live, in the meantime.

Franz walked slowly in the direction of the Hamme Market, letting the sunlight bleed the tension from his shoulders; closing his eyes and lifting his face as he passed under the linden trees, feeling the dappled shadows, like small fingers, stroking his eyelids.

'Stop!'

A surge of adrenaline boiled through his body. I'm going to throw up, he thought. He felt the familiar flex of his stomach muscles – felt his throat open in anticipation and swallowed convulsively until it passed. 'I will not be sick,' he told himself fiercely. 'I will not give them the satisfaction …' He opened his eyes and stared at a pair of horses, who stared back. They both had ugly misshapen heads like things a boy might make from soft wax. The one on the left looked stonily at him while its companion's prim mouth chewed some invisible cud, its lips writhing so disgustingly that he feared the sick cycle would start all over again. With an effort, he wrenched his eyes away from them and let his gaze travel down their bodies to the ornate, open Fiaker hitched behind. A man sat on the driver board, shapeless in a creased cape. Under a wide-brimmed hat, his face was shadowed, except for his mouth which chewed in seeming sympathy with the horses.

'Sorry for shouting, Excellency,' he said. 'I thought you'd ram the horses.'

'No … no,' Franz said quickly, 'I … I was …'

He was lost for words and gazed at the driver helplessly. Some instinct warned him against saying where he had been, and yet his rational mind countered the man must have seen the direction he'd come from. He must see the smears of masonry dust on his trousers and jacket, must smell the miasma of decay he felt he carried with him.

'You look tired, your honour. Sit in the back. I'll take you home.'

The Herr Chancellor registered the shift from Excellency to Honour and put it down to the everyday irony of the Viennese. But he was calmed by the rough kindness in the man's voice and hoisted himself into the small carriage. A sharp whistle from the driver swung the horses into the road. Their rhythmic clopping lulled Franz to lean back against the stiff upholstery.

'Not a tourist?'

'No.'

'Thought so. Not these days. Gentleman's lost, I thought. Looking for something. Bookshop. Yes, that's it. One on the corner, back there. Gone now. Very popular. Lots of customers. Intellectual types.'

He paused in his staccato monologue to swivel his head.

'Like yourself, your Grace. Intellectual, looking for a special book. That's the story, isn't it, sir?'

'Y … Yes,' Franz nodded.

'Good,' the driver replied, turning his face to the road.

'So many questions, these days,' he continued, as if thinking aloud. 'Questions, questions.'

Franz Steiner was not a worldly man, nor was he particularly wise. A life in academia had precluded him from the possession of what people called common sense. He was always mildly amazed that his daughter, Bertha, had managed to be academic and astute. But he was not a fool. Even a fool, he thought, would be hard-pressed to miss the driver's message. There was every chance that he had been observed either entering or exiting the Jewish Quarter. That tickling sensation between his shoulders had already been there before the man spoke from behind him. 'In the present climate,' his university colleagues were wont to say when they wanted to euphemise Austria of the Anschluss. God, how they riffled frantically through some internal thesaurus to avoid words like occupation, invasion and liberation and conceal their own particular political view. And how he had smiled at that. But in the present climate, he accepted, there would be watchers, and watchers evolved – no, devolved – into 'followers' and, inexorably, into 'interrogators'. He shivered and willed himself not to look over his shoulder.

'Here,' he said, and the driver reined his horses to the kerb.

'How much do I owe you?'

The driver stepped down smartly to open the little door and offer a hand to his passenger.

'Often pick up gentlemen there, sir,' he said, easing Franz to the pavement. 'Looking for that bookshop I mentioned. No, sir, you don't owe me for such a small favour.'

He went to withdraw his hand and Franz held it a moment longer.

'I think I owe you more than I can repay,' he said quietly.

'Won't see you wandering thereabouts again will I, sir?'

'No.'

MAX: HALLSTATT

His mother handled the cooking utensils as if she resented them. It was a blessed relief when she moved to the window. There, she began a commentary on the passersby, a mangling monologue that was reductive and cruel. She returned to slap porridge bowls before his father and himself. The spoon he picked from the table was already heavy with admonitions. 'The waste of good food is a sin – in Croatia, we had one bowl and took turns with the spoon.'

His father looked scrawny in his open-necked shirt, his thin shoulders harnessed with navy suspenders. While they ate, she pared the peace of the morning with cutting asides and sharp silences. He watched his father erect defences of elaborate rituals. He saw him tilt the spoon, angle it into the porridge, scrape its base on the rim of the bowl and blow across the surface. He saw him duck his head to take the porridge into his mouth, as if lifting his elbow from the table might expose him to attack. Soon, Max thought, I will escape. Karl and Elsa will be waiting for me. He knew that if he announced that fact, there would be an interrogation. His mother would hover behind his chair and ask him interminable questions. She would belittle his friends with snorts and heavy sighs.

'I'm going to return a book to Father Kyril,' he said.

He sensed his mother's stillness and saw his father hunch lower behind the palisade of his upright arms. Father Kyril's name was just another hazard in the minefield of his home. The priest, to him, was a tortured man who said mass with the desperation of someone clinging to faith by his fingertips. And yet, he felt attracted to the agony in him, finding solace in his moral rants for the conflict within himself. He knew it was Karl who included him in these outings and that Elsa tolerated him for Karl's sake. And, although their obvious ease in each other's company emphasised his own singularity, a part of him craved their company, their lightness. With them, he could sometimes risk lowering his defences.

Three more spoonfuls to freedom, he thought, and almost smiled at the image of a boy tunnelling his way to freedom with a porridge spoon. Typically, his father could never suffer silence.

'That bastard, Tauber,' he intoned. 'All that paperwork for a Jew.' He continued to shovel porridge into his mouth against the flow of vitriol that poured out, so that bits of food shot like shrapnel across the table. 'Hitler has the right of it,' he continued. 'It's time to smoke them out. Damn rats have been feeding on the Reich since Versailles.'

Two more spoonfuls.

'Once and for all.'

One more spoonful.

'They have it coming.'

Outside the door, the morning light dazzled and shamed him as if it had exposed his darkness for anyone to see. He looked around, furtively, anticipating jeers and pointed fingers. A miner trudged by, carrying sunlight on his back. Somewhere, in the distance, a cow lowed, simply to hear its own sound. The normality of it all eased him upright and he began to walk. Every step took him away from them. He felt that the atmosphere of his home clung to him and permeated his clothes with the stink of old smoke. He started to run.

★

He had to brace himself as the odour of strong coffee enveloped him. The Café Figaro was a fug of pipe smoke and spicy humidity. He was relieved to see Klaus, the mathematician, and Professor La Croix of the French department occupying their usual table to the rear of the café. Klaus waved and rose to his feet, his keen eyes seeming to measure him as he made his way through the tangle of small tables.

'The Herr Chancellor looks like a young undergraduate who has been doing some late-night research in a bierkeller,' Klaus observed.

'I must bow to your extensive experience of that, Professor,' Franz riposted, attempting a smile. His colleague pulled a chair from the table. 'Sit down before you fall down,' he said gently. 'What can I get you?'

'*Melanksch*, I think.'

'*Melanksch*?' Klaus snorted. 'Milky coffee for maiden aunts? Well, if that's your poison,' he muttered, and grumbled away to the counter. Franz angled himself so that he was upwind of La Croix's sulphurous pipe. The French professor sat hunched over his mug as if inhaling his moka. He held an open book in both hands to barricade himself against interruption. In Viennese circles, Franz mused, moka was a brew deemed suitable to French and Italian palates. Klaus, he saw from the dregs in the cup beside him, was drinking *eine türkische*, the dark coffee prepared semi-sweet in a copper pot. Semi-sweet with a bitter aftertaste; much like the man, he mused. We have a coffee for every taste and mood, he concluded, as his friend placed the cup before him. We even have one for those who suffer from sickly stomachs. He was aware of Klaus' attention and raised the cup dutifully to his lips. He sipped a tiny amount, allowing the bland concoction just a moment on his tongue before he strained it down. Despite his best efforts, the cup rattled as he replaced it in the saucer.

'Don't you have a faculty meeting to attend?' Klaus said, rounding on La Croix.

'I do?'

'You do. *Auf Wiedersehen.*'

As the Frenchman scurried from the café, Franz raised a quizzical eyebrow at his companion.

'He needs to be off the streets, anyhow,' Klaus said defensively. 'The Herr Professor is both noisily critical of the status quo and a Frenchman. Not a very safe combination just now.'

'But surely his position at the university wo—'

'Oh, for the love of God, Franz,' Klaus snarled and then quickly drank his coffee as heads turned their way. 'I'm sorry, please forgive me,' he continued, 'but you seem blissfully unaware of what is happening around you.'

'I have been ... preoccupied,' Franz allowed. 'So tell me, what is happening?'

Klaus leaned across the table and lowered his voice. 'People are disappearing,' he whispered.

'You mean J—'

'No, for Christ's sake, man, don't say it. Not here. But yes. In Vienna, we had over one hundred and sixty-five thousand before the Anschluss. According to my sources, only a fraction remain. There is more, Franz. There are others, many others, who suddenly cease to exist The ... visitors are everywhere, currying favour and culling discontent. They are in the government, the Church, even in the university.'

'The Church?'

'The dominant Church in Austria dances to Rome's tune, Franz, and Rome has positioned herself on the dance-card of every powerful leader since Constantine. Our esteemed cardinal waved a welcome like all the others, my friend.'

'But the university!' Franz protested. 'Surely you don't believe that?'

'I do believe it and you had better believe it,' Klaus said vehemently. He laughed suddenly and wiped his mouth with a trembling hand. 'I suppose we should be flattered to be considered capable of subversion.' He leaned back in his high-winged chair, as if exhausted. 'Dammit, Franz,' he said wearily, 'you are the historian. Ask yourself some questions. Ask yourself what sort of people they regard as a threat. The butcher, the baker the candlestick maker? No! They are the poor and they have been promised better times. It costs nothing to switch allegiances when you have nothing to lose. The middle class? No, for the opposite reason; they have everything to lose.'

'Which leaves us,' Franz said dryly, 'the so-called intellectuals.'

'Yes, us and the artists, writers, philosophers; the people who think for a living. The people who smile at crude, racist propaganda, who raise their eyebrows at foreign uniforms on our streets; who might even have the temerity to ask questions and make speeches.'

'How little they know of us.'

'Perhaps, but we know of them. Tales travel, Franz. They're coming from Poland, Czechoslovakia, France, Belgium and even little Luxembourg. They tell of institutions closed if they are considered unfriendly – people considered unfriendly are disappeared.'

'What should we do?'

Klaus drained his *eine türkische* and grimaced at the bitter taste. 'Survive,' he said, and Franz thought he looked ashamed. 'I have a wife and four sons, Franz. I will teach mathematics and, otherwise, keep my mouth shut. And when all this has passed I will try to live with myself.'

'There must be other options,' Franz said thoughtfully.

'Not for me. I haven't the imagination for martyrdom or the luxury to suicide. Oh, yes,' he continued, seeing his friend's expression, 'the figure now runs at two hundred per month. You see, Franz, even in this I am no more than a numbers man. My hope is that there are enough massing on the other side of the scale to overbalance this one. Or ...'

'Or?'

'Or that their Kriegseuphorie will tempt them to bite off something that will choke them.'

'Like Napoleon? You think they will—'

'Franz, Franz.' He waved a weary hand to halt the chancellor. 'You, as I said, are the historian, probably the brightest mind we've had in the university during my tenure. You don't need to spell things out, now or ever. Do you understand?'

'Yes.'

'Good. Then let me say this. You must look to your own.'

'Bertha?'

'No,' Klaus shook his head impatiently. 'Your daughter has much of your genius and little of your naiveté.'

'I was thinking about that a little earlier,' Franz murmured.

'Franz, please. This is no time to be … abstracted. I mean Kurt, your son-in-law, who is equally gifted but—'

'But?'

'You know what we're like in the common room. We gossip like old women. Who has tenure? Who is waiting for another to die? Coffee-crucifixions of ambitious colleagues. It's harmless nonsense, for the most part. But I have heard talk of unsubtle innuendo and sarcastic asides during lectures, the sort of daring talk that passes for erudition among you historians. If it reaches my ears, then you can be sure …'

He stood abruptly and dropped some coins on the table. 'You look like shit,' he grunted, and Franz's eyes smarted at the trace of concern in his voice. 'Take better care of yourself, man. You look as if you've seen a ghost.'

'I have,' Franz Steiner replied. He said it softly, as his friend left the restaurant, careful not to be overheard.

ELSA: HALLSTATT

Elsa had woken as soon as her father had eased open her door. She'd kept her eyes closed; it was important to observe the rituals and this one stretched back as far as she could remember.

'And the little girl fell into a deep sleep,' he'd whispered. 'As the sun came up, an ugly troll came down the mountain from his home in the mine.' At this point, he made grunting noises and took heavy steps to the side of her bed. 'The troll was amazed to see the little girl all tucked up and fast asleep. She was the most beautiful creature he'd ever seen. Apart from a boar he'd seen once and a very handsome weasel.'

She'd shaken with suppressed laughter under the covers as he'd continued.

'What should the troll do? Should he eat her up? No, she was tough and bony and he'd be spitting freckles for hours. Instead, he leaned down and kissed her.'

She felt the rasp of his cheek on her own.

'Did he turn into a prince?' he said, as he padded back to the door. 'Did she turn into a princess? No. She was still tough and bony and freckly and he was still a troll. Sadly, he set off for his mine in the mountains.'

'And good riddance,' she'd shouted after him and snuggled deeper. His rumbling laugh warmed her to the tips of her toes.

The girl she saw in the mirror was tough and bony and freckly. Elsa stuck out her tongue at her equally rude image, picked up her satchel and slammed the door behind her. It was such a beautiful morning, she thought. If she hadn't been such a serious student, she might have conjured the usual clichés to describe it. If she hadn't been seventeen years old, she might have skipped. 'Grüss Gott,' she wished on those she met on the path and smiled at their cheerful responses. She knew that, one day, she would leave Hallstatt for the University in Vienna but not today. Today was—? She stopped at the rim of the hill that sloped down to the village. The sky, mountains, lake and village filled her vision and she felt a surge of pure happiness. I'll come back here, one day, she thought, and teach at the school and stay for ever and ever.

Karl sat on the step outside the bierkeller. She had a few moments to observe him as she approached. He had the sort of hair that held red embers in winter and then bleached almost white in summer. He wore a blue shirt that did nothing for his pale face. She registered this before he sensed her approach and turned. He had blue eyes. Usually, they were intense, as if he was recording the details of the world around him to study later. She thought they were the sort of eyes that would look thoughtful behind spectacles when he was a lecturer at the University in Vienna and—. He saw her and smiled.

'Were you going in or falling out?' she teased, inclining her head at the bierkeller.

'What?'

'Obviously falling out,' she laughed, unslinging her bag and sitting down beside him. 'Well, what are we waiting for?' she asked. 'The mysteries of the Hallstatt Celts are waiting to be discovered.' They had planned to visit the archaeological site at the end of the lake and she'd packed sketch pads and pencils for the trip.

'Max,' he said, and she felt as though a cloud had passed across the sun.

'Why?' she asked, even though she knew what his answer would be.

'Because he's my friend, Elsa.'

There was no hint of defensiveness or reproof in his voice.

'Why?' she persisted.

'Why what?'

'Why are you friends?'

She felt she had to ask. How could two such polar opposites attract? Max was closed and cold when he wasn't being insufferably knowledgeable and boastful. Karl was – Karl.

'I – I don't know, Elsa.'

It wasn't that he hadn't thought about it, she knew that. She suspected he had reasons that he might think it disloyal to express – even to her. There had to be an element of pity, she surmised. They both knew Frau Steiger from unpleasant experience. She was the kind of mother who idolised her son and seemed a little jealous of his friends. As for his father, the policeman, even her father found it hard to say a positive word about him. She had often wondered how a man who could be invisible at home could be such a pompous ass in public. She wondered if Karl's pity for Max was the best foundation for a friendship and if it would last.

'Speak of the devil,' she said wickedly, as Max emerged from Father Kyril's house. The gaunt priest followed him outside, continuing their conversation. Although they were out of earshot, the priest's stabbing finger signalled another of the moral rants most of her age-group ignored. She saw Max bob his head, dutifully, and wondered how someone who could be so sarcastically dismissive of others' opinions could surrender himself so passively to the priest's.

She felt like a voyeur and leaned against Karl's shoulder. 'He looks like he could do with a friend,' she muttered grudgingly, and Karl pressed his shoulder to hers. He slung her bag over his shoulder and they went to meet Max. She thought Max almost smiled when he saw them. She wasn't certain; she'd been distracted by the obvious disapproval on the face of the priest.

VIENNA

Franz walked back to the university, letting his feet find their way as his head mulled over all that had happened since he had stepped off the planet and into the Jewish Quarter. He felt as if he had been plunged into an ice bath and surfaced to find his senses heightened. The baroque architecture looked somehow even more overblown than usual, like the yellowing icing on a rancid wedding cake. How could he have missed the bloody gashes of Nazi flags that bled over shopfronts and hotels? When he dropped his eyes, he saw that posters pocked the walls at regular intervals, celebrating the man who regarded himself as their liberator. And, at regular intervals, soldiers in coal-scuttle helmets stood on street corners, shifting their gaze first one way then another. Pedestrians, he noticed, crossed over the street rather than come close to these sentinels, or walked more quickly with faces averted when that wasn't an option. Within sight of the university, he began to sense the now familiar prickle between his shoulders.

For what seemed a long time, he stood in his office, pressing a handkerchief to his forehead, breathing in the comfort of familiar things.

'Herr Chancellor.'

He started at his secretary's voice and wondered how long she had been standing inside the door. Theresa Renner had been with him for over a decade. She was a petite woman of some thirty-five years or so – he couldn't be certain. In fact, he realised that, beyond the fact that she was unfailingly efficient, he knew almost nothing about her, except that she was Fraulein Renner who placed his post on the desk each morning, typed his replies and kept his appointments diary. He had overheard someone in the common room refer to her as Cerberus and deduced that she was efficient at protecting him from non-essential interruptions. He hadn't noticed that she had cornflower-blue eyes and that her fair hair was bound up behind her head in an old-fashioned knot or that the sunlight from the window behind her burnished one side of her face with a soft downy halo.

'Herr Chancellor,' she repeated and something in the tone of her voice alerted him to the fact that he had been staring. 'I beg your pardon, Fraulein Renner,' he said, 'I'm afraid my thoughts were … somewhere else.' He saw an expression flit across her face. Was it one of apprehension or disappointment? He had never been good at this sort of thing and tended to rely on his late wife to prompt him into doing the right thing and preserve him from putting his foot in it too often.

'There is a gentleman to see you, sir,' she said. That simple statement seemed to clear his mind and bring him into focus.

'He doesn't have an appointment, does he?'

'No, sir. He … he says you have been looking for him all day.'

The man who stepped into his office would have been tall but for a scholar's stoop. The Chancellor placed him at about the same age as himself. He had a few moments to register the crumpled suit, a frayed shirt-collar and a tie that dangled over the bump of his belly. The man carried a soft hat between the thumb and forefinger of his left hand. With his free hand, he picked up a chair and brought it to the desk. He sat. Up close, Franz saw watery blue eyes magnified by thick spectacles. A coating of dust was illuminated on one lens by the same shaft of sunlight that had plucked Fraulein Renner from her usual invisibility. Slowly, the man reached into his inside pocket and placed a wallet on the desk between them. He flicked it open with a practised forefinger and turned it so that Franz could see the small photograph and official stamp.

'Should I be flattered that the Gestapo has been watching me?'

'Not particularly,' the man replied in a surprisingly soft voice. 'They watch everybody – even each other.'

'They? Then you are not—'

'No. A historian should really look more closely at official documents, Herr Chancellor,' he continued with a small smile. Franz dropped his eyes again to the identity card.

'Who, or what, is SD?' he asked.

'The Sicherheitsdienst, a sister organisation to the Gestapo, although we might wish that our 'sister' had a little more refinement. To put it in terms you can more readily understand: they are the researchers, we are the ones who assess the information.'

'And your name?'

'Is not on the card, Herr Chancellor. Introductions are unnecessary. You and I are meeting now; we will not meet again. You understand?'

Franz nodded and the man returned the wallet to his pocket.

'Am I to be interrogated?'

'What? Oh no, Herr Chancellor,' the man replied, as if surprised. 'That is not the function of my department. You are aware, I'm sure, that there are others whose talents, shall we say, are more suited to that. No, there is no need for any of that unpleasantness. Besides, I already know all I need to know about you. If I may recap briefly: you held the Chair of History at the university up to ten years ago when you were appointed to the chancellorship. You are a widower who has a daughter who is an academic and is married to another academic who now lectures in the History Department.'

'It seems rather a waste of resources to collect information that is common knowledge, sir.'

'Yes, of course, you're right. But that is not all we know of you, Herr Chancellor. What is not common knowledge is that you entered the Jewish Quarter at approximately ten o'clock this morning. You met a man ... his name is Moshe Horowitz, by the way. He escorted you to meet Professor Eli Baruch. At approximately eleven twenty-eight you left the Jewish Quarter and walked in the direction of the Hamme Market where you took a Fiaker to the Stephansdom. At eleven forty-four, you met with professors Klaus and La Croix in the Café Figaro. Professor Klaus bought you a melanksch … coffee …'

'And what do you deduce from that startling item of information?' Franz interrupted.

'Oh, by itself, very little. But, coupled with the x-rays you brought to Professor Baruch – x-rays which you left in his office, by the way, together with the testimony of a consultant at the … hospital, I would deduce that you are dying, Herr Chancellor.'

Franz felt as if the tension that had been building in his body since the man first stepped into the room suddenly evaporated, leaving him at ease. A disease that is named and made ordinary in the mouths of others loses its power to confine and confound, he reflected.

'Why are you here, sir?' Franz asked calmly.

The man nodded once, as if marking the transition in the chancellor and in their discussion.

'To give you choices, Herr Chancellor.'

'Under the circumstances, it seems my choices are limited.'

'Yes, you are correct. There are times in our lives when our choices seem unlimited, such as in our youth. Eternity stretches before us and we can choose a path in the comfort of knowing that we can always retrace our steps with impunity and opt for another. In times of crisis, however, our range of choices narrows – but there is still choice, even if it is the choice between the lesser of two evils.'

'You are quite philosophical about this, sir. Do you speak from the experiences of others or from yourself?'

The man removed his spectacles and pinched the bridge of his nose between thumb and forefinger. After a moment, he replaced his spectacles, looked keenly at Franz Steiner and sighed.

'We are both the results of our choices, Herr Chancellor, for better or for worse.' He smiled bleakly for a moment and then his face became expressionless. 'You may choose to remain as Chancellor of the university for as long as your condition allows. If you so choose, my superiors desire that you supply me with the personal records of every member of staff and every student of the university. You will also facilitate the placement of our agents within the administration, forbid any criticism of the Reich and promote the closest co-operation between the university and the authorities.' He said this in a toneless voice, as if reciting some document he had memorised.

'I would become your agent.'

'Yes, if that's how you wish to name our relationship.'

'And in return?'

'In return, you will be absolved of your indiscretions in the Jewish Quarter.'

'And if I should pass on that particular choice?'

'In that case, Herr Chancellor, there will be consequences for you and others.'

'If I agree, do you guarantee the safety of those others?'

The man shook his head.

'You are an intelligent man, Herr Chancellor,' he said, rising to his feet. 'You are a historian. Ask yourself when did the victors ever need to barter with the vanquished?'

'When the victor was aware of the possibility of trading places with the vanquished at some future time,' Franz Steiner replied quietly. 'And there are plenty of historical precedents. If the Allied Powers had paused to consider that at Versailles, would we be having this conversation? However, I'm sure that an intelligent man like yourself must have considered that.'

When the door closed, Franz Steiner stood and walked to a window that overlooked the quadrangle. Through a filter of immaculate, white lace curtains, he watched the untidy lines of students make their way from one lecture hall to another. The muffled hum of young voices rose from below, punctuated by an occasion yelp of laughter. He smiled. He had loved being a lecturer, striding the dais and exhorting his students to move beyond the bare bones of historical fact. 'The man in the street buys a newspaper to find out what has happened,' he liked to say. 'We historians busy ourselves in dusty archives to find out why. Both are valid and complementary approaches to history. But both of us, citizen and historian, live in this time. We are part of the continuum of history. When you have read *The History of the*

Austro-Hungarian Empire, tear off the back cover of that textbook and attach the photographs and letters of your grandparents and parents. If you keep a diary, add that to the textbook as well, and each evening when you write in your diary be aware of adding a page of history for another generation to read.'

It was a cliché with more than a ring of truth to it, but Franz Steiner knew that history was most often written by the conquerors. They are already within the gates, he thought. They are already writing the books that they plan to use as textbooks for a thousand years.

He returned to his desk and picked up the telephone. The number he dialled was of a friend who had responsibility for teacher appointments to schools throughout Austria.

'Herr Schmidt, if you please. This is Chancellor Steiner of the university.'

'Franz! To what do I owe this pleasure?'

'There is no owing between friends, Gregor.'

'Oh, God, now you have me worried.'

'Don't be. I was just recalling our last conversation. You mentioned certain shortages in teaching staff.'

'Hell, yes. Why are teachers so susceptible to war, Franz? The bloody idiots are climbing into uniform in their droves, as if they were going on some jolly geography field trip.'

'Well, that particular syllabus is being expanded by the day, isn't it, my friend?'

'You know I hate it when you go elliptical, Franz.'

'Let him who has ears hear, Gregor.'

'Oh! Well, yes of course, we do have vacancies. Please tell me that you can magic some replacements.'

'One.'

'For which God was prepared to spare Sodom and Gomorrah. And who is this answer to prayer?'

Franz told him.

'But isn't he—'

'Yes, he is.'

'He surely can't take a sabbatical at this time of the academic year?'

'Yes he can, Gregor, especially at this time of year. And, Gregor, where do you people put someone you don't want found?'

'I'll have to check. Let me call you back.'

'Within the hour, Gregor, if you don't mind, and with the necessary papers and travel documents delivered to my secretary after the weekend.'

'You're really worrying me now, Franz.'

Franz replaced the phone and picked up his pen, sliding a blank sheet of headed notepaper to the blotter.

'My dear Bertha,' he began.

HALLSTATT

Max was a snagging shadow in her peripheral vision; someone who seemed always present when she focused on other things, and absent, in some unsettling way, when she looked at him directly. It wasn't even anything he said, although he had plenty to say. It wasn't the way he said things, though his patronising tone rubbed her raw whenever he translated her enthusiasm for the archaeological site into sterile facts and dates. What infuriated her was that his talk and tone seemed to establish a boundary he refused to cross, a Rubicon that marked engagement from disengagement. Max was with them but not present to them. There was something almost parasitic about it that made her skin crawl.

Inevitably, she was drawn into the kind of verbal duel she thought she'd outgrown. It was cut and block, thrust and parry up to the point where he'd wondered where she'd misplaced her brain. Her father had always warned her that her tongue would break her jaw one day, but her riposte was out of her mouth before she could weigh the consequences.

'The same place you misplaced your soul, Max.'

He went completely still. A small frown puckered between his eyes as he analysed her comment. Slowly, the colour drained from his face until he had the sickly sheen of sour milk. He lifted his head and looked at her. She'd anticipated the hurt in his eyes and was already readying her apology when his eyes changed. A slow malevolence seemed to crawl from inside his head and look at her through his staring eyes. As quickly as it came, it disappeared and his eyes burned with recognition and rage. She had seen something malformed at his core and there could be no going back, his eyes said. There could be no forgiveness. She tried to maintain her defiance but she felt afraid.

'You two are like little kids,' Karl said, and the spell was broken.

Later, Karl cajoled them into a sketching competition. 'Our Celtic forebears,' he declared grandly. 'The task is to draw some artifact that symbolises the Hallstatt Celts.'

He's so transparent, she thought. He thinks we'll get time to cool off and everything will be as it was.

'It's a necklace, Elsa,' Karl said when he looked over her shoulder. 'It's very fine.'

'It's an amulet,' she said tonelessly, 'a ward against evil.' Karl held her gaze until she looked away.

'And yours, Max?' Karl asked.

Max had drawn a Celtic broadsword, the outline deeply gouged into the paper so that the sword seemed to stand up in relief.

'Looks sharp enough to cut,' Karl remarked mildly. 'And you've got the Celtic U-shaped hand-guard. It's very impressive, Max.'

'Your turn,' Elsa said.

'Oh, I'm no artist,' he said, smiling crookedly. 'You know that, Elsa.'

She did know that. Karl was a draughtsman. Every line of the tree he'd drawn was to scale. Even the serrations on the leaves were painstakingly done. Karl's tree was solid and unassuming. Like Karl, she thought, as she held it up to the light. The perfect leaves obscured the upper branches and hid whatever lay within. Small birds could roost there in safety, she thought, and felt some warmth return to her body.

They returned to the village in silence, Karl striding out before her and Max bringing up the rear. The itch between her shoulder blades urged her to overtake Karl and place his reassuring presence at her side. As they climbed one of the steep staircases that linked the lower and upper sections of the village, Max broke the silence.

'Let's stop at the Karnel,' he said, and strode away towards the small chapel that flanked the cemetery. The interior of the twelfth-century chapel provided a cool respite after their climb. She wondered why Max had brought them here. The Karnel was a repository for skulls and human bones. Everywhere she looked, she saw skulls set out in neat rows on the floor and stacked on shelves; hundreds of them.

'Traditionally, a grave is rented, not owned, in Austria,' Herr Tauber had taught them. 'After ten years or so, relatives are expected to dig up the skull and large bones and free the grave for another corpse. The Karnel is an ossuary. Where does that word come from?'

'From the Latin word for bone,' she'd answered and felt warm when he'd smiled approvingly.

'Relatives could bring the bones here,' he'd continued, 'to a consecrated place. Otherwise, great grandpa's skull might be watching you from the kitchen shelf at home.'

She remembered how they'd laughed nervously. She didn't feel like laughing now. There was a terrible vacancy in the empty eye sockets, something macabre in the way many of the skulls had been painted with a date or flowers. A skull near her foot had a painted serpent that seemed to undulate from one eye socket to the other and she took a step back.

'Father Kyril says it's good for us to reflect on our mortality,' Max said. His whisper scattered sibilants to hiss against the hard stone walls. 'This is what we are, in the end,' he continued, crouching before a skull on the floor. 'All our dreams and thoughts and longings,' he murmured, tapping the skull with his forefinger, 'all gone, forever. Nothing left inside,' he concluded and dug two fingers into the eye sockets.

'Max,' Karl said sharply and the boy lurched upright.

'What?' he asked. 'I was just—'

'It's not right to dishonour the dead,' Karl said firmly.

The other boy looked like he might argue, but he smiled and raised his hands in mock surrender.

Fraulein Renner was standing in front of his desk before he had taken his finger from the buzzer. 'Herr Chancellor?' she said, sweeping a truant strand of hair behind her ear.

'I think we might clean the in-tray, Fraulein,' he said smiling, 'if you think you can bear the excitement.'

They worked solidly for the next hour; she sorted the documents and he signed them. The ritual induced a kind of peace in him and he performed the task carefully, as if it was somehow sacred. At last, he capped the pen and laid it aside.

'Thank you, Fraulein Renner,' he said.

She bobbed her head and turned to go. 'Theresa,' he said softly. She paused and turned, a look of apprehension pressing her lips together. 'Do you have … family?'

'Yes, Herr Chancellor. My sister is married in—'

'Do you visit her often?'

'Not very often, sir, what with …' – she shrugged her armful of documents – '… my duties,' she continued, 'and the choir.'

'The choir?'

'Yes, sir, we sing at High Mass in the Stephansdom every Sunday and sometimes at other services.'

'It must be wonderful to sing in a choir,' he said softly. 'Will you do something for me?'

'Of course, sir.'

'Tomorrow is Friday,' he said. 'Could you take that day as a holiday and spend the weekend with your sister?'

'Oh yes, sir,' she blurted and he was moved by the blush of pleasure that spread over her face.

'Does your sister have family?'

'Two,' she said quickly, 'a boy and a girl, sir.'

'Do they like school?'

'Oh yes, sir. Sometimes, I am able to bring them books and we read in the evenings. I … I tell them if they read a lot, they might some day work in the university.'

'Like you, Theresa,' he smiled.

'No, not like me. Like you, sir.' She hugged the bundle of

documents closer and the colour deepened in her face. Franz took a pen from his inside pocket and picked the other from the table.

'Perhaps if they had pens like these, they could work here one day, like me … and you,' he said, holding them out to her.

'I couldn't … I mean … oh, sir.' Tears began to stream down her cheeks and she bowed her head. He moved around the desk and held her shoulders gently. 'Hush,' he whispered, 'there is no need for tears.'

'It's that man, isn't it?' she sobbed. 'I couldn't stop him. I'm so sorry.'

'No need to be,' he said, shaking her gently. 'Whole armies haven't stopped men like him.' He produced a large white handkerchief and put it in her hand. 'You may keep that,' he said, smiling. 'Over the years, I must have given a thousand of them to my daughter Bertha. Time for you to be off now,' he said, leading her by the elbow to the office door.

The phone on his desk rang sharply.

'Gregor? Good of you to get back so promptly. Thank you, Gregor. Yes, I seem to remember it was a closed area up to quite a short time ago. It sounds perfect. No, everything is fine now.'

He hung up the phone. Seated behind the desk again, he plucked a pen from his store in the drawer and drew a sheet of headed paper. Briskly, he wrote a letter granting sabbatical leave to his son-in-law, Kurt Brandt, and wishing him well in his new appointment as schoolmaster in the tiny village of Hallstatt. He sealed it in an envelope and placed it in the out-tray.

'*Consummatum est*,' he whispered. 'It is finished.'

He walked to the drinks cabinet and chose a wine bottle from the rack. Seated in a comfortable armchair, he emptied into his palm the contents of the envelope Eli Baruch had given him. 'Forgive me, Bertha,' he said, 'I love you more than life but I cannot …'

With one swift movement, he brought his palm to his mouth and struggled to swallow the tablets. Franz Steiner leaned back in his chair, sipping the wine, trying to dilute the bitter taste in his mouth.

★

They stopped at the fork in the path. Max lived in the lower town, Karl and Elsa on the upper slopes.

'My mother said you could come for coffee,' Karl said. 'She's been baking.'

'Oh, thank God,' Elsa gasped. 'My stomach thinks my throat is cut.'

Max shifted from one foot to the other. 'That's very kind,' he said, formally, 'but I have some reading to catch up on.'

'Oh, for heaven's sake, Max,' Elsa exploded, but Karl cut across her.

'We'll walk with you a bit,' he offered.

Elsa saw a face emerge from behind Max's tight features and braced herself. This time, it was the face of a small boy who seemed surprised at being included. It shone, for a moment, and melted back into the mask again.

'That's not necessary,' Max said, and walked away.

'Not advisable' is what he meant, she thought, as she and Karl continued their climb to the Hamner house. Max's dragon-mother might see us together and start preparing the instruments of torture. It had been a perfect day, except for the interlude in the ossuary. There had been something deeply unsettling in the way Max had poked his fingers into the skull's eye sockets. She hated that damned Karnel anyway. Why would her beloved Hallstatt enshrine the bones of the dead when she and Karl were so alive on this lovely day? The memory of their trip to the ossuary hung behind her shoulder, like a Roman priest whispering reminders of mortality into the ear of one returning in triumph. She shivered.

'Are you cold?' Karl asked.

'No,' she said. But when Frau Hamner hugged her in welcome, she clung to the embrace a little longer than usual, as if she needed to bolster the warmth of the day and her friendship with Karl and her belief that things would always be like this. Frau Hamner held her at arm's length and looked at her keenly.

'Where were you adventurers today?' she asked.

'In Paradise,' Elsa answered.

'And did you meet a serpent?' Frau Hamner asked, smiling.

'Yes,' Elsa said, gravely.

SICHERHEITSDIENST HEADQUARTERS, VIENNA

Claus Fischer the SD man sat back in his chair and waited. Waiting, he knew, was not something most people did well. The world was overrun with pacers and fidgeters, men who made an art form out of shifting from one cheek of their arse to the other. *Cogito ergo sum* popped into his head and he smiled. When Descartes had said, 'I think, therefore I am,' it must have registered with a maximum audience of two. The rest? The rest had already moved on to the next philosopher; an oxymoron, but true. And never more true, he thought, than in time of war. Is it a characteristic of Germans alone? he wondered. Is there some burr deep in our national psyche that irritates us into constant action? Does constant activity give us the illusion of achievement?

The nation is gripped with the urge for Lebensraum – living space. This time around, we ditched the horses because they were too slow for an army in a hurry. Then we ditched the maps, because borders were too confining and we rushed into most of Europe. Austria? No, we strolled into Austria. Even if we reach the Nirvana of taking Britain – what then? Where to next? We are the child's balloon that must be puffed bigger and bigger, because the alternative is to grow flaccid and deflate. Like the Roman Empire, he thought, gobbling up the world. That thought reminded him of Steiner and he shelved it. Where to, next? he asked himself, resuming his reverie. He had asked his colleague, Theodor, that very question that morning over coffee in the canteen. Canteen was a euphemism for the grim functionality of the room they shared with other ranks. It was made grimmer for Fischer by the men who came singly and in pairs from the cellars – men who sat aloof from the other personnel and laughed too loudly. Men who had set themselves apart by the work they performed and the spots of blood they wore like badges on their boots. 'East,' Theodor had whispered carefully into his coffee. Claus had raised an eyebrow in silent query and Theodor had simply bobbed his head. They were both SD old hands. They knew, better than most, that the walls had ears. The authorisation for installing the listening devices carried their signatures. When he had drained his mug, he walked back to his office … slowly. And here he sat, waiting.

He was unsurprised to hear the heavy footsteps approach his door. The Gestapo agent clicked his heels and flung his arm forward in salute.

'What is it, Dietrich?' Fischer asked mildly. He watched the rigidity of the man's body slip a little, noted the slight twitch of uncertainty in his eyes and cautioned himself about going too far. Remember, Claus, they are well-trained dogs. They will fetch and come to heel on command, if the command is consistent. Change the pattern and you confuse the dog and one day it will bite. 'At ease,' he snapped and the man lost his look of confusion. 'Report!'

He listened carefully, head tilted to one side, eyes fixed on the dull-grey surface of the metal table. Listen for facts and feelings, his old mentor in the service had advised. Facts come wrapped in feelings, Claus. Feelings distort and exaggerate facts. Let the feelings run their course and you will be left with what matters.

Contempt, he concluded. This man is reporting the death of one he thinks a coward. Perhaps the insecure need to bolster . themselves with high-minded judgement when confronted with suicide.

'When?'

'At approximately eight-thirty this morning, sir. A cleaner, one Frau Gehert, found the body.'

'Who reported the incident?'

'A Frau Loden, an administrative assistant, called the police at exactly eight forty-five, sir.'

Fischer nodded for him to continue and the agent narrated the sequence of events up to his reporting to SD.

'I presume his daughter has been informed.'

'Yes, sir, permission to bring—'

'No. We will not expose our interest by becoming involved with the daughter or her husband.'

'And the others, sir?'

'What? Oh yes, Klaus and La Croix.' He shook his head. 'La Croix is being returned to France. It has been arranged. Klaus ... will remain at the university. He is a survivor. He will not trouble us.'

'I ... I was referring to the Jews, sir.'

Fischer sat forward. 'What would you propose, Dietrich?' God, it was the oldest trick in the book, a book this oaf should have studied and still the question threw him.

'Well, we thought we had swept the city of these ...'

The agent struggled to find the appropriate word. You almost said 'people', didn't you? Fischer thought. 'Vermin,' he offered, and the agent grasped the word gratefully.

'Yes, sir, vermin, sir.'

'Dietrich, listen to me.' Fischer lowered his voice and leaned forward, his hands flat on the table top. He was unsurprised to see the agent bend his body to mirror his superior's posture.

'We will take no action against Baruch ... Do you know why?'

'No, sir.'

Still a little truculent, Fischer noted. Now it was time to reel him in.

'Because, Dietrich,' he said, raising a finger from the table, 'vermin in a cage are harmless.' He lifted a second finger. 'They may attract their wilder brethren and bring them to our attention. And...' He folded his hands together. The agent had fixed his eyes on the rising fingers and was now forced to look up and make eye contact. It was as Fischer intended – a message delivered with eye contact tends to be more easily believed and remembered.

'Austrians are different, Dietrich,' he continued. 'They will drink their coffee and blind themselves to the disappearance of thousands. Why would they be concerned at the fate of two? Because they are the last two of all those thousands. We are not in the business of making martyrs.'

He snapped upright.

'No further action ... for now,' he said briskly. 'Tomorrow, we will inform the university council of our choice of Chancellor.'

He stood and raised his arm.

'Heil Hitler.'

After the door had closed, Claus Fischer produced a handkerchief and blotted his face. So Steiner had made a choice after all, he mused. Not a choice he would make himself ... unless. He took a deep breath and leaned back in his chair. Steiner couldn't wait for the wheel to turn, he thought, and that's where we differ. I waited for the right time to join the party, which was thankfully after the Putsch. I waited and read the runes; identified the major players and hitched my wagon to the rising star Heydrich and found myself in the SD – which may be somewhere between the Valhalla of the inner circle and the Hell of the cellars, but it is still somewhere. And I am here. I am good at waiting. But sometimes the wheel needs a nudge. He leaned forward and picked up the phone.

HALLSTATT, THE SCHOOLROOM, 1941

Herr Professor Kurt Brandt, late of the University of Vienna, consulted his fobwatch, checking the progress of the second hand. *Tempus fugit*, he thought. Time flies. Except it doesn't, he countered, at least not here in Hallstatt. It judders – yes, that's the word. It judders from now, to now, to ... He snapped his eyes away to the students hunched over their work.

He had rearranged the desks in a semi-circle near the top of the draughty schoolroom so that his charges would benefit from the stove. Also, so that they would be less conscious of the accusing empty desks stacked one on top of another at the rear wall. Like miniature coffins, he thought and tucked his chin deeper inside his greatcoat. In just a few months, the war had whittled down his students from twenty to ten. The early, enthusiastic recruits had benefited from family connections to speed their service to the Reich, despite their youth. The rest had succumbed to the inexorable cull of conscription, despite whatever influence their contacts exerted. For those who remained, apart from the girls, he knew it was only a matter of time. That word drew him back to the face of his fobwatch. He saw the second hand as clipping seconds from young lives like a silver guillotine, as it made its circuit of the dial. It was still five seconds shy of the hour when he said 'time' and clicked his fobwatch closed.

Some of the students slumped over their test papers as if they were puppets and someone had snapped their strings. Elsa and Karl remained crouched and taut while Max stretched back and yawned ostentatiously. 'Karl,' Professor Brandt said, 'if you would be good enough to collect these masterpieces and bring them here, time and sanity permitting, I'll have them corrected by Monday. *Auf Wiedersehen*.'

He turned and began to erase the test question from the blackboard, oblivious to the miniature chalk-blizzard that enveloped his head and shoulders. He had already obliterated 'Russia, the bête noire of', leaving 'Napoleon' still starkly white on the black background when he paused. He wondered how many of his students would have managed to translate the question, never mind answer it adequately. Three, he concluded; the Druckner girl, the quiet Hamner boy and that irritating Max Steiger. The rest? He looked at his chalk-frosted fingers and wondered if he should have raised them up as some form of visual clue. It would, he knew, have been a waste of time. Why hadn't anyone asked for a translation of bête noire? How many times had he told them that ignorance did not equate with being stupid; not knowing was simply standing before a closed door. Open a textbook at home or a reference book at school and the key to that door falls into your hand. If you don't know, raise your hand and ask, he'd urged them. He accepted the majority would never do that – they'd never risk losing face among their peers by seeming stupid or eager. He also knew he was delaying the inevitable.

He sighed and turned to face them. 'Heil Hitler,' he said, raising his right arm to barely above the level of his fobwatch. 'Heil Hitler,' they responded. Kurt Brandt took some consolation from the half-hearted salutes of the majority. A few snapped it off smartly enough. Only Bruno, the postman's son, managed to click his heels. There would always be some, Kurt thought, who would need heroes to fill a vacuum in themselves. In Bruno's case, he reflected, that gap was between his ears. In Brandt's opinion, the hero who was the focus of Bruno's devotion was the bête noire of Austria, but he was wise enough to keep that opinion to himself – now.

Before the Anschluss, he had written letters to the Viennese papers arguing that an Anschluss would translate into occupation and had felt a degree of satisfaction when the Wehrmacht had goose-stepped into the city. He had smiled at the fluttering flags and fawning speeches and had laughed out loud over bitter coffee with his university colleagues in the cafés, until they had stopped coming to their mocking gatherings. And until Franz Steiner, his father-in-law, had killed himself. Even now, some months later, he found it hard to understand why the abstract and amiable chancellor had done something so dramatic. Of course, according to the coroner, Franz had been terminally ill, but ...? He had found it equally hard to accept that his father-in-law had fired him from his university post and arranged a temporary teaching post for him in Hallstatt. 'It's a bloody salt mine,' he'd protested to Professor Klaus at the post-funeral reception in the university. The Professor of Mathematics had looked haunted rather than elevated by his surprise appointment to chancellor, and had been making steady progress through the brandy while they conversed.

'Franz Steiner was a cultural paradox,' the man had slurred. 'He was an Austrian in whom there was no guile.'

'Well, yes, would you like another—'

'He didn't do the rounds of the coffee covens or the sneering circles and ... and at the end, he took care of those he cared for.'

'His affairs were quite in order, Herr Klaus. Bertha will be—'

'I'm not talking about Bertha, Brandt,' the old man said fiercely. 'I'm talking about you, and if you weren't so fixated on the fluff in your navel, you'd see that. He took care of you,' he reiterated, and Kurt was alarmed to see tears in his eyes. He helped him into his greatcoat and steered him carefully to the door, where Klaus paused again and drew Kurt closer to whisper, 'And he did for me.' He snorted a half-laugh, half-sob and tottered away.

Kurt stood and watched him weave across the quadrangle. He had wondered why Klaus had turned up his coat collar and hunched his shoulders on such a mild day.

He felt someone's attention on his back and shook himself from his reverie.

Max Steiger was watching him with expressionless eyes. '*Auf Wiedersehen*, Herr Professor,' the young man said, and followed his classmates. Had he imagined something knowing in the boy's eyes? Something sarcastic in his voice?

'Paranoia is a disease that confines the mind to the self, my dear,' Bertha had said when he spoke of his feeling of always being under someone's scrutiny in Hallstatt. 'A man who considers himself watched sees eyes everywhere.'

She was right, of course, but something – the emptiness behind the boy's eyes – had shaken him.

The village clung to the slopes of the foothills of the great peaks that housed the salt mines. Occsionally, he had paused on the path to steady himself against the serenity of the lake. Today, as he did most days, he took a detour to the cemetery, walking slowly past the row of iron crosses containing photographs of the departed. Many, too many, were of young men in uniform. His eye was drawn to the wound of a fresh grave.

'Young Heysel,' a voice informed him and he started. The gravedigger was as close to a revenant as Hallstatt could conjure, he thought. The man was thin to the point of being cadaverous and moved silently among the graves to stand beside Kurt. 'Fell out of a truck in France,' the man mumbled. 'Always was a bit careless, young Heysel.'

Kurt felt rage welling up inside him on behalf of a boy he had never met. He seemed to feel the weight of the mountains press down on his shoulders and he turned abruptly away from the man with red mud caking his boots. The cemetery gate seemed to keen as it swung behind him.

★

There is a time to speak and a time to be silent, Monsignor Emil Dubois reminded himself. He read the body language of the cardinal and decided it was a time to be silent. Emil Dubois had tutored Eugène Marie Tisserant when he had been a brilliant student at the seminary in Nancy and, after the young man's ordination, had become his mentor and friend. It was he who had encouraged him to study with Lagrange in Jerusalem and to volunteer for national service when the war broke out. It was no surprise to him that the Church had recognised Tisserant's talents and promoted him up the ecclesiastical ladder until he had been appointed to the College of Cardinals, the most elite and powerful group in the Roman Catholic world. He hadn't been surprised either when his friend had asked him to serve as his secretary or that he had accepted. Part of his willingness to do so he attributed to his retirement from the university and his very real fear of being rewarded with some quiet parish in the Dordogne.

Forty years as an academic had deprived Emil Dubois of the dogmatic certainty that was the *sine qua non* the Church expected of its pastors. The people of the parish, he mused, would expect the Curé of Ars and be presented with Voltaire. He knew himself well enough to know that he didn't have a pastoral bone in his body. The university had been his life. He had dreaded the vacuum of retirement after the frisson of the endless interdepartmental intrigue of university life. He was already crafting a polite refusal to his superiors when the call came from Rome. 'Why not?' he'd considered. As a Professor of Church History, he had always been fascinated by the complexity of the Vatican and, as Tisserant's secretary, he would be at the heart of it. Also, he had missed his hot-headed and argumentative student and friend. As a friend, he knew the cardinal well enough to read his humours. This, he concluded, was definitely a time to be silent. When Eugène Tisserant was ready to talk, Emil Dubois would listen.

But the cardinal did not so much talk as erupt.

For twenty minutes, he vented his frustrations with Vatican bureaucracy in general and Eugenio Pacelli in particular. Finally, he slumped into a chair and muttered, 'He is a man possessed by his papacy.'

Emil Dubois rose quietly and poured a measure of brandy from a decanter on a side table.

'I have been wounded,' the cardinal protested, staring accusingly at the glass.

His secretary sniffed and added some more.

'Severely wounded,' the cardinal said and watched in satisfaction as the decanter tilted again. He accepted the glass and held it to his nose, inhaling the aroma of the Armagnac before taking a tiny sip. He looked speculatively at his secretary over the rim of the glass. 'You are so atypically generous, Emil,' he said slowly, 'that I suspect you are the bearer of bad tidings.'

Emil filled a second glass and returned with it to his chair.

'Very bad tidings,' Tisserant observed.

'Who did you see in the anteroom?' Emil asked.

The cardinal closed his eyes and spoke as if watching pictures pass behind his lids.

'I saw D'Arcy Osborne,' he said, 'looking anxious and English.'

'He has reason to be. And who else?'

'Pavelič, the Croatian,' Tisserant growled, 'surrounded by his Ustashe thugs and the ubiquitous papal secretaries, Kaas and Leiber.'

'We secretaries are required to be everywhere, often at the same time, Eminence,' Emil remarked mildly. 'Our superiors require it of us.'

'Touché,' Tisserant admitted. 'In your own time, Emil.'

Emil sipped his glass and regarded his friend. He knew that, like many strong personalities, the cardinal did not suffer fools gladly. His sharp mind often found expression in a cutting tongue. Whenever he moved through the Vatican, it seemed as if a forceful bow-wave preceded him and pushed people out of his way.

For his own part, he accepted that seniority and age rendered him non-threatening to the young Turks who did the donkey work in the diplomatic corps. Their commitment and ambition cut them off from normal friendships outside the Vatican's walls and made them suspicious of friendships within. The clarity of his memory enabled him to know their names and enquire after their families. They called him 'Abbé Emil' and tended to tell him things. It didn't hurt that he was also secretary to such a powerful man and might help their star ascend with a word in the great man's ear. He had become adept at sifting the self-serving from the genuine and worked hard at maintaining a balance between being Tisserant's ears and lending those ears to the ordinary human concerns of brother priests.

'The English ambassador brings letters from the Foreign Office,' he began, 'which His Holiness reads. He brings letters from other sources, including America, which His Holiness sometimes reads, when he receives them.'

'Kaas and Leiber?'

'Yes, the Vatican sorting office, as one of my young friends calls them.'

'And von Papen?'

'The usual. He conveys the Führer's respect for the Church and his admiration for the pope.'

'Bloody ventriloquist's dummy,' the cardinal muttered. 'What about the awful Pavelić?' he added.

'Learning what the pope wants to hear and becoming more adept at saying it,' Emil answered dryly. 'Today, he suggested a free and Catholic Croatia is the best bulwark against Bolshevism and asked the Holy Father to bless their national aspiration.'

'Was he questioned about actions against the Orthodox Serbs?'

'Not by the pope. Montini held a meeting with him before the papal audience.'

'Montini is in awe of Pacelli and is much too … malleable,' the cardinal said. 'He's no match for Pavelić.'

'My sources say his mouth asks the hard questions but his ears are tuned only to the concerns of the Church. He accepts Pavelić's wish that the Church does not accept conversions from the Serbian Orthodox community and recommends that the pope instructs the local bishops accordingly.'

'Well, we know what that means,' the cardinal said, lurching to his feet and pacing to the window. His reflection in the glass appeared ghostly against a bloody Roman sunset.

'Without the protection of the Church,' he continued, 'the Orthodox Serbs will be defenceless before Paveliç's gangsters. It's all coming to an end, Emil, and nothing will be as it was. And the one man who could lead us through this desert sits in a small office surrounded by layers and layers of insulation against reality. Churchmen, who should bring the truth into his presence, and dilute and distort it because they put their own national allegiance before their commitment to the Church, or they put the Church before the truth. Three of Pacelli's immediate predecessors were prisoners of the Vatican, until Mussolini signed the Concordat. But Pacelli volunteered for imprisonment and was happy to lock the door behind him.'

He looked up at the window where the sky had blackened and his reflection stared back at him. '*Kyrie eleison*,' he whispered. 'Lord have mercy.'

He returned to his seat at the desk, picked up his glass and then set it aside.

'I saw the boy in him, Emil,' he said sadly. 'I saw the boy he had been – the boy he was expected to be – a good boy and I was moved by his aloneness. Then, before my eyes, the boy Eugenio disappeared inside the shell that is Pius. Maybe I didn't try hard enough. Maybe if I hadn't let my anger get in the way, he—'

'Eugène,' his secretary interrupted, 'you are tired. There are two things you should know and then you must rest.'

Tisserant slumped in his chair.

'Cardinal Maglione's office is as porous as ever,' his secretary continued. 'So it is already common knowledge that you no longer enjoy the pope's favour.'

He raised a warning hand as the cardinal bristled.

'Eminence,' he said sternly, 'we know from our country's recent history that it is futile to confront a blitzkrieg.' He sighed and sipped at his brandy before continuing in a softer voice. 'You are such a Celt, Eugène. You become a berserker and rush to attack. If that attack is not a success, you sheathe your sword and go home. The Romans have always known how to make a turtle against us.

We – you – must learn to fight more cleverly. Mon Dieu, sometimes I think that if you had been Hector, the Greeks would still be banging on the gates of Troy.'

He relaxed when he saw the cardinal smile.

'Please don't ask me to drop down to my knees and kiss his papal ring,' the cardinal said.

'Why not?' his secretary retorted. 'The people of Israel conquered Babylon by becoming part of that kingdom and changing it from the inside. Remember, Moses was an Egyptian – only someone from the inside could have led the Hebrews out. So, yes, you will kiss his ring or his slipper if needs must.'

'I am suitably chastened, Mon Professeur,' the cardinal said, throwing up his hands in surrender. 'You said there were two things I had to hear.'

The secretary stared at him until he was certain he had the cardinal's attention.

'A message has come from a friend in Vienna,' he said. He was pleased to see Tisserant sit forward as he continued. 'Our friend, as you may remember, is in, but not of, the nunciature.'

'Do we have to play such games?' the cardinal asked irritably.

'We do. Now pay attention. Our friend has been contacted by someone in SD.'

'SD?'

'The German security police,' Emil explained patiently. 'It seems this person wishes to have an understanding with us.'

'Why?'

'He says, and here I am quoting the message verbatim, so that we will remember him when we come into our kingdom.'

'It's a paraphrase of what the thief crucified on Calvary asked of Jesus.'

'It is,' the secretary agreed. 'It's a trade, Eugène. He provides information to us and, if the Reich should falter, we will provide … eh, I think the correct term is "life insurance" for him.'

The cardinal tugged thoughtfully at his long-suffering beard.

'What kind of information could this SD person have that we would want?' he mused aloud.

'As an aperitif,' his secretary answered quietly, 'before, as it were, we sit down and dine together, he offers us June the twenty-second 1941.'

'And that is?'

'According to this person, it is the day Hitler will invade the Soviet Union. He says the codename is Operation Barbarossa.'

BOOK TWO

Kurt Brandt felt his spirits lighten and his pace quicken as he approached the small stone cottage. He had missed the high-ceilinged apartment he and Bertha had shared in Vienna. It had been the perfect base for a young, ambitious lecturer – close to the university and the coffee houses where the academic staff met and mingled and pretended they were still carefree undergraduates. Well, Kurt reflected, Franz Steiner had put a very large spanner in that particular works, banishing him to this academic Siberia. He still felt a twinge of resentment at the thought, and chided himself immediately.

Yes, he did feel like a large fish in a particularly small pond and he did miss the cut and thrust of academic life, but he was growing to appreciate some things he had been oblivious to before. Like marriage, he thought, and stopped to shake his head ruefully. Not just marriage, he knew, but being married to someone like Bertha – doing all the small, domestic and inconsequential things that married couples do. The sort of things I thought we'd do, years from now, when we were settled, he thought, and shivered at that word. And yet he was discovering a side to himself that appreciated the complex person that was Bertha Steiner.

With time, he might even grow into the kind of schoolmaster he suspected Simon Tauber had been. It was Bertha, of course, who had formed the friendships and found the facts. The facts, she reported, were tragic. The broken-hearted widower had walked into the lake. Of course, he'd argued, her primary sources were women who liked nothing better than a romantic tragedy. Persuaded by Bertha, he went to the bierkeller once a week and, although not gifted with small-talk, he did have the good sense to listen respectfully to the conversations of the villagers. Occasionally, he was forced to bite his tongue when the talk turned xenophobic. Ironically, he was relieved at its lack of focus. The good people of Hallstatt weren't particular when it came to suspecting outsiders; they had an instinctive suspicion of everyone from beyond the Dachstein Mountains. However, he did hear enough to learn that Tauber had been liked by many and respected by all. Maybe not all, he reflected. There was some murmuring about pressure from the policeman and some awkwardness involving the priest, Father Kyril, around the circumstances of Tauber's burial. No doubt he would hear it all, in detail, in time.

Behind the Soviet border, 20 June 1941

Edwin Unger timed his pull on the lines so that he skirted the edge of the forest. As the meadow rushed up to meet him, he bent his knees to lessen the impact. It took less than a minute to dig a hole for the parachute and his jumpsuit. By then, the euphoria of flying had washed out of his system and he was alert to the sounds of the world around him. He noted the sound of the Junkers aircraft banking somewhere beyond the screening trees, as it swung its nose for the airfield near Rumenov. The normal hum of a June meadow slowly elided the sound of the plane and he was alone.

Some men might crave the society of comrades on a dangerous mission behind enemy lines – but Edwin Unger was not one of them. He was a Brandenburger, part of the special operations commando unit formed at the end of the First World War by those who were prescient enough to anticipate a second war. The battalion had been rejected by the Prussian officers first time around because they considered it dishonourable to attack an enemy from behind. Happily for him, Admiral Canaris, father of the Abwehr, the German spy network, didn't share their scruples and the Brandenburgers had repaid his trust in every theatre of war. There were three attributes that qualified a man for membership of the battalion. Unger's parents had ensured that he qualified for the first by conceiving and rearing him in the

Sudetenland, on the fringes of the Reich. His Russian mother could claim sole credit for the second – a proficiency in a foreign language. His subsequent training had made him pitch-perfect in Russian and expert in recognising various Russian dialects. It had also increased his knowledge of local customs and mannerisms. Edwin Unger, his commanding officer noted approvingly, could 'spit like a Russian'. The third attribute was unofficial but just as essential for someone who was expected to infiltrate and even become the enemy. Physically, Edwin Unger was the antithesis of the blond and blue-eyed Aryans much sought after by the Gestapo and other branches of state security. Swarthy, with brown eyes and hair and the short, thick torso of the Steppe dwellers, he fitted the Russian stereotype as snugly as the NKVD uniform he pulled on in the meadow.

He retrieved two items from his compact haversack. The map, he consulted briefly and dumped in the hole with the haversack. The other item, a small wire cutter, he weighed in his hand for a moment before slipping it into his tunic pocket. Apart from the NKVD-issue pistol at his hip, the wire cutter was his only weapon. It would be enough, he thought, as he stamped the earth flat over the hole in the meadow. With that simple tool, he intended to destroy an army.

HALLSTATT, 20 JUNE 1941

Bertha was sitting in the overstuffed armchair she favoured, her bare feet drawn up beneath her. As usual, she had a book open in her lap and her free hand idly curled a stray wisp of auburn hair as she read. She was absorbed and unaware of his presence and he took the time to study her. She was as tall as her father had been, before he developed a scholar's stoop. The lantern flickered and discovered golden seams in her hair, then strengthened to cast her high cheekbones in sharp relief. Her face, he thought, was saved from severity by a soft, full mouth, crinkled with laughter lines at the corners. She looked up suddenly and his heart stuttered at the loveliness of her eyes.

He remembered trying to impress her when they'd first met, talking too much and flaunting his academic prowess. He'd offered to take her on a tour of the university library – God, what a romantic he'd been then. Midway through his manic discourse on the library filing system, she'd taken his arm and led him to one of the huge windows. 'Look at that sky, Kurt,' she'd said. 'Have you ever seen anything so lovely?' And he, who was convinced only ink ran in his veins, had looked at her profile, warmed by the sunset, and blurted 'No, Fraulein Steiner – not until now.' Even now, he felt a phantom shudder of the huge embarrassment that had flooded through him in that dusty library. She'd simply looked at him and smiled – as she was smiling now.

'Welcome home, Herr Brandt,' she said softly.

'It is good to be home, Frau Brandt,' he said, and leaned forward to kiss the top of her head. Her free hand came up to mould itself along his cheek as he inhaled the clean smell of her hair. At that moment, he was oblivious to the world that was sliding into darkness outside the window.

BEHIND THE SOVIET LINES, 20 JUNE 1941

The uniform did it. The uniform and the raised hand brought the jeep to a skidding halt. The driver, Unger judged, was about nineteen and most likely a conscript from Irkutsk. He had high cheekbones and almond-shaped eyes that had become almost round in terror as he stared at the NKVD officer. The passenger, Unger guessed, was a son of the Rodina, Mother Russia. Apart from his facial features, the way he lounged in the passenger seat marked him as thinking himself superior to his companion. The papers the driver tugged from his tunic confirmed Unger's suspicion as to his nationality. The older one affected a nonchalance his eyes betrayed. His papers listed him as having been born near Borodino.

'Company?' Unger snapped, although he knew from their insignia that they were army. They chorused a confirmation.

'Step out,' he commanded.

The driver moved quickly to stand at attention on the side of the road. The other moved more slowly. In his eyes, Unger saw the spark of suspicion, the questions already beginning to form. What was an NKVD officer doing alone in the arse-end of nowhere? It was time to push, to keep them off-balance before suspicion grew into something else.

It was vitally important that they focus their attention on him at all times. Had they looked up, they might have noticed that thirty metres of telegraph cable had been cut between the two poles that stood sentry beside the road. The sound of the approaching engine had given Unger time to complete his task and prepare his plan.

'Did you see or hear an aircraft?' he demanded.

'Y … Yes, sir,' the young one blurted, 'as we came – from there.' He gestured towards the forest and Unger suspected they had heard the banking plane, as he had.

'Good,' he said. 'It's possible the Germans have dropped supplies for partisans. Search the meadow.'

The conscript moved quickly, jumping the ditch and wading through the long grass. The other hesitated. 'Is there a problem, Corporal Antonov?' Unger asked, watching the conscript as he scanned the earth in his search. He kept his hands clasped behind his back, disdaining to look at the corporal, waiting for a reply.

'No, sir.'

'Better be quick then,' he said, 'before that idiot tramples the grass flat. Look for recent disturbances – fresh earth. You know what to look for. Call me if you see anything suspicious.'

The corporal moved after his companion as Unger inspected the jeep. Standard issue, he concluded, and poorly maintained. It was Spartan and functional, apart from a litter of orange peel under the passenger seat and a rusty trenching tool in the back. There was no radio. Uncle Joe Stalin didn't approve of radios, he knew from his briefing. The paranoid Georgian thought they were too vulnerable to interception. Couldn't fault him on that logic, Unger thought.

However, his briefing officer had been at pains to point out that the telegraph wires linking the Soviet armies at the frontier with headquarters at Brest and Moscow travelled underground only for the last eight kilometres of their journey. Where he stood now, they looped invitingly from pole to pole. Apart from the loop he had cut.

'Sir!'

He jumped the ditch and waded into the meadow, the trenching tool swinging from his right hand. The other hand he placed behind his back after fastening the empty holster.

'Something here,' the corporal said, nudging the gash in the earth with his foot.

'Dig,' Unger said, tossing the trenching tool at the man's feet. The corporal hesitated for a moment and Unger saw resentment flash across his face. Digging was for conscripts, the look said, especially fucking goatherds like this bastard. The corporal began to hack savagely at the earth, sending clods flying before the miniature mattock.

'Wait,' Unger said suddenly. 'Can you see it?'

The corporal straightened to arm sweat from his eyes as the conscript leaned forward. A flock of crows erupted from the fringe of the forest at the sharp double crack of the shots. Unger stood for a moment and listened. The only sound he heard was of flapping crows, who grumbled back to their roost and were still again. He left the bodies where they lay; the high grass would obscure them from the road. Besides, he didn't want earth on his boots or blood on the cuffs of his pristine uniform. Perhaps he wasn't as Russian as he ought to be, he mused, and filed that thought away for later.

HALLSTATT, 20 JUNE 1941

After a light supper, taken on a tray before the fire, Kurt Brandt dug into his satchel and produced the test papers. He plucked his Meerschaum pipe from the rack and puffed contentedly. The pipe had been a gift from Bertha when they'd first come to Hallstatt. 'It goes with the village schoolmaster image,' she'd said. 'Anyway,' she'd added teasingly, 'a pipe gives a man the appearance of wisdom.'

'Ah, Elsa, Elsa,' he muttered, underlining yet another purple passage in the Druckner girl's answer sheet. 'Passion, dear Elsa,' he continued, scoring the page with his pen, 'is for demagogues, a historian ought to be …'

'Tempered?' Bertha offered, without raising her eyes from her book.

'Interesting choice of words, my dear.'

She closed the book, trapping her little finger to mark the page.

'Sword-making in Toledo, Kurt,' she said. His look of incomprehension spurred her on. 'Heat and cold applied over and over to the steel until the blade is flexible – flexible enough to bend full circle, hilt to tip.'

'Where do you learn such stuff?'

'Books, Herr Professor,' she said mock-seriously, 'where else? So,' she continued, burrowing back into the cushions, 'the fiery Elsa burns with the little Corsican's passion for empire?'

'Yes, I must remember to tell her about the Toledo swordsmiths.'

'But not to douse her flame, Kurt,' she said gently. 'A historian without passion is just a recording clerk. My father always said that.'

She was thoughtful for a few moments and he closed over the answer sheet to share her silence.

'And the Hamner boy?' she asked, rousing herself.

'He writes well, more careful than she. Karl is earth to Elsa's fire, I suppose you could say.'

'He gets that caution from Rudi, his father,' she said smiling. 'You know? Measure twice and cut once. Life won't also be so straightforward for him, will it?'

'No,' he sighed, 'not for any of them, not now.'

'And Max?'

'Max is my bête noire, Bertha. The boy has genius, but just when I'm getting enthused about his potential, he changes. It's as if he can't relate to praise. I don't know. I suppose it can't be easy being the policeman's son.'

'Or his mother's son, from what I hear.'

'She's somewhat – forceful, isn't she? And very Catholic.'

'Well, more Roman than universal. She has a brother, a monsignor in Croatia. I think she would like to make a priest of Max.'

'Why, for God's sake?'

'Well, more for her own, I suspect. The way things are going, I think she just wants to keep her son.'

'Ah,' he nodded, and laid his pen aside. 'It's getting more difficult to keep sons. Sometimes, I feel relieved that we never …'

His voice trailed off and he wished he hadn't spoken as a shadow dulled her eyes.

'Yes,' she said quietly, 'sometimes.'

She flipped open her book and stared sightlessly at the page. Despite the stove, Bertha tugged her shawl more tightly around her shoulders.

Kurt scribbled half-heartedly on a few more papers before he thought of something to say.

'I've given Elsa a little research project to do at the mines over the weekend,' he said, 'that might temper her.'

'Is it safe for her to go there alone?'

'Her father is a miner, Bertha. She's been going in and out of those tunnels since she could walk. Besides, I doubt if she'll be alone.'

'You arranged for someone to go with her?'

'Heavens no, she'd be furious if I did that.'

'So?'

'So she'll arrange it herself, Bertha, and the young man will think he thought of it.'

'You're not totally unversed in the ways of the heart, are you, Herr Professor?'

'Not totally,' he agreed quietly, 'only sometimes.'

She laid her book aside and came to sit on his lap. He knew he had been forgiven, and felt a deep surge of love that was almost painful. The lantern flame trembled for a moment and went out.

★

The road was quiet. Over the next three hours, Unger encountered just two Red Army lorries. He glared at both as they passed, gratified at the way the occupants sat up at little straighter. In that period, he also clipped the required length of telegraph cable. He would now make his way east to where a small island floated on the confluence of two rivers, and wait.

He steered between two potholes on a sharp bend and stopped. The way ahead was blocked by a Red Army lorry, slewed sideways across the road outside a sagging cottage. He saw a woman run from the cottage and toss a parcel to someone in the lorry. It was fielded by a soldier and he heard the sound of raucous laughter from the body of the lorry. It was too late to reverse; soldiers were already looking his way. He engaged the gear shift and steered a few yards shy of the lorry, edging on to the grass verge. An NKVD officer sauntered up the verge and stood before the bonnet of the jeep.

'Trouble, comrade?' Unger asked, turning off the engine.

'Nothing more than usual,' the officer answered easily. 'Our directive is to move these people back towards Brest.' He was interrupted by a rifle shot. 'They are reluctant but they are leaving,' he added. Moscow, Unger deduced from the accent, probably a graduate from Dzerzhinsky Square. Is this posting a promotion or a punishment? he wondered.

'You don't look as if you need any help, comrade,' he said easily and restarted the engine. 'If you could ask your men to move the lorry, I'll be about my business.'

'What business is that, comrade?' the officer asked, walking around to the passenger side of the jeep.

'Oh, the usual,' Unger sighed. 'General Pavel is concerned about deserters and infiltrators so we tour the back roads.'

The officer strolled to the rear of the vehicle as Unger spoke.

'It seems you caught one, comrade,' he said. Unger swivelled to see a pistol in the officer's hand. The officer gestured at the passenger seat with his free hand. 'Did he request a last orange before you shot him, comrade?' he asked. 'Face front and keep your hands on the steering wheel.' Unger did as he was bid and saw soldiers running to take positions around the jeep. The officer came up beside him and pressed the pistol to his temple. Swiftly, he opened Unger's holster and pressed the release so that the magazine popped free.

'Two deserters,' he said calmly, 'or were they infiltrators? The grass in these parts is plentiful, comrade,' he continued. 'Come September, it will be cut for winter feed, or to patch a roof, or to keep the animals' feet out of the mud. In June, however, it carries a heavy burden of seeds and they cling like crazy.' He gestured at the tiny seeds that speckled Unger's tunic and trousers. 'You'd think a Brandenburger would know that kind of thing,' he added.

BEHIND SOVIET LINES, 21 JUNE 1941

They took it in relays, as he knew they would. It was textbook stuff – two to question him and then two to beat him. His right eye had given up the unequal contest and puffed shut. Through his left eye, he saw the light bleed slowly from a tear in the curtains. He had only to wait, he reminded himself. The blows kept coming, becoming more savage as the interrogators grew frustrated by his silence. He knew they would beat him to death; it's what they did. If he told them what he knew, they would kill him anyway.

When they had finished with his face and torso, they would progress to his fingers and toes. He didn't want them to do that. He eyed the sliver of dark through the curtain and made a decision. The officer came into the room as they splayed his left hand on the table. 'Enough,' Unger grunted. At a gesture from the NKVD man, the others shuffled out. The officer sat at the opposite side of the table. He tapped a cigarette from a packet and lit it with a flaring sulphur. Leaning across, he placed it between Unger's lips. 'Sorry it's not German,' he said softly.

'Doesn't matter,' Unger mumbled around the cigarette, 'been smoking Russian for two years now. They haven't killed me yet.'

The other man smiled tiredly.

'I've met you before,' the officer said, and laughed as he saw the surprise in Unger's face. 'No, not you,' he continued. 'Before – before this, I had the pleasure of meeting the Gestapo at Zacopane when we were collaborating on what to do with the Poles. We were friends then. Naturally, there were toasts to the Reich and the Rodina and to whatever else we could think of. Their sense of protocol prevailed over their good sense, except for one officer. I remember he was dressed in a Wehrmacht uniform. No love lost between the two groups, so what was he doing there? They introduced him as an interpreter, but they all seemed to speak fluent Russian. Also, I admit, his Russian was better than ours. Annoying and intriguing. Later in the evening when the vodka was — well you know — I asked my opposite number who he was and he told me. It was as simple as that. I researched the Brandenburgers in our archives in Dzerzhinsky Square. So I was expecting you, Brandenburger.'

Unger coughed and the officer removed the cigarette from his mouth. 'I know why you're here,' he said. 'My question, therefore, is when?'

'What time is it?' Unger asked.

'It's one fifteen.'

'Do you believe in God?'

The officer hesitated. 'I don't get asked that question very often,' he smiled. 'I'd need more time to think about it.'

'You have two hours,' Unger said, and tried to smile as the man rocketed out of the chair.

The frantic NKVD man left the door ajar in his haste and Unger had a partial view of the panic in the other room.

'Nothing, sir,' the ashen operator mumbled. 'Nothing.'

The officer snatched the phone from the cowed operator and pressed the receiver to his ear. Unger saw the blood drain from his face as if the vacuum at the other end of the line was sucking the life from him. 'Couriers,' he snapped.

Unger relaxed against his bonds. He knew it was their last throw of the dice and he had clipped that dice with his little wire cutter. No courier could ride that far that fast. He retreated into himself until the shouting from the other room faded into a background babble. They should run, he thought, run east and keep running until …

He became aware of the NKVD officer bowed over the table, staring into his face, and tried to focus through the eye that still worked. The man seemed to have aged a decade in the past few hours.

'It's time to run,' Unger whispered.

'Perhaps we will,' the officer said, 'if the orders come in time.'

'Nothing is coming,' Unger said impatiently. 'Nothing is coming from the east,' he added, as gently as his bruised mouth would allow.

'You know what Churchill said?' the officer asked.

'No.'

'In 1931, Winston Churchill said some countries are too big for armies. Think about that, Brandenburger. In 1812, we pulled back and back and back before Napoleon until he was too far gone to pull back. And then we turned.'

A young Red Army soldier appeared at his elbow, his rifle clutched in bone-white fingers. 'Take him to the forest,' the officer said and turned away.

The private fumbled to untie him with shaking fingers. Unger grimaced as the blood burned back into his extremities. He suspected he had at least one cracked rib and concentrated on shallow breaths. 'Move,' the private grunted, prodding him with the rifle. Leningrad, Unger concluded, amused that he hadn't lost his touch.

He shuffled across the bare ground outside the building, surrounded by the chaos of running men and revving engines. The mix of human sweat and exhaust fumes burned his sinuses and he was almost grateful for the relative sanctuary of the meadow. The forest loomed about two hundred yards ahead, a black mass with a serrated silhouette against groups of stars playing hide and seek with scudding clouds. He moved slowly, crouched over to ease his ribs, keeping his arms wrapped around his bruised torso. Inside the treeline, he felt the shift of pine needles under his bare feet. A little farther and they arrived at a small clearing. 'Halt,' the soldier said.

'Turn.'

In the sudden quiet, Unger thought he heard a rumble of thunder in the distance. A faint flicker of light backlit the trees behind the soldier and the thunder rolled again, growing in intensity. The soldier turned to look back the way they had come. 'What is that?' he whispered.

'The end of the world,' Unger said and flung himself on the man's back. As they fell, he hooked an arm across the man's throat, ignoring the agony in his own body when they crashed to the forest floor. He planted a knee in the soldier's spine and began to arch back his head, putting every ounce of his energy into tightening his forearm across the throat. Over the dying man's head, he saw a wall of fire roll towards them, heard the explosions rip up the land until their individual sounds melded into a single bestial roar. Mesmerised by the sight and sound, Unger barely registered that he was holding a dead body in his arms. Then he was shambling deeper into the forest. He fell to his knees and began to scrabble frantically at the soft loam, burrowing down from the horror that breathed fire on his back. He threw himself into the shallow depression and dragged the earth over him as the world exploded.

THE KREMLIN, MOSCOW, 21 JUNE 1941

Ambassador Friedrich von der Schulenburg, German ambassador at the Kremlin, thought the Russian was having a stroke. Molotov's face had gone from red to purple and the veins stood out on his neck like cords.

'W – What?' the Russian Foreign Minister gasped.

It was just the man's crippling stammer activated by the shock, the ambassador concluded and relaxed. In a carefully neutral voice, he recited the official message, emphasising only the phrase, 'Russian troops massed on our eastern frontier.'

Molotov had now turned bone white. 'B – But, you encouraged

me to sign the non-aggression pact with Ribbentrop,' he whispered almost plaintively. 'That was just over a year ago, Friedrich.'

Schulenburg felt a twinge of genuine sympathy for the man who was now his enemy. He himself had laced his reports to Hitler with warnings about Russia's military strength and the unassailability of its industrial reserves. But it was to no avail. Hitler had already conquered France and neutered Britain; it was inevitable that he would flex his muscles eastwards.

'Vyacheslav Mikhailovich,' the ambassador said gently, 'you know, better than most, how I have tried for the past six years to do everything I could to encourage friendship between the Soviet Union and Germany. But you can't stand in the way of destiny.'

Perhaps he had allowed some bitterness to inflect his voice on the last phrase, Schulenburg thought, because Molotov nodded as if he understood the awkwardness of the ambassador's position. That tiny gesture cut Schulenburg deeply. At that moment, he longed to be at home in Burg Falkenberg, 'Friedrich's Folly' as his friends called the castle he had taken three years to renovate as a retirement home. I could be there now, he thought, pretending to be lord of the manor and …

Molotov turned on his heel and left the room. Schulenburg took his handkerchief and mopped his bald head. He looked up at a click of heels and the Kremlin guard indicated that he should follow him.

The driver pulled over, just inside the Kremlin Gate as a procession of sleek, black ZIL limousines powered through. The ambassador watched as doors were flung open and members of the politburo scrambled out onto the cobbles. He recognised General Semyon Timoshenko immediately. A year earlier, Timoshenko had taken just two months to whip the faltering Soviet troops back into shape and bring the Finns to the negotiating table. He had cut his military teeth in the Great War and sharpened them on his own countrymen in the Civil War that followed. Timoshenko, calmy, saluted the sentries and stood at ease, waiting for the civilians to sort themselves out.

'There's Beria,' his secretary muttered, as if the Soviet security and secret police chief might actually hear him.

The ambassador took some satisfaction in Beria's dishevelled appearance. 'Probably interrupted his whoring,' the secretary whispered. It was well known among the diplomatic corps that the round-faced Georgian Stalin called 'our Himmler' was accustomed to trawling the night-time streets of Moscow for women to feed his sexual appetite. Whether they stepped or were dragged into the official limousine was immaterial to Beria.

'Who's the other general?' the secretary asked.

'Zhukov,' the ambassador breathed. 'One of their best, by all reports.' He wondered if Georgy Zhukov would survive Barbarossa or Stalin.

He leaned forward and tapped the driver on the shoulder. The car surged out of the Kremlin into Red Square. Lenin's mausoleum loomed to their right, under the red granite walls. In the distance, at the end of the square, the domes of Saint Basil's loomed out of the fog, nestled close together like exotic Fabergé eggs.

'What will we do with all this?' the secretary giggled, looking back at the citadel as they drove across the bridge.

'I'm sure Napoleon asked the same question,' the ambassador said dryly. He repented a little as he saw the young man deflate beside him. Otto can't help being young, he thought, and the young have no memories. 'He will level Moscow to the ground,' the ambassador said evenly. 'Then he will dig a big hole where Moscow stood and fill that hole with water.' The secretary searched the ambassador's face for some sign of humour, but the ambassador pressed on in that toneless voice. 'Der Führer plans to make Moscow a reservoir, Otto. No ploughing of the earth and seeding the furrows with salt, like the Romans at Carthage.' If Barbarossa succeeds, he added to himself. If Hitler survives, he added as an afterthought.

★

Emil Dubois surfaced from a dream he couldn't remember. He heard bells ringing. The monsignor stumbled into his slippers and swept a dressing gown around his spare frame. Not bells, he thought groggily, the telephone. He plucked the receiver as Tisserant bustled into the room.

'*Ja*,' Emil said, raising a cautionary finger to his lips. The cardinal hovered at his shoulder. '*Ja*', Emil said again. '*Danke*.'

He replaced the receiver.

'Well?' Tisserant asked.

'Barbarossa,' Emil said. 'It's happening.'

Emil Dubois marched up to the double doors, thought of knocking politely and then drew back his foot and kicked them. '*Merde*,' he hissed, hopping on the other foot. The door swung open and a chubby Italian monsignor glared at him.

'Holy mother, Emil,' he hissed. 'What are you doing?'

'Get Maglione out of bed,' Emil grunted, flexing his right foot.

'Do you know what time it is?'

'Yes, it is time to witness a major moment in the war,' Emil growled. 'If Maglione sleeps through it, by tomorrow you will be a pastor in some half-assed Perugian parish.'

When the monsignor hesitated, Emil leaned forward until his Gallic nose almost touched that of the Italian. 'Tisserant is coming,' he said darkly. He could hear the pounding feet on the corridor behind him.

The monsignor's eyes widened and he disappeared inside. Emil waited until Tisserant barged open the door and then followed him.

'*Buona notte*, Eugène,' Cardinal Maglione said with heavy sarcasm when he walked into the anteroom.

Maglione's hastily donned cassock was collarless and the square gap at his throat was filled with greying hair. Tisserant thought it made the Secretary of State look naked and averted his gaze. 'Time for pleasantries later, Eminence,' he said amiably. 'Russia is being invaded. Gather your minions.'

Maglione didn't hesitate. 'Luigi,' he boomed, 'call them.'

He led the way into his office as the monsignor gabbled on the phone. Maglione pulled a switch and Tisserant paused to admire the long table that took up most of the room. It was covered with a map that included Poland to the west and stretched all the way across to Siberia in the east. We look down from on high like the gods of Olympus, Tisserant thought; too exalted from the world to see the blood. Other clerics began to filter into the room. Some took up their places at the map table, others manned the telephones banked on a side table.

'When?' Maglione asked.

'Now,' Tisserant answered.

The clerics at the map table carried wooden pointers in the upright position, ready to move the flat markers that identified the various forces. The German markers were solid black, inset with a tiny red swastika. The Russian markers were blood red.

'There,' Maglione said, pointing south to the Pripyet Marshes. 'They will strike there.'

'No,' Tisserant said, taking a pointer from the hand of a surprised cleric. He snapped it down on the map so that the thick end straddled the Polish border and the pointed end thrust like a lance at Brest. 'It will be here.'

The phones began ringing as messages poured in from nunciatures, embassies and Vatican contacts. Relays of clerics moved from the phones to whisper in the ears of those who wielded the pointers. Almost in perfect synchronicity, they began to push the black markers east.

'You were right, Eugène,' Maglione conceded, as the markers representing the German Centre Army outstripped the others and swept across the map towards Brest. Maglione moved to stand beside Tisserant.

'Should we tell His Holiness?' he whispered.

'We?' Tisserant said innocently. 'You are the Secretary of State.'

Maglione looked as if he had swallowed something disagreeable.

'I think it would be more prudent to tell him in the morning,' he said tightly.

★

Behind Soviet Lines, 21 June 1941

Edwin Unger came back to consciousness. He was lying in what he had thought would be his grave. Slowly, he sat upright, scrubbing the loam out of his eyes and ears. The firestorm had passed some hundred yards south of where he now swayed to his feet. He saw the white bones of broken trees, stretching into the distance. Here and there, small fires flickered and the air he breathed was spicy with the smell of boiled resin. Apart from the crackling fires, the night was eerily silent, as if still holding its breath in disbelief. He heard a drone and lifted his face to the lightening sky. Planes: he saw wave upon wave of planes swarming east. He identified Junkers, Dorniers, Heinkels, Messerschmidts, and Stukas. Some, he knew, were heavy with bombs; others bristled with guns, ready to stitch thousands of rounds into the bodies of men and thin-skinned vehicles. The stubby-winged Stukas looked poised to scream down out of the sky to roast crews in their tanks. Edwin Unger raised his arms to them in adulation. 'Barbarossa!' he screamed. 'Barbarossa!'

10 Downing Street, London, 21 June 1941

'It is rather urgent,' the messenger from the Foreign Office insisted.

The prime minister's secretary raised an eyebrow. 'It always is,' he said. 'However, the prime minister gave strict instructions that he was to be roused only if Britain was being invaded. Are we being invaded?'

'No, sir. The Germans have invaded Russia.'

'Jolly good,' the secretary beamed. 'I'm sure Mr Churchill will address that in the morning.'

'Mr Chamberlain will expect a response to his message, sir,' the messenger said stubbornly.

The secretary loomed above the hapless man.

'I seem to recall Mr Chamberlain coming with messages before,' he said frostily. He stared at the messenger until the man bobbed his head and retreated.

'Rather a rum turn-up for the books, wouldn't you say?' the secretary remarked to an aide as the door closed. 'Be a good chap,' he added, 'and see if you can rouse some of those script wallahs from their cots. Our master will be expected to make mention of this in the Commons tomorrow.'

THE KREMLIN, MOSCOW, 5.45 A.M., 21 JUNE 1941

General Zhukov assessed the most powerful men in Russia as they filed into Stalin's office. For the most part, he judged, they looked dazed or downright frightened. He caught General Timoshenko's eyes and thought he saw confirmation of his analysis. He felt comforted by Timoshenko's unruffled demeanour. Beria, he was pleased to observe, looked scared shitless; although, as a man who had seen frontline action himself, he considered 'scared shitless' a contradiction in terms.

His train of thought was interrupted as the group suddenly went silent. Stalin had arrived.

He moved with that peculiar stiff-armed gait to his desk and sat. His head hung forward so that his eyes were screened by the great bushy eyebrows. Zhukov knew him as a man of mercurial temperament, likely to slip from coarse humour to lethal rage with frightening speed. He looks depressed, he thought and, just as his heart began to sink towards his belly, Stalin changed. He straightened his shoulders and a light came into the brown eyes as if he had thrown some internal switch.

'The enemy will be beaten all along the line,' he said calmly. 'What do you recommend?'

The civilians, conditioned to tailor their opinions to the view of their leader, vied with each other to condemn the fascists and extol the superiority of the Red Army. Zhukov noted that only Timoshenko and Molotov stayed aloof; the general inscrutable, the foreign minister looking deeply shocked. 'Perhaps,' Stalin interrupted, 'perhaps it is a mistake.'

Zhukov wrestled to keep the incredulity he felt from his face as Stalin continued.

'Some German general panicked … shots were fired … and … it might still be possible to … diplomatic solution …'

After a pause, the civilians changed tack and began to support this possible interpretation of events, but even *they* found it hard to muster any enthusiasm for the argument. Zhukov felt sweat trickle into his eyebrows as the tension built in the room, and then Molotov spoke.

'Iosif Vissaryonovich,' he said, as if spelling out a truth to someone grasping at straws, 'it is war.'

He didn't stammer, Zhukov thought, and then Stalin was screaming.

'They fell on us without making any claims,' he raged, 'making a vile attack, like bandits.'

As quickly as the storm rose, it abated and Stalin slumped back in his chair. Zhukov felt stunned, not so much by Stalin's outburst as by what it revealed. Zhukov knew regular reports had been coming from the frontier to Stalin's office, detailing the enormous build-up of German armies and armaments. He knew also that the paranoid leader distrusted his own intelligence service. No, it was more than that – worse than that. Stalin never believed Hitler would attack the Soviet Union. At worst, he believed, the Germans would rattle their sabres and make demands and he would mollify them by agreeing to modify a border here or there on his vast western frontier. He had been wrong. They had attacked – were attacking – and now the fate of millions of Soviet citizens rested on the shoulders of a man who seemed unable to grasp the fact that Hitler had deluded and humiliated him.

Zhukov risked a look at the others and wondered if the same thoughts were flashing through their minds. These were men who had survived purges, men who were adept at exploiting a weakness in others to their own advantage and who were not forgiving of mistakes. For the first time in many years, Georgy Zhukov felt afraid. Stalin seemed to read the mood of the room and turned to

Molotov, his staunchest supporter in the politburo.

'Vyacheslav Mikhailovich,' he said softly, 'you will go to the Central Telegraph Office and inform the people.'

Zhukov could feel the tension leach from the others. In one simple stroke, Stalin had shifted the onus of explanation from his own to Molotov's shoulders. In the minds of the Soviet people, the foreign minister's radio broadcast would link his name and voice forever to the disaster that had befallen them. Stalin might have been betrayed by the treacherous Führer, but Molotov had signed the non-aggression pact with the Nazis. It was Zhukov's first real taste of politburo politics and it soured his stomach.

At midday, they broke from composing directives to various generals along the frontlines and planning the evacuation of key industries farther east. An aide turned on the radio and Molotov's voice filled the office. When the foreign minister claimed that a mere two hundred men had been killed and wounded in the first air attacks, Zhukov threw a disbelieving glance at Timoshenko, but the general gave him a warning look and he listened impassively to the remainder of the broadcast.

Molotov referred twice to the fact that no claims or demands had been made. Fascist Germany, he declared, was the aggressor. True, Zhukov mused, but it concealed the deeper truth of the politburo's failure to prepare. The foreign minister went on to remind his audience of the First Great Patriotic War and promised that the Red Army and the entire people could conduct a new Patriotic War, 'for the Motherland, for honour, for freedom'. 'Our cause is just,' he concluded. 'The enemy will be beaten. Victory will be ours.'

Stalin smiled his approval, and a ripple of applause swept around the room.

Stalin immediately ordered Kaganovich, the Minister for Communications, to evacuate factories and twenty million people from the frontline areas. Mikoyan, the Minister for External Trade, he tasked with feeding and supplying the Soviet armies. As the two men hurried from the office, Stalin turned to General Timoshenko.

'General Pavlov failed to hold the line,' he said coldly. 'Remove him.'

So, Zhukov thought, the first sacrificial victim is chosen to atone for the sins of the mighty. He wondered how many more would die for the mistakes of their masters.

He hurried after Timoshenko, eager to escape the Kremlin and to face an enemy who could be counted on to stab you in the front.

RUDI HAMNER'S WORKSHOP, HALLSTATT JUNE 1941

Karl selected a plank and secured it to the bench.

'Well-seasoned,' his father remarked from where he was sanding a chair-leg. The early light turned the sawdust to golden snow as it sifted down.

By the time he started Kindergarten, Karl could distinguish the different woods by their grain and use. After school he would help his father in the workshop, learning to work with tools under Rudi's careful eye. The weight of the plane reminded him of the first time he had smoothed a plank.

'Let the plane do the work, son,' Rudi had cautioned. 'Slide, don't push. Work with the wood and what is in the timber will come out.'

Karl had wiped the sweat from his forehead and relaxed his grip on the tool. He had looked along the straight grain of the plank and started again, thinking of skating across the frozen lake and letting his knees flex to avoid gouging the ice.

'Good,' Rudi had murmured, 'much better.'

Karl raised the plane and angled his head to inspect the work. 'Did you always want to be a carpenter, Papa?'

'What? Oh Lord no. I wanted to be a miner, like all the other lads and like my father, of course.'

'Did he … did your father feel disappointed when you said you didn't want to be a miner?'

'No. He never said much anyway but it was his idea. He was a sly one, I'll give him that. He got me a job helping Johann in his workshop, during the school holidays. He said I was too young for the mines and we needed the money.'

'Johann the boatman? He was a carpenter?'

'Oh, yes, before the war claimed his arm. After that, he took to the boat and the beer, but don't tell your mother I said that. Anyway, Johann had two arms then and was twice as cranky. He worked me like a man. Lord, there were days when I couldn't lift a fork to my mouth after work.'

'Why did you stay?'

Rudi ran his hand over the back of his neck. It was what he did when he was thinking. 'I suppose … I liked it,' he said. 'I told my father. I thought he'd be angry. You know the way it was then, sons were expected to follow their fathers down the mines. He said if every son did what his father did, from Adam's day, we'd all be gardeners.' The carpenter laughed at the memory. 'I remember he said, "Life is short, Rudi. A man should find out what he likes to do and do it for a living. If he does it long enough he'll get good at it. Anyway, I have nothing to leave you so you'll have to make your own way. But, always remember, your old man gave you the sky." It was the most the old man ever said to me in one go, and it stuck.'

He was quiet for a moment, his head tilted to the window that framed the mountains. 'And you, Karl,' he said softly, 'what do you want to be?'

'I'd like … I'd like to be a teacher,' Karl said, searching his father's face for a reaction.

'Like Herr Brandt?' Rudi asked, smiling.

'Yes and no.'

Rudi quirked an eyebrow and his son continued hesitantly.

'Like Herr Brandt, yes, but also like Herr Tauber, may his soul rest in peace.'

'Amen to that,' his father said soberly. 'Say on, boy.'

'Herr Brandt is very brilliant, Papa. Elsa says he thinks sideways.' He looked questioningly at his father.

'I think I know what she means,' Rudi nodded. 'Any man can measure and cut a plank, I suppose it takes a carpenter to look at it and see a chair.'

'Yes,' his son said enthusiastically. 'He's always asking why; he says it's more important than when or how.'

'But?' his father prompted.

'But sometimes I think he'd rather be at the university, you know, with really bright students. Sometimes he can become impatient when we don't keep up with him.'

'And Herr Tauber?'

'Her Tauber liked us, Papa,' Karl said simply and turned back to the workbench. 'Herr Tauber always praised us for what we could do.' After a time, he said, 'He praised all of us. I think we worked hard to please him.'

He picked up the plane again. 'Leave it,' his father said. 'I hear Mutti coming with our coffee.'

When the door swung open, Frau Hamner's hands were empty. She read their expressions and smiled. 'Coffee is in the house,' she said, 'we have a visitor.'

'If it's that Heinze looking for his table, I told him it would be ready on Wednesday,' Rudi said, watching Karl tidy the tools away. 'Man has no patience,' he added, lifting the apron over his head and hanging it on a nail.

'It's not Heinze,' his wife said. 'Anyway, poor Heinze is just anxious. He wants to surprise Katya on her birthday.'

'Wednesday I said and Wednesday it will be,' huffed Rudi stubbornly. 'So who's come to visit us at this time of day?'

'Not visiting us, Rudi,' his wife said smiling. 'There's a lady here to see Karl.'

'To see me?' Karl said.

'Yes, so shake the shavings out of your hair before you come down to the house, both of you.'

★

'I wish he'd die.'

Max Steiger's body tightened at the thought. Not because he considered it a terrible thought to have about his father, but that it had become his first thought. It had come immediately, without intensifying from irritablility through anger and rage and all the other nuances of emotion until it had flatlined at this cold, sickening feeling. I wish he'd die, he thought again, watching the small man suck his coffee, hearing him clear his throat as a preface to yet another mindless observation on the vicissitudes of all other human beings except Policeman Steiger. There must have been a time, he thought, when I listened and marvelled; a time I glowed with the satisfaction a young boy feels at the perfection of his father. Yes, there had been such a time, he admitted, and, for a moment, that remembered feeling warred with the coldness he felt now, and lost.

'And what about your own career, Max?'

Max had been working his way mechanically through his breakfast, distracting himself with the textures of the food that passed over his tongue, leaving no memory of taste. His father's question startled him. Was it possible, he wondered, that the policeman had become aware of his own monologue, that he had actually heard himself and become embarrassed? Was it within the bounds of reason that he was interested in someone other than himself?

'I was thinking,' he began tentatively, and something like relief flooded through him when his father overrode him.

'Of course, being a policeman is a great challenge. A policeman must stand for—'

Max blazed with anger at himself. How could he have been naïve enough to think there was any space in that bloated ego for a boy's dreams? He consciously relaxed the hand holding the spoon so that the blood flowed back into his whitened fingers. The kitchen table is a perfect square, he thought. The light from the window is triangular. The spoon is oval-shaped. In this way, he created a barrier against his father until the drone of his voice was no more irritating that a wasp in the window.

*

Rudi marvelled at how the girl could talk so much without breathing. He leaned against the kitchen cupboard, his coffee mug cradled between his palms, and watched the phenomenon that was Elsa in full flight.

'Russia was the bête noire of Napoleon. I ask you, what sort of test title is that? At least half of the others wouldn't know what a bête noire was if it sat up and bit them. Well of course Karl knew and I kind of guessed. I suppose Max knew, because Max knows everything — at least, that's the Gospel according to Max. This shortbread is delicious, Frau Hamner. My father said they had loads of bêtes noires down the mine, but you know what he's like. Then he asked me to go to the mine and sketch the body.'

'Your father?' Frau Hamner ventured.

'No. Herr Brandt. And I thought Karl would help and, anyway, he needs to do his own research in the mine for his paper on the Celts. So I packed a lunch. All the stuff we need like lanterns and such are in the store shed at the mine, so we'll be off then, Karl. Oh, you'd better bring a warm sweater. It gets cold down there. And boots, definitely boots; water on the floors makes them slippery.' Elsa stood close to Karl. 'Let me look at you,' she said, like a mother inspecting her child. Artlessly she swept her splayed fingers through his fringe. 'You'll do. Thank you, Frau Hamner. You ready, Karl?'

'Yes,' Karl said in such a bewildered voice that his father had a sudden fit of choking and had to lean over the sink while his wife thumped him on the back.

'Must have gone down the wrong way,' he gasped as the tears rolled down his cheeks.

His wife gave him the kind of look that said choking is too good for you. She had also slapped his back a little harder than was strictly necessary and that sobered him. Rudi liked the spontaneous way the girl kissed his wife at the door and the way his son slung her bag over his shoulder.

They stood together at the door watching the animated Elsa chivvy their son down the path, hands and hair flying as she made some point or other.

'Poor Karl,' Rudi murmured. 'He won't get a word in edgeways.'

'You can save your sympathy,' his wife smiled. 'I think Karl is a willing victim. Did you notice how he looks at her?'

'Yes, like a rabbit looks at a shotgun.'

'He really likes her, Rudi, and I'm glad. Elsa is affectionate and full of life …'

'And young,' her husband interrupted, 'they're both very young. They have their whole lives ahead of them.'

'Life is now, Rudi,' she said, suddenly wistful.

He put his arm across her shoulders and tugged her close. 'Yes, you're right,' he admitted, 'as usual. I'm going to the mountains to draw timber but I don't have to go for an hour or two yet.'

'You could tidy up that workshop,' she said smiling.

'I could, but I won't,' Rudi Hamner said, and kissed her.

THE STEIGER HOUSEHOLD

'Are you running a temperature?'

For a second, Max felt completely disorientated. He had been unaware of his mother's presence – hadn't heard the door open or the sound of her footfall. He felt her wrist, cool against his forehead, and flinched involuntarily from the contact. With her other hand, she drew on the chain he wore around his neck and placed the tiny cross against his shirt. 'No,' she continued, 'still, it might be better to stay inside today. The wind is—'

'I'm going out,' he muttered, pushing himself up from the table.

'Where?'

'Out!'

'Who with?'

'Christ, Christ, Christ,' he raged silently, why must every single thing be marked and measured. He struggled with his coat, venting his anger on sleeves that seemed suddenly to become obdurate, erecting his barriers furiously so that her tirade seeped through the gaps in his defences as individual sentences or just single words.

'Probably that Hamner boy – too quiet and polite for his own good – miner's girl trailing after him – father soft in the head – damaged goods – a boy with your ability – careful – riff-raff – standards –'

The slam of the door cut her off. He leaned his forehead against the wood, his arms spreadeagled, and pressed his body against the door as if he could hold the awfulness inside at bay.

THE MINE, HALLSTATT

'Karl.'

'Yes.'

'Move the lantern a little to the left. The other left.'

'Sorry.'

'That's perfect. What do you think killed the miner?'

'Maybe a rockfall or a collapse of the roof.'

'Could be,' Elsa said, placing the pad on her lap and beginning to sketch. 'Any other possibilities? Remember that Herr Godalmighty Brandt thinks sideways.'

'Ritual sacrifice?'

'Could be. He's a little too well preserved to have been mashed by a few tons of rubble. Karl?'

'What?'

'You're standing in my light.'

'Sorry.'

'Just shift a little – perfect.'

'Elsa.'

'Yes.'

'You'll get cold sitting on the floor. Sit on my sweater.'

'Now *you'll* get cold.'

'It doesn't matter.'

'Thank you. You know, I like your parents.'

'You do?'

'Yes. They're just – oh, I don't know, they're just so comfortable.'

'Comfortable? Actually, Elsa, we don't have much money—'

'Ass. I mean together. You know?'

'Yes, eh, not really.'

'God, Karl, what do you use for eyes? They look at each other all the time, sending little messages, as if they have this silent language. Mine fought and shouted all the time but it was sort of nice. Even as a small child, I knew they loved each other. Karl, I can't work with you talking all the time. Do you think you might start work on your project? The Celtic staircase is about two galleries over. Follow the path behind you and turn right at the junction. Come back in an hour and we'll have lunch.'

'Fine, but not here, Elsa.'

'Oh, why?'

'I don't think it's respectful to have a picnic beside – well.' He inclined his head towards the fossilised body of the miner.

'But he's been here over a thousand years, Karl.'

'When does respect for the dead end, Elsa?'

'And what about the Egyptian mummies?'

'The same.'

She looked at him until a blush crept up his face and he dropped his eyes down.

'What am I going to do with you, Karl Hamner?' she said, in mock exasperation. 'All right, we'll eat somewhere else.'

He nodded and turned away.

'Karl, thanks for coming with me.'

'I wanted to come.'

'Why?'

'Because – you asked me.'

'And if I'd asked you to jump in the lake, would you have done that also?'

'Probably,' he said, and smiled.

His smile stopped her heart for a moment. Then she began to busy herself with the sketch.

'Are you still here, Karl?'

'No, Fraulein Druckner,' he said solemnly and walked away. She imagined some of the warmth she felt went with him. She felt an urge to call him back, but for once in her life she couldn't think of anything to say.

ON THE PATH TO THE MINES

She was waiting outside the village.

'Max,' she said, as if surprised, 'are you going for a walk?'

He watched the girl move from the shade of a birch that stood aloof from the treeline and thought of possible replies to this fatuous question.

'No, Eloïse,' he said, with heavy irony, 'I flew too near the sun and fell into the lake.'

'What?' She gazed at him with those wide, cow-like eyes. Father Kyril was right, he thought contemptuously. Girls like Eloïse were 'occasions of sin – corruption masked in soft flesh, tempting a young man's purity with fly-blown fruit'. He felt so aroused it hurt, and he walked quickly along the path. 'I might be going for a walk,' he said over his shoulder, and hated himself for his weakness.

'I might be also,' she said in a voice that seemed to lick his earlobes. He shook his head but the voice persisted. 'Our mountains must be the highest mountains in the world,' she said dreamily.

'Actually, no,' he snapped, 'the highest mountains are in Nepal. These,' he added, shaking a dismissive hand at the Dachstein Mountains, 'are just foothills by comparison.'

'Oh, you're so clever, Max. I'm not clever but I notice things.'

'Really.'

'Yes, really. I noticed your friends walking up to the mine. Karl and Elsa, Elsa and Karl,' she sang in a singsong voice that grated on him. 'They had a picnic bag, Max; isn't that sweet.'

'So what?' he said, turning to face her.

'So they didn't ask you along, did they, Maxy witzy?' she pouted, stepping up close to him. 'Probably going to kiss and cuddle in the dark. Probably going to—'

'Shut up, you stupid bitch.'

'Sticks and stones,' she sang, 'sticks and stones. Maybe I know as much as Miss Bet Noor.'

'Bête noire.'

'That's what I said. But then, she's a flat-chested boy, isn't she? And little Karl has just a little—'

'Don't talk about them like that.'

'Oh, Maxy is cross now.' She swayed closer, slowly undoing the buttons of her blouse until it fell away and revealed her full breasts. 'She doesn't have these, does she, Max? Yes, have a good look, I know you want to. Maybe want to feel them a little. Maybe want to—' She took his hand and led him in between the trees.

He came explosively and a harsh cry of exultation, mixed with disgust, burst from his throat. He rolled away and stood on shaking legs trying to cover himself.

'You're such a little boy,' she said waspishly, coming up behind him. 'Can't wait, can you? One little push and—'

'Shut up,' he snarled, rounding on her.

'Big, brave man,' she mocked, 'can't keep it—'

The sting in his palm travelled up his arm and through his body. The sound of the slap echoed away into the valley: slap – slap – ap – p – p. Her breasts seemed to swing in time to the fading sound. She opened her mouth and then snapped it closed. He heard the click of her teeth as they came together and he took a step towards her. She scrambled backwards, tripping and sprawling in the undergrowth. He saw naked fear in her eyes and began to feel a rush of warmth flood his lower belly. Abruptly, he turned and hurried away, the blaze of arousal now replaced by a dull ache of self-disgust. At a stream that fell from between the trees and fanned into a shallow pool beside the path, he scrubbed himself, using handfuls of sand and grit to abrade his skin until it stung.

★

IN THE FOREST

Rudi stepped back from the tree and shouldered his axe. He had taken an hour to decide on this one, an hour of casting about in the small copse of birches, checking the width of the boles and the height and lines of the various trunks until his eye had fallen on this one. It was perfect; he'd known as soon as he touched it, almost reverently, with the tips of his fingers. With these craftsman's fingers, he read the Braille of the tree's potential for all the things he could make – things locked away under the sleek bark. Why is it always the perfect one that's chosen for the axe, he mused? He stepped back slowly, took one last apologetic look at the crown of leaves that swayed above him and unhitched the axe from his shoulder.

THE MINES

The lantern lit the side of her face as her pencil moved across the pad. He stood in the shadows, beyond the circle of light and watched her. The soft scratching of the pencil seemed to rub at the memories of what he had done with Eloïse and he felt a weight of sadness in his chest. Darkness is my métier, he thought, my sin excludes me from the light. Elsa and Karl had happened on something he could never reclaim; a kind of innocence that permeated their friendship so that they moved together with the grace of unconscious intimacy. On the few occasions when he had visited their homes, he had felt awkward in the atmosphere of easy affection that Elsa and Karl took for granted. But, he acknowledged, he had armoured himself too successfully against the awfulness of his own home and parents to allow him to expose himself to the possibility of something different. And so he stood in the shadows while the only girl he ever saw as anything but an object sat sketching within the light. The sadness curdled inside him, souring into bitterness. Why should they have what he was denied, he seethed? When he stepped forward, some of the shadow clung to his eyes.

THE FOREST

The axe cuts were clean and economical; a specimen tree like this deserved no less, Rudi thought. His shoulders rotated with purpose as his arms guided the blade until he knew that only one cut remained. Rudi blotted the sweat from his eyes and wiped the axe handle smooth with a rag. A last, careful look measured the angle of the V-shaped wound and the likely angle of fall. He swung. The clearing seemed to hold its breath as the tree shivered and began to topple. The carpenter stepped smartly away from the base to protect himself against the kick of the severed end as the concussion snapped it clear. He leaned on the axe handle, relieved that he had read it right and that the tree had died without maiming a companion in its death fall. He always felt a mix of satisfaction and sadness when he culled timber from the forest. With the crash of the falling tree still echoing in the valley, a new thought occurred to him. His son would never deal death to a living thing as noble as this tree. He would be a teacher – and teachers, good teachers, promoted life and growth. That thought gentled his heart as he began to dress the tree for transport. Bismarck, the old nag he had borrowed from a neighbour to haul the cart, seemed to shake its withers in sympathy and settle patiently between the shafts.

THE MINES

'Karl?' Elsa cocked her head and listened. 'Come on, Karl,' she whispered impatiently, 'get in here and we'll have some lunch.'

'Is that all you'll have?' Max mocked from behind her.

She whirled to face him and he saw her relax. 'Oh, it's only you, Max,' she said dismissively. 'Well, there's enough for three,' she added without enthusiasm, turning back to pick up her bag.

'But more for two,' he said, coming closer.

Elsa looked up and frowned. 'You know, Max,' she sighed, 'sometimes you let your mouth run ahead of your brain. Do you want some food or not?'

'Not,' he said and lunged for her.

Surprised, she took a step back and swung the bag into his face. He stumbled and regained his balance, coming up in a crouch, his hand exploring the side of his face. 'You cut me,' he said, in disbelief. He held his hand out before him so that she could see the blood on his fingers. 'You cut me. I'm bleeding.'

'Karl!' she screamed suddenly.

Then Max was on her, his hands groping for her throat. 'You cut me!' he raved and her eyes grew very wide. He looked into her face and the fear he saw there sent a powerful surge through his body. Her clawed fingers raked for his eyes and missed, searing down over his face and neck. All his feelings of self-disgust and exclusion bloomed into rage, ignited by the lines of fire on his face, and he shook her violently before slamming her to the floor.

'You hurt me,' he growled, crouching down over her. 'Why did you do that? I—'

Something in the way she lay – some wrongness in the tilt of her head – sobered him suddenly. 'Elsa?' he whispered, reaching a hand to touch the side of her face. He barely brushed her cheek with his fingertips but her head rolled at a grotesque angle so that her face was bisected by the lantern light. The eye he could see was unfocused and glassy. He thought it stared accusingly at him. 'You hurt me,' he whimpered and began to back away. A sound came from within the galleries and shocked him to awareness.

'Karl', he whispered. 'It was an accident, Karl, I swear. We were—' His lips continued to move but no sound emerged. He caught the girl under the arms and began to drag her away from the direction of the sound he'd heard. As he laboured deeper into the shafts, a colder part of his brain began to reassert itself, assessing the situation as if it existed at some level removed from himself. There are sinkholes, he remembered, Elsa had shown them some, the year before, when the three friends had come here. 'Elsa, Karl and Max,' he murmured, 'Elsa, Karl and Max,' until that other part of his consciousness stilled that manic mantra. 'Left here,' it prompted, 'now right to the end of this shaft. It's a cul-de-sac, remember?' He did remember, and followed the instructions carefully. It was ink-black inside the shaft and he extended his hand until it touched the oozing wall. 'Slowly, slowly,' he cautioned himself. Easing his burden to the floor, he lay flat and inched forward until his groping fingers slid from wet rock to cold air. He retreated and when he returned, he was pushing the girl's body before him until gravity suddenly took her from him. He held his breath, straining his ears in the dark, but there was no sound apart from the blood drumming in his ears. Elsa had simply disappeared. 'You didn't mean to kill her,' the voice in his head comforted. 'I didn't mean to kill her,' he whispered, nodding. There was a moment when other emotions threatened to bleed through his calm, but he fought them into submission. At that moment, he felt something inside him give way and a blissful feeling of detachment came over him. She had hurt him and she had died, he reasoned. 'But you are alive,' he whispered. 'Yes, I am alive.'

He made his way back to where Elsa had been sketching, his sense of direction assisted by the reflected glow of her lantern on the weeping walls of the chamber. He picked up her bag and stuffed the sketching materials and sweater inside. Finally, he took the lantern and retraced his steps to the sinkhole. Carefully, he leaned out over the void and dropped first the bag and then the lantern. He watched the light recede from him until it became smaller and smaller and winked out.

★

The lantern threw spindly shadows on the wall behind the ancient staircase. Although no more that a filigree of ancient timber, Karl knew the staircase had withstood the passage of millennia. The salt, he concluded, suddenly aware that he was crouching under a mountain of the mineral Herr Brandt called 'white gold'. He imagined he heard something and cocked his head to listen, but the dead air pressing on his eardrums carried nothing. Had he imagined it? This place was conducive to imaginings, like imagining a rockfall and lying in a small sealed chamber as the rising toxicity in the air stole his life. Hastily, he scrabbled backwards and began to make his way through the galleries. Where was the reflection of Elsa's lantern, he wondered? Could it have gone out? She'd assured him there was enough fuel and he had left her the spare can. This was the chamber, he was certain. His lamp edged light across the floor, gradually revealing a shape.

'Elsa?' The walls bounced the sound back at him as he recognised the fossilised remains of the ancient miner, coiled like a foetus in the rock. He swung the lantern left and right. Where could she have gone? He fought the impulse to action and took deep breaths into his stomach. Think, he commanded himself, consider the possibilities. She could have gone outside! He decided to keep that as his last option, although his fear urged him otherwise. He resolved to do a sweep of the surrounding galleries. A sharp, scraping sound stopped his breath. An animal? he wondered, No, the miners said nothing lived down here, not even mice. 'Elsa,' he called. 'Elsa.' There was no reply. Perhaps she's injured, he thought, and making that sound to guide him.

He lost all awareness of time as he clambered in and out of the galleries, impervious to the icy water that swamped his boots, becoming more and more desperate until his lantern began to flicker and fade and his fear of the dark forced him outside. On the mountainside, he squinted his eyes against a blood-red sun that had impaled itself on the surrounding peaks. 'Elsa,' he breathed, and began to run.

In his haste, Karl forgot the basic rule he had been taught in childhood – coming down a mountain is much more dangerous than climbing up. Never run, the adults had cautioned; zigzag coming down to avoid building up a momentum. By the time he recalled their counsel, he was already out of control, not so much running as taking huge, lunging leaps as the mountain seemed to speed beneath his pounding feet. A section of shale glittered briefly before him and he was sliding, first on his feet, then his bottom and finally on his back, the edged, flat stones making ribbons of his shirt as he windmilled his arms wildly for balance. Small shrubs smacked and raked him as he slid until a stand of young firs sapped his speed and tangled him to a halt. He lay there until the sky stopped spinning and the last stone dislodged by his fall had clattered to rest.

He had tumbled into a pocket of fog that wreathed the trees as if a fire smouldered beneath the forest floor. Something moved in the mist and he squinted his eyes to draw it into focus. A shape hardened and a face swung his way. 'Max?' he gasped. The figure flinched away, like an animal surprised by a hunter, and turned again. The face was divided between light and shadow, like the chiaroscuro Herr Tauber had described when he'd shown them a print of *The Taking of Christ* by Caravaggio. Twin weals bisected it, carving long fissures that gouged from the corner of the eye to the hollow beneath the jawline.

Even as he watched, black viscous drops formed on the chin and dripped silently to the ground he seemed to float on. Blood, he thought. 'Max,' he whispered again and the fog seemed to eddy away from the word. The eyes of the figure looked into his. He saw suffering there and his heart swelled with sympathy. Before he could speak again, the pain vanished from the eyes, burned away by a consuming rage. He felt the intensity of the rage directed at himself, as if he had surprised his friend in a shameful act; in something so terrible that his observation of it could never be forgotten or forgiven. Abruptly, the phantom turned and blundered away into the trees. A feeling of foreboding surged from Karl's belly to his throat and squeezed tears from his eyes. 'Oh, Max,' he said. Ignoring the pain that clamoured from every part of his body, he levered himself upright and moved more cautiously until the path levelled. Then he began to run. 'Elsa,' he gasped, between ragged breaths, 'Elsa.'

★

Rudi Hamner eased back against the buckboard and let Bismarck set the pace. The old horse plodded along contentedly, drawing the wagon and the sections of the tree Rudi had trimmed and loaded. Rounding a bend, shielded by trees, the carpenter sat up straight and stared ahead, shading his eyes against the setting sun. A girl limped along the side of the road and, as the wagon drew alongside, he reined the horse to a halt.

'It's Eloïse, isn't it?' he said. 'Are you hurt, girl?'

She turned to look at him and he was shocked to see her right eye was swollen shut.

'Good God, girl, what happened to you?' He jumped down from the wagon. She flinched away from him, trying to shield her bruised face with her hand. He thought she looked feverish and disorientated and gentled his voice when he spoke again.

'If you'd like to sit in the wagon, Eloïse, I'll bring you home.'

She looked at him warily.

'You know me, Eloïse,' he said. 'I'm Rudi Hamner, Karl Hamner's father.'

'Karl and Elsa, Elsa and Karl,' she said, in an eerie singsong voice that sent a chill through him.

'Have you met Elsa and Karl?' he asked, speaking slowly as one would to a small child.

'On a picnic to the mine,' she chanted and stopped, her eyes widening. 'Don't let him hit me again,' she whimpered.

'Who?'

'Karl and Elsa,' she began again, 'Karl and Elsa went to the mine.'

Rudi Hamner took a deep breath to calm the frustration and anxiety that warred in his stomach.

'No one will hurt you, Eloïse,' he said. 'I promise. Sit in now, girl, and you can rest.'

She moved away from him and perched at the back of the wagon. Slowly, so as not to alarm her, Rudi climbed back on the buckboard and clucked Bismarck. He strained to make sense of the babble streaming from the girl behind him.

'Karl and Elsa went to the mine but didn't ask him. Ha! He

couldn't, could he? – Keep it up.'

She laughed brokenly and lapsed into silence. Rudi stewed with anxiety but maintained his silence as they approached the outskirts of the village. He knew Eloïse and her mother. It was common knowledge in the village that her mother had suffered a mental breakdown after her husband had left. Eloïse had run wild and there were whispers about boys taking advantage of her. Rudi shook his head, angry that two human beings should be reduced by the measurements of small minds. At the same time, he had to admit to himself that he was relieved he had no daughters, only Karl. Oh God, he thought, what if something—

'Here,' she said sharply and, in his surprise, he hauled on the reins, earning a baleful look from Bismarck.

'But you don't live here, Eloïse,' he said, climbing down from the wagon.

'No,' she said, 'don't live here. Friend lives here – woman's friend.'

He looked around and saw a path leading off into the woods. Smoke drifted up from a chimney, somewhere beyond the screening trees. The herbalist, he thought, the girl wants to – oh! The realisation struck him and he turned away in embarrassment. A secret, his wife had told him years before, is something known to one person. Even someone like himself, who had little time for gossip, couldn't have lived in Hallstatt and not known about the herbalist. He also knew she provided services for girls who got into trouble. He snorted at that foolish phrase. Why does the man never get into trouble? he thought angrily. His anger urged him to ask her again, 'Who hit you, Eloïse?' For a moment he thought she was going to answer, then her eyes slid away from his.

'He's mad,' she said quietly. 'He would have killed me.' She stepped along the path and paused. 'He hates them,' she said, over her shoulder.

'Who?'

'Karl and Elsa, Elsa and Karl,' she began again and the jingle buzzed in his brain like an annoying gnat long after she had disappeared among the trees.

★

'Elsa, Elsa.' The miner's door slammed into him and he crumpled.

'What, in God's name? Karl?' The miner swept him up like a child and bundled him on to a sofa.

'Elsa,' Karl moaned and tried to thrash his way to his feet.

'Look at me, boy,' the miner snapped. 'Look at me.'

The whipcrack voice focused him on a pair of intense blue eyes.

'Tell me,' the miner commanded.

'Can't find her — searched — everything gone — Elsa gone.'

The miner disappeared from view. Karl heard shouting outside, then a door slammed and the miner was back. He hooked a hand behind the boy's neck and tugged him forward. 'Let me look at you,' he murmured. 'Jesus, your back is— Turn on your side. Good. Drink this.'

Karl felt a glass bump against his lips and opened his mouth eagerly.

'Sip, don't gulp. Enough. I saw your father on the road, Karl. He's coming, Frau Werther too. I'll get some ointment.'

His father suddenly loomed above him.

'Papa, I couldn't find her.'

'Just tell me, son.'

The miner leaned in again and the two faces bracketed his vision.

'Elsa told me to go — see the staircase. I heard something. Went back. Nothing. I searched. Papa, I couldn't find her. I—'

'Easy,' his father whispered. 'Lie back now, son. Frau Werther will see to your back.' His father's face disappeared.

'Herr Druckner.'

'Yes, Karl?'

'Sorry — so sorry.'

The miner's face blurred as the boy's eyes filled with tears. He felt two calloused thumbs rub his tears away, so gently that it broke his heart.

★

'Gentlemen,' the policeman said, 'we need to be organised. No point in running around in circles like—'

'Shut up.'

'I beg your—'

'I said, shut up.'

The miner stood uncomfortably close. 'You don't know the mines,' he said harshly, 'I do. Don't get in my way.'

'There's no n—'

'Rudi,' the miner snapped, 'and you, Herr Brandt, search this area. Wilhelm—'

'I really think we—'

'You have been warned,' the miner said, wheeling on the policeman savagely.

'Wilhelm, Gunther and you, Gert, into the first gallery and split. If you see anything, sing out. Stefan, you and I will check the sinkholes. It is eight o'clock now. Everybody back here at nine thirty. Go!'

None of them could look the miner in the eye. 'Nothing,' they muttered, 'no trace.'

For a moment, the man's squat shoulders sagged, then he took a deep breath and straightened. 'You did your best,' he said tiredly, 'thank you. We're all tired, and tired men make mistakes down here. Safer to go home and sleep. I will be here at six in the morning with ropes. If you can help, I'll be grateful.'

They nodded and left, a few clapping the miner on the shoulder as they trudged dispiritedly from the mine. The miner ignored the policeman. He busied himself tidying away the equipment. Finally, he lifted his lantern head high and looked around the chamber one last time.

The policeman watched him go. Bloody amateurs, he fumed, they should have let him organise a proper search. After all, he was the one with the authority, wasn't he? And that fucking troll had threatened him – before witnesses. What was the fool girl doing here anyway? Ah, yes, he remembered, doing some shitty project for that fool schoolteacher. Well, there'll be questions to answer there. He swung his lantern in a circle, squinting into the shadows beyond the light. 'Bloody miners' brats think this is a playground,' the policeman muttered to himself as he paced the floor, replaying the insults he had endured and the stinging replies that he should have given. 'Bloody peasants,' he said aloud, 'I should have report—'

A tiny flash winked in the lantern light and he froze. He marked its position and crouched; duck-walking across the floor, he kept his eyes on the spot. Slowly, he stretched out his hand, sifting the thin layer of earth through his fingers. When he raised his hand, a delicate chain swung from his fingers, a silver chain with a tiny silver cross revolving in the light. He felt the air puff from his lungs as if someone had struck him, and he wavered on his feet. 'Max,' he croaked.

THE STEIGER HOUSEHOLD

'Where have you been? Max fell in the forest and hurt himself. Why are you never here when you're—'

Something in the policeman's expression stopped her tirade. He slumped in the kitchen chair and began to knead his forehead with the heel of his hand. Carefully, she drew out the chair opposite and sat.

'What is it?' she asked.

'What did Max tell you?'

'I already told you. He said he was in the forest and fell. Why? Don't you—'

'Did he say he was anywhere else?'

'No.'

'He lied,' he whispered.

'You dare call my son a liar,' she said savagely. 'My s—'

'Your son is a liar. He was in the mine and now the Druckner girl is missing and—'

'Who saw him there?'

'Nobody saw him but—'

'See, you have no proof. Some policeman you—'

'I found this,' he said numbly, dangling the cross and chain between them.

The links of the chain had trapped tiny pieces of grit. She knew that if she touched them with her fingers and touched her fingers to her tongue they would taste of salt.

'Did anyone else see this?'

'No, but you know what this means? This is Max's—'

'This,' she said, grasping the cross in her fist, her face barely inches from his, 'is a noose that could hang my son.'

For a moment, the slim chain stretched taut between them; then the policeman groaned and let go.

'Go to bed,' she commanded. 'Leave everything to me.'

'I – am a policeman,' he said stubbornly.

She stared at him with smouldering contempt.

'And how long do you think that will last if word of this gets out? We need to make sure Max can't answer any questions.'

'We could send him away.'

'No, that would only arouse suspicion. Leave it to me.'

'Where are you going?'

'I have a plan,' she said, pulling on her coat. 'There are people who will help me.'

'Who would choose to help us?' he said bitterly.

'No one,' she answered, 'at least no one who has any choice.'

THE HERBALIST'S COTTAGE

Frau Mende had learned to live with the title 'that woman'. She'd accepted that, in small towns and villages, a real name conferred a degree of inclusion, something she neither received nor expected in Hallstatt.

It hadn't helped her cause that she had come here from Salzburg. The locals had examined her through the prism of their prejudices and found confirmation of her otherness, no matter how hard she tried to adapt. And she had tried, especially in the first year when her husband had managed the mines. The status of mine-manager's wife had given her access to the small circle of professional people in the village, but she had discovered to her cost that the wives were more interested in her status than in herself.

If further proof was needed, it was readily available when he'd suffered a fatal accident and her erstwhile friends had excluded his widow from their gatherings. Did she miss them? No, she concluded, as she carried herbs from the kitchen table to her apothecary cabinet. She closed one of the many small drawers and let her palm linger on the lustrous veneer. The cabinet had been a wedding present from Helmut, who'd always encouraged her interest in herbal remedies. Truth be told, she smiled ruefully, Helmut had been supportive because he considered it something a hausfrau could do in her spare time, like a hobby. He had no idea of how adept she'd become at sourcing local herbs and blending them into remedies for the ordinary ailments country folk rarely took to a doctor. She wondered how he would feel now if he knew that her 'hobby' provided the bulk of her income and ensured his widow and son a comfortable living.

She washed her hands under the faucet and went to look in the sitting room. Gunther looked up from where he was shelling peas in a basin and smiled. It was the smile of someone without guile, a radiant look of love from a young man who would remain a child forever. He's seventeen years old, she thought, and a feeling of foreboding welled up inside her. Who will care for him after I'm gone, she wondered? That recurring worry evaporated, as it always did, in the warmth of his smile. Don't lose the moment, she reminded herself and blew him a kiss. She returned to the kitchen table and sat. It was important, she knew, to sit and reflect after she'd seen someone, and Eloïse needed to be thought of.

*

The priest's house

Father Kyril slotted the book precisely into its appointed place. He cast a suspicious eye along the row of volumes and was mollified to see they maintained a uniform distance from the edge of the shelf, their spines exactly vertical. He turned and took three paces to his desk, then sat and picked up a pen. He dipped it once in the ink bottle and scraped it once on the rim to remove the excess.

'It's an obsession, Father,' his confessor had said. 'Some priests take refuge from a painful reality in excessive scrupulosity. It can even manifest itself in the way they perform their ablutions. I remember a priest in—'

The confessor, Father Kyril concluded, had been well meaning but misguided. 'Scrupulously taking extreme care over the small things,' he'd responded, 'is what keeps the devil at bay. It is potentially lethal to the soul to leave chinks in the armour, an unguarded casement—'

'A gap on the bookshelf?' his confessor had queried.

'And the inappropriate levity of one's confessor,' he'd retorted.

The priest began to write in his journal, though he would have been offended if someone had suggested that he kept a diary. To him, diaries were the ego-driven scribbles of those who had been seduced by their hubris to consider the trivia of their lives worth recording. He kept a journal: a meticulous record of his soul's trial and triumphs as an aide-mémoire for his guidance and edification. Much like a navigator's chart, he thought, a collection of sightings and soundings that kept the barque of his soul safe from reefs and shoals. He knew from experience how fragile the soul could be and how perilous the world.

The herbalist's house

The girl was coming more frequently, now that she'd matured physically. In the beginning, her visits had revolved around mourning her absent father. Lately, she was trying to come to terms with the more immediate and painful presence of a mother who had abdicated as a parent and become dependent on her child. Eloïse was hungry – hungry for love and she was finding its forgeries in all the wrong places. 'Easy' was a word that had become attached to the girl and, like a parasite, it had sucked her dry of any respect in her local community. Today's story was just a variation of every other day's story. Not exactly the same story, Frau Mende reflected. If what Eloïse had recounted was true, this latest episode had a more sinister edge to it than the other inappropriate relationships Eloïse had been prone to. Eloïse had sensed a danger in the boy and had been terrified. Frau Mende was holding that dark thought when the pounding started on her door.

Over the years, the herbalist had honed her instinct for trouble. She had learned to read it in facial expressions and bodily postures, convinced that the body carried and communicated its distress. That instinct had developed into an awareness of sound. She could distinguish the timid knock of a worried girl from the frantic hammering that heralded an emergency. The pounding on her door she registered as 'imperious' and was unsurprised when she opened it to reveal her visitor.

'Good evening, Frau Steiger,' she said calmly.

THE PRIEST'S HOUSE

Father Kyril had met 'that woman' on a number of occasions, he recorded. One couldn't avoid meeting everyone at some stage in the tiny enclave of Hallstatt. Naturally, he'd averted his eyes but that had drawn his attention to her defective son. The woman insisted on bringing the creature with her despite the sensitivities of others. He'd tried to offer her some words of comfort because of her affliction, urging her to carry her cross with fortitude. She'd brushed his exhortation aside, insisting her son was a gift from God like any other child. He'd pretended not to hear her and had gone on to ask if she was in need of charity from the parish – considering the burden she had to carry.

'I'm a herbalist,' she had declared brazenly, 'I am quite capable of providing for my child.'

Before charity or prudence could intervene, he'd felt compelled to quote Leviticus: 'You shall not suffer a witch to live.'

At this, she had accused him of misinterpreting the text – accusing *him*, who had lectured on Sacred Scripture at the seminary in Salzburg. She'd insisted the passage referred to a woman who uses her gifts to cause harm. Well, that was Luther's legacy, wasn't it; every common person interpreting the Bible to suit themselves?

He laid the pen aside at right angles to the journal. What has brought me to this pass, he wondered? What providential plan had ordained that he should be removed from his post at the seminary and exiled among these Godless people?

'Inappropriate behaviour,' the bishop had mumbled. He had protested, but to no avail, that the young woman in question had sought him out, had forced herself on—. The bishop had scrubbed his hands together as if embarrassed. Like Pontius Pilate, he wanted to be rid of the problem and so 'it was necessary for one man to die for the people'.

'We must consider the Church above all else, Father – the importance of avoiding scandal – her parents have listened to reason – arrangements made with the nuns – to protect the unfortunate girl.'

And finally, after his sin and its consequences had been aired sufficiently, the penance.

'You need a period of prayer and reflection, Father.'

The 'period' had extended to twenty years and Hallstatt had become his Purgatory.

Father Kyril had been taught that Purgatory was a place where souls were cleansed of impurities before they were admitted to Heaven. He'd never heard from any theologian that, even in Purgatory, 'the devil goes about seeking whom he may devour'. Nevertheless, he knew that to be true – now.

The woman brushed by her and stalked into the kitchen.

'Please sit, Frau Steiger,' she invited, but whatever raged in the woman wouldn't allow for that. She saw the enormous effort it cost her to maintain a semblance of control and so stayed silent.

'I want something,' Frau Steiger said abruptly. 'I want something that will make someone ill – very ill.'

Frau Mende looked at her blankly.

'Oh, for God's sake, woman,' Frau Steiger hissed impatiently. 'I don't want to kill them, just make them sick.'

'I'm sorry, I can't do that. It's against my code of ethics to knowingly cause harm to—'

'Spare me that Hippocratic gibberish,' the other woman interrupted. 'It's not as if you're even a real doctor. More like some itinerant quack who—'

'Who has been of service to you in the past, Frau Steiger.'

The policeman's wife stopped as if slapped.

'Once,' she croaked, 'just once because I was—'

She bit off the final word.

'Anyway, it doesn't matter, I never took that stuff.'

'It was always your choice whether you conceived or not.'

Frau Steiger glanced over her shoulder as if afraid of eavesdroppers. When she looked back, her eyes were wary.

'You swore that you would never speak of that,' she said hoarsely.

'Nor have I. Nor did I need to swear. The oath was your idea, Frau Steiger, that was your need, not mine.'

Frau Steiger waved an impatient hand before her face as if erasing something.

'Will you give me what I've asked for?'

'No, Frau Steiger, I will not.'

'Do you have any idea whom you're talking to?'

'Yes, I do. You are a woman who came once before asking for a particular remedy. Under the circumstances then, I gave it to you and I think I was right to do so. You chose not to use it, as was your right. Now you are asking me for something to harm another person.'

'It's for their good.'

'I don't see how harming someone is for their good.'

'I don't have time to explain.'

'Then I bid you goodnight, Frau Steiger.'

Frau Mende moved to the door but the other woman didn't follow.

'I won't change my—'

'Listen carefully, Frau Mende,' the policeman's wife said, and the herbalist paused with her hand on the latch. 'I can bring trouble on you and, as sure as Christ was crucified, I will do so if you don't oblige me.'

'I have nothing to fear from you,' the herbalist said. 'I am a registered practitioner and my affairs are in order.'

'I'm sure they are,' Frau Steiger nodded and smiled.

Frau Mende considered she had never seen such a grotesque parody of a smile and, for the first time since the woman had invaded her house, she felt afraid.

'Your son means everything to you, doesn't he?'

'Yes, yes, of course, but I don't see—'

'Then you have everything to fear from me.'

'I really don't—'

'You think you are safe, don't you?' the policeman's wife taunted. Frau Mende tried to ignore the chill that shivered between her shoulder blades as the woman continued. 'They tell me he is the light of your life. Some say he is simple. Others use words like defective and retarded. Ah, I see you don't care for those words.'

'No, I do not and I'll thank—'

'The Germans refer to them, to those like him, Frau Mende, as Untermenschen. Are you familiar with that word?'

The herbalist nodded dumbly.

'And are you familiar with their policy towards sons like yours – policies which are now enforced throughout the Reich?'

The herbalist stared at her in shocked disbelief.

'Are you?' the woman shouted.

'Mutti!' Gunther called anxiously from the sitting room. 'Mutti!'

'It's – it's all right, Liebchen,' she answered querulously, 'nothing to worry about.'

'My husband is a policeman,' Frau Steiger continued implacably, 'it is his duty to notify the authorities of such persons. I can persuade him otherwise.'

Frau Mende turned and walked to the cabinet. She took a tiny key from its hiding place under a Meissner figurine and unlocked a drawer. Under the watchful eye of the other woman, she brought the herbs to the pestle on the kitchen table and ground them. Finally, she poured the powder into a small white envelope.

'One spoonful in a cup of water,' she whispered through bloodless lips. 'Repeat every six hours, or as long as—'

The words died on her lips and she held out the envelope in an icy hand.

She stood there for a long time after she'd heard the door close. Abruptly, she moved to the faucet and began to scrub her hands, first scrubbing one hand with the other and then with a hand brush. She scrubbed as if she could wash away the memory of what had just happened, as if she could scour the fear from her belly and the shame from her heart – scrubbing, ever harder, until she saw blood in the basin.

THE PRIEST

Father Kyril dragged his mind back to recent events. The carpenter, Hamner, had come to his door demanding he ring the church bell. Some girl or other was missing in the mines and there was need of a rescue party. The man was distraught and could be forgiven for his manner. However, when he'd explained that the bell could be rung only to summon people to mass or to mark a funeral, the fellow had simply gone off and rung the bell himself. Naturally, he had included the missing girl in his prayers but what business had a girl in the mines in the first place? It was just another example of the fraying of the fabric. That was a phrase he had coined himself and had used a number of times from the pulpit.

'We are witnessing the fraying of the fabric of our society,' he had warned his congregation. 'Long before the people of Israel rejected Christ and were condemned to perpetual exile, they built a double-woven palisade of laws in the Torah and Talmud to keep them free of contamination from the pagans who surrounded them. In our day, the teachings of Holy Mother Church serve the same purpose. Any laxity in observance – any toleration of ungodly behaviour – even the merest hint of doubt can lead to a fraying of the fabric.'

THE STEIGER HOUSEHOLD

She had carefully measured out the dose and carried it to his bedroom. She saw the apprehension in his eyes as she approached. 'This will dull the pain,' she'd said, 'and protect you from infection.'

He'd taken the cup from her hands and winced at the smell.

'Drink it quickly,' she'd said.

Now he lay on his back, his eyes wide open and unseeing. The lines on his cheek and neck stood out lividly against the pallor of his face.

'He's dying,' the policeman whimpered.

'No, he isn't,' she said impatiently. 'Let me explain it to you, again. What's important is that Max can't answer questions. Can you get that into your thick skull? This will give us time. Do you understand?'

'Yes, but—'

'No buts, no ifs. No anything from you except doing whatever meaningless things you always do. Be a policeman – leave everything else to me.'

'You're going out again?'

'Yes. I'm going to see the priest.'

'Why?'

'Because people must know Max is ill – very ill. They're less likely to become suspicious.'

'If you were a proper wife, you wouldn't go to that man,' he muttered.

'If you had been a proper husband, I would never have gone to him in the first place,' she said and left.

THE PRIEST'S HOUSE

'Pearls before swine,' he sighed.

He cleaned his pen and blotted his journal, placing it in the top drawer on the left-hand side of the desk. One final check to make sure everything was in its allotted place and he could retire for the evening. He was correcting the angle of a deviant pencil when the devil knocked on his door.

THE BIERKELLER, HALLSTATT

The men in the bierkeller sat with a stillness born of exhaustion. Kurt Brandt raised his glass with both hands to avoid slopping beer on his neighbours. He wondered how miners survived the aching cold of the galleries and if his curled fingers would ever hold a pen again.

They had done shifts at the mine — searching shafts, shining lanterns into hidden places, even lowering men on ropes into sinkholes. Nothing! And although a sense of futility had begun to sap their energy, no man would consider withdrawing from the search. Even Gert, Kurt thought, had been untiring, holding a lantern or a rope as required for eight straight hours and then manning the bar in the evening to slake the thirst of the searchers.

He saw a companion raise a finger for another drink and heard Gert's grunt as he stretched back for a bottle. He felt like smiling but didn't have the energy. He knew why they turned up each morning before dawn and regrouped disconsolately at the mouth of the shaft as the last light faded. They did it for the miner. Druckner was a man of few words, but they were attended to and appreciated by his neighbours. He was always first to the mine each morning and had lanterns, ropes and everything else they needed stacked and ready when the others trickled in.

Kurt had been taken aback the first night of the search when the miner had silenced the policeman and taken control of the operation. His surprise had changed to admiration when he saw him express his gratitude to the rescue party before they began their search and again at the end of another fruitless day. Kurt was also impressed by Rudi Hamner, the carpenter. It had been Rudi's idea to map the area to avoid various groups searching the same area twice. Every morning, he compared his map with a map of the mine. Kurt had been astonished at the size of the mine. He'd also been disheartened when others had muttered that it stretched further into the mountain than the map could reach. The miners talked about tunnels that honeycombed the rocks and sinkholes that plunged hundreds of feet to underground streams.

Rudi, he'd noticed, would always walk the miner home, sometimes persuading him to have dinner in the Hamner household. Today they had appointed Rudi to bring the miner to a meeting in the bierkeller. Kurt was finally getting some flexibility back into his fingers when the door opened.

'Rudi says you want to talk,' the miner said.

For a moment there was an awkward silence and then Rudi spoke.

'I've been studying the map. Karl says he was away from the chamber for an hour. If Elsa started walking immediately after Karl left, she couldn't have got farther than we've searched. I mentioned this to Karl and he didn't think she'd planned to leave the chamber. She was sketching when he left.'

The miner nodded slowly.

'What do you suggest?' he asked.

'I think it's time we got help – from outside.'

'Who?'

'The mountain rescue from Brunke – the army – I don't know. But time is not on our side, Tomas.'

The miner nodded again and the men in the bar stared into their drinks rather than look at his face.

'You're right,' he said, at last. 'I'll call to the policeman in the morning and ask him to contact the Brunke people. I suppose,' he added, 'I'll have to apologise to the little prick for biting his head off.'

There was a moment of shocked silence, and then the bierkeller erupted. Kurt wondered about the heartiness of the laughter until he noticed more that one man knuckle a tear from his eye.

'I'll do it for you,' Rudi said, clapping the miner on the back. 'I need to see him anyway.'

HALLSTATT, LATER

Kurt was making his way home when Rudi detached himself from the shadows and fell into step beside him.

'I think you were right to suggest outside help, Herr Hamner,' Kurt remarked.

'My name is Rudi.'

'Kurt,' the teacher said, and they shook hands briskly without breaking stride.

'I need to speak to you,' Rudi said.

Frau Steiger heard the approaching footsteps and stood in the dark shadow between two houses as they passed. A light, peeping between the curtains of one of the houses, briefly lit their faces before the dark reclaimed them and their footsteps faded. The carpenter and the teacher, she noted: strange bedfellows. She knew that anxiety tended to exaggerate the ordinary and invest chance happenings with a meaning they didn't merit. Nevertheless, she resolved to consider that particular pairing later.

She hurried on until she was standing in the shadows that pooled under the church. Light from a lantern sieved through the curtains of the small house beside it. She knocked and watched the light hurry from the window and wax stronger in the fan-shaped glass above the door.

The priest's face registered annoyance and then paled. She took a step forward and he retreated before her, the trembling lantern flicking his face with shadows as she closed the door behind her.

'What do you want?' he asked.

'I want nothing from you,' she said evenly, 'except what any parishioner has the right to expect.'

Confusion glazed his eyes.

'We will speak in the reception room,' she said.

He nodded and shambled down the short hallway. She followed the lantern into the small room with the bare table and hard chairs. She was reminded of the times she had sat here and poured out the misery of her marriage to this man. She had told him things and he had sat where he sat now and nodded sympathetically. That, she remembered, was before they had moved to his study 'because it would be more comfortable for her' and from there—. She shook her head and steeled herself to the task in hand.

'Tomorrow,' she said, 'I want you to pray for my son at the public mass. You will say that he is seriously ill and in danger of death. Afterwards, you will come to my home with a purple stole around your shoulders and give him the last sacraments. Do you understand?'

'Max is ill?' he whispered.

'Yes. Will you do this?'

'Yes – yes of course. It is my duty to—'

'There's more,' she said. 'I am sending my son to my family in Croatia to recuperate. My brother is a monsignor at the archbishop's palace and he will handle matters. When Max is ready to travel, you will accompany him.'

'But there is a restriction on travel.'

'Which is why you will be with him. The authorities will not hinder a priest.'

'But I cannot just leave the parish. I have taken a vow of obedience to my bishop and—'

'You took other vows, Father Kyril,' she said coldly, 'and you took leave of them.'

'I'll leave you two to your chat,' Bertha said, when the introductions had been made and Rudi was seated at the fire.

'Be sure to keep the fire stacked, Kurt. You both look frozen.'

After she'd closed the door, Kurt rummaged in a cupboard and produced a bottle of schnapps and glasses.

'Yes, I think I will,' Rudi sighed. 'the cold of the mines is boring into my bones. I hate to think of Elsa—' He turned away and held his hands to the fire.

'How is Karl?' Kurt asked as he poured.

'Oh, his back is healing well enough, but – he's suffering. He blames himself. Thank you,' he added as he took the glass.

Kurt raised his glass. 'To absent friends,' he said gently. 'They w— are such good friends,' he said as he sat back in the armchair on the other side of the fire.

'Yes, they are. Karl is an only child, Kurt. Oh, he's sociable enough but solitary. Does that make sense?'

'Yes, Rudi, it does. He's an excellent student, very conscientious about everything he does. But he has a stillness in him. Bertha would say he's "an old soul".'

The carpenter smiled. 'We, my wife and I, were pleased when he became friends with Elsa. I suppose it must be true that opposites attract; she is so full of life—'

Their eyes met for an instant and Kurt saw the pain and confusion in the carpenter's face.

'If there is anything I can do,' he said. 'I mean if you'd like me to talk to Karl, or anything.'

'That's very kind of you,' Rudi said, 'but I didn't really come to talk about Karl.'

He took a sip from his glass.

'It might be better if I just tell you my story. It's been buzzing around inside my head. I haven't said anything at home, what with Karl – well, you know?'

'Why do you think I can help, Rudi?'

'I hope you won't be offended, but, you're from—'

'From the outside,' Kurt said smiling, 'from beyond the

mountains. I'm not offended at all.'

'At the same time, you've been here long enough to know what village life is like.' He clasped his big hands before him. 'We live so closely together that we know almost everything about everyone else, but must pretend not to. I'm sorry if I'm confusing you.'

'Not at all,' Kurt answered. 'I often think the staff common room at the university was something like the village. Of course, everybody gossiped about everybody else but there was an unwritten rule everyone observed. We did not speak of each other to outsiders. Unless it was a matter of life or death, I suppose,' he added and smiled. Rudi Hamner did not smile. He drained his glass and began to tell his story. 'Maybe Karl saw Max in the forest. Maybe he just imagined it. I don't know,' he concluded.

After he finished, Kurt put some logs on the fire and both men watched the flames lick the wood until the resin began to sizzle.

'I've never been able to understand Max,' Kurt said slowly. 'Sometimes he seems so hungry for companionship. I've noticed him watching Karl and Elsa and wanting to be part of their circle. And then it's as if something in him can't deal with friendship. He'll suddenly say something arrogant or just – abstract himself, become remote and cold.'

'You think he might—'

'I don't know.'

'I'm going to the policeman's house tomorrow. I promised Tomas I would, but I was going anyway. I need to ask Max some questions before it's too late.'

He stood and placed his glass on the table.

'His mother will probably bite my head off.'

'Biting off two might be more than she can handle,' Kurt said.

THE HAMNER HOUSE

'Well?'

'Still the same,' she sighed. 'He just lies there. Oh Rudi, what are . . .' But her husband had already gone, pounding up the stairs to the boy's room.

'Karl,' he said, 'get up and come to the workshop.'

When the boy stumbled into his workshop, Rudi Hamner didn't waste time with pleasantries.

'Listen to me, boy,' he said. 'You lie all day in that bed, staring at the wall. Now tell me this, what have you learned from the wall?'

The boy stared blankly at him.

'Well?'

'Nothing, Papa.'

'And what are you thinking of while you're staring at the wall?'

'Of Elsa,' he whispered.

'And what do you think about Elsa?'

'I should never have left her.'

'You're right.'

'What?'

'You're absolutely right: you shouldn't have left her. You knew that as soon as you had your back turned, she was going to walk off into the galleries and lose herself. And still you left her.'

'Wha— but Papa I didn't know that. I – she was sketching and—'

'And was it reasonable to expect she'd carry on sketching?'

'Yes.'

'And was it reasonable for you to leave her?'

'Yes.'

'And none of that matters now, does it Karl?' he said gently, 'because Elsa is gone and you fear for her?'

'Y – Yes, Papa, I feel—' The boy's face contorted and then dissolved.

His father held him gently, careful not to contain him even when he opened his mouth and wailed silently – even when he arched his back and flailed at his father's shoulders. And when there were no tears left, Rudi Hamner cradled his son against his chest.

'This is what it costs to care for someone, my son,' he whispered. And lose them, he thought, but didn't say. Eventually, he tilted up the boy's head and wiped his cheeks.

'What can you do for Elsa now, Karl?'

'I – I can search for her.'

'Then you'll need your sleep. Go and kiss your mother goodnight.'

THE STEIGERS' HOUSE

We should have called before dawn, Kurt thought, just to see if the policeman appreciated the irony. The man who opened the door seemed more concerned with threading his arm through his suspenders while struggling to maintain a scowl on his face. The early hour, Kurt considered, might account for his dishevelled state but not for the furtive look that crept into his eyes.

'The police office opens at nine,' he muttered and began to close the door.

Rudi stopped it with a firm hand and stepped inside, driving the policeman before him.

'Elsa Druckner can't wait for the office to open, Herr Steiger,' he said. Kurt imagined he saw the policeman wince at the girl's name.

'Max may have some information that will help us find the girl,' Rudi continued. 'Where is he?'

'Max?' the policeman gasped. 'He's …'

He gestured towards the loft and before he could object, Rudi was taking the stairs two at a time with Kurt hurrying to catch up. 'I'm sorry to wake him,' Rudi was saying, 'but we can't afford to—'

Both men froze when they saw the boy. Max lay motionless on his back, his face made ghastly by the light that pearled through the small window set into the roof. His eyes were open, flat and sightless, and showed no reaction when his father moved protectively to the side of the bed. Embarrassed by the boy's vulnerability, Kurt gazed around the attic bedroom. His attention was drawn immediately to the bookshelves that stood to attention around the walls. There were no books on the floor, or lying open on the desk that crouched under the skylight. Spartan, he thought, noting the absence of ornamentation or bric-a-brac or any of the things that would mark this as a boy's room. The policeman's influence? he wondered and dismissed the thought when he glanced at the rumpled and perspiring man. On the other hand, the room was not what Bertha called 'woman tidy'. Even he knew what that meant. Max then, he concluded, and wondered what this 'monk's cell' revealed about the boy. Rudi pushed the father aside and stooped over the still figure.

'What happened?' he asked.

'He – he fell in the forest,' the policeman stammered. 'By the time he got home, he was …' He gestured mutely at the stricken boy.

'What does the doctor say?'

'Doctor?' The policeman opened his mouth to say more and closed it again.

'What happened his face?' Rudi asked, tracing his fingers gently down the gouges in the boy's cheek, following their path to the collar of his pyjamas.

'Scrapes,' the policeman blurted, 'from the rock he was climbing.'

'You said he fell in the forest,' Rudi remarked quietly, never taking his eyes off the boy.

Kurt heard the front door open and saw relief flood the policeman's face. A wavering light climbed the stairwell and Frau Steiger appeared, holding a candle. She paused at the top of the stairs and glared at the intruders. Kurt thought the reflection of the small flame in her eyes made them look almost feral. Wordlessly, she moved to the bed, followed by the priest. Father Kyril was encased in a black cassock that made his face seem unnaturally white. A thin purple vestment hung from his shoulders and he carried a round, silver box in his hands. At the bedside, he dipped his thumb carefully in the box and traced the sign of the cross on the boy's forehead while chanting a prayer in Latin. Frau Steiger motioned to the others to follow and they trooped in awkward silence down the stairs.

'What are you doing in my house?' she hissed when they'd congregated in the kitchen.

'We're sorry to intrude at such a time, Frau Steiger,' Rudi said. 'We thought Max might have some information about the

Druckner girl. We had no idea the boy was so ill.'

'So now you know,' she said flatly. 'My son knows nothing about that girl. I bid you good-day.'

She moved to the door but Rudi turned to the policeman.

'It's time to ask for help from outside,' he said.

They climbed steadily towards the mines, each enveloped in his thoughts. Finally, Kurt broke the silence.

'The man of the house seemed on edge,' he offered.

'There is only one man in that house,' Rudi observed, 'and it isn't the policeman.' He sighed in frustration. 'I noticed you looking around,' he said. 'What were your impressions?'

'Cold,' said Kurt, hitching the haversack a little higher on his back. 'Very tense, almost fearful. There's something going on there that I can't put my finger on. Why did you ask about the marks on the boy's face?'

Rudi stopped walking and eased his pack to the ground.

'He gave me contradictory answers,' he said.

'The policeman?'

'Yes. He said Max fell in the forest and then said he got his scrapes rock-climbing. So the question is: who was with him?'

'Why do you think there was someone with him?'

'I don't. Max is a loner and he certainly wasn't rock-climbing. One of the first lessons drummed into children's heads around here is never climb alone. That and all the other rules, like don't run down a mountain and never eat snow – especially yellow snow.'

'Why?' Kurt asked, and then smiled.

'Exactly,' Rudi said. 'Also, I know what rock scrapes look like. They're patchy, nothing at all like what Max has. Max has scratches that start near his eye and run down his cheekbone in straight lines all the way to his collar.'

'So?' Kurt prompted.

'You don't have children. Anyone who has will tell you that those marks are made by other children when they fight.'

'Could it have been Eloïse?'

'No, I don't think so. Eloïse is a timid girl and was terrified that the person who attacked her would kill her.'

'Well, we can't ask Max.'

'The people who come from the outside will ask him questions. Sooner or later, the boy will have to answer them.'

THE LAKE, HALLSTATT

Johann sat, without moving, in the bow of the boat. He was afraid that even the slightest movement would topple his head from his shoulders and it would splash in the lake. With his luck, he griped, it would make a loud splash that would wake his headache. The boy knew his moods and feathered the water with the tips of the oars so that the boat moved smoothly. Johann risked a glance at the majestic mountains, wrapped in shadow-blankets. Still no sign of the girl, he thought sadly. If she was alive and near water— He turned abruptly from that foolish thought – who could drink the water in that place?

He'd sat in the bierkeller each evening, nursing a single drink, waiting for the searchers to come in. Each night, he read the dejection in their bodies, the disappointment in their expressions. He didn't need to ask the question he'd been holding in his mouth all evening. After that, he had no good reason to remain sober. If he looked over his shoulder now, he knew he'd see them moving like wraiths along the escarpment before they climbed the last scree-slope to the mine. Instead, he focused on the small pier Erich's oar-strokes were pulling ever nearer to the boat. The early train would have paused long enough to drop whoever was coming from beyond the mountains. Two men, he decided, as the mist parted and revealed them.

The taller of the two, the boatman knew, was army; even before he was close enough to identify the greatcoat and cap. He had the straight posture and the way he spread his feet showed he knew how to wait. The other was a swirl of aimless movement, picking up and putting down his bag, checking his watch ostentatiously as if that might draw the boat to the pier any faster. Erich backed expertly on one oar and spun the boat slowly so that it nuzzled against the buffer with a gentle thump. God mightn't have put too much in his head, his father thought admiringly, but even with two hands he had never been the boatman his son was. The boy had lake water in his veins. Normally, he'd have placed the smaller man up front and put the bigger man aft, for balance. Some instinct warned him otherwise. When they were seated with their baggage stored under the seats, he nodded to his son and the boy broke the pier's embrace with the slightest shift of his wrist on the oar.

'That's a pleasant morning,' the sergeant said affably, planting his big feet firmly on the rib that ran beneath him, centring his body to help the boy on the oars.

'Better morning than they're having in Bruckna,' Johann quipped, recognising the accent. 'What brings you down from the backwoods?' he continued genially. There was a long tradition of rivalry between the two villages and, over the years, barter had given way to banter. 'Maybe you decided you'd like to try some real food for a change?'

'I think I'd have to go farther than this pissy fishing village for that,' the sergeant said easily. 'Might pick up a pinch of salt, though, if you're sure you can spare it.'

Now that each had established the other's ability to take a joke at his own expense, they moved seamlessly on to more weighty matters.

'How's this war going, then?' Johann asked.

The sergeant stared over Johann's shoulder and dropped a broad wink. It was a signal, the boatman knew, from one soldier to another. There was brass about and whatever was said should be interpreted accordingly. Sure enough, Johann saw the small man in the stern become suddenly still and attentive.

'Caught Ivan with his pants down,' the sergeant said enthusiastically. 'Panzer tanks going like a knife through butter, going so fast they're passing the queue of deserters. Luftwaffe killed fifteen hundred planes first day, and only three hundred managed to get up in the air. They say our lads will be drinking vodka in the Kremlin in a few weeks.'

He stretched expansively and hunkered forward with his elbows on his knees. Johann busied himself, rolling a cigarette on his knee with one hand. He waited until the sergeant had conjured a lighter from his pocket and leaned into the flame.

'Sounds to me like Goebbels is farting off,' he mouthed around the cigarette.

'No,' the sergeant murmured, 'that bit is all true, but it's not all "run Ivan run" either.'

'I didn't think so.'

'First day, all blood and iron,' the sergeant continued, *sotto voce*. 'North and south armies eating up the ground. Centre now's a different story. Hit this place called Brest-Litovsk, bloody fort not far from the border. The fly in the champagne, you could say. Pounded the shit out of it with artillery. When the smoke cleared, it's still there. So they sent the forty-fifth infantry in anyway.'

'Don't they always?' Johann grunted.

'Numbers I heard were twenty-nine officers gone to God and ten times that number of infantry marching after them. Mostly Austrians,' he said bitterly.

Johann spat over the side in disgust.

'We won't be hearing that on the radio,' he muttered.

'You didn't hear it from me either,' the sergeant said. 'Just one soldier talking to another, right?'

Johann nodded. 'And the lump of lard at the back?' he enquired.

'He's the one they sent to find replacements,' the sergeant whispered. 'He's got a fucking list; bastard took six from my village.'

'And Hallstatt?'

'Five.'

Johann looked over the man's shoulder to where Erich was easing up on his stroke as they approached the Hallstatt slip.

'He won't be on the list,' the sergeant said quietly, fixing his cap in place. He nodded towards Johann's empty sleeve. 'I'd say your family has done more than its share for the fucking Fatherland,' he said quietly.

Johann nodded his thanks and stood in the bow, ready to step ashore and steady the boat for the others to disembark. He knew he should feel some sense of relief but he couldn't shake the thought that his son's gain was some other father's loss, and it gnawed at him.

THE POLICEMAN'S HOUSE

'And so, you see, Herr Steiger, my superiors feel it is important that we are accompanied by the local policeman.'

The official curled his prim lips in distaste.

'It seems some people in Österreich are less than willing to serve the Fatherland.'

'Yes sir, I see, sir,' Steiger said.

'On a more positive note,' the little man expounded, 'our experience has shown that persons in authority, like yourself, tend to know their local community rather well and are therefore in a position to aid us with certain recommendations. I must emphasise that word "recommendations", Herr Steiger. The final decision in all cases would be mine. You understand?'

'Of course, sir, yes sir,' the policeman parroted, sitting up even straighter on the kitchen chair while tugging his tunic.

'More coffee, sir?' Frau Steiger asked.

'If you don't mind, Frau Steiger. It's so difficult to get decent coffee in these—.' Hastily, he dragged his briefcase to the table and extracted a document.

'The first name on my list is Erich Krauss.'

'He's the boatman's son,' the policeman said quickly.

'Ah, that fellow,' the official said. 'Seemed strong enough, from what I saw during our crossing. Very well—'

'Excuse me, sir,' the sergeant interrupted.

'Yes, Sergeant.'

'I had a good look at him on the way across, being closer to him than yourself, sir. The boy is slow.'

'Slow?'

'Simple-minded, sir. Not suitable, I'm afraid. Wouldn't pass induction standards, according to directive—'

'Thank you, Sergeant. I must bow to your experience, as a military man.'

He glared at the policeman in annoyance and made a neat stroke with his pen through the name.

'The second name on my list, you'll be honoured to hear, is Max Steiger. Your son, I'm presuming. Is the boy here?'

The stricken couple stared at him.

'Is he here?' he repeated. 'We don't have all day.'

'He is ill,' Frau Steiger said hoarsely.

'Ah well, young people get all sorts of aches and pains, don't they? Boy will get over it, I'm sure. Be right as rain by the time—'

'My son is very ill,' Frau Steiger interrupted in the same ragged voice.

'Believe me, I understand your feelings, Frau Steiger. A mother cherishes her child and so on. But I'm afraid I must see for myself what the situation is. No offence meant, of course, it's just part of official policy.'

The official pushed back from the table and brushed crumbs from his waistcoat.

'The priest gave him the Last Rites this morning, sir,' she said and buried her face in her hands.

'Oh dear,' the official fretted, 'it must be serious then – possibly contagious. I'm sure you won't mind checking the boy, Sergeant, just to, well – be about it, man.'

The sergeant heaved himself to his feet as Frau Steiger gestured to her husband to show him the way. As the pair ascended the stairs, Frau Steiger cut a generous slice of tart and placed it on the official's plate.

'Oh but I couldn't,' he protested.

'Eat it.' she urged. 'A man in your position needs to keep up his strength. It can't be easy going around to communities like ours. People here can become so inward-looking – so taken up with their own affairs. They seem to forget that there are bigger things going on in the world – that we must all make sacrifices.'

'Oh, my dear lady,' the official sighed, 'how true, how very true. You have no idea of the resistance we encounter, the excuses we hear. Sometimes – sometimes, I think if I hadn't the sergeant along, I think they might do me an injury.'

'It's a sad truth, sir, that not everyone has the same dedication to the Reich as you have. Why, I know people in this community who—. Excuse me, sir, for forgetting my place.'

'No, no, dear lady. As the policeman's wife, I'm sure you—'

'Perhaps if we looked at your list, I might be able to offer some small assistance?'

'Do you know a Rudi Hamner?'

'I know him.'

'Do I detect some – disapproval, Frau Steiger?'

'Oh no, sir. Herr Hamner is a carpenter, a strong and able man but somewhat disrespectful of authority. I don't doubt but that you will be well capable of dealing with him.'

'I certainly will, but we still need to fill the gap left by this Erich fellow.'

'Then you're in luck, sir. Rudi Hamner has a son of an age with Erich. Karl is bright and strong like his father, but I can't see Herr Hamner agreeing to—'

'Frau Steiger, it is not for Herr Hamner to agree or disagree with my decisions.'

'I know that, sir, but, as I said before, he doesn't show much respect for authority.'

'My authority is absolute in such matters, Frau Steiger.'

'It's not often we meet a person like yourself, sir. I can see now why the authorities would send someone who wouldn't be browbeaten by stubborn people or intellectuals.'

'Intellectuals – here?'

'I suppose it's truer to say someone who thinks himself an intellectual. I don't know the full facts, of course, but from what I'm told, he was a lecturer in the university in Vienna before he became schoolmaster here.'

'It seems, if you'll pardon my saying so, like something of a demotion.'

'Yes it does, doesn't it? There was talk, as there always is in small places like this, of opinions.'

'Opinions? What kind of opinions?'

'Critical opinions, I'm told. Critical of the authorities, that is. Some say he was sent here as a punishment. Others say it was to avoid military service. They say his wife is a daughter of the chancellor and that he arranged it. But I can't imagine that sort of thing would be approved of by the authorities.'

'There – there have been instances, and I tell you this in the strictest confidence, Frau Steiger, when my duty has been thwarted by—. Well, better not to say by whom. But, believe me, that sort of thing is being nipped in the bud. Österreich is now part of greater Germany and the tail will not wag the dog, Madam. I – I beg your pardon, I'm afraid I have become quite overheated.'

'I quite understand, sir, and I'm sorry if I've put you in an awkward position. I won't mention this person again.'

'His name, Frau Steiger, if you please.'

'His name is Kurt Brandt.'

'And the final name is Druckner.'

'Ah, that poor man.'

'You can't be suggesting that it is a misfortune for this man to be chosen to serve the Reich?'

'It's just that his daughter has been lost in the mines, poor girl. My husband has organised the search for her, to no avail. She was his only child, sir, and he's a widower.'

'That is … most unfortunate.'

'My husband has tried to make him see reason and call off the search but he insists. He's even talking about calling in the army to help.'

'The army? We are at war, Frau Steiger. The man can't seriously expect the authorities to send in the army to search for every stray girl.'

'Yes, but he is distraught, sir. In some ways, it might be a mercy if he could be distracted—'

'I understand perfectly, Frau Steiger. He may not appreciate the kindness we are doing him just now, but he will in time.'

'You are an unusually sensitive man, sir.'

'What? Oh, well, thank you. I do try to temper my official duties with a degree of compassion. Ah, the gentlemen have returned. Well, Sergeant?'

'I'm afraid the boy is seriously ill, sir,' the sergeant said heavily. 'I'm sorry, Herr Steiger, Frau Steiger. I can only hope he'll get better, but I suspect it will be a slow process.'

'That still leaves one place to be filled in our quota.'

'May I make a suggestion, sir?'

'Certainly, Frau Steiger.'

'My husband and I are very concerned about our son. At this moment, we have no idea if—'

'Please, please don't distress yourself, dear lady. As I said—'

'But we, I mean my husband in particular, have always considered it an honour to be of service to our community. If our son had been spared this illness, we would have been sad to lose him but very proud at the same time. Isn't that so, dear?'

'Yes, Yes of course, eh, dear,' the policeman said uncertainly.

'Perhaps it's not in your power to grant us something, sir.'

'Anything that is in my power to grant, you shall have, dear lady.'

'Thank you, sir. But as someone who has carried great responsibility within our community I'm certain my husband would be honoured to take the place of my son.'

The official felt a swelling of emotion in his chest and struggled to his feet so he could pump the hand of the policeman who looked as if he might faint.

'Anyone for fresh coffee?' Frau Steiger asked, smiling.

THE BRANDT HOUSEHOLD

'... and mittens,' Bertha said, rummaging in a drawer.

'What? Yes, dear, whatever you say,' her husband muttered absently.

Kurt was plucking books from the shelves and piling them on the rug before the fire. She could see the pile was becoming more precarious by the minute and didn't know whether to laugh or cry.

'Perhaps you should confine yourself to one book, Kurt,' she suggested.

'One book! My dear Bertha, according to the radio, the Russians are surrendering in their thousands. We'll be in Moscow in a few weeks with time on our hands.'

'Herr Goebbels is hardly a dependable source of primary material,' she said shortly, balling two socks and stuffing them into a pair of sturdy boots. 'Some commentators think otherwise,' she added cryptically. He knew she eavesdropped on the BBC from time to time, hunched over the crystal set in the attic.

'Perhaps you're right,' he said diplomatically. 'Don't forget the Meerschaum and the tobacco.'

He thinks this is some kind of faculty field trip, she thought, and rammed his precious Meerschaum into the bag. The book tower swayed and fell.

'One book it is,' he said, rescuing a single volume from the rubble.

'I can't imagine following in the footsteps of Napoleon without taking Armand de Caulaincourt along as a guide.'

'Your superiors might not appreciate the comparison,' she remarked.

While they packed, they argued spiritedly about the validity of comparing Napoleon's campaign in 1812 with the war now raging eastwards until the bag was packed and strapped and there was nothing more to do.

'I feel like I should be telling you to stay safe,' she said quietly, 'but it sounds like such a silly thing to say.'

'Look at me,' he said, and waited for her eyes to meet his own. He tapped himself lightly on the chest. 'This,' he said smiling, 'is not the stuff of which heroes are made. I am a most unlikely soldier, Bertha. My plan is to stay to the rear, keep my head down and keep a journal, though not necessarily in that order.'

'And come home,' she added.

The silence surged back into the space between them until she became aware of the clock ticking on the wall. She wondered why she had never noticed that sound before.

'It seems everything's ready,' he said hesitantly. 'Is there anything you'd like to do – to pass the time?'

'I would like to go to bed, Kurt.'

'Bed! But it's – oh.'

He was surprised by the intensity of their love-making and, afterwards, she held him in a hungry embrace. He inhaled the familiar scent of her hair and luxuriated in the warmth where their bodies touched. Sunlight pierced the lace curtains, etching patterns on their bedroom wall. He watched a shadow-flower wax and wane, dancing to some phantom breeze in the still room. Finally, his eyelids semaphored the approach of sleep and he kissed her one last time on the cheek. His last sensation was the taste of salt on his lips.

The Hamners' house

' … and winter underwear,' Frau Hamner fussed.

'It's a summer campaign,' Rudi protested. 'We'll itch all the way to Moscow. Anyway, Goebbels says we'll be home before Christmas.'

'I don't care what Geobbels says,' she snapped and burst into tears.

He sat on the kitchen chair and drew her into his lap. 'Easy, Liebchen,' he whispered, rocking her gently. 'We'll bring you back one of those Russian dolls – you know, the ones with other dolls inside –'

'I don't want anything back from that place,' she said brokenly, 'except you and Karl. Promise me, Rudi, promise me you'll bring him back.'

'I promise,' he said but she refused to be consoled.

Karl heard his mother crying and debated whether he should go to her. Then his father's voice rumbled from below and he relaxed. Swinging his legs to the floor, he paced restlessly under the window set in the gable, sometimes pausing to look out and check the progress of the sun. Night would come soon, he knew, and wondered if it was already dark in Russia, as the light retreated westwards. He crouched before the map of Europe tacked to the bedroom wall and placed his finger on Austria.

'Landlocked between seven countries,' Herr Brandt had said.

Slowly, he slid his finger to the east, passing, without hindrance, over wavy border lines and dots with difficult names until his finger pushed into the huge expanse of red that was Russia. A large dot snagged his eye and attracted his fingertip. Moscow! Just shy of the capital, a splinter punched through the map and pierced his finger. Automatically, he pinched the splinter between the nails of his thumb and forefinger and pulled. A tiny drop of blood bloomed on his skin and he blotted it on the map. It glinted for a moment and then disappeared, subsumed into the vast red landscape. Passing the window on his way back to bed, he thought he saw an early star but it was a pinprick of light in the blackness of the mountains. 'Elsa?' he whispered and the light disappeared.

THE MINES

'Elsa,' the miner called, as his lantern sparked stars from the walls of the shaft. His voice bounced away into the darkness and died. He followed the light to the chamber and sat, placing his bag on the floor between his feet.

The terrible emptiness of his home had finally driven him out. He had paced from room to room, torturing himself with the sight of familiar things. This was where she hung her coat when she came home – she put her bag here: He had followed her phantom to the bedroom. Sitting on the bed, he had caressed the coverlet for a while before lying down, drawing his knees up to his chest and clutching her pillow to his face, searching for some trace of her scent. Later he had thrown some clothes in a bag, picked up the lantern and pulled the door closed behind him. He didn't lock the door. There was nothing in his home worth protecting – not now. Tonight he would stay in the mine. It was as close as he could get to his daughter.

*

I can see and hear, Max thought. I'm not dead. When he'd drunk the medicine, he'd felt a numbness spread through his body and all physical sensation had melted away. It was like floating in the lake watching the sky spin above him. The varnished wooden sky of his bedroom did not spin. Occasionally, people intruded on that sky, looming over him with huge faces. They spoke as if he couldn't hear them, but he could, every word. He'd put together the jigsaw pieces of their words and concluded they knew, or at least suspected, he'd been involved in Elsa's disappearance. He'd felt terror building inside him until he'd learned she hadn't been found.

The ceiling darkened and brightened, marking the passage of time. Other faces had appeared and disappeared. He saw Karl's father staring at his face and reaching down to touch him, even though he'd felt nothing. Herr Hamner had been troubled by the marks on his face and neck and then his fool-father had tied himself in knots, as usual. Herr Brandt he had seen only in his peripheral vision.

Then he'd seen the frightened face of Father Kyril. Why was he frightened? Who was the soldier who had looked at him and then talked to his father, at length, about some official downstairs? And why did he tell his father how lucky he was. His father didn't look as if he felt lucky, particularly when he'd come back alone later, sobbing and shaking as if his son was going to die. He wasn't going to die. He knew that now. Knew it as a certainty because his mother had come up later, long after the buzz of voices had stilled downstairs and the front door had closed. His mother had leaned over him and looked into his eyes. She'd told him everything, from the moment he'd stumbled home from the mines to the conversation with the government official in the kitchen.

'It was all for you, my son,' she'd whispered. 'No one must stand between you and your destiny. I won't need to give you that medicine anymore. Soon you'll be yourself again.'

Then she'd kissed him on the forehead. He'd felt nothing.

He didn't want to be himself again. He wanted to remain in this unfeeling limbo where he wouldn't be tormented and disgusted by what Father Kyril called 'the thorn in the flesh'. He knew his lust and anger were powerful and terrible forces that coiled inside him until he could no longer control them and then .... Elsa, he thought, and the mouth of a sinkhole yawned in the ceiling to swallow him. 'The damned cannot even scream in Hell,' Father Kyril said but he was screaming inside, howling like someone lost forever in a labyrinth. He clung to the hope that his body would remain in this suspended state and then his little finger twitched. For an instant, he felt its pressure against the sheet that shrouded him. The ceiling blurred and a tear escaped to roll down the scars on his cheek.

THE LAKE

The women stood on the little slipway and watched the boat until it faded into the fog – watched until the dip and splash of the oars grew muted and the sound of small waves, fretting at their feet, erased every other sound. Bertha recognised the woman beside her as Frau Hamner and wondered how such a tiny frame could bear the burden of her double loss. There was no sign of Frau Steiger. Probably tending to her son, she thought. There had been no one to say goodbye to the policeman and he'd huddled in the stern of the boat as if to distance himself from the others. The miner had come, at the last minute, from the direction of the mines. Her heart had ached at the defeated slump of his shoulders. She threaded her arm through Frau Hamner's.

'Please come to my house for coffee,' she said. 'I don't think I can go back there alone.'

The carpenter's wife had looked surprised and then pleased as they turned together from the lake.

Bertha was surprised to see the herbalist and her son standing hand in hand looking out over the water.

'I'm sorry to intrude,' the herbalist said, 'I brought a few simple remedies for the men to put in their bags, but we were too late.'

'Can you join us for coffee in my house?' Bertha asked.

The herbalist looked as if she might refuse but her son stepped forward and took Bertha's hand in his own.

'That's decided then,' Bertha smiled.

THE SALA REGIA, THE VATICAN

'Barbarossa.'

'You're sure?'

Emil Dubois sighed. 'To think you were once a student of mine,' he said. 'Perhaps if we started with simpler questions. What is this room called?'

'The Sala Regia,' Cardinal Tisserant answered dutifully, 'the Regal Room.'

'Correct. And which pope thought it necessary to emphasise in this room the political clout of the papacy?'

'All of them?'

'God give me patience. Attend! Paul the Third commissioned Sagallo the Younger to design this room. You're looking at a propaganda poster from the sixteenth century. So, there we have the Battle of Lepanto and the Capture of Tunisia. For the sake of those who are less apt, Henry the Fourth of Germany submits to Pope Gregory the Seventh and Frederick Barbarossa reconciles with Pope Alexander the Third.'

'That's Barbarossa? The one crawling across the carpet?'

'The same. And for those who are slow-witted and impervious to the obvious, over there is the assassination attempt on the Huguenot Coligny and the Saint Bartholomew's Day Massacre of Protestants by Catholics. You see, Paul the Third was making a statement, "*Ego sum Caesar, Ego sum Imperator*"' "I am Caesar, I am Emperor."'

'Except it was Boniface the Eighth who made that claim, Professor. I didn't sleep through all your lectures.'

'Pedant! Do you want to know who the artists were?'

'Spare me.'

Tisserant looked around at the frescoes covering the walls. 'Methinks the pope did protest too much,' he murmured.

'Well, he did have three sons and a daughter before he became a cardinal.'

'Colourful!'

'A quality you might expect in someone who was the protégé of a Borgia pope; the same Alexander the Sixth who had, eh, enjoyed Paul's sister, Giulia Farnese.'

'May I ask a simple question, o omniscient one?'

'A simple question befits the man who asks it. Ask!'

'Why did Pius invite us here? And why did you tell me the appointment was for eleven?'

'That's two questions. I see the rot runs through history and mathematics. The answer to your second question is a simple one. I lied. I'm a secretary to a powerful cardinal. I lie for a living. Anyway, you can't afford to be late again; someone even less paranoid than Pacelli might interpret it as provocative. Your first question is a simple one but the answer is complex. The pope, like his predecessor Paul the Third, wants to show us something. We can deduce from the screen at one end of the room and the projector at the other that it is a film of some sort. As to why he invited us, the rows of chairs would suggest that there will be others. Why has he asked us *here*? Hitler speaks from the Brandenburg Gate and Stalin from the Kremlin Wall. They are both leaders on the world stage and appreciate the power of an impressive backdrop. So does our pope.'

They were interrupted by the arrival of Cardinal Maglione and his secretary, who took up positions on the other side of the throne-like chair in the centre of the front row. Gradually, the room filled with men in religious habits.

'All the major religious orders are represented,' Emil whispered, 'and, if I'm not mistaken, the others come from the Russicum and the Ruthenian College.'

'The seminaries which prepared the priests for Russia?'

'Yes, our own version of Barbarossa.'

They stood as Pope Pius XII came through the door flanked by

Swiss Guards. When the pope was seated, the Guards melted away to the back wall. The lights dimmed, the projector whirred and the screen flickered as martial music filled the room.

They saw squadrons of planes fill a grey sky. Armoured vehicles bounced towards a flat horizon as the cameraman tilted back to earth. The German narrator enthused about numbers of planes, tanks, armoured vehicles and artillery pieces. The next sequence featured huge guns lunging at the sky, then recoiling as explosions bloomed silently in the distance. Tiny figures dotted a landscape and fell over or raised their hands in surrender until the army racing east was bordered by two endless lines of prisoners shuffling west. Panzers churned from left to right and the sequence ended with the obligatory close-up shot of blurring tracks. Blitzkrieg, the narrator intoned. The brass-band soundtrack segued into slow pastoral music as Russian peasants offered bread and salt to smiling soldiers. Shots of small churches followed and an orthodox priest holding an icon to be kissed by his people.

'Religious renewal,' the narrator said reverently, 'in churches that had been converted into atheistic museums, warehouses and club rooms by the Bolsheviks.'

The newsreel faded on a long shot of the distinctive Orthodox cross, silhouetted against a bright sky. There was a moment of absolute silence before the assembled religious burst into applause and the pope rose to face them.

'We are witnessing a new crusade,' he said. 'This crusade is unlike those of old when Christian knights led armies of the faithful to conquer the heathen and reclaim the holy places. In our day, it is the heathen who wages war on other heathens and yet, by the power of the Holy Ghost, those who have strayed will be brought back to the one fold and one shepherd. Already, our brothers in Christ move across the Steppes in the belly of the beast carrying the sacraments to those who have been oppressed and dehumanised by Bolshevism. Some will achieve the crown of martyrdom but their blood will refresh the dormant seeds of faith across the Bolshevik Empire. *Resurrexit sicut dixit*, alleluia,' he concluded. 'He is risen as He promised.'

Tisserant and his secretary extricated themselves from the throng pressing to kiss the papal ring before returning to the cardinal's apartments.

Emil Dubois wasn't given to melancholy and had little patience with those who were. Brooding, he considered, was for birds and the cardinal looked like a jay sitting on eggs.

'Oh, for Heaven's sake, Eugène,' he snapped, 'you should be elated. This is your plan, even if Pacelli neglected to mention that fact.'

'It's not my plan,' Tisserant growled. 'Pius XI hatched it, his successor adopted it and then delegated it to me.'

'So you have responsibility for it?'

'It's not about "it", Emil, it's about "them"; all those idealistic young men we sent to Russia. Yes, I have responsibility for them and Pius enthusing about martyrdom does nothing to ease the burden.'

'Popes have always enthused about martyrdom – especially when it involves the martyrdom of other people. Pacelli is one of the few who said he was willing to go that road himself. He reminds me of von Bock.'

'The commander of the German Fourth Army.'

'I'm impressed.'

'I had coffee and a war tutorial with Maglione.'

'Ah! I see. von Bock's soldiers call him "*Der Sterber*", the "Grim Reaper". Powerful men like him and Pius seem very keen on dying for a cause.'

'Even if they bring millions with them,' Tisserant said heavily. 'Have I sent these priests to their deaths, Emil?'

The secretary pondered his former student for a time. He had known him as a brilliant academic and a formidable churchman. In the face of incompetence or duplicity, Tisserant was a force of nature. He was also a human being, Dubois knew, who faced and felt the implications of his decisions. At this moment, he saw the pain behind the cardinal's question and wished he could say something to console him. The truth will set you free, he resolved.

'You saw the newsreels yourself, Eugène,' he began. 'Heady stuff – people flocking back to the churches in the wake of the

Wehrmacht. However, where the flocks go, the wolves follow.'

'Wolves?'

'Yes, wolves and worse than wolves, because the animal kills only out of need. Hitler's Waffen SS make no such distinction. They hunt at the rear of the army, Eugène. If they find our priests on the way to Moscow, they will hang them as deserters. Should Barbarossa fail, the Russian commissars will hang them on the way back. They were marked men from the beginning, my friend.'

'You mean since Rosenberg?'

'Yes, since the head of the new Ministry of the East forbade missionaries from entering what he called "liberated areas". But, there is more. Our "good thief" has been in contact. He says Reinhard Heydrich will make a recommendation to Hitler in the next few days.'

'The head of the Reich's main security office?'

'The same. Our friend has seen the final draft of Heydrich's recommendation. The gist of it is that the Vatican is concentrating its entire Vatican-Russian policy in Slovakia and Croatia. The aim is to infiltrate priests into the Soviet Union who will be involved in intelligence-gathering and promoting Roman Catholicism.'

'Well it was never much of a secret, was it?' the cardinal said bitterly, 'not when it originated in this Tower of Babel. What is Heydrich recommending?'

'I can give you the exact words from memory,' his secretary said. He closed his eyes and began to recite. '"That the Reich prevent Catholicism from becoming the real beneficiary of the war in the new situation that is developing in the Russian area conquered by German blood." The recommendation is marked "top secret" and it is entitled "Tisserant's Plan".'

'What do we do now, Emil?'

'We wait.'

'Waiting is the hardest part,' Cardinal Tisserant said.

★

WEHRMACHT TRAINING CAMP ON THE RUSSIAN BORDER

'Waiting is the hardest part,' Karl concluded.

The weeks since leaving Hallstatt had been like the 'Stop–Go' game he had played as a child in the schoolyard. The rules were simple. When someone shouted 'Go' you ran, when they shouted 'Stop' you halted and froze in that position. Being a soldier, he thought, is exactly like that. He'd run from one queue to another, at the training camp outside Vienna; chivvied by bored NCOs, prodded by a doctor and measured by a quartermaster. He'd run to the armoury for a rifle and to the rifle range for target practice. Maybe it's to keep us from thinking, he reasoned, and it wasn't without its lighter moments. Luckily, he'd inherited a steady hand and a keen, measuring eye from his father and they'd both proved to be competent marksmen. He wondered if he'd feel the same puff of pride when a human target toppled over. The miner didn't seem to care one way or the other, he just slotted the butt into his shoulder and pulled the trigger until the magazine was empty. Immediately, the instructor had been shouting furiously in his face.

'What the hell are you doing, you lump of Austrian dog shit? I said to squeeze the trigger, man. Doesn't your wife ever say squeeze, don't pull?'

The laughter of the other soldiers and the instructor's abuse had stopped abruptly when the miner squared his shoulders and took a step closer to his tormentor.

'Do it your own way,' the man had hissed, turning away to vent his spite on some other hapless marksman. 'Why don't you use the other end and club the fuckers to death?' he added. 'Now, fuck off before I really lose my temper.'

Herr Brandt was another who found it difficult to shoot straight, despite his eagerness to master the rifle.

'If you keep shooting like that,' the instructor had roared, 'some of our boys won't live long enough to be killed by the Russians.'

'What an extraordinarily complex sentence,' Herr Brandt had remarked and spent the afternoon picking up used cartridge cases.

The policeman had performed like an automaton, earning

grudging praise from the instructor. In some ways, Karl concluded, the Stop–Go frenzy of induction and basic training had served its purpose as a distraction.

THE LAKE

Max Steiger sat in the stern, as far away as he could get from the glaring boatman and his idiot son. The priest sat in the bow; for ballast, the boatman had said, but Max suspected he was being malicious. A sharp breeze chopped the lake into foot-high waves and the rower pulled with gusto. Father Kyril would be drenched by the time they got to the other side. He allowed himself a moment to savour that thought.

The last few weeks had seemed interminable to him. With every passing day, the poison had leached from his system and his extremities still tingled with remembered pain. His mother had haunted his room. She had come to turn, wash and feed him and he'd hated the indignity of being touched more than he'd hated her incessant talk. She had always spoken Croatian when his father was out of the house and now she spoke nothing else, as if she never expected him to return.

'Our ancestors were nobility in Croatia,' she'd babbled, 'before the Serbs stole our country. My generation could have been teachers, even doctors – professional people, but the Serbs kept all that for themselves, the filthy heathens. But the wheel turns, Max, and there will be a reckoning.'

Father Kyril's visits had been only mildly less purgatorial. He'd come every day, after his morning mass, and observed the same rigid rituals: coffee with Max's mother in the kitchen, followed by lengthy prayers at his bedside, liberally sprinkled with warnings against the 'sins of the flesh' and 'the seductions of Satan'. No one else came to visit. He wasn't surprised. His father had never been popular in the village and his mother had never disguised her contempt for 'those peasants'.

'You'll send for me, Max,' she'd said, tugging at the lapels of the coat that floated on his emaciated body. 'You'll send for me and we'll be together, always.'

Had there been a plaintive note in her voice, he wondered? Was she experiencing some pangs of uncertainty, now that she was no longer the policeman's wife and couldn't invoke his power to cow her neighbours?

He hadn't looked back. He'd sat in the boat and looked out over the angry lake. The mountains loomed accusingly all around him but he'd kept his gaze on the water. She'd called but he hadn't answered; sitting in the stern, hunched into his greatcoat. She'd called until her voice had cracked and faded. The wheel turns, he thought, I have survived my parents.

His father had disappeared years ago inside the carapace he crawled into every time he came home. Should he feel something for the absent man, he wondered? He felt nothing for him. He knew he had survived his mother by being the son she'd wanted – the son she had created in her own image and likeness – who would be her successful surrogate and live the dream she'd failed to realise. That was the unspoken bargain and he had kept his part of it until she'd handed him a cup of poison. She had killed the old Max that day, he knew. The boy who sat into the boat and crossed the lake was no one's son – he wore no bonds of blood or obligation – his destiny would be of his own making.

'Two schillings,' the boatman said.

Father Kyril handed over the coins with bad grace. It was not the custom to charge a priest or a sick passenger, Max knew. Let the ogre have his moment of petty triumph, he thought. At the pier, he ignored the hand offered to assist him ashore. Max heard the boatman hawk and spit as he made his way from the pier, and smiled.

★

KARL: THE TROOP TRAIN TO THE RUSSIAN FRONT

After they'd been herded on to the train, there was nothing to do except wait and think. Even his father Rudi had stopped complaining about the evidence of poor workmanship he found all around him in their carriage. The miner sat for hours on end, his arms folded across his chest, staring at nothing in particular. Herr Brandt turned the pages of his book, sometimes jotting in the margins or making comments as if in conversation with the author. They were invariably in French and none of the crew paid any heed. Herr Steiger seemed to have perfected the art of invisibility. He remained mute and distant, speaking only when addressed directly and then only in monosyllables, like a monk who hoarded his silence.

The view from the window was of fields and forests; a slow-moving film strip, spliced at regular intervals by telegraph poles and underscored by the rhythmic percussion of wheels on rails. Sometimes the rocking movement lulled him to sleep and, when he woke, he felt he was looking at the same field or forest unwinding beyond the window. He preferred the tedium of his waking world to the horror of his dreams.

Dream, he corrected himself. It was always the same dream. He was in the mines, admiring the way his flickering lantern danced spindly shadows of the ancient staircase on the wall. He heard something. A shout? A cry for help? He stumbled back to the empty chamber and, in his sleep, his stomach turned over again with fear. Something moved in the shadows. 'Elsa,' he called frantically, 'Elsa, Elsa.' He was pounding down the mountain, going too fast to stop, knowing it was only a matter of moments before he f—.

He always woke with a start. Instinctively clamping his teeth around the name he had been shouting in his dream.

Sometimes the train pulled into a siding. He passed the time studying life outside the window until he'd exhausted it of interest and was relieved when they began to move again. On one particular evening, they'd halted on the outskirts of an enormous railyard and a train on a parallel track had pulled away, giving Karl the odd sensation of moving backwards. As the other train blurred by, he became aware of what looked like a stationary train, made up of cattle wagons, being revealed and concealed by the moving train until, suddenly, there was nothing to obstruct his view. The cattle wagons were dull grey and windowless. The huge door on the side of the wagon directly opposite had a small square opening divided by metal bars. He thought he saw a hand clutch one of the bars and then slide through the opening to reach out and grasp at the air. It was followed by another and another until the small space in the grey door seemed alive with fluttering butterflies. A soldier stepped into view and slammed his rifle butt against the side of the wagon. Suddenly, the space between the bars was empty again. The soldier seemed to sense that he was being watched and turned. Under his close-fitting helmet, his eyes were invisible but Karl felt the man was staring directly at him and sat back. He became aware of his companions' reflections in the window. The policeman was still an anonymous shape, hunched close to the door. The miner had turned his face to the window and his eyes seemed darker than usual. Even Herr Brandt had been drawn from his book. He saw his father standing, uncertainly, in the middle of this tableau, turn his head to exchange a look with the schoolmaster.

THE TRAIN TO CROATIA

The swaying train made Max queasy and irritable. He endured a whole day of Father Kyril's petty grievances, feigning interest long enough to conclude that Father Kyril had 'a past'. That information may be useful, he thought, and filed it away. He pretended to sleep when the priest began to repeat his sordid tale.

People came and went as the train wormed its way south from Vienna towards Zagreb. A young mother and her two small children travelled with them for what seemed like forever. Father Kyril conspired to hold her hand as she poured out her anxieties; held it long after her discomfort became apparent and she invented relatives in another carriage and fled. The priest had railed for a full hour against 'forward women' who 'took advantage' of a priest's kindness. Sleep was Max's escape from those ravings but it was a doorway to nightmares.

He was in the mines. She was sitting in a pool of light, feigning indifference to him – excluding him with her cool manner and grudging offer of lunch. He savoured again the terror that widened her eyes and saw her head loll sideways on the floor – watched, again, as her lantern was swallowed by the hole in the ground. He woke with a shout.

'Would you like a glass of water?' the priest asked anxiously.

'If it wouldn't be too much trouble,' he rasped in a voice hoarse with disuse.

THE TROOP TRAIN TO THE RUSSIAN FRONT

'Karl!'

With an effort, he tugged his attention from the scene outside.

'Come with me,' the schoolmaster said firmly.

They edged by the other soldiers who were ambling up and down the narrow corridor.

'Where are we going, Herr Brandt?' he asked, as they threaded their way from one carriage to the next.

'I am going to smoke my pipe,' the schoolmaster replied, 'and you are going to stand sentry duty.'

Finally, they came to a narrow compartment where the carriages hinged together and Herr Brandt released the leather strap to drop the window. Karl stood where he could see through the glass panels in the swinging doors that sealed the compartment from the carriages on either side.

'Some officers object to soldiers smoking on the train,' Herr Brandt explained around the stem of his Meerschaum. He flared a match and the sweet tobacco smell filled the compartment before the open window sucked the smoke and exhaled it into the night.

'Waiting is the hardest part,' Herr Brandt remarked, as if he had read the boy's mind. 'It can induce a kind of torpor that is toxic to the mind. I can remember visiting Chartres Cathedral with a friend from the faculty – it was years ago. When we'd walked around for about an hour, we decided to get some coffee at a place across the square. Coffee is not just a drink in France, Karl, it's an art form. Anyway, just as we got to the door, there was a thunderstorm and we retreated back inside. We sat on two chairs beside one of the great pillars and my friend took a book from his pocket and began to read. I remember thinking how extraordinary that was. There we were, sitting within sight of the rose window and the labyrinth and medieval masterpieces in one of the greatest cathedrals in Europe. We were at the very heart of history – and he was reading a book!'

'But,' Karl said hesitantly, 'you read all the time, Herr Brandt.'

'Good point, well observed,' the schoolmaster said, nodding enthusiastically as small tobacco meteorites flared from his pipe, 'but, not completely accurate, Karl. I also observe what is happening around me. Did you see the official offer to pay the boatman after we'd crossed the lake?' he asked suddenly.

'Yes, Herr Brandt.'

'And—.'

'And Johann refused.'

'Why?'

'I – I,' Karl stammered, and the schoolmaster raised his hand.

'There are no right or wrong answers to that question, Karl,' he assured the boy. 'Only Johann can answer it with certainty; he is our primary source. But, as historians, knowing something of Johann's history and combining that with the nature of our departure, we can have theories, yes?'

'Yes, sir. I think Johann was – offended to be offered the money. He doesn't accept money if there is an emergency, if people want to cross to the doctor or for a funeral. I think he saw our crossing as something similar.'

'Good. Now, reviewing a happening, an event, is like peeling an onion. It has many layers, so peel it a little more, Karl.'

'Johann fought in the Great War, sir. My father said that's where he lost his arm.'

'Did he say where?'

'At Ypres, sir.'

'Very good. A memory for detail is an advantage but not all-important. Please excuse my interruption. Now go on.'

'His experience there, at Ypres, may have influenced his attitude to this war.'

'Yes, "may" is the correct word to use. Historians are not seers or oracles, Karl. Clairvoyance, coupled with certainty, is for quacks. Is there anything else?'

'He, Johann, may have been embarrassed.'

'Embarrassed?'

'That we – I mean that I – was going to war and not his son Erich.'

The silence lasted so long that Karl began to wonder if he had offended the schoolmaster in some way.

'Karl,' Herr Brandt began slowly, 'we can regard our conscription as a curse or as an opportunity. The former will blind us to everything but our own circumstances. Many soldiers came home from the Great War and complained of water-logged trenches and weevils in their bread. Others, like Owen the English poet and Schnack, the German, used their experience of war to write poems of immense power. You and I had no choice about going to war but we can choose how to experience it and what to make of that experience, as men and as historians.'

'I am not a historian, Herr Brandt.'

'You have the makings of one,' the schoolmaster said firmly. 'I would like to invite you to be my student.'

'Here?'

'We are in the railyard at Cracow in Poland. If we continue northwest, we will cross the Russian border at Brest-Litovsk, Karl. So, we are on a train travelling to the war, but also travelling through a world affected by that war. At the moment, I am reading Armand de Caulaincourt's book on Napoleon's campaign, to prepare my mind for Operation Barbarossa. But I am not blind to the happenings both inside and outside this train.'

'Like the cattle wagons we saw in the railyard?'

'Yes. What did you see, Karl?'

'I'm not sure if I imagined—'

The schoolmaster stepped closer.

'Karl,' he said gently, 'many people find it difficult to accept the evidence of their own eyes. They reason that the Reich would never cut the throat of the Austrian prime minister – they would never invade or annex or whatever word you want to use another sovereign country and they would never transport human beings in cattle wagons. And so they decide not to see. We're becoming a nation of blind people. What did you see, Karl?'

Karl told him, and when he finished his story, Herr Brandt nodded.

'That is what I and the others saw,' he confirmed. 'Except for Herr Steiger, of course, who refuses to deal with reality just now.'

He tapped the bowl of his pipe against the window frame and replaced it in his pocket.

'You will read a chapter of de Caulaincourt each day and I will question you on what you have read,' he declared briskly. 'You will also keep a journal, as I do, and we can compare our observations; at least, those we are comfortable with discussing. Oh, and one last thing, Karl. As long as we're together, we are master and student, as well as fellow soldiers. I propose you address me as Herr Brandt when we are being historians and as Kurt when we are in the army. Agreed?'

'Yes, eh, Kurt.'

'Herr Brandt, if you please,' the schoolmaster said with mock severity, 'we have not yet returned to the army. Speaking of which, shall we?'

'I think I'd like to stay here a little longer, Herr Brandt.'

THE RAILWAY STATION AT GRAZ, AUSTRIA

Max stood at the carriage window, looking at the mountains that loomed over Graz. Soon the whistle would sound, doors would slam the length of the train and steam would obscure the view and scour Austria from his life. He felt nothing but contempt for his homeland and longed to leave it.

Father Kyril also moved within the ambit of his contempt but Max was learning to curb his contempt to his own ends. People like Father Kyril could be manipulated so easily. They had some need – some vacuum inside themselves that could be filled by an appropriate word or action.

He wanted to sleep again but didn't dare to. This too will pass, he reassured himself. He turned his thoughts again to the manipulation of others. His father, he reasoned, had been a street devil and a house angel – a bully who would come to heel like a dog when his mother commanded. He smiled bleakly when he thought of how his mother had lured that spineless man into her trap.

His mother, now there was a subject worth studying – a strong woman who had demanded and received. But was it her husband's authority she had wielded? Now that he was gone, whither mother? What would it be like for her to live in Hallstatt without the armour of her husband's uniform? 'Oh, the wheel turns,' he murmured, 'the wheel turns.'

Who stood out from all the people he knew as a genuinely strong person? Karl! The name popped into his mind and took him unawares. Why Karl? Unconsciously, he extended his fingers as he ticked off the reasons. Karl had not befriended 'the policeman's son', he admitted, but the boy himself. Despite his moods and coolness, Karl had remained his friend; despite his father's pomposity and his mother's disapproval. Why? Because Karl felt no need to earn their approval. He was secure in himself because he was loved for himself. His reasoning ran on before he could divert it. Because Karl is everything you wished to be and are not, his traitorous thoughts suggested. The enormity of his loss bloomed suddenly like a rampant tumour inside him. His lips peeled back from his teeth and he growled like an animal – growled at the black pain that ate at his insides and spewed out of his mouth on the compartment floor.

He saw, with awful clarity, the priest's hand spasm and the glass fall from his hand. It seemed to fall for a long time. When it hit the floor, shards exploded outwards and a small wave surged through the vomit, carrying some of the mess to coat the priest's shoes. He let his eyes travel up the creased trousers and coat and the oversized white collar until they locked on Father Kyril's eyes. He looked like someone who had seen the face of Satan. That look shocked Max back to reality.

'I'm very sorry, Father,' he whispered, 'I must have overexerted myself.'

'It's nothing,' the priest said hurriedly and retreated from the compartment. He returned, followed by a surly porter dragging a mop and bucket. The man swabbed the floor in silence and then looked meaningfully at Father Kyril. He pocketed the single coin and left without a word of thanks.

THE CRACOW RAILYARD

He moved to the window and leaned his elbows on the sill, breathing the metal and burned oil smell of the railyard. The conversation with Herr Brandt still sang in his mind and his body tingled with excitement. Perhaps, he thought, when the war is over I can go to university and become a teacher, like Herr Brandt. Buoyed up by that thought, he returned to the carriage and sat in his spot by the window. The light in the carriage made it impossible to see anything through the reflection in the window. He cupped his hands around his eyes and pressed his face to the glass. There was no sign of the cattle wagons. A cloud shifted and silver moonlight shone on the empty tracks that coiled through the railyard and disappeared into the darkness. But, he thought, there was a train of cattle wagons. And there were hands fluttering like pale butterflies outside a barred window. It was all there. I saw it.

Quietly, he picked up the notepad and pen Herr Brandt had left on his seat and began to write.

Waiting, he wrote, need not be the hardest part.

★

'I can get you another glass of water,' the priest offered.

'No, I've been enough trouble already. Why don't you sit, Father. You look tired.'

'I – I am tired, but—'

'I've been thinking, Father. I think my sickness was God's will, His way of purging my impurities. I began to realise this when you came to pray over me.'

'I did pray but—'

'And God heard your prayers.'

'God hears all prayers, my son.'

'Indeed, Father, but the prayer of the righteous man must be particularly effective?'

'I don't consider myself a—'

'Of course you don't, Father, that would be the sin of pride. But doesn't it say in the Scriptures that "the stone rejected by the builder can become the cornerstone"?'

'Yes, yes it does.'

'And that God chose people who were despised by others to fulfil his will? I don't know if I'm remembering correctly.'

'Oh, you are, indeed you are.'

Max saw relief begin to replace the fear he had seen in the priest's eyes.

'It must be difficult being a priest,' he continued, 'so many people expect so much from you?'

'This is true, my son. I remember when I lectured at the seminary—'

Max sat back and fixed an expression of interest on his face. Father Kyril is easy, he thought, there will be greater challenges. In the meantime, he would watch and wait. Waiting need not be the hardest part.

*

Brest-Litovsk marked the end of their train journey and of
civilisation. Trucks ferried them over shell-pocked roads through
Minsk and on to Orsha, on the Dnieper river. Karl relied on Herr
Brandt for the place-names. To him, they were skeletal ruins and
heaps of rubble rising from a blasted landscape. From Orsha, they
marched to Smolensk on the road to Moscow.

The troops trudged with their heads bent, concentrating on
putting one foot in front of the other. Only Kurt and Karl scanned
the mangled wreckage of tanks and aircraft that seemed to form a
ghoulish guard of honour on either side of the road. There were
bodies strewn everywhere, Karl noticed – bodies languidly posed
as if sleeping in the summer grass – bodies twisted into unnatural
shapes. Dead faces, as empty and waxy' as masks, watched their
passage with indifference or prescient horror. He saw pieces of
bodies scattered among the debris and glistening streamers of
entrails looping in the branches of a tree at the forest's edge.
Sickened, he forced his eyes to the front in time to see a dot rise
over the brow of a hill and grow two dashes, one on either side as
it raced towards them.

'Bomber,' he yelled and rolled off the road with the others,
burrowing down into any hole available. The Russian bomber
growled closer and he tensed against the concussion of a bomb, but
a snarling, high-pitched whine competed for dominance with the
bomber's bass roar and a brace of Messerschmidt fighters harried
the Russian plane away from the road and over the forest.

'Good lad,' the sergeant yelled and a ragged cheer rose up from
the troops.

They were deployed near the brow of a hill, just shy of the ridge,
and ordered to set up camp. Karl and Kurt belly-wriggled to the
crest after they'd finished their chores and looked down on
Smolensk for the first time.

In the shimmering air, golden cupolas seemed to glint like
gilded mushrooms. Karl let his gaze follow the curving line of the

medieval wall that wound protectively around what he guessed must be the old city. After all the death and ugliness he had experienced on the road to Smolensk, the beauty of the city soothed and saddened him in equal measure.

'Beautiful, isn't it?' Kurt whispered. 'This is as far as Napoleon wanted to go. He thought he could smash the Russian army here, in one big battle.'

'Inside the city?'

'Actually outside the city, here where we are. You see these cupolas? That basilica houses the most venerated icon in the Orthodox Church – Our Lady of Smolensk. The Russians believed it was painted by Luke the Evangelist, and Napoleon was convinced they wouldn't fight inside the city and risk the destruction of the icon.'

'Did they?'

'Oh, yes. Icon or no icon, Napoleon had over one hundred and seventy thousand soldiers against the Russians' one hundred and fifty. They had no intention of facing those odds on open ground. Even when he sent troops to capture two suburbs, he couldn't winkle them out. So he did what we're going to do, Karl: he hammered Smolensk with artillery until the city caught fire. Even at that, he still couldn't get inside the walls because some French quartermaster had forgotten to bring scaling ladders. De Tolly, the Russian commander, realised he couldn't save the city, so he blew up the food and ammunition stores and evacuated his army. How did that affect Napoleon's campaign, Karl?'

They were teacher and pupil again, temporarily outside the reality they had learned to live with.

'The Russian army escaped, Herr Brandt.'

'Yes, but Napoleon is chasing after them up the road to Moscow and he's still got the bigger, more powerful army.'

'But Napoleon is getting farther and farther from home and supplies, and a burned city is useless to him.'

'Excellent, Karl,' his mentor enthused. 'So now you are Barclay de Tolly, the Russian commander, and Napoleon's coming hard on your heels. What would you do?'

'I'd do the same again.'

'I'm sorry, what do you mean?'

'I'd burn everything behind me all the way to Moscow.'

Kurt was on his feet with excitement, practically dancing on the ridge and wind-milling his arms. 'Yes,' he shouted, 'that's exactly what he did.'

'Herr Brandt.'

'Oh for God's sake, Karl, call me Kurt. The lesson's over and you have excelled yourself.'

'Herr Brandt,' Karl said stubbornly, 'will Stalin do the same? I mean, will he let us destroy Smolensk and then draw us deeper into Russia?'

He was interrupted by a shout from the camp.

'Get off that ridge, you mad bastards,' the sergeant yelled. 'You think Ivan can't put a shell up your arses at that range?'

Kurt dropped flat beside Karl just below the crest of the ridge.

'You didn't answer my question,' Karl persisted, but he was foiled this time by a bass sound that built to a clattering roar as waves of bombers swept over their position.

'That's your answer,' Kurt shouted in Karl's ear. 'Watch how history repeats itself.'

Karl watched long enough to see the bundles of bombs unfold from the planes like a rope ladder between heaven and earth – long enough to see the flashes and feel the detonations shudder through his body from the hill beneath him and Smolensk begin to disappear behind the smoke of its funeral pyre. He edged away from the crest and began to stumble back to camp.

'Karl,' Kurt shouted, but the burning city behind him swallowed his voice. Karl was hunched on a camp stool in the tent, his hands covering his face. 'Karl, what's the matter?' the teacher asked. 'The artillery will start shelling any moment now and we'll have a perfect view.' Impatiently, he pulled the boy's hands aside. He was stunned by the stricken face of his pupil and the tears that traced two pink paths through the grime on his cheeks. He took a grubby handkerchief and began to dab awkwardly.

'Is Karl hurt?'

Kurt hadn't heard the miner come inside the tent.

'We've been discussing Napoleon's attack on Smolensk and, eh, drawing comparisons with the present campaign. Then the bombing started and Karl became upset.'

The miner gazed expressionlessly at the schoolteacher.

'You wanted the boy to watch people being killed?' he asked tonelessly.

'No – no, of course not. It's just that, as historians, we should observe and record such things—'

'Things like dropping bombs on families, Herr Brandt?'

Kurt Brandt opened his mouth to argue and closed it again.

'Karl is a boy, Herr Brandt,' the miner rumbled, his unblinking gaze holding the eyes of the schoolteacher. 'He has already seen more than any boy should see. This is painful for him. Do you understand?'

'Yes – I understand.'

'Good. When all the bombs have fallen, we'll be going in to kill the survivors. Perhaps you will excuse us now.'

The miner sat on the ground by Karl's camp stool and gently brought the boy's head to rest on his shoulder.

'It is good to feel sad, Karl,' he whispered. 'War is sad, Liebchen, very sad.'

Kurt Brandt backed quietly out of the tent. He considered returning to the ridge and decided against it. Rummaging in his pack, he unearthed his journal and pencil and began to write.

'A historian is more than an observer,' he wrote. 'He is also a human being. If an observer has no emotional investment in the events he chronicles, he is merely a recorder of facts. Feelings may indeed distort facts but that is a price worth paying for the authenticity it brings to the history and the humanity it preserves in the historian. A poor teacher has learned this, today, from his finest student.'

He was distracted by the belching exhausts of the Panzer tanks as they sped along the flanks of the camp and tilted over the ridge. Soon, he knew, the artillery would stop firing. Whoever was left alive in the inferno of Smolensk would face these behemoths which ground cities and their citizens under their hungry tracks. Whoever survived the Panzers faced the Wehrmacht. 'Us,' he muttered, gripping his rifle so hard his knuckles bleached. 'Us. God help us. God help us all.'

BATTLE OF SMOLENSK, JULY 1941

Kurt heard the odd gasping sound men make when they are running full tilt and trying to hold their breath at the same time. The ground before them looked frighteningly open – the sky above a blue, unblinking eye that seemed to follow their puny progress like the flat stare of a painted Madonna that had frightened him in childhood. He was concentrating doggedly on not tripping over his own feet when the shooting started. In his peripheral vision, he saw men punched back and crumple. Ahead of him, a soldier pirouetted and sank gracefully to the ground. He had to jump to avoid stepping on a surprised face. Now the intermittent popping sounds had settled into one crackling roar and the front ranks were firing from the hip as they ran. A low moan began around him that built and burst into a scream as they burst into the ruins of the first houses and rolled into the lee of sheltering walls.

A Panzer crashed into the wall beside him and an officer signalled they should move in the wake of the dragon. Kurt had time to see Karl being motioned in another direction before he became absorbed in the chaos around him. The tank moved in straight lines, punching through walls or spitting a shell at anything that barred its passage. The troops huddled in its shadow, sometimes swinging their rifles up to pluck snipers from the windows of high houses. Increasingly, Soviet soldiers stumbled out of the fog of masonry dust, some to fall before the tank, others to throw up their hands in surrender. They were disarmed quickly and pushed to the rear; no one had the time to escort prisoners.

The fire-fights came in intermittent, savage bursts when a foxhole or a machine-gun nest was encountered. He was unaware that he was firing, reloading, running and killing. His focus had narrowed to what was immediately before him and he moved instinctively to the primal choreography of a hunting pack. Occasionally, something seared its way into his consciousness. He saw a tank spewing gasoline into a cellar. The sharp tang stung his nostrils before the cellar door coughed flames, and human puppets jerked spastically as fire consumed them. An enemy soldier crawled along an alleyway, trailing purple ropes of guts behind him. He was shot in the back of the head by an officer who didn't break stride. A grenade skittered across the road and came to a halt between Kurt's feet. He braced himself for the explosion and ran on when it didn't happen.

He felt neither terror nor elation as he pushed on. An officer jumped from a personnel carrier and motioned them to stop. He saw the man's lips move and his arm rise to direct them somewhere, and then one of his cheeks deflated as the other sprayed blood in a gushing arc, a brilliant red streamer against the dust-grey backdrop. He felt himself falter and his vision narrow as tiredness gave way to exhaustion, and still they moved forward, dealing death with a mindless efficiency until they were halted in a square by an officer. He fired two shots from his pistol over their heads before they stopped.

'This area is secure,' he shouted. 'Water over there.'

Most sank to the ground where they were, as if something had scythed the strings that moved their limbs. Kurt followed the officer's pointing finger and stumbled towards the promise of water. He couldn't control his rubbery legs and crashed into the trough. Immediately, he plunged his head into the greenish water. It felt incredibly cold and he wanted to stay under the surface forever. He straightened, gasping, and shook himself like a dog. Then, like the animal, he bent again and lapped the water until his belly felt hard. He sat. He had just enough energy remaining to prise the helmet from his head and feel the chill of the air on his scalp.

From his position, he had a view across the square. Somewhere in the distance there was the sound of a vicious fire-fight. Beyond the shield of tall buildings he saw a pillar of smoke rise up from a lurid base. We are in the eye of the hurricane, he thought, and fought to keep his eyes open. They slewed and fixed on an equestrian statue, still standing on its plinth in the centre of the square. The marble, prancing horse was missing a raised foreleg and pocked with bullet holes. The stately rider seemed to be oblivious of the carnage all around him, pointing dramatically to some long-gone objective. Kurt wondered if he could hoist himself upright and step over the bodies sprawled around the plinth to read the inscription. It could be King Otto, he thought; a historian should know something like that. He imagined the conversation at the plinth. 'Let me through, gentlemen, please, I'm a historian.' He began to laugh. It began as a spastic movement in his chest and a huffing sound from his mouth and worsened, alarmingly, into a gape-mouthed wheeze. He was frightened by the physical intensity of it and the possibility that he couldn't inhale as much air as he was braying out of his mouth. A shape wavered in his tear-blind vision and his head rolled sideways with the force of a blow. 'Breathe, soldier,' someone commanded roughly and a pair of hands dragged him upright by the lapels. The hands held him in that position until he had reined his breath back to normal. He dragged a forearm across his eyes and looked at the corporal.

'Think you can stand?' the corporal asked.

'Yes.'

'We'll be pulling out in about ten minutes. Count the survivors for me – living and wounded.'

He was turning away when the corporal gripped his arm. 'Heard you couldn't shoot for shit,' he said, 'and you can't. But you survived and you didn't turn back. That counts for something. It won't be as bad next time.'

He counted twenty-five survivors, including the wounded. He was still looking for the other forty when the personnel carrier arrived to bring them back to camp.

Sergeant Kann considered himself 'old Wehrmacht'. He and his corporal agreed that the army had changed under the influence of 'the new order'. They were careful to use this coded language when they spoke. Stalin had his commissars and Hitler had the SS: fanatics who policed the purity of their vision. That's the sort of vision that gets you killed, he thought, and spat the dust from his mouth. He had survived to be an old soldier because his vision didn't involve being killed. Fight honourably? Yes. Die gloriously? No, thank you.

He extended this principle like a shield around the men under his command. His job, as he saw it, was to make every effort to preserve them, even if that meant making liberal translations of orders from vision-blinded superiors. He ran his eye over the troop and was relieved by their caution. Most of them fired on instinct. Their battle-heightened senses registered a threat and swung their rifles up to deal with it. Otherwise, they crouched, making themselves as small as possible and ducked from one protected position to another. He knew there was a fine line between the energy they needed for offence and the headlong madness of euphoria. He had seen normally cautious soldiers swept up by the sudden elation of ground gained and outrace their sense of vulnerability. In the furnace of the fighting, their humanity could be burned away and combat could turn to slaughter. That's why he moved among them; calling them by name, chanting short mantras for blood-deafened ears.

'Pick your target – shoot the shooters – only the shooters – everyone else to the rear.'

He was the cynical old man in the back of the triumphal chariot, reminding the conquerors of their mortality.

'Heroes don't go home – stay alive – stay alive.'

He sensed the relief rise from their hunched forms as he absolved their caution.

Steiger bothered him. The fucker seemed to court death as if he had no life to lose. He stood whenever others hugged the cover – pushed beyond the protective fence of cover fire.

'That bastard will win an Iron Cross,' his corporal muttered, as they watched Steiger storm another silent foxhole, daring even the dead to show some hint of resistance.

And crosses for the rest of us, Sergeant Kann thought, but didn't say.

Why us? Rudi wondered.

Why did the sergeant pick the pair of us for 'death duty'? It made some kind of sense that the miner had qualified because of his physical strength. Also, he admitted, the powerful man had seemed to shrink as they marched under that immense Russian sky.

He watched him now as he hunched over, keeping the solidity of the earth in sight. Even a friend would have to allow that the miner made a reluctant soldier. At the same time, he couldn't help noticing how the miner cradled the dead in his massive arms as if those arms had been denied the opportunity once before and found some solace in this dreadful work.

'Why me?' Rudi muttered as he laid yet another body at the end of a lengthening line and, automatically, tilted the helmet over unseeing eyes so the sun wouldn't blind them. Why detail a man who would search every fallen man's face and then grunt in guilty relief when it wasn't the face he dreaded finding? Was that the sergeant's reasoning? Did he know Rudi would touch every dead soldier as if he were Karl and carry him tenderly to the rear to expiate his guilt that it wasn't?

He found himself muttering snatches of half-remembered prayers over the broken bodies as he picked his way over the charnel house that was Smolensk.

'Eternal rest grant unto him, o Lord – but deliver us from evil.'

He didn't know when this stream of supplication had broken through the barricade of his clenched teeth. It gathered in force, coming in grunts and gasps until the miner held his arms and rooted him.

'Rudi,' he said, in that rumbling, rock-fall voice, 'Karl is not among them. He is alive. You must come and rest now – orders from the corporal.'

The miner conjured coffee from somewhere and they sat among the dead, sipping the bitter brew. The miner was badged with other men's blood and Rudi realised he must also be wearing the decorations of other men's sacrifice. He wondered if the miner's coffee also tasted of salt.

He'd had a fleeting moment of panic when the sergeant had jerked him from Kurt's side and shoved him towards a group commanded by a lieutenant.

The lieutenant looked young, Karl thought apprehensively, and then smiled at the irony. He'd watched the young officer bob his head repeatedly while the captain barked orders at him.

'Understand?'

'Yes, sir.'

A bit too prompt with his answer, Karl judged. He'd known boys in school who nodded even when they didn't know. He checked his magazine and straightened his helmet. They were at a crossroads in a comparatively quiet part of the city. The four radiating streets curved sharply after about fifty yards. Whatever or whoever came their way would come fast. He prayed the lieutenant was brighter than he looked. The lieutenant was poring over a map as the men shuffled from one foot to the other, glancing uneasily over their shoulders.

'Bastard knows as much about battle as Uncle Adolf,' someone whispered and the group shook with suppressed laughter. We're exposed here, Karl fretted; better to be back to back in one of the streets than milling around here. Impulsively, he approached the lieutenant.

'May I hold the map for you, sir?' he offered. Gratefully, the officer pushed it into his hands as if glad to be rid of it.

'Maps can be very confusing,' Karl added, 'especially when the city has been changed so much by the bombing.'

The lieutenant looked at him intently, searching his face for a suggestion of sarcasm. Then his face relaxed into a hint of a smile.

'The Russians are confined to the western section of the city,' he said. 'We are to hold this position against any breakout. What's your name, soldier?'

'Karl Hamner, sir.'

'Well, Karl Hamner,' the lieutenant confided, 'at this moment I don't know up from down.'

'None of us do, sir,' Karl replied. He bent his head over the map and whispered, 'West is where the sun is just now, sir. How would you like us to deploy?'

'Deploy? Oh yes.' The lieutenant divided the other eight soldiers into four pairs and ordered them to the bends in the streets.

'And you, Karl Hamner,' he said, when the others had shuffled off, 'I want you up there at a window to give us covering fire.' He gestured at a reasonably intact building standing like a sentinel on the crossroads. 'Stay alive, Karl,' he added and grinned.

The door was unlocked. Why would fleeing people lock a door, he asked himself? He had a sudden vision of women and children crowding the hallway he stood in – people with tight, grey faces focused on being somewhere else – families, who had held their collective breath in a city crouching under a gathering storm, waiting for the thunder to roll. But they hadn't waited. They had thrown whatever was portable on a table, trapped it all in a table-cloth and run – run eastwards, away from the terror – away from him. Why lock the door?

A Panzer didn't wait for permission to enter. Soldiers knocked with rifle-butts and boots. His own boots crunched over small objects dropped in the panic. He found the stairs lit from above by a window, still miraculously intact, and began to edge his way upwards, keeping to the sides of the steps where the wood was less likely to betray him. Light rectangular patches on the walls mourned some family photograph or religious icon tumbled in the humble tablecloth with bread and cheese. They took their history with them, he mused as he climbed higher. A house, he considered, is just a shell without its people. Wherever they found refuge, the photographs and icons would be displayed again and that place would be consecrated as home.

He had tried to read the runes of what people discarded, as the army had marched on Smolensk. He discovered that cooking utensils were jettisoned soonest – followed by a samovar – spare clothing and then the bodies of those who couldn't keep up or who just ceased caring. He'd never seen a photograph or an icon among that pitiful jetsam. On the top-floor landing he paused to listen. The distant crump of shellfire was muted inside the house as if it was too alien to enter. He leaned on the door, eased into a high-ceilinged room and stopped. A small oil-lamp burned on a sideboard, its weak glow reflecting faintly in the picture frames that crowded the walls. Within the frames, family groups stared sombrely from an ethereal, sepia fog. There were portraits of men in uniform – imperial, he guessed – that evolved as he progressed through the room to black and white studies of children and adults.

Remembering his mission, he turned to the window and froze. Someone sat in a high-winged chair by the window. Defensively, he raised his rifle but the figure remained immobile. Slowly, he followed his pointing rifle until he stood before the figure. Karl found himself looking at a very old man. He was clad in a black suit and wore a set of military medals on his coat. Fingers, like gnarled roots, rested on a cane before him. His eyes were milky blue and looked back at the intruder with interest. For what felt like a very long time, they simply stared at each other.

'Boy,' the man said. Even his heavily accented German couldn't disguise his surprise. 'Boy,' he said again, wonderingly, 'young boy.'

Karl nodded dumbly and lowered his rifle. 'Why are you here?' he asked, slowly.

The old man nodded his understanding. 'Here is home,' he said. 'Others go.'

Karl stood his rifle against the window and rummaged in his pockets. 'Chocolate,' he said, offering the squares with a shaking hand. Twisted fingers picked up a single square with impossible delicacy and placed it between purpled lips. The man chewed for a few moments and swallowed. 'Gut,' he announced, 'sehr gut.'

Karl poured coffee from his flask into its cup-cover and held it to the man's lips. He sipped a few times and looked into the boy's face. Slowly, he raised a hand and touched Karl' cheek. 'Boy,' he said hoarsely, as his eyes blurred. Karl retreated to the window and raised the lower section. He picked up his rifle and hunched down. 'Watch,' he explained, but the old man didn't reply.

They came suddenly. The two sentries at the far corner had covered only a few yards of their retreat to the crossroads when a rattle of gunfire shook them to the street. Breathlessly, Karl aimed and fired. His single shot betrayed his position and he tumbled to the floor as the window exploded, shards of glass raining around him. He saw a tiny sliver erupt from his knuckle, like a miniature stalagmite, and a spot of blood bloom at its base. He heard shouts and firing from the street below, but a constant fusillade through the window kept him pinned to the floor. As suddenly as it began, the noise stopped. He risked a look through the ravaged window and the street was empty. He heard the faint concussion of the front door as it bounced against a wall and the rising crescendo of boots on the stairs. Panicked, he swung his rifle to his shoulder and aimed at the apartment door.

'Boy,' the old man called. 'Boy.' He turned his head and saw the man gesture at a table. He hadn't noticed the heavy cloth that covered the table and hung to the floor.

'Hide,' the man said.

He was concentrating on regulating his breathing and ensuring that he was totally covered by the tablecloth when the door burst inwards and the pounding of heavy boots shook the floorboards under his knees. A man's voice said something in Russian and Karl was surprised by the strength in the old man's voice when he replied. He detected a note of deference creep into the first voice and then a barked order prefaced the sounds of departure. Whoever closed the door did so gently.

'Gone,' the old man said when Karl rolled out from his concealment. He heard voices outside, the fading clatter of boots on the street and then silence.

The old eyes regarded him with a mixture of relief and sadness. Karl found he couldn't speak; his fear seemed to have welded his tongue to the roof of his mouth and, if he opened his mouth to express his thanks, he feared he would scream. He picked up his helmet and bent to kiss the old man's cheek. A hand rose up and cradled him there so that their tears mingled.

'Life is changed not ended,' Karl remembered Father Kyril saying at gravesides in Hallstatt. It's both, he thought, as he counted the dead bodies strewn around the crossroads. They appeared vacant – that was the word. A short time past, they'd been occupied with all the ordinary energy of living – sneaking a quick smoke, pulling faces behind the lieutenant's back. Whatever residue of life remained, he knew, was what his memory projected on the dead. The lieutenant lay at the centre of the crossroads, his arm extended to the west as if he had been killed in the act of prophecy. Karl wondered if he should say a prayer but couldn't think of words that didn't sound facile. Instead, he closed the lieutenant's eyes, as he had done for the others, and sat within the circle of their bodies to watch over them and fulfil their mission.

There were three of them. Karl had just swivelled his head to check a side street and when he looked back, they were there. Two of the Russians moved ahead of a third man who favoured the shadows near the buildings.

'Halt,' Karl croaked, slotting the rifle butt against his shoulder. The leading pair froze in the centre of the street and then jerked forward a few paces and fell as they were shot from behind. Karl grunted in surprise and swung his rifle to hunt among the shadows for the third man.

'Don't shoot.'

His brain registered the unaccented German even as a more primitive part of him tightened his finger on the trigger. At the last moment, it was the lack of fear in the man's voice that saved his life.

'Don't shoot,' he repeated. 'I'm going to walk to the centre of the street and stop. I'll raise my hands over my head. My pistol will be in my right hand. When you can see me clearly, I'll drop the pistol and take two steps forward. Understand?'

'Yes.'

The muzzle of Karl's rifle tracked the man as he walked out of the shadows, came to a halt in the centre of the street, dropped his pistol and came forward two paces.

'Who are you?' Karl asked warily.

'Special forces,' the man replied calmly. 'I need to speak to your commanding officer.'

'The lieutenant is dead.'

'I was hoping to speak to someone a little more senior,' Edwin Unger said smiling and walked right past the startled boy.

The camp

Karl and his 'prisoner' ran the gauntlet of the soldiers rough good humour as they made their way to the command tent.

'Keeping that one for a pet, boy?'

'He'll never fit in the pot, son.'

A soldier with a soiled bandage around his head demanded to know why he hadn't shot the bastard and saved himself a walk.

'Erfurters are the living proof that the Weimars are sheep lovers,' the prisoner responded and the gape-mouthed soldier was buffeted by the delighted laughter of his companions.

The SS officer looked at them as if they were something that might soil his gleaming boots.

'Prisoners go that way, soldier,' he growled, jerking his head towards the forest.

'Edwin Unger, Brandenburger Regiment, reporting to General Kluge,' the prisoner said calmly and walked into the tent. The officer's right hand twitched towards his holster and then disappeared behind his back. Thwarted and humiliated, his eyes ranged for another target and found Karl.

'What are you waiting for?' he asked in a voice hot with menace, 'a fucking medal?'

Karl saluted smartly and retreated.

They were waiting for him, ranged around his frantic father like a protective shield. At the sight of him, they raised a ragged cheer and then withdrew as Rudi stumbled forward to embrace him. For an instant, Karl thought he saw Herr Steiger watching through the tent-opening and then his father swamped him in his arms. When he released him, Karl saw that his father was ashen-faced and covered in blood.

'Not mine, son,' Rudi said hoarsely, his eyes checking the boy's body for signs of injury even as his blood-encrusted fingers touched his face and hair as if to confirm his solidity. He saw his father trying to read his son's experiences in his eyes and whispered, 'Later, Papa, we'll talk later.'

The miner sat on a camp stool like a great boulder, seemingly unscathed by the storm that had raged around him. Herr Steiger had returned to the rear of the tent, hunching down on his cot and wrapping his silence around him. Kurt had tried to apologise for what had happened on the ridge and Karl had deflected it by asking his teacher about his experiences in Smolensk.

'Perhaps later, Karl,' Kurt had said quietly. 'Things like this take time – to settle.'

Karl sensed a fragility in the older man as if he had encountered a question and was struggling to find a coherent answer. 'I am very glad to see you alive, Karl,' Kurt whispered.

'And I you, Kurt,' the boy responded.

They stood awkwardly for a moment and then Kurt extended his hand. Karl thought his handshake was that of a man whose mind had already returned to some other matter.

He wandered off between the tents, taking in the sights and sounds around him. He saw a group of soldiers ignoring a whistling kettle as they argued loudly, everyone speaking at the same time. Farther on, a corporal knelt beside a young private whose eyes were focused on something far away. The corporal was trying to pry the boy's fingers from the stock of his rifle while he stroked his back with his other hand. Soldiers lay sprawled on their backs, their eyes wide open, simply staring at the sky. Others busied themselves around cooking pots and washtubs, spending their remaining energy on small, inconsequential actions as if constant movement would keep reflection at bay. He asked himself if he was doing something similar, strolling to nowhere in particular to outpace his own memories. Kurt was right, he concluded, things like this take time to settle.

He looked up and saw that the neat rows of tents were now behind him. Ahead, near the edge of the forest, lay a separate camp. It was the music that had drawn him from his reverie – a wild, jagged music that shot like shrapnel from a harmonica played by a man with tightly shut eyes and a face so red it seemed about to burst. Around the harmonica player, men gyrated and stamped their feet in a tight, angry circle. Farther back, out of the sharp music's range, two men danced together, waltzing with exaggerated care, drinking what he guessed was champagne from long-necked bottles. Nearer the trees, a man, naked apart from his boots, brandished a beer bottle in one hand and a pistol in the other. He seemed uncertain as to which he would raise to his mouth.

Karl dragged his gaze away from that disturbing sight and his eyes were drawn to a young man who was sitting outside a pristine tent. He had a dagger in his hand and was running the tip, delicately, under the thumbnail of the other. He wore SS badges on his collar, shot-through with silver lightning bolts. His face was thin and bone-white, like his close-cropped hair. The man seemed to become aware that he was being watched and raised his eyes. Karl had seen many expressions in soldiers' eyes during the battle for Smolensk. He had identified and stored all the nuances of expression from terror to unbridled elation, but he could find no category for the expression he saw now. He remembered the proverb that 'the eyes are the windows of the soul' and shuddered. There was an absence in these eyes – a desolation that stretched to infinity and their light-blue tinge could have been the sky behind the eyeholes of a mask.

'Soldier!'

His heart stopped and then banged reproachfully at his ribs. The comfortable bulk of Sergeant Kann interposed itself between him and the SS man and he felt relief melt his muscles.

'Do you know who they are, boy?' the sergeant asked in a low voice. For an instant, Karl thought he spoke like a man whispering outside a cave, as if afraid to waken what lay inside.

'No, no, Sergeant,' he managed through stiff lips.

'Waffen SS,' the sergeant said and spat to the side as if he had tasted something tainted. 'Steer clear of them, little soldier,' he continued in the same low voice. 'That bunch are just as mad when they're sober.'

He nodded dumbly and the sergeant turned him with a hand on his shoulder and nudged him back towards the camp.

'So,' he said in a more normal voice, when they had moved beyond the range of the mad music and the SS man's stare, 'who, in our collection of peasants and sheep-shaggers knows anything about wine?'

'Wine?'

'Yes, you know, wine. Comes in a bottle – choice of red or white – made from grapes, mashed under some clod-hopper's filthy feet. Wine,' he repeated, slapping Karl on the shoulder for emphasis. He bent forward, to look the boy in the eye. 'We are to be graced, blessed, cursed with the presence of the brass – and brass do not drink beer, little soldier. Beer is for farm boys who drink it up and piss it out and think it's funny when they roll under the table. Wine is for the generals and officers who think beer is beneath them. Wine is for men who read maps and draw lines and plan advances and flankings and encirclements and all the folderol that kills the beer drinkers. Now, who the fuck knows anything about wine?'

'Herr, I mean, Kurt Brandt, sir.'

'Brandt?' The red-tinged eyes narrowed dangerously. 'Tall fellow, walks with a stoop? Looks like he's got a hot-poker up his ass and can't shoot for shit; that Brandt?'

'Eh, yes, Sergeant.'

'You'd better be right, boy, because if that string of misery pours wine down General von Kluge's crotch, you'll be digging latrines all the way to Moscow.'

'Yes, Sergeant.'

'Right! In one hour, you and Brandt report to HQ in full uniform. And soldier' – when Karl looked up, he thought the vitality had fled the sergeant's face and he looked older – 'Don't come back here,' he said. 'You don't want to be downwind of those mangy curs – Burgermeisters' sons, playing at being soldiers. Remember, boy, we are the Wehrmacht, the real army. We go toe to toe with the enemy and keep fighting until he calls quits. These creatures have other rules of engagement. Stay clear of them. Some animals should be seen only through bars.'

'That's four cases of Kavanchkara and two of Mukuzani, this should make for quite a party,' Kurt said happily.

'I don't know one wine from another,' Karl protested.

'After the third glass, neither will they,' Kurt assured him.

Karl watched his friend become more animated as they stacked the crates and polished the wine glasses. There was a gleam in his eye as he held a bottle to the light that sliced through the tent flap.

'Just remember, Karl,' he said, 'serve from the right, always from the right, like a good fascist.' He chuckled at his own joke and wiped the bottle on his sleeve before putting it back in the crate.

'This is such an opportunity for us, Karl. Very few historians get the chance to sit in on the meetings of the mighty. Well, apart from Herodotus, and he listened to every bit of tittle-tattle. Gather your bottles, boy,' he laughed, 'history beckons.'

'Kurt?'

'Yes, what is it?'

'Do you think the generals would miss one bottle?'

He inclined his head meaningfully towards Rudi and the miner who sat listlessly on their cots.

'Why not?' Kurt declared grandly. 'We are all part of history. Get the cups, Karl.'

Karl chivvied his father and the miner to a vacant cot that doubled as a makeshift table. He arranged the four mugs and began to pour, carefully turning his wrist when a cup was nearly full, as Kurt had instructed. The schoolteacher raised his cup to pronounce a toast.

'Kurt,' Karl said quietly, 'we're short a cup.'

'No, we've got four.'

'Herr Steiger, Kurt.'

In the sudden silence, he realised they had forgotten the policeman, erased him from their minds as thoroughly as the policeman would have wished. The miner growled dismissively and Kurt looked puzzled, as if he couldn't recall who Herr Steiger was.

'Use mine,' Rudi said, rising, 'I'll find another.'

Karl felt a swell of pride for his father as he took a cup to the blanket-shawled figure at the rear of the tent.

'Herr Steiger?'

The man remained immobile. Karl reached out a tentative hand and touched his shoulder. The policeman winced and Karl took an involuntary step back, startled by the feral grimace that contorted the man's face. The policeman turned to face him. He looked wonderingly at the boy as if he was trying to recall where he'd seen him before.

'Max?' he whispered and a look of infinite sadness glistened in his eyes.

'It's Karl, Herr Steiger. Please, have some wine.'

A hand trembled from beneath the blanket and grasped the cup. When Karl looked back at the others, he thought they looked abashed. Only his father smiled with relief, as if he'd discovered his son unscathed all over again.

'To absent friends,' Kurt toasted and Karl touched his cup gently against the policeman's.

General von Kluge's HQ, Smolensk, July 1941

'Two generals and assorted minions,' Kurt whispered as they polished wine glasses and set them on silver trays. 'General Adolf Ferdinand von Kluge – "clever Günther" to the troops – a Prussian military blue-blood. Cut his battle teeth at Verdun in the Great War. Led the Fourth Army through the Ardennes to take France in this one. Uncle Adolf made him a Field Marshal.'

'And the other general?'

'Halder. Son of a general. A tactician. Planned the invasion of Poland. Not loved by Uncle Adolf.'

'What's he like?'

'Testy. Sergeant says Halder could start an argument in an empty tent.'

' … and then, Mannstein tiptoed through the Pripet Marshes and bit Ivan's bum.'

The tent rocked with laughter and cheers. General von Kluge acknowledged the applause with a raised glass. 'Heil Hitler,' he said, and the others shot to their feet. 'Heil Hitler,' they shouted.

We are invisible, Karl thought, scanning the faces of the men who crowded the map table. Apart from generals von Kluge and Halder, he recognised only a Panzer officer, from the insignia on his uniform. The others were strangers to him. A man whose uniform was bare of any decoration sat quietly at the rear wall of the tent. Karl's eyes widened as he recognised his 'prisoner', the Brandenburger. Edwin Unger, he recalled. The dark-haired, compact man raised his eyes and dropped a slow wink when their eyes met. He looked away to find the sergeant standing, at ease, inside the tent-flap, his sharp eyes belying his stance.

'Watch the glasses, Karl,' Kurt whispered urgently. 'Fill them before they're empty and listen, Karl, listen.'

'Gentlemen,' General von Kluge continued, 'our victory has already been hailed by Der Führer and trumpeted in the press. Congratulations are extended to one and all. Please convey them to your units. And now it is time to retire. We will need our strength for the next victory.' He raised his glass. 'Moscow,' he shouted.

'Moscow,' they thundered.

Karl counted four who remained after the others had departed in a flurry of handshakes. Generals Kluge and Halder stayed seated at either end of the map table. They seemed relaxed, Karl observed, but the length of the table that divided them could mean there were other tensions. The Panzer officer had resumed his seat and the Brandenburger moved out of the shadows to sit beside von Kluge. Five! Karl corrected himself as the sergeant straightened to something more like attention in the background. He didn't count Kurt or himself – they were still invisible. He sensed that the mood of the remaining group had distilled into something less boisterous and reminded himself of Kurt's injunction. Listen!

'Won't you have a little more of this Georgian wine, General Halder?' von Kluge enquired smoothly. 'Mannstein, eh, liberated a whole cellar of it from Ivanev's HQ. Seems he kept it under guard in case Stalin dropped by. We can't check its provenance, of course, since both the guard and Ivanev were last seen running for Moscow.'

General Halder cracked a small smile and extended his glass to be replenished by Kurt.

'Isn't Stalin a Georgian?' he said and sipped.

'Yes, General,' Kurt replied, 'and Beria also.'

General Halder glanced at him and Karl saw the sergeant stiffen.

'Well, "know your enemy",' the general continued smoothly. 'Some oriental or other said that but I suppose you know that?' he said, cocking an enquiring eyebrow at Kurt.

'Yes, General. I believe it was Sun Tzu, sir,' Kurt replied, turning his wrist to avoid spotting the general's sleeve.

'My, my, von Kluge,' Halder said innocently, 'even your waiters are omniscient.'

Karl registered the thunder on the sergeant's face and forced his concentration back to the table. He knew Kurt well enough to know that he wasn't being a show-off.

Kurt was obsessed with the details of history and presumed others shared his obsession. Even as Karl's stomach plummeted towards his boots, in trepidation, he couldn't wait to compare their journal accounts of this meeting. Von Kluge allowed the silence to stretch before he spoke.

'Generals don't always have the exclusive ownership of knowledge,' he said evenly, 'which is why we're having this meeting. Now that the euphoria of battle has evaporated somewhat, we need to take a cooler look at the lessons to be learned from Smolensk. Yes, Captain?'

'Captain, Albert Becker, sir.' The Panzer officer slicked the hair back from his eyes. Karl wondered if his fixed stare was due to battle fatigue or the glasses of Georgian wine he'd been emptying as fast as Karl could fill.

'Herr General,' the officer said, hoarsely, 'I fear Smolensk may have been a Pyrrhic victory.'

'Nonsense,' Halder snapped. 'We have taken an important city on the road to Moscow, as well as two thousand tanks and ten times that number of prisoners. How can you say we've lost more than we've gained?'

'With respect, Herr General,' the officer said stubbornly, 'five divisions of their army escaped. They'll be waiting for us up the road with Timoshenko and—'

General Halder erupted to his feet.

'This is defeatist talk,' he said harshly, 'I will excuse it because we have all had a long day, but I will not listen to more of it.' He bowed stiffly to von Kluge. 'Perhaps you and I could discuss this later,' he said and stormed out of the tent.

'I think we could all do with a refill of that excellent Bolshevik wine,' von Kluge said, as if nothing had happened.

Kurt and Karl busied themselves with the bottles.

'You too, Sergeant,' von Kluge said, smiling, 'if you're not too busy glowering.'

Stiffly, the sergeant marched to the table and accepted a glass of wine. Karl noticed the sergeant's fingers were white around the stem of the glass and nervously touched the bottle to the rim. A clear note sang from the glass and the general laughed.

'Now you're terrifying the boy, Frederick' he said. 'Relax, man, we are old soldiers jawing together. Sit!'

The sergeant lowered himself reluctantly into a chair. 'Clear up a mystery for us, Frederick,' the general continued. 'Where did you find such a learned waiter?'

'Austrian conscript,' the sergeant sniffed dismissively.

'Surely you're not denigrating the prowess of Austrians, Frederick,' von Kluge said mischievously. 'After all, Der Führer is—'

'I know, sir,' the sergeant interrupted. 'I will admit this man fought well today – or so his corporal said. But he doesn't know when to keep his fucking mouth shut. Excuse my language, sir.'

Von Kluge waved a languid hand. 'No apology necessary, old friend,' he said smoothly. He turned his attention to Kurt, eyeing him appraisingly.

'What did you do before the war, soldier?' he asked.

'I was a lecturer at the University of Vienna, sir, in the history department and, latterly, a schoolteacher in Hallstatt.'

'Some might consider that a rather drastic demotion,' the general observed.

'I did,' Kurt said, quietly, 'at the time, but not now.'

Karl couldn't contain a smile of pleasure. The general's keen eyes swung his way before he could conceal it.

'Could it be,' von Kluge said, 'that we are blessed with a historian and his apprentice?'

'Yes, sir,' Kurt replied.

'General,' the Brandenburger interrupted, 'I would like to point out that this young man, eh, escorted me from Smolensk.'

'Excellent,' the general beamed. 'Bring the bottles and sit to the table,' he instructed the bemused waiters. 'You'll have to excuse General Halder,' he said, as they sat self-consciously on the recently vacated camp stools. 'He's not much given to the study of history, I'm afraid, but a competent tactician nonetheless. Now, Albert,' he said, in a more businesslike voice, 'you think we may have trouble up the road?'

'Yes, sir,' the Panzer officer replied, leaning forward urgently. 'They – they fight well, General.' He tugged at his hair as if to help his concentration, before continuing. 'They had no answer to us at the border. Some of that could be put down to surprise and lack of organisation. But even at Minsk they'd steadied up and gave a good account of themselves.'

'And at Smolensk?' the general prompted.

'They fought for every inch, General – foxholes, tank traps, house to house and—'

He paused as if straining for the right words.

'And?'

'And – they don't know when they're beaten, sir,' Albert said. 'I saw soldiers roll under our tanks with explosives in their hands.' He drained his glass and swallowed convulsively. 'If they fight like that, all the way to Moscow …' His voice trailed off and the faraway stare returned to his eyes.

'Thank you, Albert,' the general said gently. 'Why don't you get a few hours' sleep?'

The young man hauled himself to his feet, saluted jerkily and stumbled out of the tent.

'You've heard the views of the Panzer captain, Brandenburger,' von Kluge challenged. 'Do five escaped Russian divisions a Pyrrhic victory make?'

'It's not the ones who got away that bother me, General,' the Brandenburger said thoughtfully. 'It's the ones who arrived.'

'What do you mean?'

'I mean I was there, sir, when the elite troops arrived. From what I heard, there's more where they came from and more again in Siberia. They were everything Albert described, well-trained and fanatical.'

'Stalin needs them in Siberia, to keep the Japanese quiet,' the general said confidently. 'He won't risk pulling them back from the border.'

'Unless Moscow is threatened and he has nothing more to lose. Or until the Japanese turn their attention elsewhere, or until we can persuade them to.'

'You Brandenburgers have people either side of the border, don't you?' von Kluge said slyly.

'I couldn't really answer that question, General.'

'You have,' von Kluge said smugly. 'Doesn't matter in the short term, just so much speculation. The fact is that we have taken Smolensk a full month before Napoleon did and we will follow him all the way to Moscow. Our tanks are already pushing up the road to establish bridgeheads.'

'Except he didn't want to,' Kurt interjected.

'What?'

'Napoleon didn't want to take Smolensk, sir. He wanted to smash the Russian Army outside the city. In effect, Russia would have been conquered and he could have turned his attention to England. It didn't happen, General. The Russian Army escaped and whittled his Grand Armée at every step on the road to Moscow.'

'Napoleon didn't have tanks,' the general countered.

'True,' Kurt conceded, 'but he had their equivalent at the time. Cavalry, sir. Murat, the cavalry commander, gained a lot of ground but it took him farther and farther away from the infantry and his supply depots. Tanks and horses are what give an army mobility, sir, and both need to be fed.'

'You are quite the Cassandra, aren't you Professor?'

Kurt smiled at the reference to the prophetess who was destined never to be believed.

'The Russians don't need to win battles, sir,' he continued, 'just not lose them too badly. Delay is what eventually defeated Napoleon. The Russians remember their history, General. They'll hit and run, regroup and hit again while we get farther from our home and they get closer to theirs. So delay is a weapon, General – a particularly effective one when you have a powerful general waiting in reserve.'

'Do you mean Timoshenko? Zhukov?'

'No, sir. I mean General Winter. We are already deep into August.'

'What do you think, Frederick?' the general asked the sergeant, when they were alone.

'I think I could arrange to have him shot, sir.'

'Who?'

'That Brandt bastard, who else?'

'I could provide a long list of others,' the general said heavily. He began to chuckle. 'He's right, you know,' he said eventually, wiping a sleeve across his streaming eyes. 'The parallels with Napoleon's campaign are uncanny. If we move too fast, we risk putting the armour too far ahead of the army. If we strike directly for Moscow, they'll mine the roads and burn all before us and harry our flanks every bloody step of the way.'

His good humour had left him and he looked drained.

'What will Hi — what will Berlin say?' the sergeant asked.

'That changes from one day to the next,' the general said impatiently. 'One day it's take Moscow and cut the heart out of Bolshevism – another day it's Leningrad, an important port and the cultural capital of the Soviet Union. There are even rumours of Kiev.'

'Kiev?'

'Yes, Kiev! If we push for Moscow, we have a huge army haunting our flank. Also, Kiev provides most of their armaments, not to mention all that coal and metal in the Donets Basin.'

'Doesn't do to split your forces, General,' the sergeant said doubtfully.

'I'll mention that you said that in my next communication to Berlin, Sergeant.'

'And I'll shoot your bloody historian, General.'

They smiled and raised glasses.

'There's something else, sir,' the sergeant said soberly.

'I didn't think for a moment that you were here to protect me from waiters, Frederick. Spit it out.'

'Prisoners, sir! We have two, maybe three hundred thousand prisoners.'

'And?'

'And we can't feed them, General. The bastard quartermasters say we have barely enough to feed our own and—'

'Oh, for God's sake. Go on, Sergeant.'

'There's rumours coming down the line, sir, of shootings; men with their hand up being shot – bodies along the road with empty hands and bullets in the back of their heads. There's rumours about civilians too, sir. Some of the prisoners say their brass know about this and use it to keep their boys from surrendering. Also, any of ours taken by them can expect the same. It's bad for morale, General.'

'Are Wehrmacht personnel involved?'

'Some, but mostly others.'

General Günther von Kluge sat up straight.

'You have my permission to take out a patrol, Sergeant. Anyone found involved in this kind of inhumanity must be arrested and court-martialled. We're not the SS, Sergeant. We are the Wehrmacht. We have standards to maintain. The bastards who do this kind of thing make barbarians of us all.'

The Archbishop's Palace, Zagreb

It had taken a weary three days for the train to reach Zagreb. Mercifully, his uncle, the monsignor, had dispatched Father Kyril to lodgings in the city and hurried his exhausted nephew to the Archbishop's Palace. After a quick wash and change of clothes, Max had presented himself in the dining room, even though his body longed to lie down on anything stationary. He could still feel the movement of the train through tingling feet. Max raised his head and looked at the men who sat around the candlelit table.

I am invisible, he thought. He'd always puzzled over the concept of self-effacement: how someone could make himself invisible. Surely the energy of the act would attract attention? Then he'd discovered the secret. If we behave as others expect us to, there is nothing about us that snags their attention and we become just another part of the background the eye elides as it moves from one point of interest to the next. He had perfected it with his parents, who barely acknowledged the presence of the son they imagined him to be and then proceeded to act and speak as if he wasn't there.

Slowly, he angled the soup spoon into the thick broth and scraped the underside against the rim of the bowl. They continued talking. No one looked his way. None of the others at the archbishop's table was even remotely distracted by his movement. Even his uncle had stopped glancing nervously at him, probably relieved that the country bumpkin doesn't slurp or snort disgustingly at the table, Max concluded.

There were four others present and he watched and weighed them carefully. The bishop was a small, round man who strained his cassock. Nervous energy seemed to crackle from him, like an electrical current, so that his hands spasmed regularly into fists. He spoke in staccato bursts, his bright eyes darting left and right as if daring contradiction. Above the red sash at his waist, two buttons had already given up the effort at containment and an off-white undershirt signalled the rough peasant beneath the clerical garb. The priest who sat on the other side of the host was the bishop's antithesis. He was a tall, thin man with the abstracted eyes of a scholar.

'This is our best chance to bring them into the Church,' the bishop said, heatedly, 'the best chance we've had in centuries.'

The Croatian government is in agreement with you, Bishop,' the tall man said in a dry voice. 'They've made it crystal clear that there is no place in the new state for Orthodox Serbs.'

'Rather unsubtly, if I may say so,' Max's uncle said quietly.

'Subtlety is for the Byzantines,' the bishop barked, 'it's how they stole the land from under our feet, promoted their schismatic Church and planted their heretic cockle in our Catholic wheat to cause divisions among us.'

The tall cleric raised a restraining hand.

'Please, Bishop,' he said calmly, 'that sort of rhetoric is best kept for your pulpit. Allow the monsignor to develop his thesis.'

Max detected the sly malice behind the man's seeming forbearance and wondered if his uncle would step into the trap. Up to this point, he'd acted like a careful acolyte, replenishing the glasses of the others. Max had been surprised when his uncle had made an interjection that seemed in opposition to the triumphalism the two clerics had expressed.

'I think it was – regrettable,' the monsignor began hesitantly, 'that the government banned the use of the Orthodox Cyrillic script.'

'Chicken scratchings,' the bishop snorted.

'Closing their schools,' the monsignor continued doggedly, 'forbidding intermarriage and excluding them from the professions sound to me like history repeating itself. We are doing to them what we accuse them of doing to us. That's the kind of cyclical vengeance that will keep us at each others' throats for generations.'

'Not so,' the bishop snapped, 'not for generations, Monsignor. That cycle stops now with our generation. The measures promoted by the government will force the Serbs to make a choice. They can be part of the new Croatia as members of the Roman Catholic Church, in obedience to the Supreme Pontiff or—'

'Or what, Bishop?' the monsignor prompted.

'Or suffer the consequences.'

'Gentlemen,' the archbishop interjected mildly, 'if the Orthodox are plotting to divide us, why should we assist them in that?'

'Remember,' the archbishop continued, 'our Holy Father, the pope, referred to us as a "bastion of Christianity".'

'Surely, the Orthodox are also Christians,' the monsignor protested.

'Yes, yes, of course they are,' Stepinac conceded, 'but, sadly, they are separated from the one, true Church and Christ's vicar on earth. It is commendable that you are concerned for their welfare, Drago, but I have spoken to Pavelič and I'm convinced he is a sincere Catholic. He shares the pope's vision of a Catholic Croatia where Church and state work together for their mutual benefit.'

'And what of those who are not of our Church?' the monsignor persisted.

'This is a matter for the civil authorities, Drago. Remember, "render to Caesar the things that are Caesar's and to God the things that are God's".'

'I seem to recall the Romans exterminated those who would not render unto Caesar, your Grace, particularly the Christians. I must tell you that there have been reports from some of our priests about violence against the Orthodox Serbs—'

'Propaganda,' the bishop interrupted. 'You see how the Serbs operate? They spread such stories to demonise Croatia in the eyes of the world and the Church.'

'*Pace* – peace, gentlemen,' the archbishop urged. 'We must pray that our government is guided by the Holy Ghost to do what is best.'

He looked directly at Max, as if seeing him for the first time.

'Ah, young Max,' he said. 'I hope you have not been scandalised by the fervour of your elders?'

'No, your Grace,' Max answered, 'I found the discussion very enlightening. I know a little of our history from my mother. She told me that we have been loyal to the papacy for thirteen hundred years. I hope we can be worthy of the pope's confidence.'

'*Ex ore infantium*,' the archbishop said admiringly, 'out of the mouths of babes. Well spoken, young man. And now, gentlemen, I bid you goodnight.'

The monsignor dutifully opened the door and trailed after the prelate. The bishop shot Max a sharp glance before he bustled away.

'You are an interesting young man,' the tall cleric murmured. 'Unlike many of your generation, you listen attentively when your elders speak, and when you speak, you do so in a measured way.'

He turned from the coat stand and allowed Max to help him with his coat.

'Your uncle is a sensitive man, Max, an innocent in some ways. But the wheel of history is rolling through the world just now, and when it comes to rest, the world – your world – will be changed utterly. Those who stand in the way of that change will be broken on the wheel.'

His eyes had lost any vestige of warmth and burned now with a cold fire.

'*Carpe diem*, Max,' he said, 'seize the day.'

★

The sergeant banged on the roof of the cab and the truck slowed to a halt.

'What's that noise?' he asked.

Rudi stood up beside him and cupped an ear.

'Women screaming, Sergeant,' he said, 'directly ahead.'

They roared into the village, spilling from the truck before it had braked. 'Guard the truck, boy,' the sergeant snapped at Karl. 'You four, come with me.'

Rudi and the others quick-trotted behind the sergeant until they disappeared among the low houses. The land the village was huddled on seemed to have been reclaimed from the forest. Amputated tree stumps jutted through the mosaic of vegetable gardens that had been contoured around them. Karl heard a wild squawking and a pure white goose flapped honking into a field, pursued by two soldiers. The sergeant and Rudi followed in hot pursuit. Karl couldn't hear the conversation but he saw the soldiers gradually wilt before the sergeant's tirade and drag their feet back towards the houses.

Presently, he heard a truck start up, the noise of the engine amplifying as it rushed towards him. As it passed, some of the men in the rear brandished dead fowl and round cheeses, like trophies. Sickened by such casual thievery, Karl edged his way towards the houses. He paused at a gable end and glanced into the space between the houses that served as the village square. Two women knelt before the sergeant, imploring or castigating him; the boy couldn't tell from the unintelligible language that poured from their lips. The rest of the troop stood a few paces apart, embarrassed by the spectacle. All around, he saw the evidence of mindless vandalism. A pig lay on its side, squealing in terror and pain, trying to wriggle free of a wooden stake that pinned it to the earth. Chickens lay sprawled or fluttered weakly like a fox had come among them bent on slaughter. Beyond the houses, he caught a glimpse of beehives, some decapitated, others tilting drunkenly on their wooden platforms. Abruptly, the women surged upright and disappeared into the houses.

'You can come out now, boy,' the sergeant said wearily and Karl hurried to join his companions. The sergeant kicked a ball of feathers as he walked a tight angry circle. 'Fucking idiots,' he muttered. 'Don't need the food. Stupid, mindless, fucking idiots.' He shook himself like a dog and turned to the troop. 'You two,' he said to Rudi and the miner, 'get back to the truck and bring whatever food we have. Professor and the student who can't follow simple orders, tidy up around here.'

Like everyone else, he seemed to have trouble seeing the policeman. When he did, he stared silently at him for a few moments. 'Hey, hero,' he said, 'put that fucking pig out of its misery.'

When they had tidied up to the sergeant's satisfaction, he told them to put whatever food and drink had come from the truck near the door of one of the houses. They built a fire, as far across the humble square as they could go, and sat around it sipping coffee. No one spoke.

Karl wondered if the others also felt tainted by association. He saw a door open and an old woman, shrouded and shapeless in shawls, made her way, slowly, to the pile of provisions. She chose a single item and returned to her home. It seemed to send a signal to the other villagers who ventured out, singly and in pairs, until the provisions had disappeared. The sergeant had stood and stretched, as a prelude to their departure, when the doors opened again and a small procession of women approached, holding black bread and saucers of salt in their hands.

'What's this?' the sergeant muttered.

'It's their custom, sir,' Kurt said quietly. 'Black bread and salt are the traditional gifts offered to visitors.'

'Visitors,' the sergeant snorted, 'we're not fu—'

'They'll be offended if we don't accept, sir,' Kurt said quickly. 'Again,' he added.

'A little, then,' the sergeant allowed. 'We've taken enough from these people.'

Respectfully, the men accepted small portions of what they were offered, except the policeman, whose stance caused the women to shy away.

'*Danke,*' he heard his father say.

'*Spasibo,*' Kurt said and a ripple of whispers surged through the group of women.

Karl accepted what was offered, thanked the giver and popped the bread in his mouth. It had a rich, earthy taste and he felt kernels crack between his teeth. 'Do you speak Russian, Kurt?' he mumbled, trying to shift something fibrous lodged between his teeth.

'A little,' Kurt said. 'I had a friend in Vienna who spoke it fluently. He taught me the basics before—'

Karl waited for him to finish.

'He was a Jew, Karl,' his friend said, finally. 'Would you like to learn some Russian?'

'Yes, please.'

'Good. We're in the land of Dostoevsky and Pushkin and so many great writers, musicians and artists, Karl,' he said bitterly, 'and we are illiterate barbarians.'

THE ARCHBISHOP'S PALACE, ZAGREB

'Max!'

'Yes, Uncle?'

'Can you come to my study, please? There are some matters we have to discuss.'

He followed the monsignor down a long corridor, their footsteps muffled by a thin strip of carpet. Max mulled over the intellectual's words as his eyes measured the shambling man before him. His uncle, he considered, had stood up well to the bellicose bishop and the sly intellectual. He was a brave man but, the boy reasoned, he was defending a lost cause. The other clerics were the Janus faces of the same power: a combination of steel fist and velvet glove, and his innocent uncle would not prevail. The corridor was lit intermittently by small lamps perched on low tables. As the monsignor stepped into the pool of light before his study door, it seemed to Max that his shadow climbed the wall of the corridor to loom over him.

Max automatically stacked the folders and letters piled on a chair and placed them on the study floor. They made a single neat island in the archipelago of other documents that littered the room.

'I have some good news for you, Max,' his uncle said, smiling. For a terrible moment, the boy had visions of his mother, sitting like a malign presence in the shadows.

'The archbishop is very taken with you, Max,' his uncle continued, 'and wants to arrange a place for you at the university. He thinks it would be good for you, intellectually and socially. We, old men,' he said, smiling self-deprecatingly, 'are hardly stimulating company for a bright lad like you. What do you think?'

A wave of relief washed over the boy and he stammered his gratitude.

'It will be a wonderful opportunity, Max,' his uncle assured him. 'Zagreb is not Vienna, of course, but our university dates back to 1669 and has quite a reputation. Sadly, many of our students seem to have become ... infected by extreme nationalism, but I'm sure you won't be deflected from your studies by any of that.'

He sighed and fingered the deep furrows between his eyes. 'I hope you weren't scandalised, as his Grace put it, by the ...' He leaned back in his chair and seemed to weigh his words before continuing. 'You're a bright boy, Max, I can see that now. I'm afraid I've been a rather absent uncle to you. Your mother and I – well, we were never really close. Magda always held such strong opinions, even when we were younger. Then she moved with her husband to Hallstatt and when people move from their homeland they can carry a version of its history that is, shall we say, simplistic. I hope my saying this doesn't offend you.'

'No uncle, not at all. I think my mother holds views even more extreme than Bishop Miscic's.'

'That's very astute of you, Max,' the monsignor sighed in relief. 'Actually, Bishop Miscic is a very committed churchman but his views on the Serbs are as you say.'

'And the other cleric?'

'Ah yes, the professor. The professor's stance is very similar to the bishop's but he expresses himself more subtly.'

'I thought you expressed your views very well, Uncle.'

'That's very kind of you, Max, very kind. I must admit I would have shared many of their views in the past. It would be very difficult to grow up a Catholic in this country and not think as they do. But in recent years I've come to know some Orthodox priests and their families. Prejudices don't survive actual contact, Max.'

'The government decrees sound harsh, Uncle.'

'Yes, they are,' the monsignor nodded. 'When you exclude a minority, you make a distance between them and the majority. Prejudice grows in the gap, Max, and that can lead to inhuman and unchristian acts. Some of my Orthodox friends and, indeed, some good priests of our own send me accounts of atrocities. There are so many.'

He gestured hopelessly at the chaos of paper in his study. 'They think I may be able to influence the archbishop to speak out against the injustices.'

'And can you? The archbishop strikes me as – naïve. I hope you don't mind my saying so?'

'Oh no, my boy, not at all. It's refreshing to be able to speak openly. Archbishop Stepinac is a very spiritual man – saintly even. But he is surrounded by powerful, ambitious men who would use his office to promote their own cause. That cause, I fear, is ultimately Hitler's cause. Miscic and the others think it's the independence of Catholic Croatia, but we are Hitler's creation, a pawn in his political game, and when he has captured the chessboard—'

'You have been very kind to me, Uncle. No,' he raised his hand to forestall the monsignor's protestations. 'I understand you felt obliged to accept me here because of family obligations, but your welcome has exceeded your duty. I'd like to be of help. I could collate your letters and documents, perhaps make a list of the major points so that when you present the case to the archbishop, it will be easier for him to grasp what's happening.'

'Could you, Max?' his uncle breathed.

The boy nodded. He knew he had the sort of organisational skill that would transform this mess of material into a coherent whole. He also knew that the work would give him access to information – information that Miscic, the professor and maybe even the archbishop wouldn't want exposed. Information is power. Someone with that kind of power might possibly influence the wheel of history, but he would not be broken on it.

THE PATROL

They were bumping over a rough country road and were almost at the point on the sergeant's map where they would loop around the forest and turn for home. Birds called from the trees, heralding dusk, and waves of barley rolled away to the horizon before a steady breeze. The land was so flat, Karl thought. He wondered if it stretched beyond the line he could see to another flat plain and another horizon and so on all the way to Moscow. Even the birdsong seemed muted by the vastness of the landscape. He noticed the miner had hunkered down in a corner and pulled his forage cap down over his eyes as if to shield himself from the immensity of the sky. The others sat or stood, rocking sleepily to the lullaby of the tyres. Sudden gunfire in the distance jerked them upright.

'Weapons,' the sergeant shouted as the driver accelerated.

'Could be partisans,' Kurt muttered and rammed a fresh magazine into his rifle. Above the revving of the engine and the hum of the tyres, Karl heard a wild music that spiralled down the scale in a savage glide.

'Not partisans,' he said. 'Worse.'

'*Scheisse*,' the sergeant rasped, as a plume of smoke rose lazily from a roof. 'Shit, shit, shit.'

The truck wheeled around a tight bend and slewed sideways to avoid the personnel carrier blocking the road. It continued over rocky ground before coming to a creaking halt. The village was a replica of the one they'd left, except that there were no women to kneel before the sergeant and berate him. There was no squealing pig, no fluttering chickens. Human forms lay here and there in the tiny square, like dolls discarded by careless children. At the far end, a cow was being slaughtered by two men who wore blood up to their elbows. Another was lofting torches into doorways and the smell of burning thatch itched the eyes and noses of the patrol. The red-faced harmonica player sat on an upturned tub in the middle of this mayhem. He played a final flourish on the instrument and dropped it in his shirt pocket.

'Waffen,' the sergeant hissed between his teeth.

He turned his head as something swung into his peripheral vision and froze. Attuned to their leader, the patrol mimicked his action. Five bodies swung from a single beam that spanned the short distance between the roofs of adjacent houses. Karl registered the unnatural angle of the heads and the wet patches on the ground beneath them. He turned away and vomited a mess of black bread. When he looked up again, he stared at the figure who had replaced the harmonica player on the tub. The SS officer had a girl sitting on his knee, held there by an arm across her throat. His other hand held a knife, its point dimpling the underside of her chin. The girl seemed to look directly at Karl and he was distracted from the scene around him by the startling sea-green of her eyes. He thought she looked resigned rather than afraid.

'What's this?' the sergeant asked in a strangled voice.

'Partisans,' the officer said, 'fired on us from the forest.'

The matter-of-fact tone, coupled with the expressionless eyes, sent a shiver through Karl.

'Their weapons,' the sergeant demanded.

'Ricard,' the officer called, 'did you get their weapons?'

One of the cow-butchers strolled over to stand beside the officer. 'Just this pistol, Captain,' he said. He plucked a pistol from his belt and tossed it at the sergeant's feet.

'The rest?' the sergeant asked.

'Probably hidden in the forest,' the man Ricard replied smoothly.

The sergeant bent and examined the pistol.

'This is a German Mauser,' he said, straightening, 'hardly regular ordinance for Russian partisans.'

'The partisans take them from our boys, Sergeant,' the SS officer said patiently, as if explaining to a small child. 'After they've cut their throats of course. Surely you know that?'

'And the girl?'

'Partisan,' the officer said and smiled. During the exchange, the other Waffen SS, carrying an assortment of arms, had filtered back to range themselves in a line on either side of their captain. 'Little bitch is helping us with our enquiries,' the captain continued in his languid voice, 'aren't you, Liebchen?'

The sergeant stepped forward until he was only a few paces from the captain.

'We'll take the prisoner into our custody,' he said firmly. 'This territory is under Wehrmacht jurisdiction.'

'You hear that, boys?' the captain called out mockingly. 'The Wehrmacht want to take our little prize.' He turned his gaze back to the sergeant and his eyes were shards of ice. 'I don't see any "we",' he taunted. 'I see just you, Sergeant. You and a ragbag of conscripts, old men and a boy. We meet again, boy,' he said, staring at Karl. 'You should have listened to your sergeant. Tell you what we'll do. We'll, eh, question the prisoner and then, maybe, let the boy have her. Ricard can break her in first; he's good at that, aren't you, R—'

The miner moved before the captain had finished talking and had his rifle muzzle rammed into the man's throat before any of his henchmen could react. Belatedly, they raised their weapons.

'Six against two seems like long odds,' the captain said calmly.

Rudi and Kurt moved forward quickly to flank the sergeant and the miner. Karl was barely a half-pace behind. The captain's cold eyes flicked to the miner.

'Just how many men have you killed, soldier?' he drawled.

'You'll be the first,' the miner said and smiled.

Karl stiffened his left leg to stop the trembling pulse that shook his body. He saw something flicker in the captain's eyes as he looked along the rifle at the grinning miner. Maybe he sees someone more insane than himself, he wondered – the thought spasmed through his mind in time to his shaking leg. Maybe he senses the miner doesn't care – not since Elsa. Elsa ... that's it ... the girl—

The captain's voice overrode and halted his runaway thoughts. 'Doesn't seem fair,' he said. 'Let's swap.'

'Swap?' the sergeant grunted.

'Yes, you know, we give you the girl and we take one from you. Fair?'

The sergeant didn't answer.

The captain let his gaze slide along the men before him.

'Scholar, tradesman,' he listed with uncanny accuracy before his eyes travelled along the rifle-muzzle stuck in his throat. 'Killer,' he smiled. 'No. What about the boy?'

Karl felt as if an icy pain was boring into his forehead. The pain spread and reached like a band around his head. His vision blurred and the figures around him split and multiplied.

'No,' he heard the sergeant say, as if from a great distance.

'Pity,' the captain responded. 'Now we'll have to kill each other.'

'Me,' a strange voice said, 'take me.'

Karl's eyes came back into focus. Who had spoken? Was it his father, Kurt? The miner? The captain shifted his gaze to someone behind the line of soldiers.

'Ah,' he said, 'the leper speaks – the one who is in but not of the group – the outcast. What dark deeds did you do, little man,' he asked, 'to earn your exclusion? Never mind; we'll have plenty of time together to share our secrets.'

His face angled back to the sergeant.

'Agreed?'

'Agreed.'

The captain inclined his head and Steiger moved to his side.

Almost tenderly, the captain placed his hands around the girl's waist and hoisted her to her feet. 'Off you go, Liebchen,' he said, 'we've found ourselves a new friend to play with.' The Waffen lowered their arms and began to file away towards the personnel carrier. The miner kept his rifle where it was until the sergeant ordered him to stand down.

Gradually, the deadly tableau disintegrated. Karl slumped to the ground and knuckled his temples while Rudi stood over him, protectively. The miner offered his hand to the girl, who took it without fear. She stepped away from the captain, who dusted his knees and fixed his forage cap at a jaunty angle.

'It's a long road to Moscow, Sergeant,' he said breezily, 'I feel certain that we shall meet again.'

He sauntered away, whistling tonelessly. Steiger followed in his shadow, his shoulders slumped. Karl hoped he would turn so that he could signal his thanks in some way, but he disappeared from the square without looking back. After a short time, Karl heard the engine of the personnel carrier cough, catch and drive away. Before the sound had faded fully, he thought he heard the music of the harmonica.

'I know some Russian,' Kurt said to the sergeant.

'How many languages do you speak, Professor?'

'Eh, four, Sergeant.'

'And just as mouthy in every one of them, I'll bet,' the sergeant sighed. 'Talk to the girl.' He waved a hand in disgust at their surroundings. 'Try and find out what this is all about.'

Kurt sat a few feet from the girl and angled his body away from her as if they were taking in the view and chatting casually. He began to speak in a low, slow voice, carefully enunciating each word, apologising for what had happened.

'We are the Wehrmacht,' he said. 'Those others are—' He racked his brain for the appropriate word – 'animals.'

'*Da*,' she hissed and spat.

'The boy will be fine,' the sergeant assured Rudi. 'You go and get that damn driver to bring the truck. We'll billet here for the night. Wouldn't bet on that scum not organising an ambush up the road or dropping a few landmines as souvenirs. Killer,' he said, and the miner looked up. 'Would you have shot him?'

The miner looked away.

'They'd have turned you into a colander.'

The miner smiled. The sergeant stared at him for a long time before he put his hand on the miner's shoulder and leaned in close to whisper. 'You can get yourself killed in your own good time,' he said softly, 'just not yet. We may need you to help us out of this shit. Now, go into the trees and bring back some kindling. Put it right here in the square. If they come back, they'll come to the fire. We'll have the cover of the houses so we can send those devils back to Hell.'

The miner looked at the dangling corpses.

'They're mine,' the sergeant said. 'I'm the sergeant.'

The girl was wrapped in a greatcoat and ushered into one of the houses. Kurt explained that there would be a sentry on the door and she gave him the ghost of a smile.

'Well?' the sergeant asked.

'She said they arrived and started shooting,' Kurt said tiredly, 'just shooting – everything.'

'And the partisans?'

'None – not here. They'd heard a lot of shooting in the forest for the past few days. Maybe the partisans are in there somewhere, she wasn't sure. She said some of the villagers escaped and may be hiding there.' He paused and looked in bewilderment at the sergeant. 'Why, Sergeant?' he asked. 'Why did they do this?'

'She asked you that?'

'Yes. I couldn't answer. I didn't have the words, and even if I had—'

'Neither do I, Professor. Maybe all this talk of "*Untermenschen*" and "bestial Slavs" Berlin keeps pissing from the radio gets people thinking that other people aren't—'

'Aren't what?' Kurt persisted.

'Aren't people, you know, like us?'

'Jesus.' He started as the miner loomed beside him.

'Come,' the miner said.

'Boy, you stand guard on the girl,' the sergeant said. 'The rest of you kit up and come with me.'

'I want to go, sir,' Karl said.

The sergeant led him away from the others and leaned in close.

'Look, son,' he said, 'it's been a rough day. You don't need to see what's—'

'But I do, sir,' Karl said fiercely. 'When – when that captain chose me, I was afraid.'

'Well, you weren't alone there, son.'

'I know that, but if I don't face it—' His face contorted as he wrestled with his feelings. 'I'll always be afraid,' he blurted.

'Come,' the sergeant said. 'I'll get that fat-arsed driver to stand sentry. Come, quick-time now.'

The fire in the square lit their way to the edge of the forest. They cast huge shadows that crept before them to the treeline and then vanished. A silver moon sat in the topmost branches, casting a cold, fractured light that mottled the spaces between the trees. The miner forged ahead, limned with light, and the others clustered in his shadow, keeping their eyes fixed on the reassurance of his broad back. Karl noticed a change in the quality of the light and saw the trees before him harden into distinct shadows. Some of the trees bore scars, white slashes that perfumed the air with resin. They stepped into a clearing, silvered by the unobstructed moon, and a smell washed over them in fetid waves. It was a deep smell of decay the boy associated with a neighbour's dead dog he had found festering with flies behind an outhouse.

'Here,' the miner said.

At a signal from the sergeant, they fanned out until a few paces separated one man from another. They began to walk, their eyes fixed on the ground before them.

'Here,' one grunted.

'Here,' echoed another, as the bodies snagged their boots and the tangle of the dead became impenetrable.

'How many?' the sergeant asked.

'Hundreds,' the miner said.

The sergeant hunkered down and turned a corpse to face the moon. 'Russian soldiers,' he said, 'no arms of any kind.'

He swung his gaze around the clearing and veered away, like a scenting dog, to walk the treeline that bounded the clearing. Karl saw him circle, stop and stoop. After a few minutes, he trudged back to join them. He held out a hand, palm upwards, and shell cases sparkled in the moonlight.

'Machine gun,' he said, 'heavy calibre. The prints of the tripod are still there.'

'What will we do?' Rudi asked.

'I'll talk to von Kluge,' the sergeant answered.

They watched the girl walk towards the forest. Rudi had offered her his coat but the sergeant had restrained him. 'The partisans would shoot her,' he said. At the edge of the treeline, she turned and looked back. Karl thought he had never seen such beautiful green eyes.

During the night, he woke with a start. He had been walking over bodies in his dream, rows and rows of dead soldiers stacked side by side on a road that stretched all the way to the horizon.

THE UNIVERSITY OF ZAGREB

The archbishop had been as good as his word and that word seemed to carry some weight in the university. Within twenty-four hours of the dinner party, Max found himself joining the students who streamed through the university gates. More often than not, he found himself sitting alone at lectures and in the cafeteria. He wondered if it was his Austrian accent that accounted for his companions' coolness, but noticed that the Slovenes seemed to fit in seamlessly. No matter; if he could not be one of them, he would be superior to them, he resolved, and immersed himself in his studies.

Within a short time, he felt certain that he had no academic equal in his class except for the girl. Every time he answered a question or made a point in class, she questioned or countered until the bemused lecturer sat back and allowed a debate. While he tended to be dry and factual, she employed anecdote and humour, weaving bright colours to contrast with his grey logic and bringing the student body to her side. At first he felt threatened, convinced he was being made fun of. He sharpened his anger to sarcasm. She refused the invitation to become caustic and it made him look pedantic and mean-spirited by comparison. Almost unaware, he found himself imitating her style, revelling in word play and extrapolation, forsaking dour defence and sharp attack. When the bell ended the debate and the lecturer called for a vote, he was stunned to find the vote was split evenly between them.

He thought she was beautiful. She sat near one of the high windows in the lecture hall and the sunlight painted her like a Botticelli angel. He tried to ignore her and concentrate on a lecturer who made the Mongol invasion sound pedestrian. His eyes betrayed him, playing truant over and over again to the figure and features of the girl who sat apart, bathed in light.

'Max. Max Steiger.'

'Oh! You're the Austrian refugee everyone talks about.'

'They do?'

'Yes. They say you're a mongrel Croatian.'

'Mongrels have sharp teeth and short tempers, Miss—'

'Marija.'

She appraised him with cool, grey eyes before offering her hand. It felt cold and he wondered if he was feverish.

'You can buy me coffee while you tell me about the Anschluss,' she said, and stalked away. He contemplated letting her go but his feet were already moving him in her wake.

'So,' she said, attacking him with those grey eyes over the rim of her coffee cup, 'you Austrians just rolled over and invited Hitler to tickle your tummies?'

'And you Croats just put on your ridiculous national costumes and danced for Hitler's puppet, Poglavnik?'

'Hitler gave us our autonomy.'

'The puppet is separate from the puppet-master but there is the small, significant matter of strings. When Hitler and Mussolini sing, Croatia dances.'

'We have independent relations with Mussolini's Italy, Austrian.'

'Expensive relations, Croat. They get a few Croat cities and islands and you get the illusion of sovereignty.'

He was unaware of the crowd that had gathered around them in the cafeteria until a hand fell on his shoulder.'

'Is this bastard bothering you, Marija? I could teach him a lesson for you.'

'The ability to read and write are prerequisites to a teaching role,' Max said calmly.

'Enough,' Marija said coldly. 'Back off, Miroslav. We need to develop the Austrian's brains, not knock them all over the floor – at least, not yet.'

Miroslav huffed with disappointment and withdrew, the possibility of a fight and the crowd of students going with him.

'Is Miroslav typical of the intellectual might of the new Croatia?' Max enquired.

'Hardly,' she said, 'but if you want to have and to hold, you must do more than think about it.'

He saw an amused smile twitch her full lips. While he was still parsing her last remark, she was off again, swinging the strap of her book bag over her shoulder and not looking back to see if he was following.

'A church?'

'Why not? The Catholic Church and Croatia have always been two sides of the same coin.'

He looked around at the pews packed with students.

'And who preaches the sermon Pavelič?'

'Shush,' she warned as heads swung their way. She leaned closer so that her breath tickled his ear. 'The Franciscan friars have been champions of Croatian independence for generations,' she whispered. 'Now shut up and listen.'

The hum of subdued conversation dwindled and disappeared as an overweight Franciscan grunted into the pulpit.

'It's Sancho Panza,' he whispered, and her elbow caught him sharply under his ribcage. He sat back, rubbing the sore spot. It seemed to him that, as he did so, the entire congregation leaned forward in anticipation. After the first few sentences, he understood why. The Franciscan had a *basso profundo* voice that seemed to rumble through the floorboards and tingle up his legs to his belly. The preacher sketched the turmoil of Croatian history – the various invasions, betrayals and humiliations that Max's mother had told and retold, ad nauseam. The Franciscan's voice remained emotionless, delivering the flat facts of history as if he were reading a list of parish activities. And then, unexpectedly, he lifted his head and asked a question.

'The city crest of Zagreb,' he asked, 'what does it show?'

There was a moment of silence before someone in the front rows answered. Expert communicator that he was, the Franciscan repeated the answer for his congregation.

'Yes,' he said, 'it is a castle – a stronghold – a fortified keep. But there is something peculiar about this castle. What is it?' he challenged. The silence stretched and he allowed it extend to the tense limit before continuing, his voice climbing up the scale with each phrase. 'The red doors of our castle are wide open. Why? Because we gave up on ourselves. We accepted defeat and occupation. Come in, we said to the Mongols and the Hungarians and the Serbs; make yourselves at home. Take whatever you want.'

He paused and stretched out his arms.

'This is not the crest of the new Croatia,' he shouted and an angry hum buzzed through the congregation. 'The new Croatia is no longer a way-station for other powers – an open house for those who would take our lands, our jobs, our places at the university. Oh, they may attempt to do so again, but not with impunity.'

Max heard only snatches of what the preacher said above the rising roar of the congregation. Despite his cynicism, he felt the emotions of the students in the pews wash over him and threaten to overcome him. He looked at Marija and she was rigid and pale, a pulse beating wildly in her throat. Slowly, the preacher brought them down from their frenzy.

'You,' he assured them, 'are our future. You are the ones who can take the places forbidden to your parents. Take up the cross of Croatia and hold it high and scatter our enemies. This is your birthright and your challenge.'

He disappeared from the pulpit, leaving a roil of emotions behind him. Max saw students embrace and weep or sit stunned in their pews as if puzzled by the preacher's absence. He locked eyes with Marija. 'What?' he whispered. She grabbed his hand and tugged him behind her, elbowing a path to the door.

Her flat was on the third floor, under the canted eaves of a building, sour with the smell of cabbage. She locked the door behind them and tore at his clothes; her mouth pressed to his, gnawing at him as if she meant to devour him. They tumbled into the narrow bed, exploring each other's bodies with lips and fingers until they climaxed breathlessly.

'Hey, Austrian!' The slap of her palm on his naked buttocks shocked him awake. 'Shower and dress,' she said, towelling her hair before a spotted mirror. Her breast peeked from underneath the towel and he began to be aroused. 'Put it in your pants,' she said, 'we'll be late.'

'Late for what?'

A car this size is not designed to hold six passengers, he fretted irritably, as the freighted vehicle hit another pothole. The occupants were shaken violently, so that he had to endure the unwelcome intimacy of various body parts pressed against his own. They sang songs he didn't know and one student managed to smoke a cigarette, even though he lay across the laps of those sitting in the back. Max lowered the window and ignored the protests as cold air spiralled around him. He knew from the growl of the engine that they were climbing into the mountains. The road snaked in such tight curves that it threatened to consume its own tail. He pressed his face to the cool window and saw the headlights of other cars beading the dark behind them.

The barn stood apart from the ruin of the farmhouse, a skeleton of charred timbers straddling the space where the roof had been before the fire. Black, sooty triangles hung underneath blind windows, and the breeze carried the faint memory of old smoke. Inside the barn, an iron stove battled gamely against the huge, cold space and students sprawled, singly and in pairs, on bales grown shaggy with neglect. Max raised an eyebrow at Marija.

'Wait,' she mouthed.

He was unsurprised to see a familiar figure enter the barn. Somehow, the machine gun he cradled in his arms didn't seem incongruous. The Franciscan was followed and then flanked by two armed men in black uniforms.

'Ustashe,' she whispered in his ear. 'To rise up,' he translated mentally. So this was Pavelić's über army, modelled by the Poglavnik on Hitler's SS.

The Franciscan waited for their attention to gather and focus before he spoke.

'Croatians lived in that farmhouse,' he said in a matter-of-fact voice, 'probably been there for generations, working poor land and barely scraping a living. They thought they were safe as well. For sure they had Serb neighbours, but why would anyone covet the little they had? It wasn't about the few cows or the money kept in a tin box under the hearth. It wasn't about the vegetables, or the goat or the hay, as you can see. It was because they were Croat and Catholic – that was reason enough for someone to shit in the vegetable store, kill the goat and lock the family in the house before they torched the thatch. Those who lived and died in that farmhouse were "open door" Croats, we are not. They were "turn the other cheek" Catholics; we hold to an older scriptural text, "an eye for an eye – a tooth for a tooth".'

At a signal from the Franciscan, one of the Ustashe tumbled a haybale to reveal a long, wooden crate. He tipped the lid, and the clatter as it hit the stone floor swung every eye to the guns.

The Orthodox church stood in a hollow between two hills, with the small houses of the village tucked into its shadow. They had left the cars and walked the final mile, breathing the damp mountain air, hearing nothing but the tread of their feet and the occasional squawk of a roosting bird.

Max struggled to keep up with the pace set by the Ustashe soldier in front while concentrating on keeping the one at the rear from trampling his heels. He carried a pistol in his hand, chosen for him by the smiling Franciscan. 'He who is not for us is against us,' the Franciscan quoted cheerfully, as he checked the magazine before handing it over.

The plan, set out by the priest, was simple. They would drive the villagers into the church and burn the village.

Max had seen sheepdogs working the high meadows over Hallstatt, harrying the flocks with quick feints and nips until the frightened animals squeezed into a pen. Sheep didn't scream, he thought, as the first wails rose from the houses. Sheep didn't have babies bouncing in shawls as they ran before the dogs. What sheep and people did have in common was a potential for panic. Panic, he knew, could push a man or animal against the herd instinct.

Even as that thought flashed into his head, a young man burst from a flaming door with a scythe raised over his head. The surprise panicked the hunters into a volley of shots that tore rags of flesh from his body and rolled thunder up the valley before them.

Mutely, he watched tendrils of straw that seemed to flirt with the torches before the whole roof caught and gobbled up the flames. He ran the gauntlet of burning houses, smelling his scorched jacket and the promise of agony on his exposed skin, searching for Marija, hoping to find an oasis of sanity in her eyes. Through streaming eyes, he squinted at the forms and faces that flitted in and out of the inferno around him. In despair, he turned completely around and stood rooted. The avenue of burning houses led his eyes to the church, shape-shifting in the boiling air. Above the bass, burning sounds around him, high soprano screams rose and needled into his brain – flames that had been reflected in the church windows had moved inside.

'No,' he gasped and began to run, heedless of the heat that sucked at him from either side until he stood before the church doors. They seemed to bulge rhythmically outwards, like a pulse, from the frantic pounding of those inside. The screaming escalated until his ears hurt and then a machine gun coughed explosively. It stitched a line of gashes across the door, shooting splinters to spray up and out and disappear. The windows suddenly blossomed with flame and the screaming stopped.

She was standing on a flat stone, near where they had entered the village. He hadn't noticed before how small she was. She stood with her hand shading her eyes from the glare and he stopped directly before her and waited for her eyes to focus on him. It seemed to take a long time, as if they had to come from some distant horizon. They stared at each other in silence, both bringing words to their lips and then swallowing them as inadequate. Others filed past. Max thought they looked older in the unforgiving light, their mouths hanging open as if searching for air.

Finally, there was only him and Marija. She was still standing on the stone, white and immobile, like the woman in the Old Testament story who looked back.

'You two, come with me.'

The gravelly voice of the Franciscan severed them from their trance. He led them up a winding hill path until they came to a clearing, where he turned to face them. Max was aware of the Ustashe pair closing up behind. 'Her bag,' the priest grunted and Max saw her stagger as an Ustashe man snagged the bag from her shoulder. She regained her balance and didn't protest as he emptied the contents on the grass. With a resigned expression, the big man sorted through the items with his boot. His brown habit drank the available light and looked black. A faint glimmer from the white cincture at his waist gave some explanation for the bearded face that seemed to float before them.

'Ah, Marija,' the Franciscan sighed sadly. With infinite weariness, he bent and picked a camera from the pile. 'The ubiquitous Marija,' he continued as if to himself, 'always here, there and everywhere. It was Miroslav who told us. Don't think too harshly of him, he didn't want to but he did – eventually.'

Marija gave a short strangled cry and her shoulders slumped, resignedly.

'Why did you do this?' the Franciscan asked. 'Who was it for? Catholic action? Some priest who thinks his collar makes him stateless? Who was it?' he bellowed, and she quailed before him like a slender branch before a storm. But she didn't answer.

The priest waited, his face as stern as stone, and then he nodded. In his peripheral vision, Max saw the black shape move behind her. There was a sudden gleam of steel and she crumpled to the ground. He started towards her and was pulled up short by the pistol rammed under his chin. Above the pounding of his heart, he could hear a terrible, wet, sucking sound. The Franciscan stepped into his eyeline.

'And you, Austrian,' he said, looking intently into Max's eyes. 'Confession is good for the soul. Speak now,' he whispered, bending to touch his forehead to the boy's.

'Were you lovers?' he whispered.

Max looked into his eyes and thought they seemed huge with understanding and forgiveness.

'Yes,' he breathed.

'Did you know of the camera?'

Max felt he had moved to a calm, uncaring place, a place beyond terror. He heard the wet gasps from somewhere to his left and dragged his attention back to those eyes and the sound of his own breathing.

'Did you?'

'No, I did not.'

The dark eyes held him, and cradled him in their immense well of comfort.

'Do you swear it, on your life?'

'I do.'

'I believe you,' the priest said and took a step back. As if a door had been opened, the ambient sounds flooded his ears. He heard and felt the rasp of the muzzle as the gun skidded from under his chin. He heard the small sounds of a shoe shifting on grass and the creak of leather as the weapon was holstered. And peaking above all those sounds, he heard Marija's efforts at breathing through the mouth that had been opened in her throat.

'She used you,' the Franciscan said, 'used you as a distraction. It is a sin to use another human being. Only you can absolve her.'

The realisation of what was being suggested bubbled up slowly through the sludge that seemed to have filled Max's body.

'I – I can't,' he whispered.

'She is drowning in her own blood, boy,' the priest said softly. 'It could take a long time. If you ever felt anything for her, show her mercy. We will wait for you.'

The priest and his companions trudged back along the path until they were out of sight. Max forced himself to look at Marija and at the ruin of her throat. Her eyes found his and flinched at his reaction. She tried to speak and a bubble of blood ballooned and burst between her lips. Her eyes beseeched him.

He scrubbed himself from scalp to toe with the acrid-smelling soap, sluiced his body by immersing himself in the bath water and started soaping again.

'Boy,' the bass voice vibrated through the door, 'there are fresh clothes here for you. Leave by the door at the end of the corridor.

Take two left turns and then the right turn by the shrine of the Madonna. You must never come back here. When we want you, we will find you.'

He heard the footsteps recede from the door and began his ritual scrubbing again – and again, until his skin felt flayed and there were white whorls on his fingerpads when he stumbled from the bath.

GENERAL VON KLUGE'S HQ, EAST OF SMOLENSK

The euphoria of battle had long gone. Some of the one and a half million men under von Kluge's command had already readied their weapons and kit for the next stage of the advance. Between the tents that formed a huge arc to the east of Smolensk, they congregated and spoke in excited whispers of Vyazma, Bryansk and Borodino, the major towns that beaded and flanked the road between Smolensk and Moscow. Others sat slumped on camp-stools or lay, wide-eyed, on their cots, projecting the horrors they had seen on the blank canvas wall of the tent. All felt grateful to be alive – grateful and guilty that the camp was pitched east of Smolensk and the smell blew west.

The sergeant strode, tight-lipped, down the avenue between the serried tents. Something in the set of his shoulders and the jut of his chin turned men away to concentrate on their tasks and spread a pall of silence before him.

The sentry watched the sergeant storm towards the general's tent and decided to direct his attention elsewhere. The officer inside the tent flap was not so circumspect.

'The general is busy,' he snapped, 'come back later.'

'Stand aside, Horst,' von Kluge said from the map table, 'the sergeant never retreats.'

He stood up and regarded the old soldier warily, a marker pen still clutched in his fingers.

'He's right, Frederick,' he said wearily, 'I am busy. Spit it out.'

The sergeant didn't embellish or emote. Tonelessly, he detailed the facts and waited for the general's response.

'Do you know who that Waffen troop are?' von Kluge asked.

'I know what they are.'

'They are Hitler's blue-eyed boys, Frederick,' the general continued, lowering his voice. 'They march to his drum and no other. He's even decorated their captain with the Knight's Cross.'

'He must have run out of humans to honour.'

'Frederick,' the general sighed, 'you must face facts. They belong to the golden circle. What do you expect me to do?'

'I expect you to court martial and hang the bastards.'

'And what evidence would I present?'

'A whole forest full of evidence.'

'Frederick, Frederick, climb down from your high-minded mountain, come back to the real world. We are at war. Smolensk is behind us and one big push will finish the war. That has to be our focus. I can't afford to deploy troops to lug dead bodies from a forest. Anyway, think what it would do to morale.'

'I saw what it did to morale, General. I saw good men – Wehrmacht soldiers, up to their shins in slaughtered, unarmed prisoners. They asked me what we should do. "I'll talk to von Kluge," I said. And that's what I'm doing, reporting to you on the murderers you sent me out to hunt. Barbarians, you called them, who'll make barbarians of us all.'

'Things happen in wartime, Frederick, dreadful things we would never approve of. But, at this point, I can't ask Berlin to—'

'We are not in Berlin, General, we are at the front. *You* are Berlin here. Your decision is what matters.'

'My decision is to take no further action in this matter.'

'And is that decision based on the facts or on how the wind is blowing in Berlin?'

'You overstep yourself, Sergeant.'

'General, listen to me. "We are the Wehrmacht," you said. "We're not like those Waffen SS bastards," you said, and you were right. We have codes of conduct – rules about how we treat our enemy. Ivan knows that. The Russians showed a white flag and then shot three of our men in the back. We took no prisoners for the rest of that engagement. That's fair, General; both sides understand that. But if you don't punish the Waffen for this, what message does that send to the Russians? That rules no longer apply? We've scrapped the code of conduct? That we're all Waffen bastards and whichever side happens to have the most bastards will—'

'Enough! My decision stands.'

'Then what of my patrol, General? The Waffen will hunt them down; it's what they do.'

'Lose them, Sergeant. Deploy them out of harm's way. Except for the professor; I want him on my staff.'

He picked up a slim volume from the map table.

'Did you know that Napoleon had his own historian accompany him to Moscow? Oh, yes, de Caulaincourt told the Emperor's story and it's still read by military men. The professor will tell our story.'

'All of it, sir?'

'You are dismissed, Sergeant.'

★

'Horses?'

'Yes, horses.'

'We don't know anything about horses,' Rudi said doubtfully.

'You don't know anything about guns either, do you?' the sergeant snapped. 'All right,' he relented, 'hear me out. You saw something the brass say didn't exist. That makes you wrong. They don't want you to talk about it, because if you don't, it never happened.'

'But it did happen, Sergeant,' Karl said. 'We saw—'

'You saw nothing, boy. This is the new Wehrmacht. We see no evil and, especially, we say no evil. Understand? Get that into his skull,' he said to Rudi, 'or the Waffen will put a bullet there. So you are being deployed to the horses. This is a mechanised army so no one gives a shit for horses, don't want to be any way near them. Which means you'll be invisible. Keep your mouths shut, your heads down and shovel shit and maybe you'll survive.'

Max went to the university every day and sat beneath the high window in the lecture hall, so that he wouldn't have to look for her in that place. He shunned the company of other students, taking his lunch outside under the trees and immersing himself in the library until the last student had tiptoed out and the librarian had cleared his throat and jangled his keys. 'Why not save a little for tomorrow?' the old man had remarked and then busied himself with the locks, taken aback at the blankness of the boy's stare.

He returned each evening to his uncle's study and read the bloody contents of a mound of letters, plucking them from the floor and filing them neatly in cardboard containers trying to expiate his guilt by this small service to the dead. His uncle asked anxiously after his health and then stopped asking, baffled and rebuffed by perfunctory replies.

When the archbishop summoned him to express his congratulations at his excellent end of term results, he knelt and kissed his ring and then waited until the prelate had run out of things to say and dismissed him. His uncle's study became his personal purgatory where he would allow a photograph of a Serb woman with mutilated breasts scourge him for a moment before he filed it away with the others. He did not return to himself. He reasoned that that self was no more and could not be reclaimed. Instead, he unlocked that cold place inside him – that part of himself he had kept hidden since Hallstatt – and listened to its voice.

'You were nothing to Marija,' it said. 'She used you as a cover for her activities and as a relief for her lust. At the end, you'd have shown a mangled dog the same mercy. They think they own you now, Max. Let them think that. Be dutiful, studious and invisible. They will find you again when they want something from you. Don't resist. Do what they ask and do extra. Don't allow them to have power over you. Remember, "from the man who is willing to give you everything, there is nothing you can take". Be cunning, Max, as cunning as a serpent.'

He began to make copies of every single document that passed through his hands. He savoured none of them, never felt any twinge of excitement when a file revealed Stepinac's knowledge of atrocities or the names of those in the Vatican who encouraged his silence for the sake of the Church. The Franciscan appeared in the documents and photographs on a regular basis. Sometimes he was accompanied by members of his own religious order but most often he was flanked by Ustashe militia. In one photograph, he posed with his machine gun on a mound of dead bodies. A rough map was pencilled on the back, giving the location of the ravine and enclosing a name in brackets (Fra Filipovic). He copied the map and placed it in the phantom file he kept under his bed.

THE HORSE COMPOUND, GERMAN CENTRE ARMY COMMAND

Karl wondered what the horse master would look like. He imagined he must look like some ramrod Prussian or like the centaurs, the man–horse hybrids he had seen as a child at the Spanish School in Vienna. He proved to be a short, wiry man with smiling eyes.

'You must be the volunteers,' he said wryly, when they presented for duty at the stables.

'We know nothing about horses,' Rudi insisted stubbornly. 'I told the sergeant as much.'

'Ah, but the horses don't know that,' the horse master said good-naturedly. 'I'm called Herman,' he added. He shook hands with each of them, repeating their names as if bedding them down in his memory. 'Have any of you ever worked with a horse before?' he asked hopefully.

The miner and Karl shook their heads.

'No,' Rudi said, 'unless you count Bismarck, a carthorse I took to the forest sometimes to draw timber.'

'And what did you learn from Bismarck, Rudi?'

'He had a mind of his own.'

'Yes, they're a lot like people that way,' Herman mused, 'except most horses are rather more intelligent than most people; more moral too, on the whole. Come!'

The makeshift stables were bordered by a meadow on the edge of the camp. Karl was relieved to discover that it was on the opposite end to the Waffen encampment. He didn't think he could bear to hear that harmonica again. Rudi sniffed disparagingly at the timber and tarpaulin structure but Karl was impressed by the cleanliness of the stables. He counted twenty horses and saw how each one acknowledged the arrival of the horse master. Some snorted into nosebags while others tossed their heads or craned them expectantly over the half-doors. Herman greeted each one in a soft, unhurried voice, obligingly rubbing a muzzle or scratching behind a flicking ear. The stallion was stabled at the rear and Karl was struck by the size of the animal. It tapped a hoof on the floor and nodded briefly at Herman.

'This is Roland,' he said, as if introducing an equal. 'Now, which of you fearless warriors is most afraid of him?'

'Me,' the miner said promptly, and they laughed.

'People say horses know that, Tomas,' the horse master said, 'and they're right, but Roland isn't the kind of horse to take advantage.'

He placed his hand on the miner's shoulder and led him close to the stable.

'I give you my word,' he said, 'the horse will not harm you.'

He turned the miner so that he had his back to the horse.

'Keep your hands at your side and let him sniff you out.'

As if on cue, the huge head craned forward and sniffed the miner's back. Karl saw the tension ease from the miner's shoulders as the horse nudged him gently.

'Now turn around slowly, Tomas, and rub his nose,' the horse master invited.

The horse snorted explosively and the miner hesitated before transferring his stroking hand to the animal's neck.

'You are a natural, Tomas,' the horse master said approvingly.

Karl and his father went through the same ritual with similar results, much to Herman's satisfaction. Briefly, he detailed and delegated their chores with the admonition to move slowly.

'Stay calm,' he said. 'If you two need me, I'll be seeing to a stone bruise at the other end.'

'I wonder what Kurt's doing?' Karl wondered aloud as he and Rudi shovelled companionably.

'Probably the same as us,' Rudi grunted, 'except he's shovelling a different class of shit.'

They leaned on their shovels to laugh.

To General von Kluge. From Kurt Brandt at Roslavl, 130 kilometres from Moscow

General,

Any report you receive from your officers here that doesn't include the word 'scheisse' has been edited.

At the village of Kosseki, our advance was halted and then repulsed after savage hand-to-hand fighting with the Russians, who came at us in waves. They seem to have an endless supply of men and equipment. The unit I am attached to was obliged to withdraw, abandoning tanks and artillery. The men are shamed and angry at this setback.

A short time ago, during a lull in the fighting, the broadcast from Berlin was relayed to us. It included references to Russian soldiers as 'bestial animals' etc. I overheard a young officer remark, 'We must be fighting in the wrong place.'

I am at Roslavl now, where Colonel General Guderian has amassed his tanks in anticipation of a push on Moscow. In fact, I am writing this report in the turret of a captured Russian tank. The Panzers are being whittled away, even as we advance, and fully one quarter of General Guderian's tank force is made up of captured tanks.

Remember Murat and his costly cavalry charges in 1812?

Kurt Brandt

GENERAL VON KLUGE'S HQ

'*Scheisse*,' General von Kluge hissed.

He crumpled the message in his fist and stamped away from the courier to stare sightlessly at the map table.

'Do you wish to send a reply, General?' the courier asked.

Von Kluge flattened the mangled message on the map table. He didn't need to read it again. He only needed to remember who had signed it. The name Adolf Hitler was printed in small letters after the terse message. It had been creased by his frustrated gesture and now he tried to smooth it with the tip of a trembling forefinger. 'Act in haste, repent at leisure,' he whispered.

'Pardon, sir?'

'Message received and understood,' he snapped. 'Tell the radio operators to contact the commanding officers at the front. They are to return to HQ immediately.'

'*Scheisse*,' he said again, when the courier was safely outside the tent.

There was a stunned silence after he'd read the message to them. He could see fury in some faces, satisfaction in others and caution in all.

'Could you read it again' General von Bock asked. Kluge thought Der Sterber looked like someone who had been awarded a marshal's baton only to have it snatched from him at the last minute. He did as requested in a flat, emotionless voice.

'"You are directed to halt your advance towards Moscow and regroup your forces. I have identified Kiev, the capital of the Ukraine, as our primary objective." Signed Adolf Hitler.'

Von Bock broke the silence.

'But turning south jeopardises the main operation,' he whispered.

Von Kluge was amazed to hear his commanding officer utter even an implied criticism of Der Führer and was unsurprised by Halder's forthright opinion. 'This zigzag nonsense is no way to win a war,' the general snapped.

Von Kluge turned his attention to the other two, von Mannstein and Weichs. He knew both men might be cavalier in battle but they were politically cautious.

'The Russians depend on Kiev for the materials to supply their armies,' von Mannstein said evenly. 'If we break their supply lines, we will break their armies.'

'Also,' Weichs added, 'they have a large army at Kiev. We can't afford to have it on our flank as we advance on Moscow. Napoleon failed because he failed to annihilate the Russian army.'

Eventually, all eyes in the room centred on von Kluge.

'I have every confidence in Der Führer,' he said and smiled inwardly as von Bock and Halder struggled to hide their irritation. 'We are, of course, eager to press on to Moscow, but generals von Mannstein and Weichs are correct – Napoleon did not smash the Russian army either in a definitive battle or by cutting off their supplies. We cannot allow history to repeat itself. Heil Hitler.'

The salute effectively signalled that the meeting was over and the generals filed slowly from the tent until only General Halder and Kurt Brandt remained. Von Kluge expected Halder's anger to erupt again but the general seemed uncharacteristically subdued.

'You know we underestimated them?' he said quietly.

'Who?'

'The Russians, who else? We were told they were ill-prepared for a war, armies of poorly paid conscripts. And so they were. We were told that they were a rabble and would run before us. All that may have been true, in the beginning, but now? We believed, before Barbarossa, that they had two hundred divisions. That means we've already killed or captured their entire peace-time army.' He shook his head in disbelief before continuing. 'And they come up with new armies. At the last count, they have three hundred and sixty divisions in the field. Are they well-armed and well-equipped? No! Often, we see the second wave pick up the rifles of those we've killed. Are they well-led? No, with some exceptions. Many of them probably wouldn't fight at all if the commissars didn't have pistols at their backs. But they are there We smash a dozen divisions and another dozen appear from somewhere to take their place. They're like some fucking Colossus or——? What was that many-headed monster in mythology?'

He turned a quizzical eye to Kurt. 'Waiters tend to know that sort of thing,' he said, with the hint of a smile.

'Hydra, sir,' Kurt answered.

'Hydra! Yes, that's the one. You cut off a head and it grows two more. And now the war moves south and we sit here and wait. How many heads will the Hydra grow in the meantime?' he asked, rising stiffly from his stool.

After he'd left, von Kluge produced a bottle and two glasses.

'So how do we kill a Hydra, Professor?' he asked as he poured.

Kurt sniffed the wine appreciatively before answering. 'Actually, there are a number of different accounts——'

'I think one would suffice, Professor,' the general interrupted, dryly.

'Very well. Hercules discovered the monster's weakness – one of its heads was mortal. As he cut off the others, he cauterised the wounds with fire so that no more heads could grow. When he'd isolated the single mortal head, he crushed it under a stone.'

The general nodded and sipped his wine before replying.

'So, von Mannstein is right,' he said. 'Annihilate the Russian armies and cauterise them with fire until we are faced with just one enemy target at Moscow and one mortal enemy – Stalin.'

'That is just one scenario, General.'

'I should have let the sergeant shoot you.'

'Pardon, sir?'

'Nothing.' Von Kluge held his wine glass to his forehead. 'Please, go on.'

'There are other sources which describe how the dying Hydra poisoned the rivers with its blood so that the fish died. Others say its poisoned blood soaked into Hercules' cloak and——'

'Enough,' the general said, raising his hands in surrender. 'So the Russian will burn all the food, fodder and shelter between here and Moscow and sap our strength at Kiev?'

'Yes, General. And one more thing, sir.'

'God in Heaven, what?'

'It's raining.'

ZAGREB

Could it be only three months since he'd come to Zagreb? Hallstatt seemed like a lifetime away. So much had happened. Marija's ghostly eyes opened inside his head to beseech him, as they often did, and he raised his face so that the rain would wash her image away.

Marija and Elsa, Max reminded himself, had been sent to test him. He had not deviated from his path. He had returned to his studies at the university with even more fervour and to helping his uncle. The fact that the other students gave him a wide berth didn't bother him. It was a comfort to return to the aloneness he had experienced when he'd first arrived. Sometimes, he caught his uncle looking at him anxiously, a question trembling on his tongue. It was a question he didn't ask. He asked regularly after his nephew's health but that was a ritual question – a safe question, for which Max provided a ritual answer so that their relationship continued, undisturbed. He wiped the rain from his eyes with the heel of his hand and walked on.

He didn't understand why people disliked rain. They blundered by him on the pavement, bent under the weight of protective clothing or cowering under puny umbrellas. He liked walking in the rain, partly because he knew how much his mother would disapprove, but mostly because it reduced distractions and allowed him time to think.

His thoughts turned to Father Kyril and he smiled. The limpet-priest had insisted on staying in Zagreb until Max had 'fully recovered', and the monsignor had been obliged to arrange a chaplaincy for him with an order of enclosed nuns. Max's smile widened at the irony. He imagined Kyril preaching to a metal grille and receiving his meals through a hatch in his dining room wall. Father Kyril had succeeded in surrounding himself with women while never getting to see a single one. If Max believed in God, he might have believed He had a cruel sense of humour. What was less humorous was Father Kyril's regular visits to the Archbishop's Palace. Happily, Max's schedule at the university kept him away from early morning to late evening and it was the monsignor who bore the burden of those visits.

'He's been coming at all hours and making a nuisance of himself,' his frazzled uncle had admitted. 'I'm afraid the porter wouldn't admit him last time because he suspected he'd been drinking. Please, Max, could you call or write to him – it might calm his concern for you?'

He didn't intend to do either. He saw the priest as an umbilicus that stretched back to Hallstatt and his mother. He had no intention of ever returning to that cold womb. Whatever motives she'd had for poisoning her son, the consequences had included his translation to a new life.

He was hanging his soaked coat on the stand beside the door when his uncle approached.

'Ah, Max. There you are at last. I'm afraid we have a little problem. Father Kyril came about an hour ago, demanding to see you. He was quite drunk and I couldn't put him in the reception room because we have a number of visitors waiting to see—'

'Where is he, Uncle?'

'I put him in your room, it seemed to calm him. Max! Max!'

The photographs were strewn across the coverlet. Father Kyril looked up guiltily.

'I'm sorry, Max,' he mumbled, 'they were …'

He turned beseeching eyes on the boy.

'Max, we must go home,' he quavered. 'This country – these people—'

'It's out of the question.'

'I must insist, Max. I came down here as your guardian and have a moral—'

'You have no obligation to me, Father. You did your duty and now you should return to Hallstatt.'

'No! I will not go without you. I can't leave you here, my son.'

'I'm not your—'

The look in the priest's eyes robbed Max of his breath.

'No,' he said finally.

'Don't judge us, Max,' the priest pleaded. 'We were both young – and lonely.'

'No,' Max said again, shaking his head as if he could dislodge the reality.

'I will confess my sin to your uncle,' the priest whined. 'He is a compassionate man. Then I will take you home to your mother.'

Max sat on the bed and motioned Father Kyril to do the same.

'Father Kyril,' he said calmly, 'there is no need to involve the monsignor. I don't think my mother would like you to divulge this to anyone, least of all her brother.'

Father Kyril nodded dumbly.

'A train leaves Zagreb for Vienna at midnight,' Max continued. 'We could meet at the station. I'll carry on my work here to avoid any suspicion or questions. Will you do this for me, Father? The journey will give us a chance to talk.'

'Yes, yes,' the priest breathed. 'Oh, Max, I'm so relieved. This has been weighing on my soul for so many—'

'Please, Father, you need to go now. Remember, midnight at the railway station.'

THE FRANCISCAN FRIARY, ZAGREB

'He was hanging around the safe house,' the Ustashe man said.

The Franciscan rose from his knees and wrapped the rosary slowly around his fist as he spoke.

'I told you not to go there,' he said flatly.

'I needed to see you. There was no other way of making contact. I could have knocked on all the Franciscan doors in Zagreb, but I didn't think you'd appreciate that.'

'You were right – I wouldn't have. So now you're seeing me.'

'Alone.'

The Franciscan inclined his head and the door closed behind Max.

'Well?'

'My uncle is—'

'I know who the monsignor is and what he is.'

'The monsignor has documents, letters and reports from all over Croatia. They describe ... actions, actions taken against the Orthodox Serbs by the Ustashe and others.'

'So the monsignor is "a man of letters"?' the Franciscan said, smiling bleakly at his own joke. 'They're just words, little Max.'

'They're also evidence.'

'Evidence? A letter scrawled by some Serb is evidence? I think not, not in a Croatian court. We've gone beyond words, boy, don't you see that?'

'There are also photographs,' Max said and felt an angry thrill as the big, bearded face tightened. 'There are boxes of them,' he continued calmly. 'Most are of mutilated women, but some are of people posing with dead bodies, mounds of them. There are six photographs of you, Fra Filipovic.'

The Franciscan took a sudden step forward and looped his rosary around Max's neck.

'Why didn't I kill you the first time?' he growled.

Max held his gaze.

'Perhaps you had a premonition that this day would come, Father,' he said, 'a day when you'd need me. The monsignor plans to give the material to Archbishop Stepinac.'

'Stepinac is a coward; he would never—'

'Cowards,' Max interrupted, 'especially if they are archbishops, refer everything to Rome. I know because I've read the files.'

He felt the grip of the rosary relax a little.

'I can tell you where the material is and how to get it.'

'And?'

'And you can do something for me.'

★

Father Kyril placed his bag carefully on the platform and unbuttoned his coat. He started at the bottom button and worked his way up, as he always did. His jacket pocket yielded identity papers, money and two train tickets. He replaced them and buttoned his coat, starting again at the bottom button. He looked around him for a few moments, squinting at the sleeping engines and unlit carriages in the sidings before his eyes swung back to the station clock. It was eleven forty-five. Good, he nodded, it's always best to be early – to allow for the unexpected. He detested the unexpected, took no pleasure in surprise. 'I prefer my *tempus* not to *fugit*,' he'd said to a colleague once. The man hadn't appreciated the joke or the concept. Yes, time was important and he preferred it to pass slowly.

Except, he reminded himself, the time he'd spent ministering to the strictly enclosed sisters in that awful convent. The silence there had bothered him. He was a man who appreciated the value of silence, but the profound and unending silence of the convent had reduced him to tiptoeing along its highly polished floors where even the faint creak of his shoes seemed to rebuke him. For the first time in his life, he'd felt loud. Vestments seemed to rustle loudly and crackle their starch when he put them on for mass. The spoon, tapping his egg at breakfast, sounded like a drum roll. Occasionally, he heard them, the sisters. Once it was the faint swish of a robe as someone disappeared from the sacristy just a heartbeat before he entered. Another time he heard muted laughing coming from behind the grille as he preached to his invisible congregation. It was so brief, he'd wondered if he'd imagined it and spent the whole day pondering why they'd laughed. It was like living in a haunted house, he concluded, and shivered.

He checked the clock again. It was eleven fifty. Max would be here soon and they would leave this violent country where women could be brutally desecrated and tossed into ravines or herded into churches to burn. He didn't want to think about that. Max would come and they would sit on the train and talk and all would be well.

He was distracted by a sound, a shuffling sound that intruded on his reverie. It seemed to come from the canal of shadows that flowed beyond the edge of the platform where the trains ran. Cautiously, he took a few steps forward and squinted into the darkness. He saw nothing. Finally, against all his instincts and the warnings repeated in childhood, he stepped to the edge of the platform. As his eyes adjusted, he saw the outline of a man crouching between the faintly glimmering tracks. 'Excuse me,' he said and started back as the man lurched upright. He saw a bright flash and something struck him in the chest. His knees buckled and he slumped to the platform. Father Kyril felt no pain. He wondered if his coat would be soiled by the gritty platform and why he had such difficulty breathing and when Max would come.

THE ARCHBISHOP'S PALACE, ZAGREB

'Ah, still working, Max.'

The monsignor sank into his favourite chair beside the fire and stretched his legs. 'It's been a long day, nephew,' he sighed, 'delegations and invitations.'

Max nodded sympathetically and continued to file.

'A Muslim group came from Glina begging the archbishop to intercede on behalf of the Jews. I must confess, I never thought I'd see the day.'

'Historically, the Muslims tended to treat the Jews very well,' Max offered, 'especially in Andalusia. I don't think we Catholics can claim the same.'

'We did have some popes who were very well disposed towards them,' the monsignor said, 'but not many and certainly not the present incumbent. Pacelli has been curiously silent on that question. He does make vague references, but the world needs a more vigorous voice.'

He sighed and held his palms to the fire. 'Our own government isn't any better,' he confided, 'truth to tell, they're much worse. I have reports of the Ustashe identifying Jews for the Germans and even doing the round-up themselves.'

'Where do they take them?'

'No one seems to be sure. I've heard rumours of holding camps and labour camps dotted throughout the country. Someone mentioned a place called Danica but the name means nothing to me. There aren't enough hours in the day, Max. I feel like that fellow in mythology – pushing a boulder up a hill every day only to start all over again the next day.'

'I'm afraid you're not at all as cunning as Sisyphus, Uncle,' Max said gently. 'Here, come and see.'

He opened one of the black cardboard boxes and rifled his finger over the neat ranks of files.

'I've numbered and labelled them,' he said. 'Also, there's a list of contents on each file cover. This,' he added, tapping a black box, 'is where the photographs are filed. Just another few days, Uncle, and you'll be ready to put all this before the archbishop.'

'You've worked wonders, Max, thank you,' the monsignor said gratefully. 'Now, I really must go to bed.'

'Let me lock this lot up in the cupboard before you go,' Max said quickly. When all the files were safely locked away, he handed the keys to his uncle.

'Better safe than sorry,' he said.

LATER

When he was a little boy, his mother would call up the stairs, 'Go to sleep, Max.'

Even then, he would puzzle over that injunction. Is sleep something you can do? Is it like scratching your head or tying your laces? Something you can perform? Surely, the harder you try to sleep, the more sure you are to be awake, tensed up by the effort? As for 'going to sleep', isn't it obvious that sleep comes for us, taking us so softly that we can't remember the moment?

Sleep would not come for him this night and he turned his mind to other things. He replayed the instructions he had given the Franciscan. His uncle slept very soundly. The duplicate key was under the carpet just inside the door. They'd assured him that they had lock-picks for all the doors. 'Take some other things,' he insisted, 'it must look like a burglary.'

He woke some time later, and coughed. Groggily, he swung his legs out of the bed and groped for the glass of water on his bedside locker. He coughed again and the spasm seemed to shake him into awareness. Smoke! He lit the lamp and saw smoke eddy under the door. 'Fire,' he shouted, and continued shouting in the corridor, until he realised he'd inhaled smoke and he dropped to all fours. By instinct, he found his way to the door of his uncle's study and clawed at the handle. How could it be locked? He slammed it with his shoulder and rebounded. 'Uncle,' he shouted, 'Uncle.' He imagined he heard a sound from inside and pressed his ear to the door. Faintly at first and then gathering in intensity, he heard the unmistakable, hungry sound of flames. Looking down, he saw a thin pulsing strip of light that increased in intensity even as he watched. He jerked away from the door as the inferno inside stung his cheek through the wood. Someone grabbed him from behind and he tried to shake them off – straining to get back to the door, trying.

Even before his eyes cleared, he heard a clanging bell and a rumble of voices. He had a sensation of movement and blinked away tears to find he was on a stretcher. It halted and a face appeared above him.

'Max?' the archbishop said anxiously.

'I'm fine, your Grace,' he said hoarsely and the prelate seemed to shiver with relief. He was swathed in a voluminous dressing gown and Max noticed that he was wearing his little skull cap. He was about to smile at the incongruity when he remembered something.

'My uncle?' he asked.

The archbishop's face melted into a mask of anguish. 'My poor Drago,' he whispered and the stretcher-bearers moved on. He saw Ustashe men running with hosepipes and keeping the crowd at bay.

An Ustashe militia man stood beside the ambulance door and helped the attendants load the patient. Before the man climbed down, he caught Max's hand in his own. 'Rest in peace,' he whispered. Max distracted himself from his burns by listing the possible interpretations of 'rest in peace', when he remembered the pressure on his palm. The scrap of paper was already smudged with soot. As the ambulance moved off, he tried to steady his hand so that he could read the note.

'He who is not for us is against us.'

He knew it was a boast and a threat. The boast he would simply file in his mind under 'vengeance'. He could not ignore the threat. Up to this point, he had survived by being 'all things to all men': a chameleon who adjusted his camouflage to the particular background. Those days were gone and that ploy would no longer preserve him. He needed to be acceptable to the forces of light and darkness to play them one against the other so that he could amass information, contacts and influence.

While he had excelled at his university studies, it was the paper trail scattered in his uncle's study that had aroused his passion and drawn him to discovery. Of all the players who strode the Croatian stage, it was he, the Austrian, the Auslander – Outsider, who had the overall view of the drama. He had his uncle to thank for that, even though he had manipulated that innocent man into supplying the access and had inadvertently brought about his death. He felt neither guilt nor remorse. The encounter with the Franciscan had taught him that feelings are failings in those who pursue a goal.

To achieve that goal, he needed a champion, someone strong enough to protect him from factions, someone who would promote him on a grander stage. Bishop Miscic? No! The bishop's deep-seated hatred of the Orthodox Serbs was a piece of petty bigotry that had been tolerated by the Reich because it was congruent with their own sense of Aryan superiority. If Hitler prevailed, Max could not see him espousing the maxim 'The enemy of my enemy is my friend.'

For the same reason, he dismissed the candidacy of the professor. He might be polished and urbane but his heart was as coarse as Miscic's, his vision, not supple enough to adapt to a wider arena than Croatia. Stepinac? Yes, he concluded. The archbishop was politically naïve and so dazzled by the possibilities presented by the Poglavnik Pavelič for the Church that he failed to see the bloody consequences of that relationship. But he was the Vatican's viceroy in Croatia and whoever hitched his wagon to that star would have every opportunity to shine.

He cleared his mind and opened himself to the tutelage of his body. Pain is a consequence of being alive, he told himself. It is what earths us in the present moment, anchors us in the now. Pain, he knew, could also serve as a weapon to bend the will of any man or woman, often by the mere suggestion of it. Even the Franciscan had baulked from the implied threat of exposure. That was the friar's Achilles' heel and Max vowed to keep a sharp lance poised above that vulnerability. He put the scrap of paper in his mouth, chewed it thoroughly and swallowed.

'Would you like to receive Holy Communion?' an earnest young priest enquired later.

'I've already received,' he said.

Stepinac came in a flurry of nurses and priest attendants. After the exchange of greetings, enquiries about his health and his own assurances that he was fine, the archbishop dismissed his retinue and sat at the bedside.

'Poor Drago,' he said sadly, 'such a loss. He was always so busy – so concerned for those in difficulty. He never refused to help anyone. He made no distinctions.'

He paused and fiddled with his pectoral cross.

'Did your uncle ever mention documents?' he began awkwardly. 'It's just that he intimated, on a few occasions, that he had some evidence of … irregularities and would put them before me.'

'He never mentioned documents to me, your Grace. If he did have such documents – well, the fire—'

'Yes, yes of course,' the archbishop said quickly. Max wasn't sure if his expression was of relief or disappointment. 'Such a tragedy for you, my boy,' he resumed sympathetically, 'to lose Father Kyril as well.'

'Father Kyril?'

'You didn't know? How clumsy of me. I assumed—'

Anger tightened his normally placid face for a moment. Max thought it didn't augur well for one of the prelate's minions.

'I'm sorry to be the bearer of more bad news, Max. Father Kyril was shot and killed at the railway station last night. According to the authorities, it seems he was waiting for a train and disturbed a saboteur. An explosive device was found on the line. The police say it is a type used by partisans. I'm very sorry.'

'Thank you, your Grace.'

'Naturally, the diocese will see to repatriating his body. And what about you, Max? Do you want to continue your studies here or would you prefer to go home?'

Max let a few seconds go by as if he were contemplating that offer.

'I would like to stay here, your Grace, but not as a burden to you.'

'Nonsense, it has been a pleasure. I hear nothing but the highest praise from the university.' He paused, his lips moving as if he was tasting his words before speaking. 'Now that your uncle has gone to his reward, I wonder if you would consider becoming my secretary. I wouldn't allow it to interfere with your studies, of course, but I would be very grateful if you could accede to this request.'

'I'd be honoured, your Grace, but isn't it customary for a priest to hold that position?'

'Yes, it is,' the archbishop said, smiling. 'That is something else I would ask you to consider, during your recuperation.'

Time passed, dragging the sunlight from one window to another until dusk and then dark replaced it. He lay unmoving, allowing his thoughts free rein. Nurses came and went to change his dressings. He endured the pain and their enquiries, stoically, and they left him alone for longer and longer periods. 'Be careful what you wish for,' he reminded himself. He had gained a protector in Stepinac but that shield came at a price. Priesthood? Who were his models? Kyril, Miscic, the Franciscan and his late uncle. What was it about the priesthood that had attracted such different personalities? Perhaps the priesthood was catholic, after all, in the universal, all-encompassing sense of the word. If the Franciscan was anything to go by, it could also be – accommodating. He lay back, inviting sleep and, presently, it came.

THE HORSE COMPOUND, EAST OF SMOLENSK

It's raining,' Rudi said, as the drumming started on the tarpaulin roof. 'Better go and ask Herman if there's anything he wants done.'

Karl chucked the grey mare under the chin and she shifted sideways to let him by. Under Herman's gentle direction, he had grown more comfortable with the horses, even Roland, the daunting stallion. That feeling had gradually segued into affection as he curry-combed and brushed their coats, feeling their quivers of contentment tremble through his hands. It became a matter of concern rather than duty for him to check their shoes for loose nails and their shins for stone bruises.

When Herman asked him to stay with the horses when they went to the meadow, he'd been puzzled. Who'd be foolish enough to attract the ire of the Wehrmacht by stealing their horses, he wondered? Even the partisans, who sometimes attacked a night sentry, wouldn't be so foolhardy. He'd never asked and Herman hadn't elaborated, and now he shook his head ruefully at how foolish his question had been. His 'eureka' moment had arrived the first evening he'd led them into the meadow. As soon as the traces were loosed, they'd bounded away and kicked their heels, shaking off the confines of the stable, as if to say grass below and sky above is our natural element. He'd watched them weaving galloping patterns up and down and around each other until his head spun and his heart sang. There was something so uncomplicated about their joy that it settled like a balm on his heart and distanced him from the war and the terrible things he had seen. After that first evening, he'd noticed soldiers coming, singly and in pairs, to sit at the meadow's edge. For the most part, they were silent, simply sitting and watching, and he didn't begrudge them a share in his pleasure.

In the same way, he'd come to treasure his time with the horse master. It compensated, somewhat, for Kurt's absence. Herman had an encyclopaedic knowledge of horses and the kind of infectious enthusiasm that is the hallmark of the true teacher. Karl was amazed to discover how widely read he was and they spent long hours discussing many topics. Herman had a special fondness for all things Russian and spoke admiringly of their customs, religion and iconography, sometimes slipping, unconsciously, into Russian phrases. Over time, the boy began to develop an awareness of the Russian people that was deeper than the labels to which the soldiers used to reduce them.

He pulled back the canvas flap that served as a door to Herman's quarters and stuck his head inside.

'My father sent me to tell—' He stopped and stared. Herman knelt before a packing case. A candle, upright in a hardened puddle of wax, glinted on the crucifix, the tiny silver cup and the morsel of bread on a silvered disc. Karl's eyes shifted to Herman's and saw sadness and resignation there.

'It's raining,' he breathed.

'I know,' Herman said, rising, 'please come in.'

Herman sat on an upturned feed bucket and gestured Karl to the stool. When the boy was seated, he began to speak.

'Karl, I am a priest.'

Karl opened his mouth to say something and then shut it again.

'Better to hear it all,' Herman said. 'I joined the army so that I would be part of Operation Barbarossa; it's a long, complicated story. My plan is – was – to wait until we came to a village or town that needed a priest and stay there when the army moved on.'

'Desert!' Karl gasped, 'but they'd shoot you, Herman.'

'They'd have to catch me first,' the horse master said, smiling bleakly. 'My hope was that they'd be too busy conquering Russia. It's a big country, Karl.'

'I – I don't know what to say,' Karl stammered. 'What about the horses?' he blurted and felt foolish.

'Rudi, your father, has a way with the horses. I think he'll manage very well, with you and Tomas, of course. Look, Karl,' he said, leaning forward earnestly, 'I understand perfectly well that you may feel it your duty to report this to the sergeant. I won't stand in your way or think less of you if that's what your conscience tells you to do.'

'No,' Karl said immediately, 'I wouldn't do that.'

'If they find out that you knew, they'll punish you as an accomplice. I'd rather give myself up than risk that.'

'That's my decision and my risk, Herman.'

Herman nodded his gratitude.

'Will you tell me when you're leaving?' Karl asked.

'No. You would have to lie if you were questioned. It's best that you don't know, for your own protection. Now,' he said rising, 'we must get ready.'

He pinched the wick of the candle and packed everything into a small rucksack which he stowed under his bed.

'Ready for what?' Karl asked.

'Why, for a miracle, of course,' Herman said, clapping his hands and laughing like a schoolboy. 'What did you come to tell me, Karl?' he asked teasingly.

'It – it's raining.'

'Yes, my boy,' Herman said happily, grabbing him by the shoulders. 'And rain is the Russian word for mud.' He pronounced the word slowly as if relishing the taste of it on his tongue. 'Any moment now, the Wehrmacht, the fastest army in the world, will come begging for horses. We must be ready,' he declared, and charged out of the stables.

'Here comes another hero,' Rudi grumbled, as a truck roared towards them. 'Slow and steady, man,' he growled in exasperation as the driver gunned the engine. A bow wave of mud rose up from the road before the bonnet of the truck and the engine coughed and died. Wearily, they coaxed the horses through the hock-deep morass until they reached the stranded vehicle. The miner waded to the front to attach the ropes while Karl and his father angled the horses. With the miner pushing and the others urging the floundering animals, they managed to clear the road.

'Clear for the next hero,' Rudi said fatalistically. They brought the horses to a relatively dry patch of ground and gently peeled mud from their legs. It was a pointless exercise, Karl thought, trying to split the mud casts that encased all three to the thighs. They would have to wade into that brown soup again to rescue the next driver who refused to believe that the roads were impassable. He slumped beside the horses and distracted himself from his discomfort by counting the vehicles they had rescued. Twenty, he estimated, between trucks and jeeps and a Panzer that had wallowed and snorted steam like a hippo. Most of the motorcyclists had managed to drag themselves and their vehicles from the mud's clutches and spent their time smoking and laying bets against the next slithering vehicle.

'Will it be like this all the way to Moscow?' Karl asked his father.

'No,' Rudi answered. 'Someone said there's a paved road up ahead, but getting there will be the hard part.'

'Maybe it will freeze,' Karl said hopefully. 'If it does, the road won't be a problem.'

He saw his father and the miner exchange a glance.

'Be careful what you wish for, son,' his father said grimly. 'Will it freeze?' he asked the miner.

'Nights are colder,' the miner said cryptically.

THE KREMLIN, MOSCOW

General Zhukov followed the Kremlin guard down the long corridor. His glowering eyes picked at the fancy uniform before him, like a babushka disapproving of a grandson's shiny new suit. Toy soldiers, he fumed, throwbacks to tsarist times. He deliberately increased his pace until he was snapping at the guard's polished heels and he grunted vindictively when the man tripped and fought to regain his balance.

'The Secretary of the Supreme Soviet will see—'

Zhukov was through the door before the guard could finish his sentence. Stalin sat, hunched at his desk, a huge, grubby handkerchief to his nose. He blew it loudly and examined the contents of the handkerchief with his habitual suspicion. Satisfied that it held no evidence of anything bourgeois plotting in his nostrils, he swung bleary eyes to the general.

Looks drunk, maybe hungover, Zhukov thought, and then revised his diagnosis as a thunderous sneeze shook the secretary. A head cold, he concluded in amazement; what germ would dare?

'Kiev,' Stalin said thickly. 'He's going to Kiev.'

Zhukov felt a jolt of shock followed quickly by a tremor of satisfaction. He had warned them, spelled out all the reasons why Hitler would divert his blitzkrieg to Kiev and destroy the army shadowing his flank and the industries that sustained the Russian resistance. He had given Stalin and the grey suits of the politburo chapter and verse from the intelligence reports right down to General Jodl's remark that Moscow gave Hitler a sinister feeling; that by breaking off for Kiev, he was stepping off Napoleon's path and out of the stranglehold of history. He drew a deep breath and relaxed his shoulders.

'Yes, comrade Secretary,' he said.

The rheumy, brown eyes under the bushy eyebrows frisked him for any hint of sarcasm.

'Kiev cannot fall,' Stalin said.

'It will, comrade Secretary,' Zhukov countered. 'The army at Kiev will delay the fascists, at best, but they will not hold them.'

'They must,' Stalin rumbled.

'They cannot,' Zhukov insisted, 'they are outnumbered and outgunned. Richthofen and the Luftwaffe will bomb holes in their defensive lines without them firing a single shot in reply. Guderian's Panzers will close about them like a claw and snap them into pieces and whoever remains standing after that must face the Wehrmacht.'

He realised his voice had been rising in intensity through this exchange and curbed his anger.

'Pull them back,' he urged. 'Burn the city and booby-trap the industries. Let the fascists have a hole in the ground but don't bury our army in it.'

'Kiev is the capital city of the Ukraine,' Stalin hissed. 'If it falls, what will the other cities think? What will the whole country think?'

'What we tell them to,' Zhukov raged. 'That it is a strategic necessity if we are to lure the fascists to Moscow and destroy them.' He groaned aloud as he fought for control. 'Comrade Secretary,' he gritted in a tightly controlled voice, 'we have no choice. If we move divisions to defend Kiev and Kiev falls, the road to Moscow lies open. Let them tire their soldiers and use up their armaments against a token force at Kiev and when they are overstretched, smash—'

'No, I have made my decision.'

'Why have generals at all if you will not listen to their counsel?'

Zhukov suddenly found it difficult to draw air into his lungs. It was as if that simple sentence had burned off all the oxygen in the room. He had a vision of his daughter's smiling face when she'd woken up that morning and found him at home. Stalin's face had gone deathly white, so that the patches around his eyes looked as if they'd been shaded with charcoal. He stood up from his desk and the sudden movement seemed to surge the blood back into his features.

'Why indeed?' he breathed and the general heard a whisper of death in that voice. 'I have listened, comrade General,' Stalin continued remorselessly, 'and I find your advice defeatist.'

He spat the word from his mouth like something rancid. 'You will vacate your present position and confine your concerns to the reserve armies. Another will take your place, a general who will not counsel surrender to fascism.'

Perhaps being shot was not so bad, Zhukov thought. He knew colleagues who'd been taken to the Lubyanka and executed. It was certainly quick and, most likely, painless. Demotion and exile, on the other hand, seemed a more painful option, almost like a prolonged execution. His thoughts were racing and he had time to consider who might replace him. Yeremenko? Good, dogged commander but not—? What? What did the Motherland need now? What kind of commander of armies did the day demand? Me, he thought immediately and anticipated some feeling of embarrassment at what might have seemed like hubris on his part. He felt nothing except a great calm, as if the acceptance of the reality had freed him of all conflicting emotions, especially fear. He saluted and left.

Word would already have weaseled down the corridors of power that he was yesterday's man. Yet his calm conviction radiated from him like a force field so that Kremlin guards snapped to stiff attention as he passed, like flags in a bracing wind. It might also have been the smile. It was the smile of a man who had looked death in the face and found it had a head cold. He stepped into the courtyard and breathed the air deeply, like a man surfacing from a dark pool. To his left stood the captive churches of the Kremlin and, beyond them, the crenellated walls. And beyond them – Russia, the Rodina, the Motherland, a vast ocean slumbering around the shores of this fragile atoll.

'When the day comes,' he whispered fiercely, 'when the day comes ...'

GENERAL VON KLUGE'S HQ, EAST OF SMOLENSK

'Kiev is ours,' General von Bock announced, and the tent seemed to billow with the force of the applause. He allowed himself a rare, indulgent smile and then his features stiffened into the mask that had earned him his sobriquet, the Grim Reaper.

'Our orders have come from the Führer.'

He paused and Kurt thought he detected a glint of mischief in his eyes. He knew von Bock had been against the diversion of forces to Kiev.

'We are to take Moscow,' the general said.

In the ensuing silence, Kurt scanned the faces ranged around the map table. There were some who looked exultant and others who looked apprehensive. General Hoepner, the Panzer commander, who had taken Guderian's place until 'Fast Heinze' made his way back from Kiev, shifted uncomfortably on his stool. Kurt wasn't surprised when the crusty general was the first to speak.

'Our supply lines are stretched to breaking point, General,' he objected.

'Then you must get to Moscow all the faster, General Hoepner,' von Bock quipped, and a burst of nervous laughter shivered through the others. Hoepner was not so easily dismissed.

'We will need to throw a wide noose around Moscow,' he persisted. 'We must encircle the reserve armies and supply lines; otherwise we run the risk of a longer campaign.'

'No,' von Kluge said emphatically, 'a tight noose strangles faster.'

He stepped up to a map pinned to the tent wall behind von Bock.

'With your permission, General,' he said, picking up a pointer as von Bock stepped aside.

'They have two major groups of armies between us and our objective. They are located here and here.' The pointer rapped on the locations of Bryansk and Vyazma. 'Our best intelligence suggests the Russians have almost a million soldiers divided between these two strongholds.'

There was an audible intake of breath by the assembled commanders. Von Kluge turned his wrist and snapped the pointer into his armpit, like a field marshal's baton.

'Gentlemen,' he said, smiling reassuringly, 'we have one and a half million men, five thousand artillery pieces, fourteen hundred aircraft and a thousand tanks. We can encircle and annihilate their forces in Bryansk and Vyazma and strike directly and swiftly for Moscow.'

He replaced the pointer on the table.

'If you run out of fuel, General Hoepner,' von Kluge said wickedly, 'we'll send the horses back for you.'

Delighted laughter broke out again and some of Hoepner's neighbours clapped him on the shoulder. Von Bock had to repeat himself to bring them back to order.

'The operation will be called Typhoon,' he said and dismissed them.

LATER

'Typhoon, isn't that a storm of some kind?' von Kluge asked.

'Actually, it's a hurricane,' Kurt answered.

He thought the general's tent resembled a miniature hurricane – orderlies and officers constantly swirling in and out delivering messages and departing with orders. Von Kluge seemed able to handle the intense level of activity effortlessly.

'Then we're going to huff and puff and blow the Kremlin down,' von Kluge said as he scrawled his signature on a document, which was replaced immediately by another.

'Yes,' Kurt said, 'eventually.'

'Why do you have to qualify everything?' the general demanded, petulantly.

'A hurricane does have incredible power, General,' Kurt continued, 'but it actually moves quite slowly, at about ten miles per hour, I think.'

'Faster than Hoepner then.'

'That's the speed it maintains over water, General.'

'Speaking of water,' the general said, 'the rain seems to have stopped. I always said a good night's frost would harden up the road to Moscow.'

'And,' Kurt continued, pedantically, 'a hurricane quickly decays as it passes over land.'

'But that was exactly my point,' von Kluge said, enthusiastically. 'As soon as Bryansk and Vyazma are neutralised, we can strike directly for Moscow.'

'There is the small matter of Borodino, sir.'

'Borodino is history,' von Kluge said dismissively. 'Yes, I know, I know,' he continued when Kurt looked sceptical. 'Napoleon failed to crush them at Borodino and it came back to haunt him, but, God in Heaven, Professor, after Bryansk and Vyazma what will they have left to throw at us in Borodino?'

Kurt didn't answer and the general was forced to confront his own question.

'Brandenburger,' he snapped, and a shadow detached itself from the wall of the tent, about three paces from where Kurt sat, making him start.

'The elite troops you saw in Smolensk – we need to know if Stalin can conjure any more of them. He's pulled off that trick once or twice along the way and I wouldn't want to be surprised again. Find out what you can and report back.'

Kurt was struck by the ease with which the general could order a man to go alone into the camp of the enemy and at how easily that man accepted such a fraught assignment. The Brandenburger nodded and disappeared as unobtrusively as he had appeared.

'Like a thief in the night,' Kurt murmured. He looked around and was surprised to find that he and von Kluge were alone for the first time that night. It was now five forty-five and the lanterns ranged around the tent worked steadily to keep the dark at bay. The general tugged his tunic straighter and adjusted his peaked cap.

'Let the hurricane begin,' he said.

OPERATION TYPHOON, BRYANSK–VYAZMA, 2 OCTOBER 1941

We are in the eye of the hurricane, Karl thought. He remembered his old schoolteacher, Simon Tauber, sweeping thick spirals on the blackboard, holding the chalk horizontally so that it produced broad concentric circles.

'Here,' he'd said dramatically, stabbing the tiny space at the core of his chalk whirlpool, 'is the eye of the hurricane. No wind screaming around you,' he'd whispered, 'no rain lashing you from every side and only blue sky above.' At this, he'd raised his head and looked up at the ceiling. Unconsciously, Karl raised his head. The sky was lightening in the east and a vast shoal of aircraft droned out of the dark, in that direction.

The horse handlers stood on a small mound, which seemed to Karl to be the only elevation on a great plain, as men and machines moved around them. Tanks clawed the earth as they rumbled on and he placed a reassuring hand against the mare's neck. His father and the miner were close by, Rudi speaking softly to his charges while the miner simply stood between two horses, his outstretched arms lying across their backs. The crackling sound as the big guns prodded the sky was superseded by the screech of rockets that flew in high arcs to disappear in the distance. Karl had a moment in which to marvel at the silent, tulip-shaped clouds that rose up to mark their fall before the concussion flexed the ground beneath him. He saw Herman stand beside the great bulk of Roland. The priest's lips were moving and, in a lull between salvoes, he heard him chant, 'Kyrie eleison, Christe eleison – Lord have mercy, Christ have mercy', the only prayer from the East that had survived in the Western mass.

The horse handlers and their charges walked in the devastated wake of Operation Typhoon, travelling wordlessly over a mangled landscape. Karl saw it as a jumbled jigsaw – a world of parts and pieces, randomly scattered. Fragments of trees cracked under their boots as their stumps bled resin into the empty spaces above them. Parts of humans lay everywhere and he felt again the fear that had paralysed him in the Waffen-ravaged village. He swallowed convulsively and concentrated on putting one foot before the other, marching to the lethal drumming of bombs and shells that beat a terrible tattoo to the east.

'Like rats in a barrel,' the soldier said around the bread he was ramming into his mouth. A farmer before the war, he had followed the smell of the horses to their camp in search of some normality.

'Brass says we have them surrounded,' he continued, speaking rapidly and tonelessly as if to himself. 'Bastards try to break out in small groups … ring of steel … tanks and machine guns … blow them up and knock them down. Rats in a barrel.'

Karl wandered into the camp to find Kurt. The sentry looked him up and down and decided he was no real and present danger to the brass.

'If the general comes back, you get the fuck out of there, and fast. You hear me?' he whispered as he pulled back the tent flap. Kurt was hunched on a camp stool, his journal angled to the light of a lantern. Karl saw the pen wriggle from left to right across the page and it was such a familiar and comforting sight that he felt tears prickle his eyes.

He coughed politely, and his friend looked up. Kurt's face had changed, he thought. It wasn't just the layer of grime that everyone wore, it was something deeper than that. Kurt's face had always been made up of flat pale plains and prominent cheekbones. His skin seemed tighter, Karl thought, as if someone stood behind him holding the back of his head in a tight grip, but the biggest change was in his eyes. He had the eyes of someone who has seen too many bad things and who now squints permanently as if in anticipation of further horrors. Karl saw eyes like those every hour of the day in the camp. He saw them in the sliver of mirror he used himself, but it hurt him to see Kurt like that. As if aware of the boy's scrutiny, Kurt knuckled his eyes quickly.

'Karl,' he said happily and the boy was relieved to see some traces of the old sparkle resurface. 'Did you bring your journal?' Kurt asked, and smiled as Karl fished the battered notebook from his tunic pocket.

Sitting in the pool of light, they compared notes with growing enthusiasm until Karl arrived at his most recent entry.

'I hope you don't mind, Professor,' he said awkwardl. 'I – I can't share this part just now. Perhaps later.'

Kurt looked at him keenly.

'That's our agreement, Karl,' he said, 'and I respect it. However, if it's something that bothers you – something you've seen or heard that you found particularly upsetting, I think it would be wise to discuss it with your father.'

Karl looked into that worn, earnest face and was sorely tempted. He knew if he could only wrap words around the things he had seen, heard, smelled and felt they wouldn't have such power over him. 'Language gives control,' Kurt had assured him while loading him with lists of words to study so that he could extend his vocabulary. But what words would ever be sufficient? he wondered. Were there enough words in all the languages of the world to capture what he had seen and tame his terrors? Murder, massacre, rape, dismemberment – all these words, once so foreign to his experience, had grown familiar and inadequate.

He accepted that he had always been shy and introspective, not as monosyllabic as the miner but much more aware and respectful now of why he was that way. Oh Kurt, he thought, as his eyes blurred with sudden tears, I could tell you such things. He cleared his eyes with his sleeve and looked at the earnest, innocent face of his teacher. It's not fair to burden him, he concluded. Even as that thought occurred to him, he felt a pang of guilt. It was not the whole truth. Deep down, he knew he was afraid – afraid that if he attempted words, they would peter out into silence and he would sit there with his mouth open, keening wordlessly, like a child who has gone beyond tears.

'Perhaps later,' he whispered.

Kurt sighed. 'Karl,' he said, slowly, 'we are historians. We read about wars all the time. I think we could study war forever and still not—'

'Good evening, General von Kluge, sir,' the sentry bellowed from outside the tent. 'I see you're back, sir.'

'And I see your grasp of the obvious is as keen as ever, Dirk,' they heard von Kluge reply and then he was in the tent.

'Ah,' he said, 'the master and his apprentice. Been filling the boy in on all our doings, have you, Professor?'

'No, eh, I mean, yes, sir.'

'In that case,' the general said, slumping down on a stool behind the desk, 'I'll give the sergeant permission to shoot both of you. Oh, at ease, boy,' he smiled as Karl stiffened to attention. 'What unit are you with now?'

'The horses, sir.'

'Thought so,' von Kluge said, wrinkling his nose. 'The sergeant chose wisely. Well, you distinguished yourselves during the rainy period; let's hope we won't need to call on you again. Dismissed.'

As the tent flap closed behind the boy, they both heard the angry voice of the sentry and Karl's mumbled apologies.

'Is he bright?' von Kluge asked.

'Very, sir. Just lacking in confidence.'

'How fortunate that he found you, Professor.' Von Kluge leaned back and sighed. 'They won't surrender,' he said flatly. 'Beaten all ends up, pounded from every side and starving to death – and they still won't surrender.'

'Perhaps they're afraid to,' Kurt suggested, 'because of the commissars.'

'Yes, perhaps.' The general didn't sound convinced. 'At least, I hope that's the reason. We could leave a token force to hold them there until they get hungry enough or angry enough to shoot their bloody commissars, but it could be something else.' He tugged vigorously at his earlobe as if trying to dislodge a niggling thought. 'You remember what Albert Becker said after Smolensk?'

'Yes, General. He worried about how ferocious the Russians could be, even when the odds were stacked against them.'

'Yes, he did. And they've become even more ferocious the closer we've got to Moscow. I also worry about those elite troops that turned up in Smolensk. It seems they gave a good account of themselves in Kiev as well. If Stalin has more where they came from—'

'But the Brandenburger is going to—'

The general held up his hand. 'Careful, Professor,' he smiled, 'how many times can the sergeant shoot you? But the answer is yes. When we get to the gates of Moscow, I'd prefer not to receive a warm welcome. After Kiev, Bryansk and Vyazma, we're stretched to the limit. Ah, well,' he sighed, pulling a sheaf of papers from the pile, 'one last push and we're there. Or so the Führer promised.'

THE ROAD FROM BRYANSK–VYAZMA TO SMOLENSK

The Waffen weren't a wolf pack, Steiger concluded. A wolf pack hunted and lived together. The captain's group, he'd discovered, were rogue wolves who preferred to hunt singly and in pairs and who came together only when commanded by their leader. Rooting out the partisans and their supporters behind the lines seemed to be their primary task, though they had a broad definition of 'partisan' and assumed all Russians were partisan sympathisers. Hanging, they considered, sent a warning to either group and they rarely passed through a village without leaving one grisly calling card at the end of a rope. News of their depredations travelled before them and they came upon more and more recently evacuated villages. Like animals bereft of their prey, they circled closer to larger, more concentrated food sources – prisoners.

There seemed to be an unending supply of prisoners – Russian soldiers who had surrendered at Smolensk, Bryansk and Vyazma, or those who had simply walked out of the forests and thrown their weapons away. These men knew they could never go back; deserters and escaped prisoners alike were accounted traitors by the Supreme Soviet and suffered the appropriate punishment if they fell into the hands of their own countrymen.

Steiger could appreciate the Soviet logic – a man who left his post or who allowed himself to be captured by the fascists could never be trusted again. Forgiveness or rehabilitation were not words in the Soviet vocabulary and that iron certainty encouraged the serving troops to hold their positions and fight to the death. They had nowhere else to go, he reasoned, like himself. He had seen how quickly the prisoners had gone from being paraded as war trophies to being perceived as nuisances or worse. The German High Command hadn't factored over a million prisoners into their plans for Operation Barbarossa and there wasn't clothing, shelter, or sustenance for anything like that horde. And so they started to die. The wounded were the first to go, often from minor wounds that became infected through lack of medical aid. They were followed by those who drank dirty water, those who had something another prisoner wanted and those who simply gave up the will to live. And, of course, those who came to the attention of the Waffen. In a short space of time, the prisoner compounds became Waffen killing grounds, as they indulged their every sadistic whim on those helpless and hopeless men.

Steiger had seen more casual slaughter than any mortal man should see and, though he had shielded himself with apathy, the smell of death seemed to follow him like a miasma. He had been relieved when the captain had ordered him and four others to the Bryansk–Vyazma front to escort prisoners from that campaign to Smolensk and he now steeled himself for the morning ritual.

Just before dawn, they prodded the prisoners out of their

barbed-wire enclosures and organised them into groups of a hundred. On the order 'run', they ran. Those who completed the two-hundred-yard dash, encouraged by whips and batons, were judged fit to march to the next holding camp. Those who could not were shot and rolled off the road. Steiger moved, robotically, up and down the line, dealing blows from the butt of his rifle and death from the other end. He dragged an unresisting corpse across the road, by the heels, and added it to the rising wall of the discarded dead as if he was stacking firewood.

A sound rang out in the still air, a natural sound that was worlds away from the grunts and groans that clotted his ears. He looked up and saw a horse rear and whinny in the meadow that bordered the road. It was a sound and sight that brought him back, momentarily, to a world he had known and, like his prisoners, could never return to. The horse shimmied sideways and a boy appeared. He recognised Karl and the breath caught in his throat. Even at a distance, Steiger could see the boy's joy in the animal's beauty. The horse whinnied again and the boy's laugh touched Steiger's heart with the promise of absolution. He dropped his gaze and saw the dead man staring at him. The Russian's skin above his beard was already tinged a blue/green and his body sprawled limply. His stare held no rebuke; the flat eyes simply mirrored the man who had dumped him there. Steiger reached out a trembling hand and closed the eyes with a thumb and forefinger.

'Herr Steiger.'

He swung up his rifle before his brain seized on the voice and words.

'Karl,' he whispered, 'Karl.'

The boy stood on the other side of the piled corpses. His skin was ivory and two feverish spots burned on his cheekbones.

'Herr Steiger,' he said, 'can you come back?'

The boy offered his hand as if he would help the policeman cross the barrier of the dead. Steiger wondered what it would be like to be among the living again. He remembered the coldness of the others and his heart flinched. But the boy had given him a cup of wine and touched cups with him. Even as his heart and hand ached for some echo of that kindness, he remembered the man with the empty eyes, and the man who made wild music, and the man who took young Russian girls into the forest and stayed there until the screams stopped. He was theirs, branded with their mark. Should he stray, they would find him and find the boy.

'You're a good boy, Karl,' he said hoarsely, as if regurgitating broken glass from his throat. He turned away and shambled back to the damned.

Edwin Unger was a perfectionist: scrupulous attention to detail was what kept him alive. The Russian uniform he was wearing was the best of a bad lot, salvaged from a pile of corpses in Bryansk. If he ever wrote his memoirs, he imagined that his description of a bored quartermaster holding the tunics of dead men against his frame for size, like some ghoulish tailor, would be dismissed as fiction. Then again, he mused, as he stepped over another corpse on the road, that's what he was – a fiction. Today he was Vladimir Chernov, a lieutenant in the Red Army. According to the piece of paper in his breast pocket, he was twenty-nine years old and a native of Kursk. At this moment, he was more comfortable with his Kursk accent than he was with his trousers. The previous occupant had lost a foot and the pants cuff crackled with dried blood. Someone sharp enough to spot that little detail would ask to see his wound. It took him a few minutes to locate a likely candidate in the throng of prisoners. The young soldier leaned drunkenly on the shoulder of a comrade as the pair weaved to the rear of the column. The gap between them and their compatriots was beginning to grow. Unger knew it measured the distance between life and death; the guard was already peeling the rifle-strap from his shoulders.

'Let me, comrade,' he offered, taking the wounded man from the Good Samaritan's shoulder. Quickly, he closed the gap and saw the guard relax. The last-minute reprieve wouldn't last indefinitely, he realised, as he examined the soldier. Something, maybe a piece of shrapnel, had pared a large flap of flesh from the man's skull. There was a hint of white in the wound, and a steady trickle of blood had drenched the collar of his tunic and was soaking down the garment as if his uniform was sucking him dry. At the next resting place,

Unger laid him on the ground and folded the flap of flesh over the wound. He knew the blood wouldn't clot and bind before the order came to march but he had already benefited from the man's misfortune. That benefit was the bloodstain on his shoulder. Even the most suspicious NKVD officer would accept that Vladimir Chernov had been helping a wounded comrade before he'd escaped.

'Can anyone help this comrade,' he said in a low voice, 'I'm going to make a run for it.'

The exhausted men sitting about him hardly seemed to register what he was saying, then someone said, 'Fucking hero's going to get us all shot.'

'So,' Unger countered, 'you think the fascists are going to wash your face and send you home to Uncle Josef?'

Some of the prisoners grunted appreciatively. One of them turned his head and looked at the wounded man.

'He's finished anyway,' he said sadly. 'A bullet would be more merciful. Just let him lie.'

'I'll help, comrade,' a voice said from behind the Brandenburger. He stiffened and turned slowly, his brain shrilling an alarm. It wasn't what the man had said, it was the way he said it – too carefully and precisely, like someone who had learned the language. The man looked wiry and capable and he looked at Unger with smiling eyes. He let his own eyes check the man for clues. The uniform passed muster and the boots were regular Red Army issue – no one could counterfeit that level of poor workmanship. The man stretched out his hand to check the wound and Unger saw it. He stared at the hole in the fabric of the tunic, like a black island in a tiny sea of dried blood. You wouldn't last a minute with the NKVD, he thought.

Unaware of Unger's scrutiny, the man took a clean roll of bandage from a small rucksack and began to bind up the injured man's head, wrapping it expertly around the crown so that the flap would be held in place. Prisoners dump their guns, Unger thought furiously; guns are always the first to go. And then, as they're herded down the road, they litter it with everything else until they're left with the clothes on their backs. The clean bandage and the rucksack were pieces of the jigsaw that just didn't fit. Whoever you are, he thought, you're as fucking Russian as I am.

'Walk,' the sentry shouted, doing up his fly buttons as he emerged from the trees.

'*Spasibo* – thanks,' Unger grunted to the stranger and immediately tripped over his rucksack. 'Sorry,' he added before he made his way to the edge of the column. A rucksack is a heavy item for a prisoner to carry on a forced march, he thought. A rucksack with metal items in it is … ?

The guard was still attending to his modesty when Unger kicked him in the privates. A ragged cheer wafted after him into the trees.

THE STABLES

Karl went to put a straw in his mouth and hesitated. Herman always said if you sucked a single straw you were sucking the whole stable. 'Adults have an answer for everything,' he sighed and dropped the straw. He'd built a little hideaway of hay bales where he liked to sit and think when all the chores were done. Karl sat in his sweet-smelling cave and thought. Herman said it was important to think. 'Otherwise, we're just blue-arsed flies bumping into the same window over and over,' he'd said. 'Think about a job you have to do and you do it smarter in half the time.'

Herman had a repertoire of sayings, proverbs and admonitions. Some of the latter were more enigmatic and less edifying than others.

'God never closes a door but he catches your fingers in it,' he'd said one time when the mare had stood on Karl's foot.

'But my mother always said God never closes a door but he opens a window,' Karl had protested.

'Yes, I know that one,' Herman had grimaced. 'Your mother is a good Christian woman, Karl. But sometime in the past she was hurt and disappointed and someone tried to turn her hurt into an opportunity. That same someone didn't have to deal with your mother's hurt, did she?'

On another occasion, he'd stunned the boy by remarking that shovelling horse shit was good for the mind.

'But it's boring and smelly,' Karl had declared.

'Exactly,' the horse master had said with satisfaction. 'Boring and smelly divert the mind to think about other things – to winnow the wheat of what matters from the chaff of everything else and feed the mind.' He'd paused before adding, 'My father never saw it quite like that.'

'Didn't you like your father, Herman?'

'There were things I didn't like about him,' he'd answered. 'But there was more to my father than his faults. That's true of most people.'

Was that true of Herr Steiger? Karl wondered. He knew his father and the miner didn't like him, but the policeman had looked grateful when he'd shared the wine with him that time. And he had saved him from the captain. He eased himself out of his hideaway and watched the mare lower her head to the manger.

'It's all very simple for you, isn't it?' he said as he ran his hand over her shoulder. The mare turned her head and gave him such a lugubrious look that he burst out laughing. 'I know,' he said, 'your belly makes more sense to you than my brain does to me.' He slapped her playfully on the rump and she reciprocated by raising a hoof.

'Herman!'

Karl swept back the sack curtain and stepped inside. For a few days after Herman's disclosure, he'd stood outside and coughed prior to being called inside. 'Look, Karl,' Herman had said eventually, 'every time you cough like that I get a sudden urge to hide something under the bed. I know it's a bit awkward for you; I mean we can't just go back to normal. Well, not to the normal we had, anyway. I don't know how much longer I'm going to be around and it seems a pity to waste time on such formalities. Why don't you take the risk of coming right in and finding me singing a solemn High Mass and I'll take the risk that you're not the sergeant? Agreed?'

'Agreed.'

Herman wasn't there. It was more than that, Karl knew as his eyes roved the small space. The campbed had been stripped and the sheets and blankets folded neatly on top. Lengths of tack were coiled and ready for use and he found the identity papers on an upturned feed bucket. There was no note, not a single slip of paper where Herman might have written 'goodbye' in his slanted script. Suddenly, Karl felt angry and lashed out at the feed bucket which tumbled over and rolled into a corner like a chastened dog. He set it upright again, sat on it and flicked the identity card open. 'Mueller, Herman,' was printed under 'Name'. He'd never known his second name; from the beginning he'd always been 'Herman' or 'the horse master'. Having a second name seemed to reduce him, somehow, make him ordinary. 'Not to me,' he whispered. He sat on the feed bucket and held the identity card in both hands, with the same reverence with which Herman had held his mass book.

'Not to me,' he whispered again, to the small space.

The sergeant picked up the identity card and seemed to weigh it.

'Where did he go?' he asked of no one in particular.

The miner looked straight ahead impassively. Rudi appeared puzzled and threw a questioning look at Karl before looking away again.

'Never thought of him as deserter material,' the sergeant said, stuffing the papers inside his tunic.

'He's not a deserter,' Karl snapped impulsively.

'So, where's he gone, boy?'

'I don't know, Sergeant.'

The sergeant walked a slow circle around the cramped quarters until he came face to face with Rudi and the miner.

'So which of you two is going to be our new horse master?' he asked.

'Him,' the miner said promptly.

'Well,' the sergeant said, 'I can hardly resist such a resounding recommendation now, can I? Maybe Don Quixote and Sancho Panza would like to see to the horses?'

When they were alone, the sergeant stepped before Karl and looked him in the eye.

'Where's he gone, boy?' he asked again.

'I don't know, sir.'

'You wouldn't lie to me?'

'No, Sergeant.'

'I believe you,' he said and sighed. 'What kind of man decides to run and then tidies his hut so the next poor bastard doesn't have to?'

'A good man, Sergeant.'

'That was what they call a rhetorical question,' the sergeant growled. He rubbed his jaw with a roughened hand. 'Why would he leave his papers?' he wondered aloud. 'Without his papers, he's nobody out there and anyone can kill him.'

Karl had no answer for that. He remembered one of the many conversations he'd had with Herman which had circled back to religion. The horse master seemed to have almost as much enthusiasm for the Bible as he had for horses. Karl had been critical of the Church's wealth and Herman, rather than countering his argument, had supported it, wholeheartedly, with chapter and verse.

'And He sent them out without purse or sandals – like lambs among wolves.'

Karl shivered at the word 'wolves'. Herman had wonderful inner strengths, Karl knew, but he would be no match for wolves.

'You left me, boy,' the sergeant said, and Karl was jolted back to the present. 'You know we're moving up today. Make sure to keep yourself – I mean the horses – to the rear.'

He paused and looked intently at the boy.

'You might take a minute and write to your mother,' he said gruffly. 'I'll see it gets into von Kluge's mailbag.'

THE BRANDENBURGER. BETWEEN BRYANSK AND BORODINO

Deep in the forest, hunched against the bole of a tree, Unger consulted his map and then buried it in the humus underfoot. He turned east and began to trot, keeping on the balls of his feet, keeping the sounds of his passage to a minimum so that he could listen to the forest. After an hour, he caught the scent of wood smoke and followed his nose to a clearing. Someone had hacked out a rough rectangular space from the forest. Maybe the same person had built the timber cabin that squatted under a thin coil of smoke from its rudimentary chimney, he conjectured. The only thing he knew for certain was that a salvo of artillery shells had chewed the trees on the eastern side and spat out a mess of tangled trunks and broken boughs, which might also explain the deep tyre marks that started near the cabin and ploughed across the clearing and out of sight. First gear all the way and pedal to the floor, he surmised. Yes, an artillery barrage can have that effect on people. Though not on everybody, he concluded, eyeing the cabin.

He followed the paper trail of discarded documents from where the truck had stood, all the way through the open door of the cabin. The radio set on the table burped loudly and Unger tensed. He relaxed again when the Russian army officer didn't move from his sprawled position across the table. He heaved him upright in the chair and slapped him.

'Major,' he said, 'wake up.'

The major's eyes opened with infinite slowness and tried to focus on who had roused him to this new and painful reality. Unger wondered if the man was injured and began to unbutton his tunic to check for wounds. The major belched and Unger took an involuntary step back. Vodka, he guessed, and smiled. 'Bastards ran,' the major confided and toppled forward again on the table. He stripped the unconscious man to his socks and shorts and dressed himself in the uniform. Carefully, he checked him from head to toe for distinguishing marks, easing the wedding ring from his limp finger to his own. The identity papers he scrutinised and placed in his tunic pocket. After a quick scan of the strewn documents, Unger dragged a chair to the doorway and sat in the sunshine, letting his mind adapt to his new persona as his body became accustomed to the sit of the borrowed uniform.

It would be nice to stop, he thought tiredly, simply to rest and be Edwin Unger, instead of the multiple characters he morphed into and out of all the time, like some fucking incubus.

'But Edwin Unger is a fiction too,' a sly voice insinuated in his head. 'Why else would he have signed up for this charade? For the Fatherland?' No, he admitted. His German father had exhibited all the worst traits of the 'über Volk' and none of their virtues. No, his mother had been his role model. It was she who had acted the Hausfrau to perfection while secretly bringing up her son in her own cultural image and likeness. From an early age, he had learned to play the part of the son his father had wished for, and the old man had died happy. His father had always stressed the importance of 'becoming someone', as if his own exile in the Sudetenland had diminished and devalued him in some way. His son had achieved that goal and surpassed it by becoming not just someone but anyone. 'Except Edwin Unger,' the voice whispered. Abruptly, he leapt from the chair, gathered the papers from around the cabin and mounded them around the former major. He blessed the pyre briefly with vodka and tossed the match.

The tyre marks led him to the far end of the clearing where they veered into the forest. Behind him, the burning cabin spat furious sparks into the sky and he lengthened his stride and breathed the tree-spiced air. He was Major Yuri Bodanov and he was going to Moscow.

THE BRANDT HOUSE, HALLSTATT

'It's so frustrating,' Frau Hamner said as she blotted tears with a tiny, embroidered handkerchief. 'Rudi's letters are full of – timber,' she said and laughed brokenly.

Bertha nodded sympathetically and the herbalist patted Frau Hamner's arm. Sitting at the table, surrounded by books and papers, Eloïse pretended to be doing her homework. The regular gathering had been Bertha's idea. No woman should read a letter from the front alone, she'd decided, especially a letter that might come from her husband's unit commander. The letters had become just another part of their coffee morning and the three women had become friends.

Bertha had taken Kurt's place in the schoolroom and Eloïse had been encouraged to do her homework at Bertha's kitchen table. She could also have regular meals at that table since Frau Brandt insisted she could never get used to cooking for one.

'Please ask Erich to shift the green timber into the drying shed,' Frau Hamner read, 'and there's a stool somewhere in the workshop for Conrad.'

She looked up in exasperation at the others. 'I know they can't write about what they're doing or where they are,' she complained, 'but why do men never write about their feelings?'

'Perhaps,' the herbalist offered gently, 'it's because they know the letters are read by others. The censors draw a line through anything military, don't they?'

'Yes,' Bertha said. 'They seem a bit confused by Kurt's letters,' she continued wryly. 'They're full of details about the war, just not this war.'

The women laughed and Eloïse smiled uncertainly until a look from Frau Brandt bent her head to the books.

'Is Karl the same?' Bertha enquired.

Frau Hamner smoothed a single sheet of paper on her lap, and Bertha was touched to see how gently she stroked the creases from her son's letter.

'Horses,' Frau Hamner announced.

'They have horses?' the herbalist said, surprised. 'I thought horses belonged in the last war?'

'This one also,' Bertha said quietly, 'if the weather—'

The sudden apprehension in Frau Hamner's face silenced her.

'Come,' the herbalist said brightly, 'what does Karl have to say?'

Frau Hamner's eyes moved down the page until she found something she could read for the others.

'I like being with the horses, Mutti,' she read, 'they are such simple creatures. The rain made the roads impassable for a while and we worked with the horses, dragging stalled trucks from the road until we were covered with mud. I think the miner liked that.'

'I presume he means the miner liked being covered in mud,' Bertha commented and they laughed. 'He has a good vocabulary, doesn't he?' she said admiringly.

'And a sense of humour,' the herbalist added.

When all the delft had been washed and stored, Bertha walked her friends to the door.

'I haven't seen Frau Steiger recently,' she said. 'I wonder if she has anyone to share letters with?'

She saw the look that passed between Frau Hamner and the herbalist and decided to let the matter drop. It was common knowledge in the village, she reflected as she returned to the living room, that the Steigers weren't the happiest couple, but what was it like to lose your husband to the war and lose your son to—? Where did Max go, she wondered? She resolved to call on Frau Steiger and invite her for coffee. Buoyed by that resolution, she leaned over Eloïse's shoulder to inspect her work and then hugged her gently. 'Oh, well done, Eloïse,' she said, 'well done indeed.' Eloïse tensed and then her face relaxed into a shy smile.

When the girl had gone, Bertha sat with her book cradled in her lap, looking at the chair on the other side of the fire. God in Heaven, she thought, Kurt could be the most maddening man in all creation but she missed him. She wondered if other war wives suffered phantom pains; the agoraphobia of the half-empty bed, the automatic setting of a second place for dinner? She had seen that bright, impossible man go off to war. She wondered what kind of man would come home.

'Come home, Kurt,' she whispered, 'no matter what the war makes of you.'

THE BRANDENBURGER

Riding his luck and the cab of a truck, he charmed or bullied his way through innumerable checkpoints to the suburbs of Moscow. He could have gone all the way, as part of the confused tangle of retreating vehicles and soldiers funnelling back to the capital from the ruins of Bryansk and Vyazma, but for the plan to work he needed to be interrogated. At the next checkpoint, he jumped from the cab and demanded to see an NKVD officer. The startled soldier waved him into a small office redolent of strong tobacco. The NKVD officer who entered was thickset and swarthy with long-suffering brown eyes. Probably a Georgian, Unger guessed, and was vindicated when the officer spoke.

'Where have you come from, Major?'

'My HQ was east of Bryansk,' Unger said smoothly. He strode to the map pinned to the wall behind the officer and tapped the spot with his forefinger. 'Our orders were to estimate the Panzer strength around the Bryansk pocket and advise the commander on where breakouts might be possible.'

'And—'

'Artillery,' Unger spat. 'I think they spotted us from the air. When the barrage started, my staff – evacuated.'

The NKVD man nodded knowingly. 'And your radio?' he enquired.

'Out of action.'

'Did you salvage any documents, Major?'

'No. I memorised the important information and burned everything. There were enemy forces in the area. I didn't want the documents to be discovered.'

'What information did you memorise, Major?'

'It is highly classified information intercepted before the Bryansk pocket closed.'

'I am an NKVD officer, Major.'

'Yes, but you are not Boris Yulanov.'

This was the name German intelligence had supplied. During his briefing, he'd asked if Boris Yulanov was 'one of ours'. The intelligence officer had smiled enigmatically. 'Let's just say he is a security specialist,' he whispered. 'They trust him, Edwin. See that he, and he alone, hears what we've told you.' Whoever or whatever Boris Yulanov was, Unger prayed his name would mean something to this NKVD officer. He was gratified to see a tiny tightening around the other man's eyes.

'You will excuse me for a few moments,' the officer murmured and left.

He returned a short time later, looking very much paler.

'I am to take you to Comrade Yulanov,' he said.

THE YULANOV HOUSE, MOSCOW

There was little sign of the recent bombing in this section of the city, Unger noticed. The streets seemed to be crawling with armed NKVD patrols and he wondered if they were there to defend against the Germans or to control the local populace. A city occupied by its own army, he thought, as the official car halted before a three-storey house. They were ushered into a waiting room and, a few minutes later, a tall, patrician man entered. Unger noticed the deference shown him by the NKVD officer, who bowed forward to whisper in his ear and was dismissed.

'How did you know my name, Major?'

'I didn't,' Unger replied calmly, 'the Bryansk commander directed that you should be apprised of the information he sent us.'

'Go on.'

'I am to tell you that the Bryansk and Vyazma pockets are closed and surrounded by Panzers.'

'We know that.'

'In his last communiqué, the general said to inform you that the fascists plan to strike directly at Moscow. They do not anticipate a delay at Borodino; in fact, General von Kluge believes the Red Army will withdraw from Borodino to make a stand before Moscow – like the Russians did with Napoleon.'

He saw interest quicken in Yulanov's eyes.

'He said General Hoepner wanted to make a wider sweep to capture the reserve armies, but von Bock and von Kluge prevailed. The general also said they do not expect the Bryansk and Vyazma armies to continue their resistance. If they do, it will seriously weaken the German offensive.'

'Where did he get that information?'

'From a German officer captured at Vyazma before the pocket closed.'

Yulanov stared at him and stroked his upper lip.

'Come,' he commanded.

'My wife and stepdaughter,' he said absently, waving a vague hand at a middle-aged woman who was hemming curtains and a young woman reading at the table. Without another word, Yulanov walked out of the room.

Mrs Yulanov beckoned him to sit at the table.

'Boris is always thinking about something else,' she said apologetically. 'Please sit. Rosa, a brandy for the major.'

The young woman placed a marker in her book and went to fetch a tray from the sideboard.

'Have you been wounded, Major?' Mrs Yulanov asked anxiously, staring at his shoulder.

'What? Oh no, ma'am. Someone else, I'm afraid. A comrade.'

'Where were you stationed, Major?' her daughter asked as she placed a glass before him and began to pour.

'I'm afraid I can't tell you that, Miss,' he replied politely, 'it would be a breach of security.'

'Nonsense,' she snapped. 'It's not as if it makes any difference. Everyone knows the Germans will be strutting around Red Square in a few days.'

'Rosa,' her mother exclaimed, 'the major is quite right. What a question to ask. What would your father say?'

'My father is dead,' Rosa replied sharply. 'He died in 1939, Mother – don't you remember? It was shortly after he'd opposed the Molotov–Ribbentrop Pact.'

'That will be enough, Rosa,' her mother said firmly. 'I do apologise, Major—'

'Please,' Unger said, 'these are difficult times for everyone.'

Mrs Yulanov shot him a grateful look and Rosa returned to her book.

'May I ask what you're reading?' Unger asked.

'Rilke,' the stepdaughter replied without raising her eyes from the page.

'In translation?'

'In German.'

'Rosa is a linguist and translator, Major,' her mother confided.

'Don't boast, Mother,' Rosa said, but he could see she was pleased.

'I think I read somewhere,' Unger said, 'that reading something in translation is like looking at a tapestry from the back.'

They looked at him with such surprise that he blushed and continued. 'I think it means that you can see all of the design but none of the colours.'

'That is very clever of you, Major,' Mrs Yulanov said. He noticed she was staring at her daughter, who seemed to be regarding him with more approval.

'What do you read, Major?' Rosa asked.

'Mostly badly written reports,' he confessed, and she grudged him a faint smile. 'Before the war, I liked to read Pushkin and Dostoevsky.'

'In translation?

He felt a stab of shock before his brain registered the mischief in her tone.

'Now you've offended the major again, you wicked girl,' Mrs Yulanov complained.

'No, no,' he laughed shakily. 'I thought you were going to say that everyone reads Pushkin and Dostoevsky.'

'They don't,' Rosa said promptly, 'and it's a great pity. They might actually discover that we once had writers in Russia who didn't write to order—'

'Rosa,' her mother said in exasperation, 'you are much too free with your opinions.'

'She has a point,' Unger interjected. 'It's never a good thing to reject the past or dismiss it just because it's not modern and fashionable. I'm sorry' he added quickly, 'my wife always said I'm opinionated.'

Mrs Yulanov sat back and smiled while her daughter seemed to wilt a little.

'Ah, you're married, Major?'

'I was, Mrs Yulanov. I'm afraid I mean nothing to my wife now. The war, you know.'

He saw her daughter perk up again as Mrs Yulanov said sympathetically, 'It is as you've said, Major: these are difficult times for everyone.'

Boris Yulanov strode into the room, dressed in an NKVD commander's uniform.

'Come with me, Major,' he said. 'You also, Rosa,' he added, almost as an afterthought.

THE KREMLIN

'It is impressive, isn't it?' she whispered.

He realised he must have been staring.

'Yes,' he breathed. 'Have you been here before?'

'I'm afraid I can't tell you that, Major; it would be a breach of security.'

The official car had swerved into Red Square and pulled up before the Great Gate of the Kremlin. Sitting up front, beside the driver, Yulanov leaned out the window and displayed his identity card. The guard snapped off a crisp salute and waved them inside.

They were preceded down echoing corridors by an expressionless Red Guard who did some complicated stamping before saluting smartly and opening a door. They entered a small auditorium with raked rows of seats fanning up from a dais. Most of the seats were already occupied and the guard motioned them to some at the back. Unger was surprised when Rosa squeezed his arm briefly and went to the microphone stand at the front. A projection screen hummed down behind her and clicked into place. When Stalin entered the room, the entire audience sprang to their feet as if they had been tightly coiled. The lights dimmed and the projector whirred.

After the first bar of martial music, Unger knew it was a

Wehrmacht newsreel. The surging tanks, lock-stepping soldiers and fervid commentary set his teeth on edge. He watched the pincer movement of the Panzers that had choked off the Bryansk pocket and fast cutaway shots of lifeless Russian soldiers littering the landscape. He felt the tension heighten in the auditorium as lines of soldiers shuffled across the screen and the camera zoomed into a big close up of a conscript's face. From Siberia, he guessed, basing his hunch on the almond eyes and elevated cheekbones. The expression in the young soldier's eyes was one of utter hopelessness. The face seemed to stay on the screen for a long time, staring out into the darkened auditorium.

Rosa's translation, he thought, was efficient and inflectionless. Her lack of emotion was all the more powerful when she listed the huge numbers of dead and captured. The audience gasped involuntarily, and Unger saw a much-decorated general lean forward to grasp the back of the seat before him. When the lights came up again, Rosa moved quickly from the dais and settled into the seat beside him.

The audience hushed as Stalin and turned to face them.

'This morning, I went to the train station,' he said, expressionlessly. 'I was advised ...' He paused and let his gaze range along those in the front row. 'I was advised to leave Moscow,' he continued. 'I did not go. Those of you who want to go – go. The rest of us will smash the fascists.'

The clapping was thunderous, with none clapping more enthusiastically than those in the front row, Unger saw, and smiled.

'We will send for Zhukov,' Stalin said, and Unger felt the smile wither from his face. Swiftly, most of the audience began to file towards the exits; others hurried to form a queue of those who wanted to speak to Stalin. Unger saw Yulanov whisper in Stalin's ear and felt a trickle of sweat on his spine as the brown eyes swivelled to stare at him. Stalin said something to Yulanov and the NKVD man beckoned Unger to approach.

'You have served the people well, Major,' Stalin said. He leaned forward until his mouth was just an inch from Unger's ear. 'Take heart,' he whispered, 'Siberia has proved too cold for the Japanese. Now you will want to return to the front.' He turned to Yulanov.

'Arrange a car for the major,' he growled. Stalin leaned forward and grasped the startled Unger in a bear hug. 'Remember, Moscow is behind you,' he said fiercely.

Unger felt a tug at his sleeve and saw Rosa tilt her head towards the exit. He'd no idea of how long he'd been standing there transfixed. He managed a salute and withdrew to the car. 'My stepfather will come home later,' she informed the driver, and they sped from the Kremlin. 'You're very quiet,' she murmured. He'd been playing and replaying the same scene over and over in his head and still couldn't make sense of it. There was something he'd missed – something vitally important.

'I'm sorry, Rosa,' he sighed, 'it's just—' A wave of tiredness swamped him and he fought to keep his eyes open.

'You need a short bath and a long sleep, Major,' she smiled. She leaned forward and whispered something to the driver, who nodded and gave Unger a knowing look in the mirror.

'Well, at least they haven't blown up the power stations yet,' she said as she tested the temperature of the bath.

'Yet?'

'They're all packed with explosives,' she laughed grimly. 'The secretary has left little surprises all over Moscow. The towel is clean and the fresh uniform is hanging in the wardrobe.' When he looked surprised, she added, 'My stepfather is efficient, I'll give him that much.'

He had dozed in the bath and now his muscles felt like jelly. He tied the bathrobe and padded into the bedroom. She lay on her back, the quilt pulled modestly up to her chin.

'Now you smell of soap,' she said, 'as opposed to just smelling.'

'I'm sure that sentence suffers in translation,' he said and eased in beside her.

Sometime during the night, he woke to find her caressing his chest. Their love-making was fierce and urgent as if the ticking of the clock on the bedside locker was nibbling away at the morsel of time they had left together. She cried out as he entered her and he hesitated until her hands gripped him by the waist and tugged him frantically.

Dawn was just an hour away when he woke with a start and sat up. During the night he had dreamed of running over snow – desperate to get to a ridge that stood knife-sharp against a cobalt sky. Grunting, he'd tugged his feet from the yielding drifts, clawed his way up the incline until he stood at the top. He'd felt a tingling in his bare feet that vibrated through his body to the tips of his ears. Two armies confronted each other on the plateau beneath him. They were arrayed in all the colours he had brushed on his toy soldiers as a child. As he watched, the army farthest away was slowly erased by a white cloud. When it had passed, the army had disappeared. 'That's it,' he whispered and flung himself from the bed. He was struggling into his trousers when he became aware of her. She stood at the high window, looking out at the waxing dawn. She was naked and the diffuse light gave her a ghostly appearance.

'I must go,' he said lamely. He thought she wasn't going to answer.

'You know, you talk in your sleep,' she said sadly.

He froze in the act of pulling on his coat.

'What did I say?'

'I could tell you,' she said, 'but it would suffer in translation.'

He walked up behind her and put his palms on her shoulders.

'Rosa,' he began but she turned and put a finger to his lips.

'War is difficult for everyone,' she said and took her finger away to kiss him lightly. 'You'd better go,' she said, 'before it's too late. '*Es schneit*,' she added, 'it's snowing.'

THE RUSSIAN DEFENSIVE LINE BEFORE MOSCOW

The heavy car gripped the road confidently as they roared out through the Moscow suburbs. All too quickly they were off the paved road and slewing through virgin snow. Miraculously, the driver seemed to have some intuitive grasp of where the road lay and they made good time. Checkpoints were a regular irritation, only slightly ameliorated by the shock he saw in sentries' faces when they recognised the scrawled signature on his pass. That too had been a miracle – something that had appeared in the tunic pocket of his new uniform. He had to admit that Yulanov might be a cold fish but he was efficient.

He felt and heard the big guns some time before they reached the front. The pounding seemed to shiver through the tyres from the road and grew louder and louder until he could only mouth his thanks to the driver. Then he was slogging, shin-deep, through a blizzard that blew a tattered white curtain across the landscape.

He fell into a trench and managed to soothe the startled soldiers, who directed him to their HQ. It was a cave hollowed into an embankment, and he ducked low to enter. The officers hardly looked at him as they bustled about shouting into telephones and moving markers on the wall map. He traced the tiny tank markers and gasped. The Panzers were in Kallinin. Christ, if they—. His mind raced and seemed to seize. He stood perfectly still, unaware of the snow that was melting from his coat to puddle around his boots. If they stall in this snow, he thought, even for a few days, the elite troops from Siberia will be here.

Stalin had said that Siberia had proved too cold for the Japanese. How many armies had the Japanese withdrawal freed up? How many divisions were travelling west at this moment? If the offensive stalled? He groaned aloud and an army officer looked up. 'There's coffee in that flask,' he said helpfully, 'you look like you've seen a ghost.'

Unger forced himself to nod and filled a cup from the flask on a side table. The bitter drink burned his tongue and kick-started his train of thought. Von Kluge needs to know this, he thought, swallowing the fiery liquid. If he gets this information, he'll dig in along the line and wait for spring. If he pushes on—

He put the cup on the table, using both hands so it wouldn't rattle. His hand strayed to his holster, only to pause and return to succour his other hand behind his back. The chances of killing all of them and getting to the radio were slim, he thought, reasoning calmly now, weighing the odds as his training kicked in. Slimmer if you factored in how long it would take for gunfire to fill the HQ with soldiers from the trenches and for him to find the right frequency on the radio and—. He was out of time.

He turned on his heel and stamped out into the trench. No time, he thought, no time for weighing the odds or waiting for the propitious moment. No time for caution. He had to get a message to von Kluge. That raw imperative pushed him to the end of the trench and into the blizzard. He tensed the muscles in his back against the bullets that didn't come. The wind tried to buffet him sideways but he leaned into its force, tacking as straight a line as he could manage. A sudden squall lifted the white veil for an instant and he saw a ridge rising in the distance. Some instinct assured him that the Wehrmacht were close. 'Just over the ridge,' he muttered through freezing lips. The gradient threatened to buckle his thigh muscles and he threw himself forward, clawing his way upwards. He collapsed at the top, peering through the falling white dots that rendered whatever lay behind them into the vague shapes of an abstract painting. 'There,' he grunted, as a grey blur moved in the distance.

Icy air burned his throat as he clambered upright and began to tumble down the other side of the ridge. His body was cast in snow and the weight of it dragged him down again and again. He squinted through frosted lashes and the grey blur seemed to become a more solid outline. He was certain it was the familiar shape of a Wehrmacht coal-scuttle helmet and began to laugh with relief. He tried to shout but his lips refused to move, turning his words into an animal sound. He trapped his upper lip between his teeth and bit down hard. Warm blood flooded his mouth and his lips began to tingle.

The words sprayed from his mouth, '*Nicht schiessen* – don't shoot – Edwin Unger – Brandenburger – *nicht schies*—.' The bullet spun him around and slammed him down. 'I am—,' he whispered as the cold point in his chest expanded to squeeze his lungs. His lips moved slowly to form a name he couldn't remember. Snow fell on his upturned face. It touched his cheeks with feathery, cold fingers and clotted his eyelashes. He no longer felt cold, just tired. I have come so far, he thought. Time to stop.

★

Even the snow failed to comfort him. At home, in Hallstatt, the first snow had always woken him early, a pale luminescence diluting the colours of his quilt and teasing his eyelids open. Snow ushered in a time of transformation, when the house, garden, village and lake – everything – was magically altered. Overnight, the lake seemed to become sullen and grey, its familiar shores swollen to a different configuration. Roads, paths and small fields filled and overflowed their fences, suddenly conspiring against the small creatures that tracked across them. From the church steeple to the humblest village roof, every building wore a similar bonnet as the leaden sky imparted an equal benediction. His first sense of awe quickly melted into action. The toboggan was roused from its summer sleep in the woodshed and pushed to make twin furrows down the hill behind the house – furrows that smoothed and hardened until the toboggan hissed with breathless speed and bucked its load into a yielding drift. He remembered Max, angular and overdressed, like a tailored scarecrow, pretending an absorption in individual snowflakes while he and Elsa—.

Russian snow is different, he thought, to distract himself. It comes down relentlessly like an assassin bent on smothering; fast and thick and denser still until it erases the known world, reducing his horizon to an impenetrable curtain as close to his eyes as the tips of their lashes. It was cold – so cold.

His father had asked the sergeant about winter uniforms and provoked a stream of obscenities. Karl had listened carefully and distilled the sergeant's ranting into one crystal clear fact. There were no winter uniforms. The brass, the sergeant raged, had budgeted for a summer war. The winter gear mouldered in German warehouses while the Wehrmacht shivered in thin-soled shoes and lightweight uniforms or gambolled naked in the snow for propaganda pictures for the press who had been ordered by Goebbels to edit the word 'snow' from their reports. It was the apprehension in his father's eyes more than the sergeant's expletives that had driven him to brave the blizzard and find solace among the horses.

They had run out of fodder for the horses two days earlier, and the quartermaster hadn't been sympathetic.

'The frontline troops fight on a few grams of bread and fat per day, soldier,' he'd snarled. 'Nothing's coming through; not bullets, shells, rockets or reserves, and especially not winter clothing. Humans first and then horses, that's the pecking order. If it gets any worse,' he'd added darkly, 'we won't eat the troops.'

He pulled a sack from inside his jacket and trudged into a stand of birches that made a hedgehog of a small hill. The snow was lighter under the branches and he foraged for twigs, pushing them quickly inside the sack so that when it froze, he wouldn't have to wrestle with it to get them out again. No shortages for the quartermaster and his cronies, he thought bitterly, not with that fat belly. He swung the sack angrily over his shoulder, pirouetted and sat with a thump. In a foul humour, he started on the return journey to where the horses were tethered.

Mercifully, the snow had stopped falling and he slogged, head bent, to benefit from the tracks he'd made on his way to the wood. The snowball caught him square in the forehead and he dropped the sack in surprise. The second slapped him just above his breastbone and he felt some of it slither under his shirt and down his body. Furious, he looked up to see his father and the miner crouched near the horses, scooping up snow to compact it for the next salvo. With a roar, he rushed forward and tackled Rudi, tumbling him to the ground. They wrestled and rolled to the bottom of a short incline and then stood apart, cuffing snow at each other until they were both sugared in white and laughing breathlessly. 'Oh, oh,' his father grunted and moved back a few paces.

'Coward,' Karl yelled.

Rudi smiled. Karl whirled around to find the miner just a few paces away. He was carrying an enormous snowball in both hands. 'Surprise,' he said, and chucked the snow boulder.

Karl back-pedalled furiously, tripped and landed on his back. With awful clarity, he watched the missile reach its zenith and begin its downward trajectory. He was waving his limbs wildly, like a beetle on its back trying to escape the inevitable when the world went white. He couldn't breathe. Snow filled his mouth, blinded his eyes and muffled the sounds of laughter from the others. He sat up and spat snow while the miner thumped his back and his father fetched the sack. He could hear them trying to smother their giggles all the way back to the camp and tried to resurrect some of his previous ill humour. It seemed to have melted away. For the first time that day, he noticed the sky was cobalt-blue and the sun made bright, shaggy halos around the horses' heads. For the first time in a long time it felt good to be alive.

Von Kluge's army, 18 kilometres from Moscow

Kurt Brandt had never really considered snow. Snow in Vienna tended to be decorative for a few days and a damned nuisance after that. Of course, people could bundle up good and warm if they really had to go somewhere. Because he had rooms at the university, he never had to go far. He tended to build a fire and hibernate among his books. He hadn't been long enough in Hallstatt to experience winter there but he remembered one bright morning when he'd looked at the gleaming peaks of the Dachstein Mountains and wondered what Hallstatt would be like when those high, white copes let down their hems and clothed the valley. Maybe it was happening already, he mused, although Bertha hadn't mentioned it in her most recent letter. It had been a very welcome letter; in fact, he'd been walking on it for two weeks.

The sergeant had been adamant.

'Any scrap of paper you get goes in your shoes for insulation. Canvas and tarpaulin you put inside your tunic or under your cap. Straw you stuff down the legs of your trousers.'

'What about ticks, Sergeant?'

'Let them bring their own straw. Every man coming off sentry duty, stand among the horses until you warm up.'

Karl had developed a method for keeping the horses warm. He'd rounded them into a solid circle and rotated them so that every horse got a spell on the inside where it benefited from the body heat of its companions. The soldiers had been keen to adopt his idea even though Karl had insisted it was a Russian custom.

De Caulaincourt, Napoleon's historian, had written of sentries found frozen to death and, one hundred and twenty-nine years later, Kurt knew that rigid bodies were a regular occurrence. Cold, he thought, was such an inadequate word. It was a word rubbed smooth of significance by its ubiquity in Central Europe. The same held true of 'temperature'. Minus thirty-five degrees, he'd discovered, was something the brain liked to engage with while the rest of the body simply endured. Russian cold seemed to freeze the marrow and work its way out to the skin and extremities. He had started making a list of descriptive phrases and hoped to compare the list with Karl. Among them were:

When the hairs in your nose make a crunching sound.

When your breath freezes on your beard, moustache and eyebrows.

When it hurts to breathe.

When you can't steady your hand to write.

When you dip the nib in the ink bottle and it bends.

When you stop on the way to somewhere and just stand there until a comrade pushes you on.

He had begun to feel guilty about the comforts associated with being on the general's staff and had assuaged that guilt by 'redeploying' various items to Karl, Rudi and the miner. The last had so many discarded memos from various field commanders stuffed inside his clothes that the others christened him 'Top Secret'. Kurt had become so adept at salvaging the dregs of wine and brandy glasses and the discarded pieces of bread and chicken in the general's mess tent that von Kluge had enquired slyly if he was 'keeping pigs'.

He laughed and watched his breath plume before his face. The sentries had given up sluicing the snow from von Kluge's tent, and the captured Russian stove gave only a grudging warmth. Even the crush of bodies didn't make the temperature any more than bearable and Kurt thought it plummeted further when the commanders began to report.

Kurt remembered one of the few times he'd attended mass in Vienna. It was more to soothe his parents' anxieties about their atheistic son than for his own edification. But he had felt uplifted by the sonorous Latin phrases and the majesty of the Palestrina motets. Suddenly, it had seemed to him, the main celebrants, in their gold-encrusted copes, had retired to the rows of seats that flanked the altar and a priest in a plain surplice and soutane began to read from the lectern. It had been in November and the priest had read the names of the dead. As the list went on and on, Kurt thought the magic of the ceremony and his own sense of exhilaration had seemed to trickle away out under the door of the cathedral. He thought of that now as the various commanders took turns to inform von Bock of their casualties and shortages. Just when he imagined the dreadful tolling of their voices would go on forever, von Bock interrupted.

'Enough! We are within thirty miles of Moscow,' he muttered so that von Kluge, Halder, Hoepner and the others bowed forward to hear him.

'Our Panzers are outgunned by their T34s. Our artillery fires and freezes. We light fires under our trucks and personnel carriers at night so that they can slide into drifts come morning. The men—' He placed a hand over his eyes and continued speaking as if he couldn't face the pictures he himself was conjuring. 'The men are beyond exhaustion. They push forward on a few morsels of bread they must chip with a bayonet if they want to eat. Coffee freezes in their flasks.'

He stopped again and took the hand from his eyes. Kurt saw the naked rage there and tried to disappear behind von Kluge's broad back.

'No winter uniforms, no boots, no food, no glycerine for the engines or the guns, no reserves. Nothing except the imperative to take Moscow. With what?' he asked despairingly. 'I had a call from Berlin,' he said and Kurt sensed a frisson of energy pulse through the audience and everyone sat up more straight with anticipation. 'They asked if I could say exactly when we would take Moscow – the Führer wants to know. I explained our circumstances and the impossibility of giving an exact time. They insisted. It seems the capture of Moscow has already been trumpeted in the German press. The Führer may wish to make a broadcast. He may even march into Moscow at the head of his victorious troops, as he did in Paris.'

The general shook his head in disbelief.

'I asked to speak to Der Führer directly. He listened to everything I had to say and wished me a happy birthday.'

He made a strangled sound that was half-laugh, half-sob and turned away for a few moments. When he turned to face them again, Kurt was struck by the weariness in his face. Von Bock waved a hand in von Kluge's direction.

'General von Kluge, as you know, was summoned to the Berchtesgaden to report directly to the Führer on the situation at the front. General?'

Von Bock slumped in his chair and ceded the floor to the younger man. Kurt had watched von Kluge walk a tightrope across the chasm between the frost-bitten reality of his army and the expectation of triumph from Berlin. He'd seen him cajole the brass on the telephone and then explode in private. He had few illusions about the man he'd shadowed and observed from Smolensk. Von Kluge, he knew, had a soldier's heart and a politician's head but the crucible of Russia threatened to grind him to despair. The summons from Hitler had engendered a rare calm in the volatile general – a fatalism that seemed to move him beyond concern for his own position to a commitment to bringing the truth home to Hitler, whatever the personal cost. As he strode to take his place before the assembled commanders, Kurt tried to read the runes in his face, but the normally expressive and spirited man seemed somehow tentative and diminished.

'The Führer received me very graciously,' he began. 'I explained our situation, detailing the difficulties that many of you have brought to my attention. The Führer said he found it hard to understand why it was taking so long to capture Moscow and why we hadn't anticipated fighting in winter. I conveyed our suggestion that we should withdraw and dig in along a defensible line.'

The audience shifted nervously in their seats. Kurt had been privy to many of the meetings von Kluge had had with the various commanders and had been shocked by the vehemence of the criticism of the brass in Berlin and the direction of the war by those who were distant from the realities of the front. While they had been almost unanimously in favour of withdrawal and retrenchment, it seemed to shake some of them that von Kluge had declared their hand so openly to Hitler.

'What did he say, General?' Heinrici asked.

'He said no,' von Kluge said flatly. 'He said there must be no retreat. We must stand fast. Not a single step back.'

It seemed to Kurt, in that instant, that the intense cold outside had broken through the flimsy barriers of canvas and flooded the tent. He felt a numbness climb from his toes and settle in his belly.

'That's it, then,' Halder muttered as von Kluge sat. 'We push on for Moscow.'

It was as if someone had dropped a flaring match in straw. Various commanders shot to their feet demanding supplies and reinforcements. Others complained of the impossibility of progressing in arctic conditions or painted vivid pictures of reduced troop strengths and the emaciated condition of the men. The cacophony built in intensity until von Bock rose from his chair.

'One final push,' he said, and some of the old fire seemed to burn in his eyes. 'One last push,' he repeated. 'In war, it often comes down to one division, one troop, one man willing to keep going, no matter what, to tip the balance and grasp the prize.'

VON KLUGE'S TENT, LATER

'Are we at the tipping point, General?'

They were alone and the general had moved closer to the stove and unbuttoned his coat.

'Yes, I think we are,' he said. 'Von Bock has that "do or die" look in his eye and Halder – Halder has decided that obedience is the better part of valour.'

'And General Hoepner?'

'General Hoepner thinks if I can get my army up to join his Panzers at the Volga Canal, we have a chance.'

'And what do you think, sir?'

Von Kluge placed his glass on the map table and ran his finger around the rim, listening to the high, whining sound it made. He picked it up abruptly and swallowed the contents.

'I think the view from a tank is severely limited. I'm sending Captain Schmidt and a small patrol up there to get an infantry man's perspective. I'd like you to go with them. Your memo from Guderian's bridgehead was helpful. You seem to have a nose for *scheisse*, Professor.'

'Thank you, sir.'

'You know we all read de Caulaincourt,' the general continued. 'Does history repeat itself, Kurt? Every time I open de Caulaincourt's damn book, I think he's been writing my reports since June. I know how the story ends, of course, but I find myself reluctant to read the last chapter.'

It was the first time the general had called him by his name. He wished he could say something that might offer von Kluge some small measure of comfort or reassurance. The man had threatened more than once to have him shot but they had eased into a friendship of sorts on the road to Moscow. Kurt Brandt found, to his surprise, that he had run out of words.

The troop could have passed for Russians. Kurt held back the tent flap and stared. Four Russian soldiers swung from their card game to stare back.

'I'm Schmidt,' the tallest soldier said. 'Heinz, Friedrich and Hellmuth,' he added, gesturing at the others. 'You must be the professor.'

'Y – yes,' Kurt stammered.

'Don't worry,' Schmidt said, smiling, 'we're dressed for warmth not infiltration. We have a spare uniform if you want it.'

When Kurt had clambered into the rough-spun uniform, Schmidt tossed him a pair of snowshoes.

'Your friend, Rudi the horseman, made those for us,' he said.

'Oh, and that pack is yours also.'

Hellmuth helped him into the snowshoes.

'Ever worn those before?' he asked.

'No.'

'Try to walk like a pigeon,' Hellmuth said helpfully.

'Rest here,' Scmidt said, 'I'll scout ahead.'

Kurt dropped his pack and sat on it, resting his back against a tree. They were huddled in a copse that fringed a hilltop and afforded them some relief from the blinding snow. One of his companions hunched before him and stared into his face.

'What?'

'Just checking you for frostbite,' Hellmuth said casually. 'We check each other regularly for signs. How are your feet?'

'I think I left them a few miles back.'

Swiftly, Hellmuth stripped him of his boots and socks and examined his toes carefully. 'No problem there,' he said, straightening. 'It might be best not to move around too much on that pack.'

'Why?'

'Grenades.'

'No signs or tracks,' Schmidt huffed when he returned. 'Guderian is east of us. I could hear his Panzers running their engines. Damned tin boxes won't start in the morning otherwise. Flat ground before him all the way to a railway embankment – good for tanks – a killing ground for infantry. I'll have a closer look at dawn. There's a sentry smoking on the embankment. They could be just strung out along the railway line but it's best to be sure. In the meantime, we need to talk to some locals. There's a small village northwest of here, about two kilometres. How's your Russian, Professor?'

'I can get by.'

He smelled the village before the huddled houses loomed out of the shadows. The air carried the sweet and sour tang of wood smoke and pigs.

'One hour,' Schmidt whispered. 'Check their papers first, it's what Ivan does. Food, yes, vodka, no. You hear me, Heinz? Professor, you get that house in there among the trees. It's just far enough away from the others to have a teacher or some other bourgeois. It'll suit you. I'll call for you on the way out. Go.'

'Papers!'

The eye he could see in the crack of the door looked more puzzled than frightened. 'Please,' he added and the puzzlement gave way to a wary amusement.

'Stamp your feet and come in,' she said. Her voice was husky as if unused to speaking. It also carried a quiet authority. She was waiting inside to help him out of his greatcoat and hang it on a nail behind the door.

'Sit by the stove,' she said, 'you look like a snowman.'

Guided by a glimmer from the stove, he found a chair and eased into it, gratefully. 'Walking like a pigeon' over two kilometres of fresh snow had tightened his thigh muscles to screaming pitch. The sudden comfort of the chair and the warmth of the stove made him clench his teeth against groaning. He was aware of her moving at the other end of the room and then a wick flared and steadied into a lambent light as she covered it with a clear, glass globe. He had time to register the silver frosting in her short dark hair and a strong face, saved from severity by large, brown eyes before his gaze swung away to the books.

'What is it?' she asked.

'Books,' he whispered, as he moved towards the shelves that filled one wall of the room.

'Don't you want to see my papers?'

'No – yes – later,' he said absently, trailing his fingers along the spines of the volumes, tilting his head back to let the titles settle on his eyes.

'Pushkin, Dostoevsky, Gorky,' he whispered reverently, until he came to Rilke's *Duineser Elegien – Duino Elegies*.

'You read Rilke?'

'You don't look like NKVD.'

'I'm not.'

'Then, yes, I read Rilke.'

'So do I,' he said, 'whenever I doubt the value of human existence.'

'Do you do that often?'

'Yes, now more than ever. Lately, I've been reading de Caulaincourt.'

'Ah, yes, Napoleon's Boswell,' she said. 'The chronicler of imperial hubris, military details and death, wartime reading.'

'Yes. I miss Rilke.'

She moved up beside him and took the Rilke book from the shelf.

'There was a time in my life when I couldn't read,' she said thoughtfully. 'I thought I'd starve to death. Later, I tried to read everything at once, like someone who hasn't eaten for a long time. It confused me. A friend gave me this book. "Just hold it," she said. "Some day, when you're ready, you'll read it, but every day you will know that you can. Rilke will wait for you."'

She put the book in his hands.

'Sit by the stove,' she said, 'I have some coffee.'

He resumed his seat, keeping his palm on the leather-bound book in his lap, as if earthing himself. The room became rich with the smell of coffee and that, combined with the silent company of books and the presence of a gentle woman, transported him to home. 'Home,' he whispered and the word hummed in his chest. Oh Bertha, he thought. A tear splashed on the book cover and he tried to soak it with his sleeve. 'I'm sorry,' he whispered. 'I'm very tired.'

She placed a mug in his hands and he held it under his nose to savour the aroma and let the steam soothe his eyes. They sat in a companionable silence that was interrupted only by the irregular ticking of the stove, before she spoke again.

'I am Anna Lunts,' she said. 'I work as a surgeon in Moscow. For the past few weeks I have been marooned here by the war. It gives me time to read and think.'

'Do you live alone?'

'Yes – now. My husband, Lev, was a writer. Some of his books are on the shelves. The lower shelves,' she added with a small smile. 'He insisted. Writing can be a hazardous occupation in Russia,' she continued, 'particularly if you are also a Jew. He was transported for – re-education. I was also rewarded with that opportunity.'

'That was when you couldn't read?'

'Yes – well, not the approved texts anyway. Marx is worthy but he isn't Rilke.'

'And after you were released?'

'Released? I'm not sure that word is the correct one. I was allowed to come back here, yes, and permitted to take up my position at the hospital. There's a scarcity of cardiac surgeons in Moscow and, surprisingly, some members of the politburo have hearts.'

'Your husband, Lev?'

'No. When I said the authorities had hearts, I meant they have aortas, valves and chambers, all the mechanical parts I'm trained to mend. Lev did not come back.'

'I'm very sorry.'

'Thank you.'

The silence stretched between them again. Kurt felt a huge sense of gratitude to this woman. For a blessed interval she had provided a place of safety and warmth where he'd been able to recover things he'd never fully appreciated until they'd been taken from him. He'd seen such terrible things that he'd begun to doubt if he could ever go home again. How could he bring that tainted part of him home to Bertha? It had been such a long time since he'd wept. The realisation that he was still capable of tears gave him hope.

'I must tell you,' he began, 'I—'

'No,' she said, firmly, 'you mustn't. I think I know who you are – who you really are. You came into my home with a love of books and, I think, of someone else. I haven't felt so blessed for a long time. I want you to have Rilke's book, as a token of thanks.'

'But – but, I can't possibly. It's such a precious thing.'

'Too precious to be burned,' she said sadly. 'The Germans will come soon, won't they?'

'Yes.'

'Then I ask you to save Rilke, as he saved me.'

'I haven't anything to give you in return.'

'You read de Caulaincourt,' she said, 'you know our army will burn everything from here to Moscow.'

He nodded.

'I would ask you to leave me your pistol. Please,' she added, smiling through her tears.

BORODINO, 16 OCTOBER 1941

The pistol lay between them on the table.

'You know what that is?' Zhukov asked.

General Rokossovsky looked up at the man who towered over him. Zhukov's face was just a few inches from his own and he flinched from the fury he saw there. Zhukov was notorious for his short temper and long memory. Some men burn off their rage in sudden eruptions and are calm again. Zhukov was not such a man. Nor was he a ranter or a berserker. Zhukov was a rumbler and those within his volcanic reach trod carefully. Rokossovsy tried to stay still. His stomach roiled with acid and he was afraid he might soil himself.

'It is a pistol, Comrade General,' he whispered through bloodless lips.

'Yes,' Zhukov grunted, 'it is a pistol. It has a barrel, a chamber, bullets, handgrip and trigger. It is not one of our icons that has only two dimensions we can see and a third dimension we are invited to imagine. Take it in your hand.'

General Rokossovsky snatched the pistol from the table and held it in a trembling hand.

'Put it to your temple.'

Rokossovsky put the muzzle to his temple and cringed involuntarily.

'If you retreat again,' Zhukov said, 'that cold kiss on your temple is the last thing you will ever feel.'

He rocked on his heels and turned his back, dismissively.

'I would suggest, General, that you borrow a backbone and muster your men for my inspection,' he said coldly.

Rokossovsky dropped the pistol and surged out of the tent.

'Do you think he was suitably terrified?' Zhukov asked.

'*I* was suitably terrified,' his long-serving and longer-suffering adjutant replied. 'Would you have shot him?'

'God, no. He's not really a bad general – just indecisive.'

'Is that a capital offence?'

'In wartime? Yes. Especially now. Also, he's Uncle Josef's current favourite. Give it two hours and Iosif Vissaryonovich will be on the phone, drying his tears and offering a present of two or three reserve armies.'

'They were coming anyway, weren't they? You knew that all along?'

'Yes, but he didn't. What news from Moscow?'

'The four major theatre companies have been evacuated.'

'You know, Yuri, sometimes I wonder about your priorities.'

'Comrade Beria has gone to the east to check on security there.'

'And your taste in sarcasm.'

'There have been riots and some looting in the city.'

'And the bad news?'

'We're falling apart, aren't we, General?'

'No Yuri, we're hanging on by our dirty peasant fingernails.'

'And the fascists are—'

'Freezing, starving, and dying – short of everything and feeding our patriotic Russian lice. We are like two drunks fighting in a village, Yuri – too tired to strike the knockout blow, both hoping to keep standing long enough for the other to fall. One hundred and eighty thousand men died here in 1812.'

He rubbed his face vigorously with both hands.

'Now I must go and tell men why they must do the same.'

*

'How old are you, Comrade?'

'Seve – sixteen, Comrade General.'

'That's a fine uniform, very fancy. Are you some kind of tsarist officer?'

'No, Comrade General. I am a cadet, at the Training College. I – I won the prize for operating a machine gun, sir.'

'Good. We compete for a bigger prize today, soldier. Be steadfast.'

They seemed to get younger and younger as he walked down the ranks and he felt older with every step. He thought the Cossacks looked as they must have done when they rode against the Tartars in the fifteenth century. The uniforms might be a shade less ostentatious but a wildness still imbued the horsemen and seemed to crackle through their spirited mounts. They cheered wildly when the adjutant led out the white stallion and Zhukov vaulted into the saddle. He was no Cossack but he had little patience with fractious people or animals and horses seemed to sense that.

'The fascists are at our gates,' he shouted. 'Like the Poles, the Tartars and the Hungarians, they would topple the walls of Moscow. They have burned our villages and hanged our villagers. They have starved our captured comrades to death. The stain of their swastika stretches all the way from our borders but it stops here. Borodino shines in our memories as the place where Napoleon stumbled before Moscow. The men of Borodino sapped his strength as he passed to Moscow and their spirits watched him pass again with his Grande Armée on the long walk home. That is history – an old story. Yesterday you cadets were boys and students. Today you are men and soldiers. Yesterday you Cossacks were overshadowed by bombers, tanks and artillery. Today you are the frontline and the last line before Moscow. For all of you, this is the day when you write your names in the history books and in the heart of the Rodina – the Motherland. Ru,' he yelled.

'Ru,' they chorused, 'Ru, Ru, Ru.'

It was the primitive war cry of generations of Russian defenders and it rolled once more around the battlefield of Borodino.

The sky was a wall of flame arched with rocket trails as they coaxed their fretting animals through deep drifts. Now that the roads were impassable and mechanical vehicles were as useful as dinosaurs in an Ice Age, the horses had become the new personnel carriers and ambulances. The sleds Rudi had made from raw timber hissed behind them as if emphasising the urgency of their task. War's brutal logic dictated that the wounded had precedence over the dead; those who had some hope of being mended and returned to the front were given a second chance at death. The others had run out of options and would lie where they fell until the death detail arrived later or the snow came first to cover them in anticipation of a grisly spring.

Oblivious to the percussion of death all around, they crouched and lifted, steeling themselves against the missing limb or the trailing intestines, quickly tying off the former and heaping the latter back inside its cavity – moving like purposeful wraiths to salvage what war had chewed and spat upon the blood-soaked snow.

'Here,' the miner said and Karl crabbed to his side. The boy was sixteen or seventeen years old, Karl guessed. He lay curled on his side with his arm beneath his head and his legs tucked up, as if asleep. He wore a perfectly fitted uniform and high, glossed boots and he was Russian. They had decided to take whomever they found and risk the wrath of the brass later. This had caused some contention among the ranks until a young officer had enquired loudly if they intended saving civilians as well. 'Yes, even civilians,' Rudi had answered calmly. 'Even you, sir,' he'd added.

The boy had no obvious wound and, at the nod, they lifted him from his snow-nest to place him on the sled. He whimpered, as if they'd disturbed his dreams, and turned over. Half his face was missing, as if someone had split a marble head with an axe. Karl leaned sideways and vomited. He wiped his sleeve across his mouth and nodded to the miner. They moved on. They were bending, lifting and stacking broken men, moving through the steps of their dreadful choreography – so focused on the present need and moment that they didn't know it was over. The sergeant hauled both of them upright. 'We're through,' he said. 'Take a break.'

'Later,' the miner said and turned to his task. Karl moved immediately to shadow him.

They found the Cossacks near the trees, tangled among dead and screaming horses. Rudi moved ahead of Karl and the miner, raising and firing his rifle, now loud in the silent aftermath. The horses bucked once and lay still. The abstracted, analytical area of Karl's brain puzzled over the improbability of cavalry, even as his body bent and lifted. Cossacks belonged to a bygone era, he thought as he cut the reins wrapped around a fist and used them as a tourniquet around the jetting stump where the other wrist had been. Cossacks are the staple of Russian state occasions, he argued with himself. What were the sabre-wielding anachronisms doing in this iron war?

He noticed the mare had begun to limp and nudged the miner. The horses, ill-fed and hardly rested to begin with, made heavy weather of dragging the loaded sleds through deep snow. For their handlers, there was the added freight of the unattended; those who whispered, screamed and called as the sleds ghosted by. At the field hospital, orderlies helped to unload and triage the casualties. The long hospital tent was a Bedlam. Attendants shoved bodies to one side to make way for the wounded as surgeons in bloody aprons worked with scalpel and saw to save as much as they could of men who had once been whole.

Finally, the sleds were empty. There was no water to sluice them clean and the weary trio led their horses to their quarters at the edge of the camp. Karl heard the dull crump of exploding grenades and didn't look up. He knew they were blasting holes in the frozen ground for graves. He fell asleep while brushing the mare and woke to find her nuzzling his pocket. 'Sorry,' he said, 'there's nothing.' The miner, stripped to his underwear, straddled a smoky fire of green sticks. Someone had told him it was a primitive method of de-lousing. Muscles in his arms and back jumped under his undershirt as if the needling cold was testing his reflexes. Karl thought he looked thin – his shoulders still retained their impressive span but the rest of his body tapered down to his waist and the undershirt billowed around him in the wind.

Rudi, who had always been wiry rather than broad, was now whipcord thin. Sometimes, at the end of the day, he looked as if his eyes were retracting into his skull while his cheekbones were pushing out. Karl slumped on his cot, his head hanging down until his father rolled him in. Rudi tucked the coat around him and rubbed his hair.

'It will be over soon,' Rudi whispered, 'one way or the other. Then we'll go home to Mutti.'

Karl heard equal measures of longing and anxiety in his voice.

'Yes, we will, Papa,' he said and felt his father's hand relax momentarily on his head. If what his father had said was a lie, he could forgive it. Hopes and lies were bedfellows in war, he knew.

'Love you, Papa,' he whispered.

'Love you, son.'

Even that short sentence carried all the weight of his father's fears. He was still weeping, silently, when he fell asleep.

THE PRISONERS' COMPOUND, BETWEEN BRYANSK–VYAZMA AND SMOLENSK

'Max!'

The young man turned and smiled uncertainly. He was not Max. The frost had eaten one side of his nose and frozen pus filled the hole. He held out his hands to the wire and moaned. His fingertips were blackened, as if he had been picking berries. Max picked berries, Steiger remembered. Karl and Elsa had come for him and he'd gone with them, despite his mother's talk of thorns. He'd come back in the evening with a bowl of bulbous blackberries and a brightness about him that Steiger had never seen before and never saw again. 'Maggots. There's always maggots after rain,' she'd said and tipped them in the bin.

Slowly, he unwound his scarf and pushed it through the wire. The Russian snatched it and bound it tightly around his head. Only then did he begin to shiver. Steiger walked on, pacing the perimeter of the prisoners' compound, trying to breathe through his mouth to lessen the impact of the stench.

He knew he smelled; everyone did. When everybody smells, nobody notices, someone had remarked in the mess. Not of him, of course. They tended to move away from him as if he carried the powerful smell of the compound. Powerful? Yes, that was the correct word, he nodded as he pulled up his collar to compensate for the loss of the scarf. Even with the blazing cold that seemed to cauterise his sense of smell, he could hardly endure the odour of human rot that came in waves. He was on his second circuit when he saw the boy again. He was lying on his back, near the fence, one hand tangled in the wire as if he had been reaching for something. There was no sign of the scarf and the dead eyes seemed to reflect a depth of disappointment. As Max's had, that day he brought the berries, Steiger thought. Pity, he knew, was a mistake. In a place where a scrap of cloth can mean life or death, kindness kills.

Farther on, a group of prisoners crouched together and he eased the rifle from his shoulder. They did that sometimes, drawn like filings to the magnetism of some fanatic who raked their apathy into rage until they flung themselves against the wire. Most times, a shot over their heads was enough to shock them quiet again. Sometimes it wasn't. He always tried to identify the leader and bring him down. He paused and pretended to examine the wire where it clutched a stanchion. The man at the centre of the group was less emaciated than his disciples. He had lank, brown hair, a thin frame, and an energy that aroused the policeman's suspicions. He saw a rough deference in the way the prisoners leaned in to listen and heard the measured tone of the speaker, even though he couldn't hear the words. His scrutiny was rewarded when the speaker raised his hand and signed a cross over the others in that peculiar Orthodox way. The meeting broke up and the policeman prolonged his inspection of the wire for a few moments before he walked on. The young Russian was still lying in the same place. He had been stripped and a chunk of flesh was missing from his right thigh. Even as Steiger's brain processed the evidence, the bile was rising in his throat. He turned away and vomited. When he turned back, the man who had blessed the group of prisoners was bending over the body. He said a few words in Russian and raised his hand in benediction before closing the soldier's eyes.

'They are eating each other,' he said, in accentless German.

'Who are you?' Steiger demanded.

The man hesitated and then his face relaxed into a look of resignation.

'I am Herman Mueller,' he said. 'I am a priest.'

'You are German.'

It was a statement and the priest didn't contradict it. 'Yes,' he said, 'I was the horse master in von Kluge's army.'

'You are a deserter.'

'Yes, I came to serve as a priest in Russia. The only way I could get here was with the army. When I saw the prisoners, I—'

'Why are you telling me this?'

'They need food and clothing. We have no help for the sick and no place to bury the dead.'

'That's not my business.'

'Perhaps not as a soldier, but as a man I think it is. Do you have sons? Would you let another man's son rot like this—'

He grunted as the muzzle of Steiger's rifle punched him in the chest.

'I could just shoot you now, deserter,' Steiger growled.

'If I live through this, they'll shoot me anyway, either our own army as a deserter or the Russians as an infiltrator,' the priest said. 'I have nothing more to lose but I might be able to save someone – anyone – with your help.'

Abruptly, Steiger withdrew his rifle and shouldered it. The next time his circuit brought him to the compound gate, he saw the Waffen captain and Harmonica Man waiting for him. The captain looked more skeletal than he had before but his eyes seemed to have expanded to accommodate even more madness. He looked away from those eyes and examined Harmonica Man. He'd wondered why their arrival hadn't been heralded by his terrible music and now he had his answer. Harmonica Man's nose was completely black and his lips bubbled with suppurating sores. He seemed unaware of his surroundings and gazed at the prisoners like a bored child at the zoo.

'Where are the others?' Steiger asked.

'Oh, checking the papers of those in Purgatory or Jew-hunting in Hell; who knows,' the captain said, airily. 'What's the news from Hades?' he asked, inclining his head towards the compound.

'None.'

'None? I see you're as voluble as ever, Herr Steiger. What? No news? No young Russian killed for his Wehrmacht scarf? No older man conversing with Herr Steiger at the wire?'

'They're starving.'

'My, oh my,' the captain sneered. 'Herr Steiger has found his long-lost heart.'

'They're eating the dead.'

'That solves the food shortage, doesn't it?' the captain said. 'It doesn't matter; we move them on tomorrow.'

'They'll die,' Steiger insisted stubbornly.

'Of course they will, dear Steiger,' the captain laughed. 'That's the point, surely. No matter where you drive the flock, the journey always ends in the abattoir.'

Steiger sat when they'd gone. He knew that if he continued to sit, the cold would climb up his body and kill him. He'd seen it happen, soldiers just sitting down either from exhaustion or simply not caring any longer. Other soldiers took terrible wounds and lived. Why? They were the ones with photographs in their wallets, he'd discovered. He had no one to return to, no one to live for. He climbed to his feet again and began to patrol the dead.

THE ARCHBISHOP'S PALACE, ZAGREB

'*Ite, missa est.* Go, the mass is ended.'

'*Deo gratias.* Thanks be to God,' Max intoned with more relief than fervour. The archbishop, he'd discovered, was prone to scrupulosity. He seemed compelled to parse every word of the ritual before pronouncing it. Sometimes he repeated a phrase as if he might elicit more magic from it with a different emphasis or inflection. Max found it tedious but didn't let that show on his face. He was careful to shadow the celebrant, keeping his movements to the bare minimum – anticipating when the cruets should be presented and the water poured. He was the perfect altar-server in that he did nothing to distract from what happened at the altar. The monsignor, he reflected, had been the same, even though he acknowledged that poor Uncle Drago had acted out of conviction rather than calculation. The archbishop relied on him to handle the worldly matters that threatened to sidetrack him from his quest for holiness. Max accepted that this was a symbiotic relationship. The archbishop was the big fish that moved majestically through deep waters, and he was the pilot fish, the remora, insignificant and unnoticed. In that capacity, he could nudge the archbishop to focus on one matter rather than another and could feed on the scraps of information the prelate ignored or left undigested.

His stomach rumbled, reminding him that he'd been fasting from midnight. Silently, he hung the vestments and stored the sacred vessels while the archbishop hunched on his prie-dieu. He knew from experience that his mentor was loath to leave the mystical for the mundane and eased the sacristy door closed behind him.

The morning mail overflowed the small table in the hallway and he carried it into the office adjacent to the breakfast room. Hunger sharpens the senses, he reminded himself as he riffled through the pile; breakfast could wait. At the bottom of the pile, he found a letter addressed to himself. The handwriting was not his mother's. Mercifully, the spate of letters from his mother had slowed to a trickle and stopped. Perhaps she had intuited that he shoved them, unopened, into the stove. He slit the bulky envelope and spilled its contents on the desk. The short letter was signed by a Franciscan friar of the Dubrovnik monastery. The friar begged him, in memory of his uncle, to present the enclosed material to the archbishop.

He was about to feed it to the stove when he turned it over and saw a postscript on the other side. It recounted a story told by a visiting Italian journalist who had interviewed Pavelič, the Poglavnik. During the interview, the journalist had remarked on a wicker basket Pavelič had on his desk, enquiring if it might contain some delicacy or other. 'No,' Ante Pavelič had replied, cheerfully, 'it contains a gift from my devoted Ustashe.' He'd flipped the lid and the horrified journalist saw that it contained human eyes. 'Forty pounds of them,' the Poglavnik had assured him. Max had inured himself against Ustashe atrocities and considered this as just another item for his files. The enclosed photographs revealed the usual mutilations, except for the last one which slipped from his nerveless fingers and seesawed down to the desk. He screwed his eyes shut and concentrated on breathing through his mouth. Finally, he opened his eyes and bent to examine the photograph. The pile of bodies was indistinguishable from all the others he had seen except for one detail. Marija was sprawled at the top of the grisly mound, her dead eyes locked on the camera. The black and white tones gave no hint of her lustrous, raven hair or the shimmering whiteness of her skin. The photograph did nothing to soften the wound in her throat or the small, black hole in her forehead. He stuffed the photographs in the envelope and dropped it in a drawer.

'Enter,' the voice murmured and he moved across the carpet to place the mail beside the toast rack. He retreated and sat on a straight-backed chair to await instructions. He wondered if some of his mother's poison hadn't lain dormant in his belly. His skin felt ice-cold and the room seemed to pulse in and out of focus. He closed his eyes and concentrated on breathing deeply into the pit of his stomach. You are alive, he reminded himself. Photographs are nothing more than frozen moments from the past. That past has no hold over you now. The image of Marija surfaced and sharpened one last time in his mind. Was that reproach or gratitude in her eyes, he was wondering when the archbishop's voice intruded.

'The nuncio is troubled,' he said.

Max nodded and allowed the pause to lengthen. The nuncio was a Benedictine who'd been plucked from delivering philosophy lectures at the Angelicum in Rome and deposited in Zagreb as the Vatican's eyes and ears in Croatia. Max had seen photographs of him attending military parades and Ustashe rallies and thought he looked permanently confused.

'Why send such a man to Zagreb?' he'd asked his uncle.

'Why indeed,' Uncle Drago had muttered angrily. 'Why would anyone send a man with no diplomatic experience whatsoever? We need a wolfhound to track Paveliç and his pack, and Pacelli sends us this amiable sheepdog. The Poglavnik rewards him with a private plane and permission to go anywhere in Croatia.'

'Why, Uncle?'

'Because you can take a blind man anywhere without fearing

what he'll see.'

'It doesn't make any sense.'

'It does if it's Vatican policy not to see, hear and especially not to report any evil from Croatia.'

What could have changed to worry the compliant nuncio, he wondered? Was there a faction in the Vatican who took a different line on Croatia to the pope's? As if prompted by Max's question, Archbishop Stepinac provided the answer.

'Cardinal Tisserant has been urging the apostolic delegate to investigate alleged atrocities by the Ustashe against the Serbs. I met Tisserant once, in Rome; a wonderful churchman, of course, but a little abrasive.'

Max's attention fastened on the name. If this Cardinal Tisserant could provoke anxiety from the passive nuncio, and do so without regard to Pacelli's disapproval, he must be a very powerful man indeed. He might be the sort of man Max should cultivate or avoid. What was the Chinese curse Simon Tauber had liked to quote? 'May you come to the attention of the authorities.' That kind of attention, Max knew, was a two-edged sword. It was a blade he felt ready to grasp with both hands. The archbishop twitched the nuncio's letter anxiously. 'Danica,' he whispered, as if trying to recall where he'd heard the word before.

'Danica was mentioned in some previous correspondence, Your Grace,' Max said helpfully. 'It was alleged the Ustashe had interned Serbs there.'

The archbishop took a sip from his cup and grimaced as if the coffee had grown cold and sour.

'What am I supposed to do?' he asked plaintively. 'You know how busy I am, Max.'

'If Your Grace can spare me, I could investigate the place.'

'Ah, but I don't spare you, Max,' the archbishop fretted. 'I work you too hard as it is.'

'If it will put your mind at rest, I'll be happy to go. I can take the train and bring my textbooks.'

'Would you, Max?'

There was a mixture of helplessness and hope in the archbishop's voice which reminded Max of his uncle and he felt a fleeting pang of guilt.

'I'll go tomorrow,' he said.

East of Borodino, on the Road to Moscow

'I'm sorry,' the sergeant said. 'Even the security divisions, cooks, quartermasters and armourers have been called to the front.'

Rudi nodded. 'What about the horses?' he asked.

'Quartermaster wants them.'

Rudi walked into the stable and the mare snickered a welcome. There was just one other mare and the stallion, Roland. Intense cold, lack of fodder and the exhausting retrieval of the wounded had cut a swathe through the herd. The mare snickered again and moved to the horse master. He could see she was dragging a hind leg and took her head in his hands. 'Sorry, old girl,' he said helplessly, 'if Herman was here—' He took some bread from his pocket and let her nibble it from his palm. It was his ration for the day but he knew what had to be done and it robbed him of his appetite. One at a time, Rudi led the mares to the forest. They were both lame and it took a lot of time and coaxing. When he came back to the stable, he left the rifle outside the door. The stallion followed him as he retraced the tracks he had made with the mares. When they were screened from the camp, he halted the stallion and cradled his huge head, teasing him behind the ears with his fingers.

'They have Cossacks,' he whispered brokenly. 'They're tough soldiers but they value horses – which is more than our army did. Take your chances, old friend.'

Walking back to the camp, he tensed his shoulders, listening for the sound of hooves behind him, dreading what he would have to do if Roland didn't go. At the stables, he turned and looked back. The stallion was gone. Rudi Hamner didn't know whether to laugh or cry. He stood in the silent stables and slapped his hands against his sides. He had taken off his gloves to rub the mares' noses before putting the rifle muzzle between their eyes and his hands were frozen. He thought he would never be warm again.

OUTSIDE MOSCOW

'This is our last throw of the die, Frederick. If this doesn't work, the cup is empty. Pray to God they fold before we do.'

'And if they don't, General?'

'Hitler says we hold, Sergeant.'

Von Kluge moved away from the table to stand before the sergeant.

'Should things not go according to plan, I want you to have a good look around. If Hitler isn't there, you're the superior officer.'

He smiled and extended his hand.

'I'm sorry I wasn't always the general you deserved, Frederick.'

'No other general would have put up with me, sir. Why do you think I'm here?'

If the orderly expected the major to show some alarm, he had brought his message to the wrong man. Major Brodsky was known among the ranks as a maverick, a brilliant tactician and leader of men. He was also a man who did not suffer fools gladly – of whatever rank. Which, the mess tent sages concluded wisely, was why he was a major in the Red Army and likely to remain so.

'Please escort the general inside, Anton,' Brodsky said.

'He has an adjutant and two other generals with him, sir.'

'We'll need some more chairs then, Anton.'

'The irresistible force is about to meet the immovable object,' one of Brodsky's staff whispered and the men around the table laughed before stiffening to attention.

'At ease,' Zhukov said and extended his hand to the major.

'Major Brodsky, I presume?'

'Yes, sir.'

'Allow me to introduce generals Govorov and Rokossovsky. We have spent the morning supervising the liberation of Dedovo. Do you know it, Major?'

'No, sir.'

'Neither did we until this morning when it became imperative to drive a handful of German soldiers from two houses they occupied at the other side of the ravine from the village.'

'I presume this Dedovo was of strategic importance, General?'

'It was – to someone.'

The men around the table stiffened to attention again. There could be only one 'someone' in all of Russia who had the power to command three of his generals to undertake such a task while Moscow was being attacked, in the certain knowledge that they would obey.

'Well, it seems you have already won a battle and not lost a war – yet,' Major Brodsky said dryly.

For a moment the space between the two men seemed to crackle with danger. Zhukov laughed and the moment passed.

'Tell me, Major,' he asked, 'can the Germans win this war?'

'Yes, General.'

'How?'

'If they were to retreat to a defensible line and dig in until the spring. In the meantime, they could tighten their supply lines, bring up reserve troops, regroup their Panzers and build some airfields. That would be a start.'

'And will they do that?'

'No, sir. Hitler has already made it clear that they cannot retreat. The winter and their present circumstances make it impossible for them to simply stay where they are. They have no option but to take Moscow.'

'And will they?'

'No, sir, not unless the Germans take Tula and von Kluge succeeds in destroying our forces here.'

'So you stand like the Spartans against the might of Hitler?'

'With some important differences, General. The Spartans had three hundred battle-hardened warriors against a huge but undisciplined army. I have considerably more men, artillery and tanks at my disposal.'

'I didn't see any tanks or artillery on my way in here, Major.'

'Good! Neither will the Germans, sir. Also, the Spartans were not expecting allies and so they fought to the death. We are willing to do the same, but I don't think we'll have to.'

'Well, let's see,' Zhukov said and strode to the map table, moving instinctively into commander mode. 'They'll put their heavy machine guns on this small hill,' he said, stabbing his finger in a small whorl of lines on the map. Extending his fingers, he dragged them towards himself. 'The massed Panzers will come right up the middle. That's how they'll keep your front flat. The tanks will be ready to exploit any weakness along the line. Even if one tank gets in behind you, well, you know what they're capable of. They won't move up until their artillery drop their calling card. Call yours up early and catch them before they get rolling. Now—'

'With respect, General,' Brodsky interrupted, 'I don't have enough armour for that strategy.'

'I can't give you any more.'

'I'm not asking you to,' Brodsky said, and motioned the general to step aside. Bemused, Zhukov ceded his position at the table with a small bow. 'Marshal Brodsky,' he said smiling.

'We haven't the armour to handle them if they come en masse,' Brodsky began, 'so we've mined the centre to force them to the sides. The mines are laid about a third of the distance from the hill to here. That means they'll come that far as a phalanx and then split, exposing their infantry. We'll harass their flanks about two hundred yards from the embankment and drive them back to the middle.' He paused and looked at Zhukov. 'You're right about the artillery, General,' he conceded, 'ours will limit their bombardment to the hill and the area to the rear of it. We don't want them blowing up our own mines.'

'Have you forgotten the Luftwaffe, Major?'

'No, just dismissed them, General. Even Richthofen can't fly in a blizzard.'

'What happens when the tanks come to the centre of the embankment?'

'I can answer that question in private, sir.'

There was a moment of stunned silence before General Govorov reacted. 'This is preposterous,' he raged. 'A mere major does not withhold information from a superior officer.'

'I am quite prepared to disclose that information to the Supreme Commander of our forces defending Moscow, General,' Brodsky replied coolly. 'It is his prerogative whether or not he shares it with his staff.'

Govorov looked as if he might object again and Zhukov stilled him with a raised hand. 'Gentlemen,' he said, 'it has been a long day. Why not avail of the hospitality in the mess while the major and I conclude our business?'

Govorov bristled and then smiled. He liked nothing better that sitting somewhere with a vodka bottle while Zhukov destroyed an upstart underling. With a light step, he led the puzzled Rokossovsky and the remaining staff from the tent.

'Tell me,' Zhukov said, and Brodsky told him. The general looked appraisingly at the major for a long moment before he took his hat off and wiped his forehead.

'If this works, Major,' he breathed, 'I'll make you a very happy man.'

'That's what my wife said when I fixed the plumbing in our apartment, sir.'

'And did she?'

'No sir, she ran off with the plumber who really fixed it.'

'Have you found someone else?'

'No sir, not yet.'

'Good! Then you have no reason to retreat, Major. Remember, Moscow is behind you.'

'I hope you put manners on that young pup,' Govorov said when Zhukov rejoined the generals.

'When this is over, I want Major Brodsky with me,' Zhukov said.

'In Moscow?'

'In Berlin.'

Lieutenant Gerhard Hauptmann stepped out of the hovel he shared with forty other men. The cold bit him to the bone and he welcomed it, welcomed the empty blue sky and the cleanliness of the snow all around. He had been fastidious about cleanliness from childhood and the squalid quarters and its complement of filthy, lice-infested soldiers was a torment. They huddled like rats under tarpaulin when the fighters came, sniffing above their heads while they camouflaged the guns – coming in low to snap tracer at their heels as they scrambled for shelter.

The major took a tracer round through the head at the second pass. Gerhard had heard the fighter planes coming, a monotonous droning sound that built and built until it sounded like an animal screaming. He'd lain on his back, waiting for it to end. Some men curled into a foetal position on the ground; others clung to companions or wept or prayed. The major had sat at the table as if waiting for his dinner after a day in the milking parlour. His round farmer's face had swelled around the exit wound and reset into the features of an old man – an old man infinitely weary of life who had given up on outrunning death.

Gerhard had been reluctant to lie with his face in the filth and had seen it happen. The tracer punched angry eyes in the wall and shredded everything at head height. The major tumbled suddenly, as if a prankster had pulled the chair from under him. Gerhard had turned to look at him and the major's left eye had looked back with an expression of mild annoyance. His other eye was somewhere among the wreckage. The major's blood was already frozen on Gerhard's sleeve as he inspected the guns. Crews filed out from their shelters and began to light small fires under the breeches. With luck, they might fire a salvo or two before freezing again. Their peripatetic contribution seemed to focus the Russian's fire power and they were being whittled away.

The field telescope drew his eyes and his feet followed. He liked to look through it in the early morning. It gave him access to a wider world before his own world contracted again to this dirty square of oil-smudged snow. For a few minutes he rubbed the eyepiece vigorously. The unwary or impetuous could leave their eyelids on the frigid metal. Satisfied, he bent and looked. At first he saw what looked like an impressionist painting, a mass of daubs and distortions. Patiently, he forced his fingers to tease the focus-ring until the view resolved into hard lines, like the photographic paper he'd seen change from ghosts to familiar faces in his father's darkroom.

His breath caught in his throat and the picture wobbled as a tremor rushed through his body. The foreground was a mushy whiteness that gradually bulked into buildings until, at the highest point in the frame, he could see domes. 'The Kremlin,' he whispered, and staggered back from the telescope.

'What is it?' someone called anxiously.

'I can see the Kremlin,' he said.

There was a ragged cheer followed by the sound of racheting as the crew elevated a long barrel. 'Loaded,' someone barked and he covered his ears automatically, so that he felt rather than heard the shell crack the cold air. He leaned forward to the telescope again as other guns barked eagerly. He saw a tiny burst of smoke above the domes and then another and another as the pack of guns belled around him. He wanted them to stop. They would wake the giant and draw his attention. Even without the benefit of the telescope, he could see T-34 tanks already snarling towards their position. The gunners were yelling like children, crab-walking the shells across the snow to the smoking breeches. He saw the paint melt on the metal and freeze into stalactites below the barrel. It was his sudden stillness that sucked their energy and froze them into a ragged tableau.

'They're coming,' he said.

PANZER TANK COLUMN, VOLGA CANAL ROAD, EIGHTEEN MILES OUTSIDE MOSCOW

'Back!' the tank commander shouted. He had wiped his eyes, unaware that his side-locks were already stiff with frozen tears. Goggles grew crystals in the humid tank and he had pulled them off an hour ago. With streaming eyes, he'd looked through the aperture and seen the T-34 nose towards their flank. 'Back,' he shouted again and felt the shuddering of the brakes. The Panzer bent down on its tracks and slewed sideways. He saw the tank to his right take the shell intended for him and burst into flames. 'Traverse and fire,' he yelled, even as he watched a burning man exit the hatch of the blazing tank. Again he shook as his own gun fired. The shell bounced from the sloped front of the T-34 and he swore. 'Forward and fire at will,' he ordered. Although undamaged, the Russian tank reversed at speed and the road was clear. Up ahead lay the Moscow–Volga Canal road. Von Kluge and Heinrici had been in agreement during the briefing.

'Punch through and get behind them,' he'd been told. 'Moscow is just down the road.'

Yes it is, he thought, as he scanned his flanking tanks and their clusters of infantry – if we can maintain our momentum and avoid more casualties. He forced his mind away from the shortage of fuel and the danger of frozen turrets and all the 'ifs' and imponderables that haunted every tank man. He could see the foxholes in the hills on either side of him and prayed the infantry could keep them occupied. 'House at eleven o'clock,' he said tonelessly and watched it implode. The crest of the hill was coming up and his stomach tightened. Crests meant exposing their underbelly for a few vulnerable seconds while their gun pointed uselessly skyward. The thump of the tracks on solid ground released his pent-up breath. 'There it is,' he shouted. 'There's the fucking road!'

They were steaming along a paved highway and he opened the turret to glory in the experience. Russian soldiers glanced uncertainly at the juggernaut as it roared by. He saw an officer salute and smiled as he returned the unexpected courtesy. Trucks wobbled as they came up behind them and then wove to the side of the road for sanctuary. A sign flashed by and he translated it. 'Eighteen miles to Moscow,' he whooped, 'eighteen – Stop!'

Ten yards from where the tank stopped, the road ended. A black hole stretched for another twenty yards to where the road resumed. The Soviets had run for home and rolled up the road behind them. 'So close,' he muttered as he wriggled from the turret and dropped to the road. 'So close, so close,' he repeated in a frantic mantra as he scrambled up the incline at the side of the road. At the top, he raked the land ahead through binoculars. '*Scheisse*,' he grunted and the single word seemed to empty his lungs of air. He descended the incline in giant, dangerous leaps. 'Radio,' he gasped and the startled operator glued himself to the bulkhead to give him room. 'General von Kluge,' he barked.

'Sir, we are on the Moscow–Volga Canal road.'

He heard the faint sound of cheering over the static and gritted his teeth.

'General, sir,' he continued, overriding the congratulations coming from the other end, 'the road has been blown. It means detouring through heavy drifts. Yes, it's possible. General, there is something else. I've looked ahead through the glasses. There are armies coming our way – and tanks. Yes, I am certain, sir. No, I hadn't time to assess their strength but there are thousands, sir. Yes, thousands.'

The Last Battle, Outside Moscow

'They'll drop the sky on us any minute now,' the sergeant said. 'Let's get organised before we dig in. The centre of the hill is mine, Ludwig feeds my heavy machine gun. Rudi and Tomas to my left – thirty yards. Your field of fire starts at the edge of the plain and sweeps to the middle. Simon and Rupert to the right – same distance, same firing orders. Questions?'

'What about me, Sergeant?'

'Karl, you wait at the foot of the hill behind me. If I have instructions for the others, you're the carrier.'

'I want to be on the hill, with the others.'

'You're the carrier, dammit.'

'I'm not a fucking pigeon, Sergeant.'

The other men drifted away to save the boy embarrassment. Karl noticed the miner shunt Rudi after them. The sergeant took a deep breath. 'No, you're not, boy,' he said, 'but—'

'And I'm not a boy.'

'You're right,' the sergeant conceded, 'a boy could never have come so far, so bravely, but I need a carrier who's fast and you're the fastest I've got. If we lose a gunner or a feeder, you can come up to the line. Agreed?'

'Agreed.'

Karl dug a shallow pit on the lee of the hill and coiled inside. The snow was coming down thickly and sweeping sideways before a freshening wind. He tried to pray but couldn't dredge up the appropriate words. He wondered if the other men felt the same, and whether the Russians prayed. That was his last coherent thought before the sergeant's augury came to pass and the sky fell.

The sky fell and his ears rang with the sound of its screaming. Shells and rockets climbed to their zenith and lost their grip, to fall earthwards. A thousand hammers battered into the hill and he quivered in his snowhole, trying to fold himself tighter, pushing against the snow beneath him, like a burrowing animal. He was deafened, blinded and pummelled by the harbouring hill as it groaned and shuddered under the blows. Some part of his mind registered a keening sound that built in intensity under the merciless barrage. He realised the sound was coming from himself and bit down on his panic, trying to blank his mind, willing himself to become as elemental and unfeeling as the snow that cradled him.

It was over. His ears still rang, his eyelids were frozen shut and his body twitched with phantom fears. Like a newborn colt, he staggered from the snow-womb, tottered, fell and rose again to a different world. He saw two shapes emerge from the snow to his left, and gasped in relief. Through the whining in his ears, he could hear the metal on metal sounds as the sergeant racked the machine gun on its tripod.

'Karl,' the sergeant called, 'to me.'

He stumbled up the slope towards the voice and almost collided with the sergeant before he saw him. 'Ludwig?' he asked.

'Loop the bandoliers around your arm,' the sergeant said calmly, 'and be ready to feed.'

He could hear the rumble of the Panzers as they moved on the plain before him. 'Infantry are using their cover,' the sergeant said, squinting through binoculars. The wind gusted and the sergeant kept up his commentary as an occasional squall lifted the hem of the white curtain that blinded them to the battle. 'Steady progress,' the sergeant murmured, 'almost a third of the—' The shockwave rolled back and they both ducked instinctively. 'Mines,' the sergeant growled, 'fucking mines. The—'

Again the dull crump was followed by a blur of fire and a warm wind touched their faces. 'They're pulling left and right,' the sergeant reported and Karl heard the anxiety in his voice. 'Follow the tanks,' the sergeant bellowed suddenly, 'follow the tanks.'

He ducked down to his gun as machine guns chattered from the other end of the plain. 'Fuck,' he said and elevated the barrel with a savage jerk. 'Maybe they're on the embankment,' he said, 'we'll fire high.' The bandoliers jerked and sped through the boy's hands as tracer-lines chased each other from the muzzle of their gun. The snow thinned, momentarily, and the sergeant eased up on the trigger. 'Take the glasses, Karl,' he ordered, 'tell me what you see. If you see Ivan, call it on the clock. Eleven o'clock high or five o'clock low – understand?'

Karl watched the bulky tanks steam on either side of the plain. The leading tank, on the left, juddered sideways and began to lean over. 'Anti-tank at eleven o'clock high,' he roared and the gun bucked in the sergeant's grip. Karl was aware of tracer rounds streaming from his left and knew Rudi and the miner had followed their lead. 'Converging on the front of the embankment now, Sergeant,' he called and paused, fiddling with the focus wheel of the binoculars.

'Keep calling, Karl,' the sergeant urged as the picture sharpened into focus.

'Branches and – stuff,' he shouted, 'packed before the embankment. The tanks are crossing it. They're through, Sergeant,' he yelled excitedly.

'No,' the sergeant said, 'God, no.'

'But they're—'

Fire filled the binoculars and he jerked his head back. He could hear the crump of artillery competing with the puffing sound of anti-aircraft guns and instinctively looked up.

'Fucking trap,' the sergeant swore and snatched the binoculars from Karl. 'Brush and boughs, soaked in gasoline,' he recounted in a dead voice. 'Big guns and ack-ack camouflaged behind. The poor bastards.' He threw the binoculars away in disgust and stood for a moment as if at a loss.

'Sergeant,' Karl called anxiously, 'Sergeant.'

The sergeant shook himself and sat behind the gun. 'We can't fire yet,' he said, 'or we'll kill our own infantry on their way back.' The sound of gunfire swelled as they huddled together behind the gun. Tracers and shells glowed and screamed over their position as the Russian gunners swung from the doomed Panzers and began to harvest the infantry. Karl buried his face in the sergeant's shoulder as screams competed with the flailing ordinance until the guns paused in their bloody work – paused and popped infrequently as the stragglers and the wounded drew their fire.

'Get the others,' the sergeant said, in the sudden silence. 'Go on, soldier.'

When the men were assembled, the sergeant seemed lost in thought. He straightened up suddenly and turned a full circle before facing the men.

'What is it, Sergeant?' Rupert asked.

'Nothing,' he said quietly. 'Just looking for Hitler.'

The men were still exchanging puzzled glances when he spoke again. 'They'll be here soon,' he said. 'Best be gone. See if you can join up with some other units. Back there – somewhere, the brass will regroup and dig in. Go on now; we're finished here.'

'Aren't you coming, Sergeant?' Karl asked.

'No.'

'Why?'

'Because I'm the fucking sergeant, that's why,' he shouted. 'Go on,' he said, in a more reasonable voice, 'I'll hold them as long as I can.'

★

Max boarded the train early and spread his books across the grubby seats in the compartment. The archbishop had arranged a black suit and greatcoat and the combination of strewn books and the austerely garbed young man deterred other passengers from entering. Meticulously, he arranged his books and notepad before placing his travel papers on the seat beside him. The dry, dogmatic theology books he studied would be his travel papers to a sphere of power and influence beyond Croatia and he immersed himself in them as the train left the suburbs of Zagreb.

At various stations along the way, Ustashe militia slammed the compartment doors open and demanded papers. Without raising his eyes from the book, he indicated the papers on the seat beside him. They were snatched up and then replaced, almost reverently. Sometimes he was aware of a salute and the softly closing door. Most of the time he was too preoccupied to notice and was surprised when a voice announced, 'Danica.'

The wind shifted as he approached the gate and his step faltered. He felt as if he'd stepped inside an abattoir and the stench of blood and rot burned the back of his throat. Only the leering faces of the militia peering through the wire forced him to continue. They looked like men who fed on the slightest sign of weakness and he refused to throw them a scrap. He pushed the papers through the gate and looked over their heads at the rows of cabins that receded into the fog. Danica, he thought, had a kind of taut silence, the kind of silence that followed a scream and anticipated another.

The gates opened and he trailed a militia man to a well-kept cabin, set apart from the others. The Ustashe knocked and walked away. Max pushed open the door and stepped into a fug of tobacco smoke and alcohol fumes. A single lantern burned on the scarred table, painting light and shadows on the face of the man who sat behind it. Max would have recognised that face in any light.

'To what do we owe the pleasure?' the Franciscan drawled.

'To the authority of the Archbishop of Zagreb,' Max replied evenly as he sat down.

'Stepinac's writ doesn't run here, little Max,' the Franciscan grunted.

'Is that the message you would like me to convey to his Grace?' Max said, in the same dispassionate voice, 'a message he is certain to relay to his friend the Poglavnik.'

The Franciscan's eyes hardened as he leaned forward.

'I could disappear you, Max Steiger,' he murmured. 'I could have you skinned alive, your balls and ears cut off and your eyeballs gouged from your head.'

'I'm sure the Poglavnik would appreciate a matching pair he could add to the wicker basket on his desk,' Max said as he rose from the chair. He walked out of the cabin and tried to suppress a smile of satisfaction when he heard the heavy footsteps behind him.

He thought the first cabin he entered contained corpses, until one of the rigid bodies, stacked on wooden bunks, turned his head slowly to stare at him. Those eyes held a look of total resignation and he moved away to count the inmates. One hundred, he estimated, as he walked the narrow passages between the bunks; one hundred humans, or what remained of them, lay side by side, like the planks of timber he had seen in Rudi Hamner's curing shed. He counted an even hundred in the next two cabins and he multiplied that number by the remaining cabins. Fifteen hundred were stored in the dilapidated buildings. Whether they were alive or dead, male or female, he couldn't tell. He guessed that the smaller forms he had seen were children and didn't count them. Apart from the staring eyes in the first cabin, not a single one had stirred or acknowledged his presence. He began to walk towards the rear of the camp and the stench pushed against him like a resisting hand. A human hand fell on his shoulder and spun him around.

'Go back, while you can,' the Franciscan said. 'If you go beyond this point, you will be faced with two options. Either you will tell the truth, in which case Stepinac will not believe you, or he will choose not to believe you. In either case, you will have to run home to Austria and hide with Mama. Or you can choose to lie to him and he will burnish your star.'

Max brushed the hand from his shoulder. He walked on through the fog until the ground fell away before his feet and he was looking into a pit. The burning church in the mountains was a mere sideshow to the horror that confronted him. A mound of corpses rose above his head and flowed down to the edge of the pit. Everywhere he looked, legs and arms intertwined in untidy intimacy. Almost all the corpses showed empty eye sockets and slashed throats.

He became aware of two Ustashe militia sitting on either side of the mound. As he watched, two wraiths were herded forward to kneel before them. Both Ustashe leaned forward, like confessors, and seemed to converse with the prisoners. Almost casually, one of the 'confessors' slashed his hand sideways and a prisoner fell. Before the body had settled on the mound, the executioner jumped up and punched the air in triumph before walking away. By the time Max had swung his eyes to the other man, he'd already dispatched the elderly man he'd been interviewing. This Ustashe hunched forward, his head in his hands. Max forced his feet to move over the corpses until he was standing over him. He thought the man looked as if he had waded, waist-deep, through blood.

'You can ask him any question you like,' the Franciscan whispered in his ear. Max remained silent.

'Why have you stopped, Ernst?' the Franciscan asked.

The man raised his head and Max was stunned by how ordinary he looked. He had a round face, sprinkled with snow-white stubble, and his eyes were an innocent blue.

'It was a competition,' he said in a flat voice. 'First to a thousand. Piotr won.'

The effort seemed to exhaust him and his head began to droop.

'Show the visitor what you have in your hand, Ernst.'

The Ustashe turned his right hand palm-upwards and Max saw a razor-edged arc of steel nestling in a leather sheath.

'What do you call it?' the Franciscan prompted.

The blue eyes crinkled at the edges as the Ustashe seemed to puzzle over the question and then his face relaxed.

'We call it the Serb-cutter,' he said softly. He stood and began to walk away.

'What did you say to the old man?' Max asked suddenly.

The Ustashe didn't turn.

'I said he should say, "All praise to the Poglavnik."'

'What did he say?' he asked.

'He said, "Just do your work, child."'

Max wasn't sure why he had asked the second question. Did he hope to hear something that would shed some light on the heart of darkness or was it that he needed words to explain why an ordinary-looking man with blue eyes had just cut an old man's throat.

THE PRISONERS' COMPOUND

He woke and stretched on his own patch of floor. Thirty men filled the remainder of the dank room that had previously been a Russian kitchen. Exclusion has its benefits, he thought, grimly. He wondered what had become of the Russian family they'd evicted.

The old man had withered them with silent contempt while the young woman had keened as her children clung to her skirts. She'd composed herself and organised the children to hunt for the possessions the soldiers had tossed in the snow. Their single spread blanket displayed the bits of their lives they could salvage; a pot, old photographs, scraps of food and two icons. She'd gathered the four corners of the blanket and swung her world on her shoulder before facing them. He'd expected spits and curses but the interpreter relayed her request to the sergeant. 'Shoot the dog,' he muttered, 'please.' At least the sergeant had waited until they'd disappeared into the trees before granting that small mercy.

Steiger had no room left in his soul for guilt. He considered he carried a full pack already in the silver cross and chain he wore against his skin. He looped it out of his shirt and held it before his face, as he did at the start of every day. He let it drop again inside his shirt and hunched his shoulders against its weight.

He collected his four grams of bread and fat from a bag guarded by a surly man and began to walk. The path to the compound took him through a corner of the forest and, sometimes, he touched a tree as he passed, not out of superstition or for luck but to make some brief contact with something living. Some instinct brought him up short at the edge of the forest. He could see the compound, latticed through the branches, and it looked unchanged. He remained standing beside a frozen birch until the answer presented itself. It was the silence. The world that radiated from the camp was always profoundly silent. No birds sang here and, if there were animals, the smell and spoor of men had constrained them to hunt at night. He had seen signs in the snow, the confident print of bears and the dimpled tracks of wolves. Wolves! They're back, he thought.

His first clear sight of the camp caused him to unsling his rifle. The prisoners were massed inside the gate, standing in complete silence as if drawn or driven there. Scattered over the rest of the compound, bodies sprawled lifelessly where the frost of the night before had claimed its measure. Some, who were sick, enfeebled or apathetic, sat unmoving in their misery. The captain stood with his back to the gate gazing out at the forest.

'Good morning, Herr Steiger,' he called, without turning.

Steiger circled him warily. 'Where's the other one?' he asked.

'The other one? Oh, you mean Theodor. Poor Theodor couldn't hunt anymore – his nose dropped off. Poor beast had begun to whine.'

He lifted a pistol to his head. 'Bang,' he said, as Steiger's heart lurched in his chest. He turned away from the captain and his heart stopped beating. The priest was spreadeagled on the gate, his outstretched arms and legs bound with wire. He moved his head and moaned and Steiger's heart hammered back to life. Reluctantly, he shuffled a few steps closer and saw the bullet holes in the bare hands and feet.

'Behold,' the captain said, 'a sheep in sheep's clothing.' He laughed wildly and a rumble arose from the figures massed at the gate. 'He came to the gate, whining,' the captain continued. 'They have no food. They sicken even unto death. What is that to me or to thee, deserter?' He spun on the last word and spat it at the priest. Slowly he approached Steiger, who stood frozen by those arctic eyes. 'I brought him forth and showed him the kingdoms of the world,' he whispered. 'All of this will be yours, I promised him, if you follow me.'

He leaned forward until his face was inches from Steiger's and his carrion breath wreathed his face. 'But he would not,' he confided sadly. 'It was necessary for one man to die for the people, Herr Steiger.' He leaned back and extended his arms. 'And so I raised him up – as a sign to the heathen.' The captain spun on his heel and stalked away to gaze again at the bleak landscape. A groan pulled Steiger to approach the priest. Fresh blood oozed from the black pits of his feet and palms and thin tendrils of saliva hung frozen from his chin. His eyes – only his eyes – reflected his agony as they found the policeman and focused.

In one smooth movement, Steiger swung the butt of the rifle to his shoulder and fired. The crack of the rifle shot severed the priest's hold on life and sent a shockwave through the prisoners. Steiger leaned his rifle beside the gate and fumbled in his pocket. His gloves proved awkward and unresponsive and he peeled them off with his teeth so that he could hold the key. It burned his skin and he welcomed the pain. The lock yielded and he pulled the gate back gently, mindful of the freight it carried.

'Steiger,' the captain barked.

The pistol was rock steady in the captain's hand, the muzzle-mouth gaping to bite Steiger's heart. Good, he thought. It had begun to snow again and he lifted his face to feel – just to feel. He was in Hallstatt and a boy held his hand. His fist closed instinctively at the memory. 'Look, Papa,' the boy said, 'I caught one.' A single snowflake nestled on the bright-red mitten. Slowly, it began to crumble and fade at the edges until it blurred into a drop the mitten drank. He had swept the boy into his arms and rested his cheek against that small, sad face. 'There are millions more, Max,' he'd whispered. He'd tilted back his head and the boy had mirrored his movement so that their chins touched and the flakes fell on their upturned faces. He remembered the hectic, red spots on the boy's cheeks and the snowflake that nestled in the declivity under his nose, and his eyes, wide and wondering as a Russian sky. Sheep, the captain thought as he looked down at the prisoners, and then a sheep moved. Where one sheep went another followed, he thought and swung the pistol towards the errant one. Another stumbled forward and then another and another and his pistol wove from side to side, like a dog confused by a scattering flock. At some unspoken signal, the Russians moved as one, bulging through the gate, flowing on either side of Steiger, who seemed unaware of their passing. The captain saw no anger in those frozen faces. They were as emotionless and implacable as any hunter and he was their prey. Even as he put the pistol to his head, he was surprised to sense a new emotion in himself. It was fear.

Steiger returned reluctantly from that other place. It was a journey tinged with a sense of loss that was reflected in the agony of his unresponsive body. He forced his limbs into grudging, short movements and pain seemed to razor every part of his body, as if his iced blood had sheared into a thousand cutting blades. His mind put together the evidence of the open gate and the stream of footprints that had marched out and disappeared into the distance. Something broken stained the path of their passage, like it had been worried by wolves and then discarded. The falling snow had already shrouded the tattered flesh and broken bones and cloaked the figure hanging on the gate. He thought of bringing him back to the troop for burial and discarded that thought. They had shown more mercy to a dog than they would have granted a deserter. Nor did he consider putting him in Russian ground. The priest had hung between those two worlds and he wouldn't take him down.

Herr Steiger retrieved his rifle and eased the strap over his shoulder. He turned east to where the light was burning and began to walk.

DANICA CONCENTRATION CAMP

He sat in the passenger seat of a truck driven by the Franciscan. In the side mirror, he saw two other trucks follow their dust. They were grey and anonymous under canvas coverings. He stood on the station platform and watched the militia ferry long, wooden boxes from the trucks to the train. Inside the compartment, he heaved his bag of books on the luggage rack and stood at the window as the train sighed and began to move. The trucks, the Franciscan and the Ustashe slid by the window and disappeared.

'It's over, Max,' the professor said quietly. 'Why don't you sit down?' Max showed no surprise at the professor's presence. He doubted if he would be surprised by anything ever again.

He remained standing a while longer, watching fields of snow roll by the window as the land rose and fell, wondering at the ordinariness of fields and hedgerows and the telegraph poles that wiped across the window at shorter and shorter intervals. He felt like kneading his eyes until they bled but weariness seemed to suffuse the marrow of his bones and he sat.

'I know you would like to curl up and sleep,' the professor said, softly, 'but it won't do any good. Croatia slept for hundreds of years and woke up to the nightmare you saw in broad daylight in Danica. And yes, before you ask, it is of our own making. Should we beg forgiveness? Who can forgive, Max? We can't – they won't. And now circumstances overtake us. Very soon, I think, the Allies will be here. How can we ever explain Danica to an American soldier? They have no history, Max, how will they ever …?'

He looked very old and profoundly weary. Max hoped the man would just sit in silence all the way to Zagreb and let him sleep. Nightmares, he'd discovered, came day or night, so what did it matter if he—.'

'The Germans are in retreat,' the professor said, and Max felt a surge of adrenaline that sizzled new energy through his veins.

'What?'

'Yes,' the cleric nodded, 'Operation Barbarossa has failed and the Americans are in the war. Hitler plans to send General Model east to prop up the Wehrmacht and hold the line but it's over. Hitler will be caught between the upper and nether millstones of the Russians and the Americans, and Germany will be ground exceedingly fine. When Hitler falls, so will his puppets – Mussolini, Pétain and our own beloved Poglavnik. Pavelić won't wait for the inevitable; he's already negotiating his retirement with friends in Rome.'

'Do you have friends in Rome, Professor?'

'I hope to have friends there, Max, at least one good friend. At the moment, my task is to smooth the Poglavnik's passage to the safest sanctuary money can buy. I fear – I fear he may not remember me when he enters into his kingdom.'

Max sat back and studied him. The professor could be irritatingly patronising and sharply intuitive in equal measure. He talked of fear but Max saw no hint of it in those cool, appraising eyes.

'How may I be of service?' he asked.

The older man nodded.

'There is a college in Rome under the auspices of the Vatican – the San Girolamo. The authorities there are kindly disposed to our cause. When the time comes, it will provide sanctuary for some.'

'Some?'

'Yes, some. As for the others, Scripture tells us that the birds of the air have nests and the foxes have dens. Those others, like our Franciscan friend, will find they have neither, and will be hunted to extinction. Only those of us who are favoured by the Vatican will survive. But Vatican favour does not come cheaply. You saw the trucks at the railway station?'

'Yes.'

'And?'

'And I wondered what could be in Danica that was worth saving; apart from eyeballs for Pavelič, of course.'

'Ah yes, that little sidebar in an Italian newspaper may yet hang the Poglavnik – if they catch him.'

'It will hang everyone who knew of it, Professor.'

He watched the urbane mask slip and savoured the moment before pressing home his advantage.

'As you say, the Vatican does not come cheaply. What's in those boxes, Professor?'

'Gold.'

The word seemed to buoy his confidence, so that he spoke with a trace of his usual cynicism.

'Serb gold,' he elaborated, 'but of a high quality and value for all that.'

Max remembered a tipsy Croat priest regaling the palace kitchen staff while he'd been trying to read a book by the stove. 'Those Serb peasants have so much gold in their teeth that they can't close their jaws,' he'd said. 'It's their dowry. I swear to you, they carry their dowry around in their mouths.' He wondered how many gold teeth made a gold bar and how many men the dowry stacked in the luggage carriage would ransom from the rope. He blinked the thought away and looked up. The professor was holding a white envelope.

'Stepinac has decided to send a delegation to Rome to allay Tisserant's misgivings,' he said. 'He's nominated Miscic and a doctor called Rusinovic and you. All the details are here,' he said, holding the envelope out to Max. 'This letter grants the bearer the power to use the gold at his discretion. It also contains the name of a bank official who is – discreet. Your task will be to prepare the way. Are you ready to accept this responsibility, Max?'

'Do I have a choice, Professor?'

'Yes. You can accept and this fortune will open doors for you at the highest level in Rome. You can refuse and the choice will be at which station on our journey the partisans attack the standing train and murder Stepinac's secretary.'

'You can arrange that also, Professor?'

'It pays to hedge one's bets in a time of war, Max.'

'I'll remember that,' Max said and leaned across to take the letter. The professor didn't release it.

'There is one other thing,' he said, smoothly. 'The Vatican has a preference for dealing with priests. I'm sure you can understand why. A priest's first and overriding loyalty is to the Church. Stepinac will ordain you tonight.'

'Does he know that?'

'He will,' the professor said and released the letter. 'Perhaps you'd like to compose yourself for the remainder of our journey. You must be quite certain of your response when he asks if you are willing.'

*

'Are you willing?' the archbishop asked.

'*Volo, cum gratia Dei*, I am willing, with the help of God,' Max replied.

Bishop Miscic and the professor had shepherded Stepinac through the hasty ordination ceremony and now it was over. Max had knelt, bowed and prostrated himself, as instructed, and he felt nothing but relief. The black suit and white Roman collar he put on in the sacristy were simply props – as important as the travel papers and the plain white envelope in his jacket pocket.

There had been one surreal moment during the ceremony and he grimaced as he remembered it. As the ritual dictates, the archbishop had asked if anyone present knew of any reason why the candidate should not be raised to the priesthood. In the ensuing silence, Max imagined he heard a fading scream and the wet, sucking sound of someone breathing through a torn throat. The ceremony had proceeded but he'd had to wipe the sweat from his face.

'Max.'

The archbishop beckoned and he went to sit beside him.

'I'm sorry,' Stepinac began. 'This should be the happiest day of your life. You should be surrounded by friends and your mother—' He seemed to gather his strength before continuing. 'Concerning … that place, Max: we haven't had time to speak of it and I think it's best we don't. The query came from Cardinal Tisserant and I think it would be proper protocol if you address it with him. If he asks, that is.'

Max saw the deep unease in the archbishop's eyes.

'Of course, your Grace,' he said, 'you can depend on me to do the right thing.'

*

She woke at dawn and closed her eyes again to harbour her dream. She saw a young girl teeter from the back door of a farmhouse, carrying a bucket of smoking ashes. The bucket swung in her right hand, like a censer. It puffed the incense of yesterday's fire into the frigid air. The girl was swaddled in her father's greatcoat. It smelled of tobacco and chafed her bare ankles. At the rim of the slope that fell away to the frozen stream, she used the overhang of the sleeve to insulate her hand and tilted a sparkling avalanche into the snow. Embers sizzled furiously for a few seconds, glowing a fierce, final red before they turned black. She placed the bucket on the ground and glanced off to her left. The ashes of the day before and the day before that and all the days since winter had claimed the valley, hummocked the boundary of their meagre farm. Yesterday's pile was already aged with snow, the ash-piles farther on already shrouded. 'They warm the seedlings underground,' her father had said. He'd pulled up the collar of the coat so that it armoured her ears. His breath had been spiced with old beer from the night before, from the pilgrimage he made to the inn every night to blunt his wife's sharp tongue on the rough talk of other men.

She turned from the small graves of winter's fires to chores that measured her days from dawn to dark. Her brother might have helped, she thought, if God hadn't called him to the seminary in Zagreb, called him away from the endless fetch and carry of the farm and the cold absence that was their mother. She pirouetted suddenly and flung the bucket before her. It tumbled over and over, leaving bite-marks in the snow, snapping its handle in protest.

Frau Steiger opened her eyes and rolled out to kneel beside her bed. Her prayers left an aftertaste of ashes in her mouth. She slapped her feet on the wooden stairs as she descended to her kitchen, sending the silence of the empty house cowering into corners. When she sat at the kitchen table, the silence surged back and threatened to steal her breath.

Frau Steiger watched the window. The postman came and passed. Later, the teacher's wife and the herbalist passed the window and knocked on her door. She sat while they loitered and knocked again, remaining immobile until their footsteps faded. She went to close the curtains and saw her mother's face reflected in the window. She pulled the curtains and it disappeared.

She spent the afternoon cleaning her house from attic to kitchen. In the attic bedroom, she pushed a book into alignment with its fellows and lay on the bed for a time watching the light dapple the ceiling. Downstairs again, she scrubbed the kitchen and returned everything to its proper place. Finally, she drew the herbalist's envelope from the kitchen drawer. She plucked a glass from the dresser and filled it at the faucet. The powder slid from the envelope and mounded on the surface of the water. Slowly, it sifted down like black snow until it had all dissolved. She drank the mixture, rinsed the glass and replaced it in the dresser before resuming her seat. 'Ashes in the snow,' she whispered before the silence came to claim her.

THE ROAD FROM MOSCOW

Karl kept the sun behind his shoulder as he ran. Back there was east and the growing sound of pursuit. They had rested until just before dawn, sheltering within a stand of trees. The rising light revealed an open expanse before them and the promise of sanctuary in the forest. He'd climbed a tree to look back and his stomach had churned with hunger and at the sight of their pursuers. Cossacks! Even the word sent a visceral shiver through his guts and he'd half-climbed, half-fallen through the branches to the quizzical expressions of his companions. 'Cossacks,' he whispered and saw the shadow of his own fear in Rupert and Simon's faces. They were from Hamburg, city men who cringed against the open spaces. Both jumped up immediately and began to gather their rifles.

'Wait,' the miner said.

'For what?'

'Snow,' Rudi answered. 'It's coming, I can feel it.'

They hunkered down again but Karl could see the tension twanging in their restlessness.

'How far back?' Rupert demanded.

'About a half-mile,' he answered.

Rupert swung his head towards the forest, his eyes devouring its comforting cover and shortening the distance between. He lurched upright and broke into a run, his impetus dragging Simon just a pace behind him. The others tensed and angled their heads to listen. At first, they heard only the floundering sound of the two fugitives, punctuated by their laboured breathing. Then a horse snickered somewhere to the left of where they crouched and Karl saw a look of regret cross his father's face. A single snowflake drifted down between them.

'Wait,' the miner breathed. They heard the hoof beats of horses ploughing through deep snow and saw two riders standing up in their stirrups, seeming to tug their mounts from one leap to the next. The distance between hunters and prey shortened quickly and the miner steadied his rifle on a low-slung branch. The leading Cossack leaned out from his saddle with his sabre extended and bore down on the trailing man. The miner's shot punched him from the saddle and the horse shied sideways, dragging the bouncing corpse by a foot caught in the stirrup. The miner wrestled with the branch to correct his aim and, in that brief interlude, the second Cossack swept from the side. His sabre flashed twice and the screams were cut short, like those of an animal in a killing snare. Karl thought the miner had shaken snow from the branches as a cascade of white showered on them. 'Snow,' his father said, 'thank God almighty.'

They crept in single file from the trees. The miner walked in front, breaking a path for Karl and Rudi, moving with a hand anchored to a companion's shoulder, like blind men in the blizzard. The miner ploughed a trail that arced around the killing ground but Karl could hear the snorting horses as the other Cossacks cast about for tracks. A shape emerged suddenly from the blizzard and swung. The miner parried instinctively with his rifle barrel and followed through with the stock, cleaving the Cossack from the saddle. The sudden shock galvanised them into a mad scramble.

Panic surged adrenaline through Karl's body and he veered away from the fallen rider, seeing nothing but the snow before his face, hearing nothing except his own harsh breathing until his knees buckled and he sprawled headlong. He lay perfectly still, trying to coax his breathing back to silence, every sense attuned to the movements or sounds around him. A shape stamped by within an inch of his outstretched hand and he bit down on a scream. Deep at the base of his skull a voice urged him to run and he tensed for flight only to relax again. They can't see you, his reason soothed. The snow is your ally, let it cover you.

★

Had he slept? Or had he just slipped into that fugue state that paralyses all movement and makes an animal inert in times of extreme danger. He sent his senses to quest around him and they came back empty. Tentatively, he raised his head and sniffed the air. It was innocent of the smells of horses or men. It took a frighteningly long time for him to free his body from the snow's grip. He had to imagine where his feet were before those phantom limbs would move. In the confusion of flight, he had lost his left glove and the rifle burned his palm. When he thought he should have reached the forest's edge, he was still facing into an icy emptiness. Lost. He stopped and a tiny whimper bubbled up from his stomach. 'Papa will find me,' he whispered to tame his fear. 'Papa will find me.'

Rudi hadn't stopped talking since they'd lacerated themselves ploughing through low branches at the edge of the forest. The miner found it hard to hear him clearly because of the scarf his friend kept wrapped around the lower part of his face. He leaned closer.

'He had his hand on my shoulder,' Rudi was saying, 'I felt it. Then that Cossack came and he was gone. I panicked, Tomas. I ran—'

His voice cracked and the miner put a hand on his shoulder to steady him. His hand seemed to sink through the thin coat before it grasped bone. It felt as fragile as an eggshell and he lightened his grip. He noticed that Rudi didn't take his hands from his pockets while he spoke. He racked his brain and couldn't remember when he'd last seen him gesture. Whenever Rudi was excited or animated, his hands tended to move as if constructing a more tangible form of his idea or emotion.

'Hands,' the miner said.

'What? Tomas, Karl is missing and you—'

'Hands.'

Rudi's eyes contested with the miner's for a fierce moment and finally conceded. Slowly, he took his hands from his pockets and held them before his friend. The miner had seen what the earth could do to the unwary. Crushed and mangled limbs were a regular consequence of working underground and he had never winced before a wound until now. Rudi's hands weren't wounded, he thought, as he examined them with a grim fascination. They were blighted. He knew enough about what grew overground to recognise a tree or a plant that had been burned by frost. Rudi's hands resembled a bundle of twigs that had been too green to burn completely. His fingers were twisted and vivid red weals fissured his palms as if his blood had boiled. Slowly, he began to unpeel his own gloves.

'No, Tomas.'

He ignored his friend's refusal, easing the gloves around the unnatural angles of his fingers as gently as he could. He took a deep breath to steady himself and let it out on a single word.

'Scarf.'

The agony in his fingers had robbed Rudi of resistance. He raised his hands in a small gesture of surrender and helplessness. The miner reached up and drew the scarf from his face. He steeled himself not to look away from the ravages of Rudi's face. His left cheekbone seemed to have pushed a hole through his face and he caught a glimpse of white in the space. His bottom lip hung down like the petal of a black flower, and there were glistening, green threads invading the exposed roots of his teeth. Casually, the miner bunched the scarf under his chin as he bent forward to examine the damage and his nose confirmed his worst fears. Gangrene. A man could barter with gangrene for a leg or an arm – but not for his head. Tenderly, he rewound the scarf and sat back.

'Must find Karl,' Rudi began again. 'Hand on my shoulder—'
'East,' the miner said.

The miner cast around in the snow. He bent and examined the unbroken surface while his friend caught up. Starvation, exhaustion and the added weight of frostbite were too much for Rudi's thin frame to carry and he teetered left and right as if balancing a boulder. 'Rest,' the miner whispered, pointing to a straggle of trees on the ridge ahead.

Rudi collapsed against the bole of a tree and seemed asleep before his body curled in the snow. The miner wormed on his stomach to the edge of the cover and scanned the space before him. On the other side of the plain, yet another forest stained a hill and he was wondering if Russia was an archipelago of forests on a vast white sea when his eyes snagged on a hummock in the snow. He opened his mouth to call Rudi and closed it with a snap when something flickered in the trees that fringed the forest. Two figures emerged from the trees and moved across the snow's surface without difficulty. They moved in a sort of slow, sliding gait, leaning left and then right as they approached the mound that had caught the miner's attention. He began to edge back to Rudi and his rifle. Feverishly, he pushed rounds into the chamber only to have his fingers betray him and drop the bullets in the snow. He thought of waking Rudi but he resisted the urge. What if he panicked and ran out there? What if they were too late or off target and Karl was shot before their eyes? He bent again to his task and concentrated, willing his thumb and forefinger to co-operate and lift the bullets from the snow.

Karl had never grown tired of the sky's immensity. Other soldiers found it oppressive and the miner seemed to burrow into every available crevice to escape it, but he had grown up under the bulk of the Dachstein Mountains. Their comforting presence was at the expense of the sky. The Hallstatt sky was a peak-ringed bowl of blue. The Russian sky made him feel like he was lying on the skin of the globe and could fall at any moment into infinity.

A bearded face occluded the sky and he squinted in surprise. The man's head was almost submerged in hair so that his eyes were the only evidence of the face beneath. Those eyes were as cold as the snow beneath him. He snarled something and withdrew. He was replaced by another face and the contrast between the two was startling. She had an oval face made severe and bloodless by the cold. A blonde wisp of hair played truant from her fur cap and swayed in the wind before her face, concealing and revealing green eyes. The startled flash in those eyes reflected his amazement. She inclined her head and barked something at the man, who grunted in reply. Karl heard him move away as she bent to look closely at him. A tiny frown furrowed between her eyebrows and disappeared. She smiled and he felt his own mouth attempt the same. Without closing her eyes, she bent to kiss him on the lips. He couldn't feel her lips on his but her green eyes seemed to expand to the dimensions of the sky. She drew back and smiled.

'*Danke, junge,*' she said slowly. 'Thanks, boy.'

For an instant, her eyes held his. He saw gratitude give way to sadness in her expression and then she was gone. He lay there, trying to retrieve and order fragments of memory. He could remember a village, bodies swinging from a beam, a girl with green eyes and a wolf. He was still trying to make the connection when the miner's strong arms lifted him from his grave.

The Sala Ducale, the Vatican

'I abominate this room,' Tisserant growled.

His secretary looked up from where he was arranging papers on an ornate desk.

'I suppose as a linguist you'd prefer calligraphy to frescoes? When you become pope, you can commission some fancy scribblers to write all over the walls and ceilings, like the Muslims did in the Hagia Sophia. You're an iconoclast, Eugène, a smasher of statues, a defiler of images.'

'That's not funny, Emil.'

'No, you're right. Even the thought of you becoming pope

should fry my brain.'

'Why do we have to meet the Croats here?'

'Because it is the Sala Ducale, Eugène,' Emil said patiently.

'Cover that one,' Tisserant said, stabbing a document with his finger.

Emil placed a blank sheet over the document and continued without missing a beat. 'The Renaissance princes of Europe came here to haggle with the pope. Imagine the scene, Eugène. They swagger in from the corridor, full of hubris and bad wine, and *alors!*' He swept his arms up to the ceiling. 'Above them, Hercules slays the giant Cacus for stealing his cattle from the Capitoline Hill. *Nemo me impune lacessit.*'

'Nobody injures me with impunity.'

'Precisely. And two papal coats of arms as well, to suggest that princes come and go but popes go back a long time. Look, there in the corner they would see the Four Seasons by Brill and—'

'And what about that drape thing over the arch with the naked angels?'

Emil slumped in a chair and sighed theatrically.

'Where to begin?' he murmured. '*Attend*, dullard,' he snapped. 'The drape, as you call it, is by Bernini. I presume you've heard of—'

'Yes, yes, everybody's heard of Bernini, obelisks on elephants, dolphins in fountains and Saint Theresa looking like a wanton.'

'I would tremble for your soul, Eugène, if I thought you had one. The drape is a masterwork of stucco and the naked angels are actually *putti* who pre-date the angels.'

'And the point of all this?'

'Awe, Eugène, awe. By the time the princes reach the negotiating table they are like clay in the hands of the papal potter. What are you looking at?'

'Winter,' Tisserant said quietly, looking up at the fresco in the corner.

'Ah yes, winter,' Emil echoed, suddenly serious again.

'They're in retreat,' Tisserant continued as if he hadn't heard. 'The invincible Wehrmacht are retracing the footsteps of Napoleon's Grande Armée. The reports say it's minus thirty-five degrees.' He shivered and drew his cloak more tightly about him. 'In God's name, how can human beings survive such cold?'

'They can't,' Emil said flatly. 'The wheel has turned, Eugène. Zhukov, Timoshenko and the others are out for vengeance. Tanks, bombers, rockets – even Cossacks are hunting soldiers in summer uniforms.'

'Any word of—'

'No!'

The silence stretched between the two old friends, whose thoughts stretched thousands of miles beyond the Sale Ducale to the Russian spaces and the priests they had sent there.

'The Russians are coming, Emil.'

'Yes, Maglione is buying little lead soldiers by the gross. His monsignors are all aflutter, painting them red and pushing them across the map to Berlin.'

Tisserant gave a pained laugh.

'He'd better corner the market on American ones too.'

His eyes swung back to the winter fresco and Emil saw his face become bleak again.

'The Russians took eight hundred thousand German prisoners in the Great War,' he said, 'and only a fraction of that number was ever seen again. I sent those priests out as lambs among wolves. What kind of shepherd would do something like that?'

Emil knew Tisserant well enough to know that it was a rhetorical question. The cardinal had never been one to shirk a painful duty or to accept easy answers or consolation for their consequences. Emil checked his watch. 'Five minutes, Your Eminence,' he said formally.

★

Max watched the reactions of the others with bemused detachment. Bishop Miscic, in full episcopal regalia, stamped loudly along the marble corridors, hunching his shoulders under the burden of Renaissance and Baroque art that blazed and hung from the ceilings above him. Rusinovic sweated like a peasant in his stiff collar and tight frock coat. Both men fixed their gaze on the back of the Swiss Guard who marched before them. Max wondered how the news from Russia and the repercussions for Croatia weighed on them.

On the journey from Zagreb, he'd seen evidence of increased partisan activity. He didn't doubt it was generated by Barbarossa's retreat and the advance of the Americans. The San Girolamo College had been strangely subdued and one whole section of the student quarters had been closed off 'for repairs'. He checked the watch, which was an ordination gift from Archbishop Stepinac. One minute, he noted, as the Swiss Guard opened double-doors, saluted and departed. His companions looked at each other and nodded. They stepped into the Sala Ducale and Father Max Steiger followed a few paces behind, as befitted a humble cleric.

Emil had done his research. The Vatican archives held files on every bishop in the world, updated every four years when they made their *ad limina* visit to Rome to report on their diocese. He had other sources of information among the diplomats and monsignori, even among the drivers, cooks and cleaners who populated the tiny Vatican state.

The identikit picture he had put together of Bishop Miscic was not flattering. It was well documented that he was a rabid nationalist who championed the conversion or displacement of Croatia's Orthodox Serb population. But the Vatican curia, like bureaucracies all over the world, knew there were some things best kept secret. Emil had access to the secret archives but he had discovered that the best secrets were hoarded by people. In the humdrum, day to day of Vatican life, they could be exchanged as titbits of gossip to flavour and facilitate co-operation between colleagues. In times of crisis, they were hard currency.

Tisserant had many contacts among the Muslims and Orthodox Serbs. The information that flowed from those sources carried no price tag. The layman, he concluded, was the joker in the pack. The medical doctor, Rusinovic, was a dupe who had been led to believe he'd become the ambassador to the Holy See when the Vatican shifted its favour from the exiled Yugoslav royalty to the new Croatian state. Emil already knew the name of his successor. He didn't doubt that the man would lie for his country, like all ambassadors.

He switched his scrutiny to the young priest. For once, his sources had come up dry. Father Max Steiger raised no eyebrows, rang no bells and the secretary had only the barest details. Steiger had been ordained just a few days earlier. A high-level delegation from the Croatian Church and state comes to Rome and includes a jumped up altar boy. Why? The older ones, he observed, kept their eyes downcast as they approached the cardinal. The boy was— The boy was doing what he was doing – observing the opposition. Careful Emil, he thought, this boy could be more than he seems, the real wildcard in the game.

So that's the famous Tisserant, Max thought. He saw him sort the papers before him on the desk as if the delegation wasn't worthy of his attention. Tisserant's bulk was impressive and made even more formidable by his robes and skull cap. And the one who hovers at his shoulder? 'Dubois – Emil Dubois the monsignor at the San Girolamo had informed him over an early breakfast. 'Emil is Tisserant's eyes and ears,' he'd mumbled through his muesli. 'The doddery and avuncular façade masks the sharpest mind in the Vatican. Rather you than me, boy.'

They halted behind the three chairs set six paces back from the cardinal's desk. Max was quite certain that the position of the chairs was strategic– the distance emphasised the gulf in authority that existed between those behind the desk and those before it.

'Sit,' Tisserant said, without raising his eyes. Clever, Max thought. No fraternal greetings or formal introductions. We are in the Colosseum and the lion has entered.

'I asked the papal nuncio in Zagreb to investigate certain matters,' Tisserant said coldly. 'I understand the nuncio relayed my request to Archbishop Stepinac and he has thought it ... appropriate to send this delegation.'

'Letters can be intercepted and fabricated,' Miscic said hurriedly.

'That is not our experience,' Tisserant growled.

'His Grace, the archbishop, thought it, eh, appropriate that we could best respond to your Eminence's queries by coming to Rome.'

'It may be appropriate in Croatia to send a bishop, a medical doctor and a newly ordained priest to represent a papal nuncio and an archbishop. For us, it is a novel experience,' Tisserant said with heavy sarcasm. 'Nevertheless, you are here now. You may speak.'

The bishop launched immediately into a prepared speech in which he accused Serbs, Jews and 'disaffected clerics' of blackening the reputation of the Croatian Church and state. Tisserant's raised hand cut him off.

'You are here to speak for the Croatian Church, Bishop. I'm sure the representative of the state is capable of speaking for the Poglavnik.'

Masterful, Max thought, admiringly – divide and conquer. As if to confirm his observation, the bishop looked nervously at Rusinovic, who glared at him in return.

'Please address yourself to my specific queries, Bishop,' Tisserant continued remorselessly. 'Are you aware of Catholic clergy who are involved in acts of violence against Orthodox Serbs?'

'No,' Miscic answered, 'such things do not happen in our country.'

'Which is it, Bishop? Is it that you are unaware of such acts or that they are not happening?'

'They are not happening.'

'There is no possibility, then, that they could be happening without you being aware of them? And may I remind you, Bishop, that you speak with the voices of the papal nuncio and Archbishop Stepinac.'

Miscic mopped his forehead and upper lip with a handkerchief before replying. 'Rome has been misled by Serb propaganda,' he said.

Tisserant leaned forward and fixed the man with a glacial stare.

'I know for a fact,' he said, 'that Franciscans, for example Father Simic of Knin, have taken part in attacks against the Orthodox population in order to destroy the Orthodox Church. I know that the Franciscans have acted abominably, and this pains me. Such acts should not be committed by educated, cultured, civilised people, let alone by priests.'

'Propaganda,' the bishop whispered.

Tisserant swept up a document from the table.

'I also know,' he continued, 'that one single concentration camp holds twenty thousand Serbs and that three hundred and fifty thousand Serbs have disappeared.'

Miscic opened and closed his mouth like a suffocating fish.

'Your Eminence,' Rusinovic interjected, 'foreign journalists were invited to visit the concentration camps. When they left, they declared that the camps were perfectly suited to regular habitation and satisfied the requirements of hygiene.' He leaned back with a satisfied smile. 'Your Eminence should not rely on Serb propaganda for such spurious statistics,' he added admonishingly.

'You are correct, Doctor Rusinovic,' Tisserant conceded and the delegate's smile broadened. 'I should not rely on Serb or, indeed, on Croatian propaganda. These spurious statistics, as you call them, come from the German High Command in Croatia. I presume I can rely on your allies to be correct in this matter. This meeting is ended.'

RETREAT FROM MOSCOW

The miner carried Karl on his back and insisted that Rudi hold on to his arm. He knew their weaving trail reflected their growing weakness. It would also serve as a beacon for pursuers. The Cossacks had not given up on them, even though the forests were alive with Wehrmacht soldiers. He wondered if their code of honour demanded vengeance for a fallen comrade, and smiled. He hoped he had killed the second one. They could only kill him once.

A Russian fighter plane zoomed over and he ducked his head. He took it as a sign that they were nearing a major road and, rather than giving in to his instinct to hide, he trusted his intuition and pushed on. They had eaten rabbit that morning and he distracted himself from the weariness in his body by remembering that novelty. Under Rudi's slurred tuition, he had worked some twigs into the semblance of a snare. No one had been more surprised when it trapped their supper. He'd skinned and gutted the scrawny animal with his bayonet and cut it into thin strips which they chewed raw. Karl had been lucid enough to chew and swallow without choking and now his head lolled on the miner's shoulder. Apart from his left hand, the boy wasn't injured. He'd been carrying his rifle in his left hand and not wearing a glove. In the intense cold, his palm had become welded to the weapon. At some stage during their flight from the Cossacks his rifle had disappeared, taking most of the flesh from his palm with it. The miner had managed to staunch the bleeding and keep the wound from being infected but he had no antidote to the black spots that were beginning to speckle the boy's fingers. He suspected he had some frostbite on his own nose and cheeks and his bare hands had suffered greatly since he'd pressed his gloves on Rudi.

Karl sometimes sank into a delirium and he muttered odd fragments of unrelated sentences. Occasionally, he muttered about a girl with green eyes, but once he had shouted 'Elsa, Elsa,' and the miner had to stop and breathe deeply before he could continue. He leaned into an incline and pushed Karl higher on his back. Rudi plodded gamely beside him and the miner was so relieved to reach the summit of the ridge that he stood there for a few moments to savour the sight of the road.

It seemed like a river of bobbing, shambling bodies flowing west. An occasional truck teetered precariously on the frozen, polished surface of the road, nosing the retreating soldiers to the sides. Not every soldier returned to the centre to resume his march. The miner saw men crouching or lying on both sides. He wondered if they were wounded or just too sick in their souls to continue. A straggle of tents mushroomed from mud at the other side of the road. Perhaps there might be a medic. A premonition forced his head around. He thought they looked less fearsome in the light of day and wondered if he could hold them off on the ridge until help arrived from the road. He turned back and saw that Rudi had followed his gaze.

'Give me your rifle, Tomas,' Rudi said quietly.

'No.'

'Please, Tomas,' Rudi begged. 'They'll kill my child.' He moved closer and the miner could see what looked like tendrils of black ivy climbing up under his skin from the ruin of his mouth. 'Let me hold my son while you dig a foxhole in the snow.'

The miner handed over the boy and used his bayonet and the butt of his rifle to dig a hole in the snow. He could hear Rudi whispering to the unconscious boy and he hacked at the hole through a blur of tears.

'Thank you,' Rudi said as the miner took Karl on his back again. 'Tell Karl—' He gasped and faltered.

'Yes,' the miner said and pulled his friend into a one-armed hug. 'Rudi,' he whispered and let him go.

He was trying to run without tumbling on the slope when he heard the shots and a horse scream from the other side of the ridge. Rudi wouldn't like to shoot a horse, he thought. There was another fierce flurry of shots and then silence.

'Medic,' the miner said to a young lieutenant who was chivvying a group of men to push a truck off the road. An orderly in a blood-soaked apron barred his way. 'The doctor's resting,' he protested.

'Wake him,' the miner said as he pushed inside the tent.

The doctor washed his hands, lit a cigar and slumped into a chair. He was a tall, gangly man with more salt than pepper in his hair. He looked like a worn sixty, but the miner knew, Russia aged a man early.

'These things will kill me,' the doctor said, waving the cigar in a languid hand, 'but they're the only thing that can cut the smell of gangrene. Oh, no,' he added quickly, when the miner started. 'The boy has frostbite but no gangrene. I've patched him up as best I can and pumped drugs into him against infection. Someone in a proper hospital could probably save his hand. I can't. Sorry. Whose army were you with, soldier?'

'Von Kluge's.'

The doctor took a long, slow pull on his cigar and seemed to tug the smoke all the way down to his toes.

'I hear he's going to see Hitler,' he confided. 'All one-way tickets on that plane.' He laughed harshly and coughed. 'Plane goes from a small airstrip about two kilometres up the road. If you know someone—'

★

Steiger moved into the 'Death-Lane' and sat. He had walked his way through the soles of his Wehrmacht-issue shoes about two miles back and had walked barefoot in the snow for a mile after that. He could have stripped a pair from a corpse. He might have, if he hadn't seen a soldier take an axe to a Russian corpse's thigh because he couldn't drag his boot off. It didn't matter. He'd rest here a minute and push on.

He passed the time scanning the faces that passed by. Exhaustion and starvation did strange things to human beings, he mused. Some performed a parody of a march, swinging legs and arms. Others shambled, trudged, staggered – he hadn't enough words in his vocabulary to describe the procession of fleeing soldiers. They all had one thing in common. Their eyes were a thousand miles ahead of them – fixed out there, somewhere, anywhere but here. Nothing broke that stare, not the truck that broke down in their path or the Russian fighter planes that came in low to rake the road with tracer. They walked around any obstacle in their path and dropped in the ditch until the planes zoomed by. Then they walked and stared until the planes banked around for a second pass. Most wore Russian uniforms and felt boots. Steiger thought they could have passed for some of the Russian prisoners he had seen in the compound. He closed his eyes on those memories and opened them again. Except that one, he decided.

'Miner.'

The miner swerved to the side of the road and looked around.

'Miner.'

Steiger staggered up the road and swayed before him.

'It's me. Steiger.'

The miner's expression didn't change.

'Rudi?' Steiger asked. The miner shook his head and saw the policeman's eyes shift to Karl. 'Karl,' he said, 'Karl.'

The boy raised his head from the miner's shoulder. 'Papa?' he whispered.

The miner glared at Steiger and tried to push by him but the man resisted. 'Please, Tomas,' he begged, 'I've been searching for you. There is something I must tell you – both of you. Please,' he screamed and dropped to his knees. The miner stood rooted to the road by the man's anguish.

'Put me down, Tomas,' Karl said quietly.

The miner thought about it for a moment and then set Karl on his feet. When he tried to straighten, his spine refused to come all the way up and he crouched before the policeman. Karl took a few tentative steps forward. 'Herr Steiger,' he said, 'I'm glad you're safe. My father – he won't be coming home,' he said in a small, quavering voice and turned his face away.

Steiger stretched his hand and touched him on the head. His Adam's apple bobbed in his throat and his lips seemed to writhe as he struggled to form words.

'It was Max,' he gasped.

'What?'

'It was Max,' he repeated, his voice soft with the tears that trickled through the stubble on his cheeks. When the boy continued to look at him in confusion, the words spewed from his mouth as if he was vomiting them like poison from the pit of his stomach. 'Max was in the mine,' he shouted, 'the day Elsa—'

At the mention of her name, the miner clenched his fists and stepped forward.

'No,' Karl said.

'Max was in the mine,' Steiger whispered, 'when – when the girl disappeared. He came back.' He splayed his hand and drew it down his face. 'He was marked. Said he'd fallen.' He shook his head. 'He didn't fall,' he whispered.

'How do you know he was in the mine?' Karl asked.

The miner drew the silver cross and chain from under his tunic and held it up before Karl's eyes. 'I found this in the mine,' he said. 'It belongs to Max.'

Karl swayed on his feet.

'Why, why didn't you tell someone, Herr Steiger?'

'Because he is my son.'

'Come,' the miner said, taking Karl by the arm.

'Please, Karl,' Steiger said, 'take this.' He reached up and placed the chain around the boy's neck. When he stepped back, he seemed diminished, just another small and weary man. They moved around him and walked on. Karl looked back to see him sitting among the other listless men beside the road.

The airstrip was already humming with tension. Crowds of soldiers circled a Storch aircraft, eyeing it hungrily from behind a ring of military police. Every time a figure passed through the barrier and boarded the aircraft, a moan of frustration and anger rose from a thousand throats. The miner shouldered his way to the entry point and stared at the frazzled officer. 'Papers,' the man snapped.

When the miner didn't respond, he turned away dismissively. The miner drifted sideways and placed himself to the rear of a group who were tossing snowballs at the military police. The aircraft's engine turned over and caught. He could see the pilot poring over charts behind the perspex. His eyes shifted to the guards and their rifles and measured the distance to the plane. 'Down,' he said, and Karl slid down his back.

He watched in fascination as the miner walked forward and bumped a man to the ground. 'Sorry,' the miner grunted and hauled him to his feet. He began to dust him down and the man pushed him away angrily. 'What was that for?' Karl whispered.

'This,' the miner said, and fired three quick shots into the air. He threw the pistol aside as the crowd surged forward suddenly and broke the barrier. 'Up,' the miner urged, holding out his arms. He clutched the boy, one-handed, and strong-armed a passage around the melee of police and rioters. A policeman spun and raised his weapon. Without breaking stride, the miner punched him in the face and the guard dropped away. He saw a man stand in the hatchway of the aircraft and begin to close the door.

'Kurt,' he bellowed.

Kurt Brandt had been writing in his journal when he heard someone call his name. He capped his pen carefully and made his way to the door of the aircraft. 'A minute,' he said to the attendant, who shrugged and abandoned the hatch. In the distance, Kurt saw a riot of bodies and broken barriers. In the foreground a man ran towards the aircraft, carrying something in his arms. 'Kurt,' the man shouted.

'Miner,' Kurt whispered in disbelief. 'Tomas,' he yelled and the sound of his name seemed to add energy to the miner's legs as he barrelled across the airfield. Kurt saw guards peel away from the riot and come in pursuit. 'Hurry,' he whispered frantically, 'hurry.' One of the guards halted and dropped to one knee. 'No,' he screamed. The guard rammed the butt of the rifle to his shoulder and sighted down the barrel. The miner was just a few yards from the doorway, holding out the burden he carried in his arms. 'Don't shoot,' Kurt screamed, 'don't sh—'

The bullet slammed the miner forward against the hatchway opening. 'Tomas,' Kurt whispered, dropping to his knees and extending his arms, 'Tomas.' Tenderly, the miner rolled the boy into his outstretched arms. 'Karl,' he gasped and fell away.

'We're already overloaded,' the co-pilot protested, 'this soldier will have to wait for—'

Kurt placed the dazed boy in a vacant seat and approached the curtain that divided the cabin. 'General von Kluge,' he shouted. An adjutant whipped the curtain aside and closed it behind him. He shoved Kurt, roughly, in the chest. 'How dare you—'

'General von Kluge,' Kurt shouted louder and the adjutant began to fumble with the strap on his holster. The curtain parted and von Kluge stepped through.

'Professor?'

'General von Kluge, sir, 'Kurt said, 'my student is wounded and I request passage for him.'

'We're already overweight, sir,' the adjutant protested. The general raised a quizzical eyebrow at Kurt. 'It seems we have a logistical problem, Professor,' he said and turned away.

'Sir,' Kurt said hurriedly, 'I believe I can solve that problem.'

'How do you propose to do that?' von Kluge asked over his shoulder.

'He can have my seat, General.'

Von Kluge turned slowly and stared at him. He waved the adjutant away and stepped closer. 'This is the last plane out of here, Kurt,' he said quietly. 'You are aware of that?'

'Yes, sir.'

'Would Napoleon have left de Caulaincourt behind in Russia?' the general asked.

'No,' Kurt replied, 'but if de Caulaincourt had requested that he do so, Napoleon would not have dishonoured both of them by refusing, sir.'

The general held his gaze for a long moment.

'No,' he said flatly.

'But, General, I—'

Von Kluge raised his hand and cut him off.

'If we leave the professor behind, who will teach the student?' he said. 'If we leave the student, who will become the professor? Germany will need teachers more than she needs generals, Kurt. Heinrich!' he snapped and the adjutant reappeared. 'Find a seat for the boy.'

'But General, we are already overweight.'

'I have two adjutants,' von Kluge said coldly.

'Yes, sir.' The Storch shuddered and began to roll. The pitch of the engine wound up to a howl and it bounced into the sky. Kurt cradled the weeping boy against his shoulder.

'We're going home, Karl,' he whispered. 'Going home.'

BOOK THREE

SAN GIROLAMO COLLEGE, ROME 1942

Max left Bishop Miscic to lick his wounds and compose a letter to Archbishop Stepinac. He didn't envy him that task. He made his way to the blocked-off wing of the San Girolamo and climbed the stairs. All around him he heard the sounds of hammers and saws as invisible workmen renovated the students' quarters.

On the top storey, he paused to get his breath back. The professor had delivered the final part of his briefing at the railway station in Zagreb. He'd stood close to Max as the train hissed a cocoon of steam around them. 'The man you will contact in the San Girolamo College is Krunoslav Dragonovic.'

'But he's a Professor of Moral Theology in Zagreb University.'

'He is also a Franciscan, a colonel in the Ustashe and the confidante of Ante Pavelíç, our beloved Poglavnik. Please, Max,' he'd admonished, 'it is indecorous for a young priest to stand in a public place with his mouth open.'

'What is he doing in Rome?'

'Like John the Baptist, he is preparing the way. The San Girolamo must be readied for those who will free Croatia if Hitler falls. Krunoslav Dragonovic is overseeing the renovations at the college and persuading various Vatican officials to receive the Croatian elect into their bosoms. Some say he is negotiating with the intelligence service of the United States to look the other way in the event that the war goes badly and our refugees seek sanctuary outside Europe. It would not benefit President Roosevelt if the Vatican was exposed in this matter. I believe the Catholic lobby in America is not something the president wishes to alienate.' He stepped even closer and used an embrace to cover his final injunction. 'I must warn you, Max, that Dragonovic is also a bully and a boor. He is a wolf in wolf's clothing. Tread warily.'

Max took a deep breath and knocked on a door. A gruff voice bade him enter. The man behind the desk glared at him.

'What?' he demanded.

'I am—.'

'I know who you are,' the priest interrupted, 'you're that young pup Stepinac sent with the other two idiots.' He snorted contemptuously. 'Had your asses kicked all around the Sala Ducale, I hear. Serves you right for trying to bluff Tisserant.' He laughed suddenly and relaxed. 'I know *who* you are, Father Max Steiger,' he said. 'I'm still trying to work out *what* you are.'

'This may help,' Max said and slid a white envelope across the desk. He watched the priest's face become guarded as he read the letter.

'So you're the paymaster,' he said slowly. 'Do you know what it's costing to renovate this shithole for our guests? And what it's going to cost to house those snot-nosed students all over Rome?'

'Viterbo,' Max said.

'What?'

'Send them to Viterbo – tonight.'

'What the f—.'

'Students talk, Father Dragonovic,' Max continued, overriding the livid cleric. 'Spread them around Rome and you may as well advertise your affairs in the *L'Osservatore Romano*. Send them to Viterbo.'

'And lock them up?' Dragonovic suggested sarcastically.

'Why not? It's where the cardinals were first locked in conclave in the thirteenth century. It'll be instructive for the students and convenient for us.'

'Us? So we're going to pay for this, are we?'

Max took a notebook and pen from his pocket and placed them before the priest. 'Write your bill,' he said. 'It will be paid within the week.'

'You have big balls for such a small man,' Dragonovic said, admiringly. He scribbled in the notebook and pushed it back.

'Sign it,' Max said.

'Maybe Stepinac is not such a fool after all,' Dragonovic observed as he scrawled his name. 'What now?'

'Now I'll have my pen back. I'll add ten per cent to the bill in case you have unforeseen expenses, personal expenses.'

Dragonovic nodded but his eyes remained wary. 'And in return?' he asked.

'Information,' Max replied. 'Where will I find the man named in the letter?'

'With a name like that? At the Vatican Bank, of course. Pacelli likes to keep things in the family.'

'Will he see me?'

'See you? They're broke, boy. He'll kiss your fucking feet.'

'Thank you, Father Dragonovic,' Max said, rising.

'That's all?'

'For the moment.'

'What do you think Tisserant will do now?'

If Max was surprised at the question, he didn't show it.

'He'll take his findings to His Holiness.'

'And?'

'And the pope will do nothing. The Russians are coming, Father, and Croatia is still the last Catholic bastion in Eastern Europe.'

'But for how long?'

'Long enough for our guests and the Americans to arrive.'

'Speed the day.'

'Be careful what you wish for, Father Dragonovic. My father always said that.'

'Said? Is he dead.'

'Yes – a long time.'

Father Dragonovic played a soft tattoo with his fingers on the desk. He'd got all he wanted from the cocky little bastard – and more. But something tainted his sense of satisfaction. Father Steiger had been efficient and accommodating but he'd also been preternaturally cold. Why hadn't he sweated, even a little? The ordination oil was still fresh on his palms, and already he had Tisserant and Pacelli analysed. Best to sup with a long spoon when you dine with this devil, he cautioned himself.

The door behind him opened and a young woman stepped inside. She was slightly built, with blonde hair pulled back into a tight bob behind her head. She wore an expensive outfit, tailored to conceal her full figure and a white blouse gleamed from inside the sombre black jacket.

'You heard?' he asked.

'I heard.'

Her voice had a metallic timbre that irritated his ears but he concealed his discomfort.

'He's in over his head,' he said, with more conviction than he felt. He knew it was bluster and he hated himself for it but this woman made him nervous.

'Maybe, maybe not,' she said. 'Your little paymaster speaks softly and carries a big stick, Father. He's someone to watch.'

'I thought the American Secret Service watched everyone,' he said and attempted a smile.

'We do,' she said and his smile faded at her tone. 'We watch and we weigh, Father. And when the war is over, we decide who is worth keeping alive. That's something you'd do well to remember, Father Krunoslav Dragonovic.'

When the door closed behind her, his fingers were still drumming on the desk. He pulled his hand back and grasped the edge of the desk to still his trembling.

CARDINAL TISSERANT'S APARTMENTS, THE VATICAN

'And he said?'

'He said he'd examine the documents carefully and recommend the appropriate action.'

'Which means he'll do nothing, Eugène.'

'Nothing is what he does best, Emil. We have the most sophisticated network of spies in the world. Oh yes, we call them nuncios and apostolic delegates but they see, hear and report to Rome. Except our man in Zagreb, of course; all of his information comes directly to Pacelli's desk. Ambassador Osborne translates the BBC broadcasts and hand-delivers them to the pope. And still nothing. He refuses to speak for fear of alienating monsters like Mussolini, Hitler and that butcher Pavelić. Instead, we are distracted from the truth by delegations of the calibre we met today. Time is running out for us, Emil. What do you think will happen when the war ends?'

'Do I look like a prophet?'

'You're a historian, for God's sake. Throw the bones, read the runes. Make an educated guess.'

'Very well.'

Emil Dubois sighed and sat back in his armchair.

'It will be Versailles all over again,' he said quietly. 'The Allies will carve up Europe between themselves and the Americans will, most likely, go home. It seems they suffer from homesickness when they move from one state to another. Europe is far too foreign for their comfort.'

Tisserant didn't smile and Emil sighed again and continued more soberly.

'It's only a matter of time before Hitler falls. Our hope is that he'll step aside and allow Model, or one of the other generals, to negotiate a peace, to avoid a prolonged war and the invasion of Germany.'

'He won't do that, will he?'

'No. A sane man might. They'll have to march all the way to Berlin. Even if he did abdicate, they'll still take Berlin. They have scores to settle – especially the Russians. The Russians will stay, Eugène; Uncle Joe will never risk another Barbarossa. Berlin will mark the borders of the Soviet Union.'

'And the vanquished?'

'History tells us that the generals always survive. They present their swords, sign the documents of capitulation and go to the officers' mess for coffee and cognac. The politicians? Some will hang and others will write their memoirs.'

'What would you do if you were Pavelić or any of the Germans who might expect to hang?'

'I'd find a place of sanctuary, some place where I could expect hospitality, especially if I could pay for it.'

'Where in the world would you go?'

'The world is a big place, my friend. Africa and South America are big enough to hide a multitude of sinners. If you're asking where I'd go in Europe, the answer is simple. I'd come here.'

Tisserant stared at his secretary for a long moment.

'You know something, don't you?'

'Not yet,' Emil said slyly, 'but from what I hear, not all delegations coming to Rome these days come to be roasted by Cardinal Tisserant. The Church has a long history of granting safe spaces to former tyrants, Eugène.'

'I can't see either of those two bastards we met today having the wit to save their skins.'

'There were three, Eminence. Surely you noticed the boy-priest?'

'The Sala Ducale didn't exactly fill him with awe, did it?'

'No. Nor the formidable Cardinal Tisserant either, if I may say. I had the feeling he'd anticipated how the interview would go and was enjoying his countrymen's discomfort.'

'Why would Stepinac send him to Rome?'

'If Stepinac did send him. Perhaps some other person or persons needed someone to smooth their passage?'

'What could he possibly have to offer?'

'Now that's the question, isn't it? What could Father Max Steiger have to bargain with?'

THE VATICAN BANK, ROME

'Eighty million dollars.'

'Pardon?'

'In gold.'

The banker removed his steel-rimmed spectacles and polished them carefully with a chamois before returning the cloth to his spectacles case and clicking it closed. Max had endured a long wait to see this man. A dapper, older man had encountered him in the foyer and enquired how he might be of service. When Max had told him, he'd disappeared and been replaced by an even older man, who had looked the young priest up and down before announcing, in reverential tones, that the 'Signor' was busy.

'I'll wait.'

This response had provoked much hand-wringing and whispered conversations and Max's eventual translation to a door on the top floor. The bank official had moved before him like a devout monsignor leading an imaginary procession. He'd tapped softly on the door and backed away. Max wouldn't have been surprised to see him perform a triple genuflection. This was obviously the Holy of Holies and he was about to enter the presence of the High Priest.

'If I may say so, Father,' the banker said, in a dry whisper, 'you seem rather young to have such a sum at your disposal.'

'You seem rather young,' Max replied calmly, 'to hold such a senior position in the Vatican Bank, if I may say so.'

He was rewarded with a faint blush of colour that stained the banker's alabaster face before his normal pallor reasserted itself. The banker touched the letter on his desk with a tentative finger.

'Your bona fides—'

'Are notarised,' Max interjected. 'The accompanying letter is also signed and witnessed by persons whose bona fides are well known to this institution and the Church it represents.'

'Quite,' the banker said softly.

He never raises his voice, Max mused. He acts like a man twice his age and is accustomed to deference. In any other bank, he could be the owner's son and heir. The only certainty was that such a degree of consanguinity did not exist in this circumstance.

'The Vatican Bank will be happy to accommodate you in this matter, Father,' the banker whispered, 'pursuant to the usual checks as to provenance etcetera.'

'*Buongiorno*, Signor,' Max said, calmly, and rose from his chair.

'However,' the banker said, as Max turned for the door, 'under the exceptional circumstances, the bank is prepared to waive the usual requirements.'

'*Grazie*, Signor,' Max said as he resumed his seat.

'*Prego.*'

'Naturally,' Max continued, 'I would expect to compensate the bank for any inconvenience caused. The principals have also instructed me to offer a token of their esteem and gratitude for the part you have played in expediting this matter. Shall we say two per cent?'

The brown eyes blinked behind the steel rims and Max willed his features to remain expressionless. This, he knew, was the tipping point, the acid test as to whether or not the information he'd received about this man's personal financial circumstances was reliable.

'The Vatican Bank is run by half-priests,' his informant had assured him, 'that's why they're on half-pay.'

The fingers reached across the desk again to realign the letter.

'I have the necessary documents to hand,' the banker said and Max felt a swell of triumph in his chest. 'Please sign here and here.'

Max scrawled his signature and returned the pen.

'If you would put your signature under mine, Signor,' he suggested. After a brief pause, the banker took the pen and signed. He blotted his signature carefully and capped the pen before rising from his chair.

'You are German, Father?' he enquired.

'No, I am a priest of the Roman Catholic Church,' Max replied. He leaned forward and read the banker's signature.

'As you are a director of the Vatican Bank,' he added and smiled. The banker held his gaze for a moment and nodded. 'Quite,' he said and extended a pale hand. 'If there is some way I can be of service, please—'

'Actually, Signor,' Max said, 'there is.'

CARDINAL TISSERANT'S APARTMENTS, THE VATICAN

'Rome has robbed me of the possibility of surprise,' Emil Dubois liked to say. Notes found in his pockets or pushed under his door were not unusual. He was known to have the ear of Tisserant. The folded note under his coffee cup intrigued but didn't excite him. He concealed it with the cup and leaned back in his chair to cast a speculative eye over the religious scattered around the tables of the Vatican cafeteria. João, the plump Portuguese bishop, was a likely candidate. He revelled in Lisbon's reputation as a 'hotbed of espionage' and buzzed happily from table to table, pollinating the various national groupings with the latest gossip.

Whatever he'd imparted to the huddle of German monsignori in the far corner seemed to have deepened their gloom and João smiled sunnily when he caught Emil's eye. Not João, Emil decided. Experience had taught him that João liked to play the spy. Whenever he'd dropped a morsel of information for Emil, it had been accompanied by an inexhaustible repertoire of winks and nods. He switched his scrutiny to the flurry of gesticulations that was the Italian table. Obviously, the news of Mussolini's senility and summary dismissal by the Fascist Party was being discussed. The fact that General Badoglio had taken up the sceptre and was attempting the dangerous balancing act of placating the Axis while negotiating with the Allies added some spice to their cooling cappuccinos. 'Please, God,' he muttered, 'don't let it be another "love note" from Sister Bibiana.' The ample sister was, at that moment, pressing coffee and her unwelcome attentions on a Polish priest from Archives. Emil thought the cleric looked like a rabbit confronted by an amorous stoat. He palmed the note to his pocket and left.

'San Bartolomeo all'Isola. Twelve noon. The Good Thief.'

He pressed the message flat on the desk and read it again before tearing it into tiny pieces which he stowed in his pocket. Was the SD man about to 'cash in his chips', as the Americans put it, he wondered?

Emil crossed the Ponte Sestio to Tiber Island at eleven thirty, nodding respectfully at the two ancient heads carved on the bridge. As he walked, he draped a hand over the parapet and dropped a flurry of paper pieces into the waters below. The island was boat-shaped and, as a historian, he knew it had once boasted marble structures at either end, carved to resemble the prow and stern of a ship. The Church of San Bartólomeo, dedicated to one of the lesser-known apostles, brooded over the central piazza and he stepped into its gloom at eleven forty-five. Apart from an elderly Roman matron supplicating at a side altar, the church was eerily empty. He sat in the front pews and waited. As the bells of Rome announced noon, someone eased into the seat behind him.

'I wonder if you'd hear my confession, monsignor?' the man whispered. 'I believe the confessional to your left is vacant.'

Emil slid the screen open and kept his eyes averted, as a confessor was obliged to do.

'You are not a young man, monsignor,' the man observed from the shadows on the other side of the grille, 'and I do not wish to burden your remaining years with my sins.'

'That is a burden I would willingly share.'

'Thank you. Perhaps some other time. There is something I believe the cardinal should know. General Heydrich convened a meeting at Wannsee outside Berlin at the request of Adolf Eichmann.'

Emil started involuntarily. He'd seen that name in dispatches from contacts in Germany.

'I see you're already familiar with that name,' the SD officer continued, 'and with his part in the solution of the Jewish question.'

Emil had a moment to consider the awfulness camouflaged by the euphemism before the man pressed on, in a flat emotionless voice.

'Eichmann pointed out that there were fifty-eight thousand Jews in the Italian sphere of influence and ordered their immediate deportation. It seems our Italian allies are made of softer stuff. Not a single Jew has been deported from Italy or from those parts of Yugoslavia and Greece that the Italians control. Heydrich has complained to Mussolini which Italians don't understand the Jewish question.' He gave a dry, mirthless laugh. 'That lack of understanding seems to afflict Field Marshal von Kesselring also. Since the occupation of Italy, von Kesselring has made no move against the Jews; on the contrary, he has thwarted Berlin's plans at every turn. He protests that he hasn't the resources to carry out that order. The cardinal must be informed that von Kesselring is about to be overruled. I'll leave a transcript of the Wannsee discussions under the kneeler.'

'When will this happen?'

'Soon. I'm sorry I can't be more exact. I have definite information about *where* it will happen. It will happen in Rome, monsignor.'

'The pope would protest,' Emil gasped and had time to reflect on his words in the silence that followed. 'I'll relay the information to His Eminence,' he added.

'Aren't you going to give me a penance?' the dry voice enquired.

'Yes,' Emil said, after a pause. 'There's a priest in the San Girolamo who is not what he seems.'

'Only one? A name would narrow my search, monsignor.'

'His name is Max Steiger.'

Emil heard the confessional door creak and listened to the sound of footsteps recede across the marble floor. He had acted on impulse, setting the SD officer to hunt Steiger. A deeper instinct filled him with foreboding. The Good Thief had kept his end of the bargain. Should he have offered to grant him sanctuary at the Vatican until he could be spirited to some neutral country?

He was still agonising over that question as he bent to retrieve the documents 'the penitent' had left in the confessional and didn't see a shadow detach itself from an alcove and glide noiselessly from the church.

THE VATICAN

The Swiss Guard checked Max's pass and ushered him through the bronze door into the Apostolic Palace. He was handed over to a monsignor, who led him to Cardinal Maglione's office. His informant had described Maglione as 'an Italian bear with a Machiavellian mind' and he stood before the desk as the prelate assessed him with shrewd, peasant eyes.

'His Holiness is walking in the Vatican Gardens,' Maglione said. 'He may speak to you or he may not. You will not speak unless you are spoken to. Is that clear, Father Steiger?'

'Yes, Eminence.'

'Come.'

Maglione positioned him at the side of a gravelled pathway. 'Wait here,' he grunted and shambled off. After a short time, he saw the pope walk slowly in his direction, reading from his breviary. He walked past him and paused, trapping his forefinger in the prayer book.

'I believe you have been of service to the Church, Father.'

His voice was inflectionless and barely rose above a whisper.

'That is my purpose, Holiness,' Max replied.

'You wish to found a new religious order within the Church,' Pius continued, 'The Fratres – The Brothers.'

'With your blessing, Holiness.'

'We live in troubled times,' the pope said, as if musing aloud. 'We have known great trials and even greater trials await us. In the past, the Church could rely on men to step forward from the ranks of the priesthood and serve the Church in her hour of need.'

'Men like Francis, Dominic and Ignatius, Holiness,' Max prompted.

'Yes,' Pius said wistfully. 'Sadly, their followers seem to have become distracted from their purpose. Which of the three would you and The Fratres try to emulate, Father?'

'Ignatius and the Jesuits, Holiness,' Max replied promptly.

'Why?'

'Because he emulated the early Christians, Holiness.' Max said enthusiastically. 'They converted Constantine and the Roman Empire turned to Christianity. In their own times, Ignatius and his followers influenced those who had power in society and through them their nations. The Fratres would dedicate themselves to a crusade to convert and create a new Christian Europe with Rome at its heart.'

'Your vision of a new crusade is truly edifying, Father Steiger,' Pius said, 'but I may not be the pope to champion it. There are those who say I should not have stayed silent during this terrible war.'

'Yours was the only voice for peace, Holiness,' Max assured him. 'When the warmongers are no more, it is your voice that will be remembered.'

The pope stood lost in thought for a long time.

'You will be informed of my decision on this matter, Father Steiger,' he said and walked away. Max saw the car at the end of the pathway and the driver drop to his knees as Pius approached. He stepped into the car and sat on the gilded throne that took up the space where the back seat had been.

Max stood on the silent path long after the pope had disappeared, dissecting their conversation. Should he have placed more emphasis on the loyalty of The Fratres to the papacy, he wondered? No, he concluded. Pius might be autocratic and susceptible to flattery but he was no fool. He shuffled from one foot to the other as he raised internal arguments and answers until his head buzzed. Finally, he took a deep breath to calm himself. 'This is my destiny,' he whispered. 'Nothing and no one will stand in my way.'

KARL: MILITARY HOSPITAL (THE FROSTBITE WING), GERMANY

The sky was reduced to a small square. It hung on the mustard-coloured wall, bracketed by a white window frame. The sunlight advanced across the floor of the ward in bright battalions that curved and lengthened as the afternoon wore on. He thought the ranks of beds looked barricaded against the light with high screens. There were no pictures on the walls; pictures had reflective surfaces. Everything else – the lockers at the bedsides, the table and chairs, hunched together in the central space – had matte, gunmetal-grey surfaces. His left hand twitched awake under the dressing and he began to breathe deeply, anticipating and then channelling the pain into a hot, bright ball that hovered over his left shoulder. Slowly, agonisingly slowly, that molten ball dimmed and faded and disappeared. His left hand had become dormant again. He swung his feet to the floor and towelled the sweat from his hair with his right hand.

'Pain is not your enemy, Karl,' Doctor Heller had told him on her first visit.

'It's no great friend either,' he'd countered through clenched teeth and she'd smiled. It was a smile that acknowledged the truth of what he'd said and he'd not felt offended.

'No, not a friend,' she'd conceded. 'A friend would never—'

She'd stopped and gone silent again, as if she'd intuited that this was not an analogy she should develop.

'Think of it as a proof,' she'd suggested, 'a proof that your hand is alive, that it feels. I can give you something to take the pain away for a while, if you wish.'

'No,' he'd said. 'No, thank you, Doctor Heller.'

He was a man now and didn't want to be protected from reality – didn't want to be left behind in the village or at the foot of the hill. He pressed the towel to his face and inhaled the salt-tang of his pain.

'Karl?'

The nurses always announced themselves from outside the screens and waited for permission to enter. It was hospital policy. Most of the men behind the screens would appreciate some time to brace themselves against the reflection of their injuries in the reactions of others.

'Come in, Anna,' he called.

He'd discovered she was from a farm in Bavaria and that her fiancé had been with Guderian. 'Captain Albert Becker?' she'd whispered. It was against regulations. She shouldn't ask and he needn't answer.

'I poured a glass of wine for him in General von Kluge's tent, after Smolensk,' he'd whispered.

'I – I got a letter from General Guderian,' she'd said, her voice wavering. She'd covered her face with her strong hands.

'I remember him as a very intelligent officer.'

His mouth had tasted of ashes. A tear leaked through her fingers. It followed the curve of her ring and sparkled before it dropped on the white coverlet.

Anna looked him over critically. 'I'm to change your dressing and tidy you up a bit. Doctor Heller is on her way with a visitor.'

'A visitor?'

'I never said that,' she said, with a warning look.

He concentrated on that tiny square of sky while she worked, remembering an oval face, ice-green eyes and a phantom kiss.

'*Danke, junge*,' he breathed as she tied off the clean dressing.

'*Bitte*.'

She stood back to give him an appraising look. He was certain she must have younger brothers in Bavaria who squirmed before that look. Briskly, she tugged the pyjama top straight and flattened his collar. Finally, she ran her splayed fingers through his hair.

'You'll do,' she said.

He was in the kitchen at home and Elsa was regaling his parents. His mother's eyes glowed with admiration and affection. Rudi leaned against the dresser, holding his coffee mug with both hands, watching Elsa with a look of wry amusement. He saw himself take her bag and swing it over his shoulder. As he straightened, tenderness warred with anxiety on his father's face. Elsa was looking at him critically. She pushed his fringe out of his eyes with splayed fingers. 'You'll do,' she said.

When he came back from his reverie, Doctor Heller was sitting by his bedside. He guessed she might be in her early forties, but her eyes were older. Doctor Heller never stood at the foot of the bed like some of the other physicians. She never held a patient's chart as a protective breastplate or raised her voice to protect herself against the possibility that a patient might confide in her or ask an awkward question. She preferred to sit at the bedside and speak slowly and softly to create an intimate space. Rudi, he recalled, had been a good listener, a man unafraid of silences who gave his full attention and spoke only when he had heard and digested what the other person had to say. Doctor Heller had all of these qualities and the courage to accept and absorb whatever horror might be entrusted to her.

'You were somewhere else,' she said gently.

'Sorry.'

'For what?'

'For being rude – for keeping you waiting.'

'Rude is when you consciously ignore another, Karl. I don't

think you were doing that, were you?'

'No, Doctor Heller.'

'What were you doing?'

'Remembering.'

'Good,' she nodded. 'Remembering is a chance to relive something. It can be something sad or happy or frightening. Was it frightening this time?'

'No – not this time.'

'Our minds take little trips, Karl, like someone who needs to go back somewhere until he needn't go back anymore. Do you understand?'

'I think so.'

'It's important that you do. Some men don't go back – won't go back, because it's too painful for them or they just want to forget the past and get on with life.'

She sighed.

'I'm afraid it's not possible to forget important things. If they're not sorted, they become like some enormous suitcase that must be lugged around forever. It can take great courage to revisit the past. A man who does so is worth waiting for.'

She allowed a few moments so that he could digest this before she continued.

'You have a visitor, a Major Gerhard Hauptmann. May I bring him in?'

He knew he could refuse and the major would be escorted, politely but firmly, to the door. The nurses whispered of a general who had thought it a good idea to 'cheer up the men' with his war stories and had found himself at the sharp end of Doctor Heller's tongue.

'Yes,' he said, 'I'll see him.'

Karl heard the major before he saw him. Through the open door, he heard the unmistakable step and drag gait of a man who had lost a leg. And an eye, he noted, as the major came to his bedside. A black eyepatch covered the hole where the eye had been, but not the crater of pink and puckered flesh that surrounded it. He looked like someone who had put his eye to the hole in a furnace door. As if aware of his thoughts, the major raised his hand and touched the eyepatch.

'I was foolish enough to spy on a sleeping dragon,' he said. 'It sent a T-34 tank to punish my hubris. The leg,' he added, 'I left in some field hospital on the way back from Moscow.'

The major eased his artificial leg to a more comfortable angle.

'I have something for you,' he said. He took a box from his tunic pocket and flipped the lid. Karl saw a medal glinting on a bed of black velvet. The velvet seemed to drink the available light and he looked away.

'You are awarded the Winter medal for your services on the Eastern Front,' the Major said, formally. 'Do you accept?'

Karl knew that the 'Old Wehrmacht' called it the 'Frozen' medal. His first instinct was to reject it, because to him it was a symbol of waste and loss. At the same time, he wondered how many times the major had had it thrown back in his face.

'I accept,' he said and bent forward so that the major could loop the ribbon over his head. As he straightened, the medal swung against his skin. 'It's cold,' he said.

The major cocked his head to look at him with his good eye.

'The German High Command has discovered irony,' he whispered and smiled. The smile twisted his face in two. The unmarked side reflected a young man who talked of dragons. The other was the face of a man who'd met one.

'It gets worse,' the major grinned. 'I am to inform you that you've been promoted to the rank of captain. The recommendation was made by General von Kluge.'

He tilted his head and looked at Karl like an inquisitive hen.

'You knew von Kluge?'

'No, I couldn't say that,' Karl said. 'I know he liked to read de Caulaincourt.'

'Didn't they all?' the major said quietly. 'For all the good it did any of us. Sorry,' he added, dragging his errant leg towards the chair and struggling upright. 'I'll be going now, Captain Hamner.'

Karl saw him hesitate and wondered if he was considering an appropriate salute.

'Thank you, Major,' he said and held out his hand. 'I'm glad the dragon didn't get all of you.'

'Me too,' the major said, shaking it firmly, 'most times.'

★

'Home?'

'Yes, home,' Doctor Heller said. 'How do you feel about that?'

'I – I think—'

'I didn't ask you what you thought, Karl,' she said firmly. 'I asked what you felt.'

'Apprehensive.'

'Which is as near as a man can get to saying "afraid",' she smiled. 'And what do you fear most?'

'That I might not survive. That I might never be happy again.'

'May I take your hand?'

'Yes, yes of course.'

Instinctively, he offered her his right hand.

'If you don't mind, I should like to hold your left hand,' she said.

Slowly, he extended his left hand and placed it on the hand she had laid palm upwards on the coverlet. She cradled it gently.

'No one survives a war, Karl,' she said. 'No one can ever go back to who they were before the first shot was fired. People long to go "back to normal". It's an understandable longing, but it's a wish that can't be granted.'

He became aware of tears on his face and went to rub them away.

'Don't wipe away your tears, Karl,' she said gently. 'You must grieve for those you've lost and for the boy you once were. As for happiness, I think it's greatly overrated. We associate happiness with pleasure and, mostly, we find pleasure in gratification. There's nothing wrong with that. I think there's a deeper sense of gratification when we do something for others; not that we neglect the self but that we develop a deeper part of it. Perhaps that part is what people refer to when they speak of the soul. Does that make sense?'

Karl thought of his father in the snow-hole and the miner's last act of heroism.

'Yes,' he whispered.

'I see you're wearing a glove,' she said slowly. 'It may not be warm enough.'

'It's a Wehrmacht glove, Doctor Heller,' he said tightly, 'standard summer issue.'

He realised he'd spoken more harshly than he'd intended and she deserved.

'I'm sorry,' he said, 'it's just I—'

'No, Karl, there's no need to explain.' She reached up and kissed him gently on the cheek. 'I have saved your hand, Karl. Only you can save your soul.'

Hallstatt

He stood on the small jetty that jutted out into the lake. The fog became pearlescent as the sun struggled over the peaks of the Dachstein Mountains and he felt diminished by the immutable forces all around him. The jetty offered a few paces of creaking boards and, beyond that, the possibility of nothingness. His hand began to throb like a tentative heartbeat, and he heard an echo in the dip, sweep and feather of Erich's oars. A tremor ran through his feet as they docked and he saw the boatman harden from shadow into substance as he approached.

'Karl?'

He took off his cap. 'Hello, Johann,' he said.

Johann stepped closer and stared at him intently. Almost wonderingly, he raised his hand to ruffle Karl's hair and let it drop on his shoulder instead.

'I'll never call you boy again,' he said hoarsely. 'Rudi and Tomas,' he added, squeezing Karl's shoulder until it hurt. He shook his head in disgust. 'Even Steiger,' he said. 'He was a bastard but he was our bastard.'

It felt strange to knock on the door of his own home but he didn't want to startle her. After a long time, the door opened a little way and he was struck speechless by the small, frightened face of his mother. Her eyes widened at the sight of the uniformed figure on her doorstep.

'Is it Karl, officer?' she said breathlessly. 'Is my son—?'

'Mutti, it's me.'

She fell into his arms and he swept her up like a child, a child who has been wakened from a nightmare and is too exhausted to do more than whimper. He placed her in her chair by the stove and turned up the lantern before he sat at her feet. Her trembling fingers touched his cheek and forehead and traced the contours of his ear, as if he were a newborn and his mother needed to satisfy herself that he had come into the world unscathed. 'Karl,' she whispered, over and over, 'Karl,' breathing his name and savouring its sound.

After a time, he made them coffee on the stove, his eyes and heart snagging on Rudi's mug as he took two others from the dresser. He put the mug in her hands and pressed them between his own until their trembling lessened, then sat again where she could see his face.

'An officer came,' she began and continued in broken sentences to tell him how she'd heard the news. When she'd finished, she began again. He'd seen comrades do the same after Smolensk, Bryansk and Borodino, tell the same story over and over again as if repetition helped to make the experience real. He sat at her feet, allowing her the time to trace the threads of their torn tapestry. Later, he would add some threads of his own.

The telling and retelling became a lullaby that soothed her to sleep. He tucked a blanket around her and brought logs to freshen the stove. Slowly, he stripped to the waist and began to bathe himself in a basin. There was a soft knock and the door swung open. A woman stepped inside and averted her face in embarrassment. 'Please forgive me,' she said and turned to go.

'Please, come in Frau Mende,' Karl said, struggling into his shirt. He turned away to wrestle with the cuff-button at his right wrist.

'May I help?'

'No, no thank you. I can manage – eventually.'

He turned and she saw beads of sweat between his eyebrows.

'I thought we might sit with your mother while you visited Bertha and Kurt,' she said.

'We?'

'You can come inside now, Gunther,' she called.

A boy stepped shyly from behind the door. He was backlit by sunlight and his downy hair seemed like a halo around his thoughtful face. He looked around the kitchen until his eyes fell on Frau Hamner. 'Ta,' he said, and his face creased into a smile. He walked over and kissed her on the forehead. Then he turned and put a warning finger to his lips. 'Shush,' he whispered.

'Won't you say hello to Karl?' his mother prompted.

The boy nodded and offered a soft hand to Karl, who shook it solemnly.

'Hurt,' Gunther said.

'Pardon?'

'Hand hurt.'

'Yes, Gunther,' Karl said, 'my hand was hurt in the war. Will you mind my mother for me while I visit my friends?'

'Ta.'

He excused himself and left them in the kitchen.

His bedroom seemed to have shrunk. The miner would love this, he thought, and stopped with a sock-drawer half open. He was still thinking of Tomas in the present tense, still expecting Rudi to call up the stairs or saunter in from his workshop. He felt reluctant to go to the workshop. He might be tempted to sweep up the shavings and tidy the tools and those little acts would reflect an acceptance of his father's absence and that would be a betrayal. The pragmatist in him knew that he would have to make decisions about the lumber and the equipment, but not yet, not yet.

When he returned, he was dressed in his captain's uniform.

'I'm really grateful, Frau—'

He was interrupted by a low moan. Gunther's face had gone the colour of clotted cream. His eyes, fixed on Karl, brimmed with tears and he moaned again. 'Hide,' he quavered.

'It's me, Gunther,' Karl said, stepping forward. He froze as the boy's lips curled back in a rictus of fear. Frau Mende took Gunther's shoulders and turned him to face her.

'It's Karl, our friend,' she soothed and drew him against her. Karl stood awkwardly until she motioned with her head to the door. As he left, he heard her murmur, 'We will make coffee for Ta when she wakes and you can play with Karl's toys.'

The boy had stopped moaning. As Karl shut the door, he heard him whisper 'hide'.

Bertha was bent over in the garden, contemplating tiny blue flowers that had pushed through the crusted snow in a sheltered corner. She turned as the gate creaked and her face blossomed into a smile. She had always struck him as – distracted. Yes, that was the word. As if she had left a book open somewhere and would return to it as soon as possible. It was an expression his mother wore when there was something in the oven that needed watching. He smiled at the notion of the bookish Frau Brandt ever leaving a book to check a pot roast.

'Karl,' she said.

There was something in the way she spoke his name that touched him deeply. The single word seemed to encompass his friendship with Kurt and the unique position he held in their lives.

'Good morning, Frau Brandt,' he said politely.

'I would like you to call me Bertha,' she said. 'I believe we shall be friends. Come, there is coffee on the stove. Kurt is doing an archaeological dig through a trunkful of papers in the study. He'll only fret if I interrupt him.'

He sat at the kitchen table and let the room soothe him. There were books everywhere, stacked in the unlikeliest places. He saw books peeping out from between the dishes in the dresser and books spreadeagled on the table. A large volume was bookmarked with a meat skewer and another leaned against the sugar bowl. A parcel lay open on the table and four volumes, bound with leather, gleamed like chestnuts released from their pods. He tilted his head to read the spines – Rainer Maria Rilke. He must have spoken aloud because she turned from the stove and followed his gaze.

'That's a story he'll tell you himself,' she said, placing his coffee before him and sitting opposite. 'Sometimes he starts to talk and stops mid-sentence,' she continued, quietly. 'In the beginning, I'd prompt him and he'd find some excuse to be elsewhere. It's very disconcerting. Kurt was never one to be lost for words. I feel – excluded.'

'Frau Br— Bertha, he began, 'in Russia, words were the first casualty. I – we saw so much, so quickly. During the early days, I wrote in my journal every day: long, careful descriptions of everything I saw and heard, even the most ordinary things. Kurt said that's what a historian should do.'

She nodded and smiled ruefully.

'As we moved east,' he continued, 'I found it more and more difficult to write until I was just scribbling half-sentences and phrases and then single words, pages of words. Before the last battle, I wrote the word 'snow'. I filled two pages with that single word.'

He paused and she wondered if he would ever come back from whatever place his eyes contemplated. Finally, he gave a small shudder and resumed.

'Soldiers speak less often as a war goes on. It becomes easier to do things – clean a rifle, do some laundry, anything to remain distracted. Later, actions became necessary to staying alive. It sometimes took twenty minutes to dress before going to the forest for kindling and twice that time to become warm enough to put the sticks in the stove. Talk became a burden, dangerous even, because you had to uncover your mouth.'

His hand floated up to cover his mouth and she waited.

'I remember a book in our schoolroom,' he said, so softly that she had to lean in to hear him. 'I think it belonged to Herr Tauber. It was about how man evolved from the primates. I don't know why, but I liked to look through the pictures from the back to the front, so that the man became hairier and more hunched. In the pictures, they began to do more practical things. There was one picture I remember quite well. It was a drawing of a group of stone-age people, living in a cave. The fire was near the mouth of the cave and, in the distance, beyond the flames, I could see the shapes of huge creatures. Every person in the picture was doing something. Most were keeping the fire alive but others were scraping hides or sharpening weapons. In the top, right-hand corner of the picture, there was a separate chamber. There were two figures in the chamber, drawing bison and aurochs and deer and stick figures of hunters on the roof of the cave. I think that's what Kurt and I did in our journals. We kept a record of experiences that were too awful for words. And—'

'And?'

'And that's the most I've said to another human being in a very long time,' he said apologetically.

She reached across the table to cover his hand with her own. 'I wish Kurt would do that,' she said.

'He will,' he assured her, 'when he's ready. The war was very difficult for him. Perhaps he thought that being a historian would distance him from the reality. It didn't. History washed over us like a flood, Bertha, and swept all our objectivity away. Everything we considered normal became twisted and abnormal. That was very frightening. We did everything we could to keep the new normal at bay. I notice my mother has the house exactly as it was when my father left it. This morning, I turned his chair a little from the table and she turned it back. Kurt and my mother and I must try to make a new normal.'

He wondered what it would be like meeting Kurt, after everything they'd experienced. His chest was tight with apprehension as he and Bertha stepped into the study. Would Kurt revert to the schoolmaster–student relationship? Would he take refuge in book talk or the delights of some article he was reading? His first impression was that Kurt had become smaller. He was hunched by the stove, a book splayed on a small coffee table beside him and a notepad open in his lap. Kurt looked up and spilled the notebook to the floor as he stood. 'Karl,' he whispered.

For a moment he stood staring, as if at a loss. Then he came forward and engulfed Karl in his arms. Karl could feel the tremors running through his upper body and a wetness where Kurt's cheek pressed against his own. He saw Bertha move to the door to grant them privacy but Kurt extended his arm and called her into the embrace. The three stood together until they had no more tears to shed.

'To absent friends,' Bertha toasted as they touched glasses around the stove.

'I have a gift for you,' Kurt announced and went to rummage in a pile of books and papers. He returned with a small package, wrapped in brown paper and held together with a delicate blue ribbon. Karl steadied it between his knees and picked it open with his right hand.

'It's your journal,' he gasped, 'I can't take—'

'You can and you must,' Kurt insisted. 'Naturally,' he added, with a self-deprecating laugh, 'I've made a copy. You know what we historians are like when it comes to primary sources.'

Karl laid it in his lap and stroked the battered cover reverently. He lifted the cover and read the inscription in Kurt's distinctive scrawl.

'To my dear friend and colleague.'

'I have a gift for you, also,' Karl said sheepishly. He plucked an identical package from his tunic pocket and passed it across. It was wrapped in a paper napkin and tied with coarse twine.

'Paper was a scarce commodity at the hospital,' he said wryly, 'and I – I didn't have someone I could ask for a ribbon.'

He smiled at Bertha, who seemed to have found a fresh reservoir of tears. Kurt accepted it with both hands.

'I know what this is,' he said quietly, 'I'll cherish it.' His voice broke and he fumbled with the wrapping until Karl's journal lay revealed. 'You know von Kluge sent me his papers,' he said. 'He wants me to be his de Caulaincourt.'

'That's wonderful, Kurt.'

'I wrote back to him and said that I couldn't be objective, that he should give the task to some other historian.'

'What did he say to that?'

'He said that if he'd wanted objectivity, he'd have given the task to a historian. He said a waiter would create something more interesting and readable. We could work on it together, Karl,' he added enthusiastically. 'That is, if you feel ready.'

Karl didn't feel ready. Could he read the battle reports without reliving the horror and the terror? Would it be possible to read the letters from Berlin without becoming inflamed? How, in God's name, could he face the lists of casualties without seeing Tomas dig his father's grave in the snow or hearing the grunt that exploded from the miner's mouth when the bullet punched him between the shoulders? He turned his head away and his eyes met Bertha's. Her eyes didn't plead. They were full of compassion, as if she understood the pain that awaited him in these papers.

'Yes,' he said. 'This is something we should do together – after everything.'

'Do you know how long you'll be here?' Kurt asked anxiously.

'Until they send for me,' Karl said.

Spring exited as demurely as she had entered and ceded Hallstatt to her more opulent sister. Karl brought his mother her morning coffee and sat with her in long companionable silences. Both accepted that their time together was measured by forces beyond their control and bent their energies to living fully in the moment. Mostly, they talked of local matters – the ordinary, everyday things that sustain people who are conscious of living in the meantime.

Sometimes his mother spoke of his father, the person Rudi had been before Karl was born. She seemed to wait until he was fixing a hinge or doing some other small task before raising the subject, allowing him to eavesdrop on her thoughts.

Later, they walked arm in arm to the Brandts' cottage and Bertha took his mother shopping or to visit Frau Mende and Gunther. He and Kurt used the morning to sort, file and read von Kluge's papers. Once the ground rules for their research had been agreed, there was little need for conversation as they went about their tasks. After lunch, Karl and his mother would retrace their steps. He noticed she seemed to walk more slowly each day, as if her old vigour was ebbing away. He enquired of Frau Mende if his mother needed medication or a tonic.

'Nothing works for phantom pains, Karl,' she answered quietly.

'What should I do?'

'Exactly what you are doing: give her a reason to be here.'

'And when I'm gone?'

'Perhaps it'll be enough for her to know you'll come back. How did you survive Barbarossa, Karl?'

'I had reasons – my mother and father, Kurt and Tomas.'

'People survive for a reason. A mother will survive for her child, I know that.'

'Does Gunther still fear me?'

'No, just the uniform. I'm glad you've stopped wearing it but I don't want him to stop fearing it. Do you understand?'

'Yes.'

'But it hurts you?'

'Not everyone in uniform is a Nazi.'

'I know, but it's hard to tell when they come calling.'

'What would you do?'

'Ask Bertha,' she replied cryptically.

'The mines,' Bertha said, after a pause. 'We've been going, once a week, to search for Elsa. We bring provisions in a picnic basket but never have a picnic. At this stage, we've quite a cache of food stored away up there.'

When the evenings shortened and the white caps on the peaks lengthened into snow capes, his mother died. He buried her near the grave of Simon Tauber; he thought she'd like that. Later, when the grave had settled, he paid a mason to erect a stone to her memory. He had his father's name carved beneath hers with the simple inscription: 'Rudi Hamner, loving husband and father.'

A few days later, he went back to work with Kurt in the mornings, as usual. In the afternoons, he went to the mines.

He heard a horse snort as he left the village, and the memory of Cossacks twisted his guts. It took some time for his heartbeat to rein back to a canter as he sat by the stream that bordered the path. After he'd ducked his face in the water and sluiced the bile from his mouth, he began to climb. He felt the pine needles move beneath his feet, like velvet rubbed between the fingers. Fir and spruce rose tall and impossibly straight from the canted terrain and he savoured their resinous perfume as he passed beneath the benediction of their upraised branches.

Almost abruptly, the sights, smells and sounds of the forest muted into the silence of lichen and shale. He'd always loved the simplicity of the higher places and placed his feet as carefully as a man walking in a cathedral. But the black hole in the mountain was not the Porta Coeli – the Gate to Heaven – of the medievalists. The opening to the mine, he knew, led down into the dark and to the contemplation of whatever demons a man brought with him.

His ritual was as defined as any pilgrim's. It began when he entered the great chamber, holding the lantern low before him, like a votive candle to guide his steps. He placed it reverently where he remembered Elsa sitting and retreated to where he'd been that day. Slowly, he moved through the familiar choreography, stepping around the lantern as he whispered their last dialogue. Finally, he left for the catacomb of corridors, carrying the lantern before him, looking back once and imagining Elsa etched in light. He sat near the ancient stairway and listened. Had he heard her call? Hurriedly, he returned to the chamber and her aching absence forced him to his knees. 'Elsa,' he whispered, 'I'm back.'

Something tapped against his chest and he snatched up the lantern. The silver cross swung in the light and the sight of it ignited his rage. Rushing from deep in his belly, it scalded into his throat and burst from his mouth in a roar, an animal snarl that boomed around the sparkling walls and echoed back to feed upon itself until he was lost in its torrent. He must have banged his hand when he toppled forward to pound the floor. Bright pain flashed behind his eyes and earthed him back to reality. She was gone. Elsa was never coming back. Max had—

Something dark and foetid uncoiled inside him and he willed it back to rest. He could not hate Max. Max had wrestled with his demons and Elsa had been a casualty of that conflict. He couldn't hate the boy who had run from the mine in terror. He knew what terror could do to grown men and began to feel the first stirrings of pity for the haunted boy. Slowly, he kissed the tips of his fingers and touched them to the spot where he'd last seen her alive. '*Danke, junge,*' he whispered. '*Auf Wiedersehn.*'

Johann shifted on the kitchen stool until Karl took pity on him and produced the bottle.

'There's a carpenter over in Kirchham willing to buy the lumber,' he said after he'd downed the first glass. 'It's a good price.

Everybody knows Rudi chose well and didn't take shortcuts with the seasoning. Says he'll make a bid for the tools as well.'

'I'll leave it to you, Johann,' Karl said. 'Take whatever covers your trouble and give the rest to the Brandts for the school.'

'I don't charge friends,' Johann said stiffly and was mollified only when Karl refilled his glass. 'Better take a refill yourself,' he grunted as he slid an envelope across the table. Karl pinned it to the table with his left elbow and slit it open with his right thumb.

'Well?'

'They want me back.'

'Tell them to fuck off,' Johann advised. 'You've done your bit and lost more than most. I know a doctor in—'

'No!'

'Why? It's only a matter of time before the Yanks or Ivan come sailing over the lake.'

When Karl didn't answer, Johann drained his glass and stood.

'I'll be ready to cross in an hour,' he said gruffly. He paused at the door. 'Look,' he said, 'I know the drill. You can't go around blabbing about orders, but just tell me they're not sending you back to—'

He couldn't bring himself to say 'Russia' and Karl filled the gap. 'Rome,' he said, 'they're sending me to Rome.'

VON KESSELRING'S HQ, ROME

Field Marshal von Kesselring was in full flight when Karl slipped into the back of the conference room. He ducked into a chair beside the door and concentrated on being invisible.

'The Appenines, gentlemen,' von Kesselring thundered. 'The mountain range will slow them and we'll shred them in the passes. Any questions?'

'Can we expect any assistance from General Badoglio?' a lieutenannt asked.

'The commander of the Italian forces insisted on hugging me

when we last met. I could feel him checking my spine for the knife. Does that answer your question, Ulrich?'

The officers laughed and von Kesselring smiled indulgently. Karl could see why his troops referred to him as 'Uncle Albert'.

'Go on, dismissed,' von Kesselring said and the officers filed from the room.

'Who the hell are you?' he barked.

'Hamner, sir. Captain Karl Hamner.'

'Ah, von Kluge's protégé. Bet you think a posting to Rome is like a furlough on the Riviera, right?'

'It's warmer than Borodino, sir.'

'That it is. How far did you get, Captain?'

'Almost to Moscow, sir.'

Von Kesselring's eyes strayed to Karl's left hand and returned to his face. Karl searched those eyes for any trace of pity and was relieved to find warmth.

'Von Kluge says you're a historian?'

'Yes, sir.'

The field marshal put his hand on Karl's shoulder and steered him to a window.

'What do you see, historian?' he asked.

'Rome, sir.'

'Look again. Some of my officers see a conquered city. They see the Romans as excitable and incompetent, a people who make marvellous pasta and indifferent allies. They joke about the Roman propensity for fancy uniforms, even the traffic policeman looks like an escapee from Grand Opera, they say. You don't find that amusing, do you, Captain Hamner?'

'No, sir.'

Karl looked out over a skyline that was mounded with domes and spiked with spires.

'This city is over two thousand years old,' he said softly. 'The original Romans had to fight the Etruscans for it and then fight all the other tribes to conquer Italy. Their armies went on to push their borders as far north as Hadrian's Wall and all the way south to Libya. Yes, they were conquered and occupied at various times by the Carthaginians, Goths, Vandals, Lombards and Napoleon, but—'

'And by us, Captain,' von Kesselring interrupted.

'And by us,' Karl conceded. 'But they're still here, Field Marshal. Where are the Etruscans? Where is Napoleon?'

Von Kessselring nodded thoughtfully.

'D'you see that big dome to your right, Captain?'

'Saint Peter's Basilica, sir. It's—'

'Please,' von Kesselring said, raising a weary hand, 'spare me the lecture. I know it's the biggest church in the world, the powerhouse of the Roman Catholic Church and a focal point for half a billion believers. As the military commander of Italy, I see that dome as a dormant volcano and that basilica as the plug that stops the crater. That's why I insist on old Wehrmacht soldiers, mostly Roman Catholic, under my command here. That's why we tiptoe around the Vatican and give a wide berth to the one hundred and fifty-eight properties it possesses throughout the city. You know that Model is in Russia, trying to hold Zhukov and Timoshenko. Rommel is in North Africa trying to contain Montgomery. So why am I in Rome? My objective, Captain, is to ensure the silence of a single man. One word of criticism from Pius XII could trigger the volcano and cause eruptions all over Europe, even in Germany.'

He turned away from the window and slumped behind the desk.

'And today,' he continued, 'Berlin has sent someone who will unplug the volcano, someone who will undo all the hard work we've put in to keeping the pope silent. And not because we've bombed churches or executed priests, but for seven thousand Jews.'

A tap on the door interrupted the field marshal and a lieutenant stepped inside.

'Major Kappler to see you, sir.'

'Show him in, Ernst.'

Von Kesselring motioned Karl to a chair beside the window. The SS major strode into the room and flung his right arm forward in salute.

'Heil Hitler,' he snapped.

'You may sit, Herbert,' von Kesselring said.

The major moved to a chair and sat, ramrod-straight.

'My orders are to collect seven kilos of gold from the Jews of Rome to procure new arms for the Reich,' he said stiffly.

'So,' von Kesselring said with a wintry smile, 'we are reduced to taking donations from the Jews for the war effort.'

The SS major flushed angrily.

'I have instructed the president of the Jewish Council, Signor Foa, to meet with me at the embassy. In the event of ... unrest, I would be grateful if you could provide a military escort.'

'A military escort to meet a single Jew, Herbert? It's understandable, I suppose. I recall that you had an escort of over two thousand troops when you, eh, visited the ghetto in Warsaw and they kicked your arses. I trust you don't plan on recreating that debacle in Rome? Request denied, Major. My men are committed to tasks befitting soldiers. I do not intend to deploy them as escorts for looters.'

The SS major shot to his feet.

'May I remind you, Field Marshal, that my orders come directly from General Heydrich.'

'May I remind you, Major, that my orders come directly from Adolf Hitler.'

Major Kappler snapped off a furious salute and turned for the door.

'I did not dismiss you, Major,' von Kesselring said icily. 'Sit!'

Karl saw the anger in the rigidity of the major's body when he turned. His eyes burned in the ivory mask of his face as he resumed his seat.

'I will allow you to requisition a military staff car and driver from the motor pool,' von Kesselring said evenly. 'Captain Hamner will accompany you as a representative of the military command. He will be my eyes and ears and bear my authority during your negotiations. Is that clear, Major?'

'Yes, Field Marshal.'

Von Kesselring opened a file on his desk and spent a full minute poring over a document. He looked up, as if surprised that the SS officer was still present.

'You are dismissed, Major,' he said.

The brown-robed monk paused on the landing and armed sweat from his eyes. Would the SD man keep his promise? he wondered. The bastard had materialised in his room like some fucking golem in a brown rumpled suit. He'd always prided himself on his ability to read faces. It had helped his promotion from guard to interrogator at Treblinka. Usually it had taken him just a few minutes to separate the sheep from the goats on the railway platform. The sheep answered questions truthfully, almost eagerly. They seemed dazed with hope and readily produced the valuables they'd concealed from the collectors in the sheds. Remarkably, they sustained that hope all the way to the showers, convinced that if they could deny reality it would pass them by like the Avenging Angel. It didn't.

The goats, on the other hand, lied magnificently, but he could read their eyes and the tell-tale, facial tics that betrayed them. Sometimes he'd had to shoot one of them before the others decided to become sheep. 'You have a talent, Caspar,' the kommandant had said, approvingly. It was the same talent that had led him to the conclusion that the war was lost. While his comrades had fastened on upbeat propaganda and been seduced by the forcefulness of words, he'd read the faces of the brass and come to his own conclusions. From that moment he'd become a squirrel, laying up a store of jewellery, currency and an assortment of gold teeth until he had enough, enough to secure a furlough, false papers and the name of a priest.

He'd persuaded a friend to come with him, a friend who resembled him in terms of his physical build. After a night of many beers, mostly consumed by the friend, he'd assisted him back to their cheap lodgings. As the man lay comatose, he'd stripped him of his clothes and identity tags and replaced them with his own. It had taken just a few moments to topple the lantern and wait until the bed began to burn.

The priest had hardly looked at his face. Within a month, he'd run through the relay of religious houses until he'd found sanctuary in the San Girolamo. The college authorities didn't ask questions. As soon as the money was in the drawer, he'd been given a room, a cassock and the title Brother Lazarus. 'Because you've been raised from the dead,' the rector had said, without a hint of irony.

It had all gone according to plan until the SD man had placed his battered ID on the table and flicked it open with his thumb.

'How did you find me?' he'd whispered.

'My purse was deeper than yours, Caspar. The priest takes a cut off both ends.'

He'd searched that face for signs of weakness and found none.

'You can't touch me,' he'd said, with forced bravado, 'I have sanctuary.'

'It works only as long as it suits them, Caspar. We'll keep calling until they decide you're not worth the trouble. Anyway, we have bigger fish to fry.'

'You want to trade, don't you?'

'I knew you were a bright boy. There's a priest here, a Father Max Steiger. We want to know him a little better. Documents would be good. We can copy them and put them back before he knows they're missing. You have twenty-four hours.'

A floorboard protested under his foot and he froze. After a tense moment, he worked the lock and slid into the room. Nobody lives here, was his first thought. There were no pictures or personal items; the bed looked as if no one had ever slept in it. His eyes ranged over the desk, chair and wardrobe and nothing snagged his attention. He began to quarter the room, pacing silently until he felt a faint movement underfoot. Slowly, he crouched and inserted a lock-pick in the join between two boards. The thin, metal filing box was filled with documents and he stuffed them into his cassock pockets before replacing the box in its lair. Methodically, he retraced his steps, scanning the room for the smallest clue to his presence. Satisfied, he locked the door behind him. Standing on the silent landing, he became aware that his body was running with sweat and he cursed his cassock.

★

Karl's first impression of Signor Ugo Foa was that he was a man unacquainted with care. He lounged before Kappler's desk and waved a languid hand as they arrived. The major seemed off-balance as if Foa had stolen a march on him by occupying his office.

'Well, Major Kappler,' Foa said cheerily, 'when are you coming for the Jews of Rome?'

'What?'

'It's a reasonable question, Major. We've been here since Julius Caesar was a pup and a lot of people have come for us in that time empires and popes and suchlike. You could say we've grown accustomed to a visit every time a new master comes along.'

'It's your gold we want,' Kappler said brusquely, 'to buy arms for the Reich.'

'Well,' Foa said, shaking his head in mock regret, 'Rabbi Zolli will be disappointed; he's convinced you're coming to deport us. Not an unreasonable assumption, I suppose. You seem to have deported Jews from every other part of Europe.'

Major Kappler opened his mouth to protest but Foa waved him into silence.

'Major Kappler,' he said soothingly, 'we're talking about a people who paid for a pope to return from exile, a people who financed the Roman Carnival to avoid the ritual humiliation. I told Zolli it's business as usual. How much?'

'Fifty kilograms.'

Foa pursed his lips and nodded a few times, as if he was totting up fifty kilograms of gold.

'When do you want it?'

'In thirty-six hours.'

'Will we get a receipt?'

Kappler bristled. 'To the enemy who is being relieved of his arms, one does not give a receipt,' he said.

'Then I'd better go and break the news to the Jewish Council,' Foa sighed.

Karl followed him outside to the pavement. 'I have a car, Signor

'Foa,' he said, 'let me drive you to your meeting.'

Foa looked at him keenly before shaking his head.

'I must decline, Captain,' he said. 'Rabbi Zolli's already convinced I'm collaborating with the SS.'

'I'm not SS, Signor,' Karl said. 'I'm Captain Karl Hamner of the Wehrmacht. Field Marshal von Kesselring sent me to represent him at the meeting. Please accept my offer.'

'Will the fare be added to the fifty kilograms of gold?'

'No,' Karl smiled.

CARDINAL MAGLIONE'S OFFICE, THE VATICAN

'His Eminence will see you now,' the monsignor said and ushered Max inside.

'You may sit, Father,' Maglione said, without looking up from the document he was reading. His skull cap lay discarded on the desk and he ran a gnarled hand through his unruly hair.

'Everyone wants something from the Vatican,' he muttered, tossing the document aside. 'What do you want?' he asked, fixing Max with shrewd, measuring eyes.

'To serve the Church.'

'Donkey shit,' His Eminence pronounced slowly. 'A man does not marry a woman for her sake. I'll ask again. What do you want?' He raised a warning hand. 'Consider well before you answer,' he growled. 'The pope is a saintly man, a man easily swayed by idealistic claptrap. I am not. I have a peasant's suspicion of those who come bearing gifts. I was not cultivated in some Roman hothouse for service to the Church. I was never the protégé of a dying pope, elevated at every opportunity, through the ranks of the hierarchy and positioned to succeed to the throne. The pope thinks you may be a visionary. Visionaries come and go around here, but it is peasants like me who keep this place running. When someone with another agenda gets in the way, I drive right over them. If your answer doesn't satisfy me, I will be your enemy and do all in my power to kick your upstart arse back to that piss-poor village in Austria. Do we understand each other, Father Max Steiger?'

'Yes.'

'Then answer my question. What do you want?'

'I want what you have,' Max said calmly.

Maglione looked startled. 'You want to be a cardinal?' he spluttered.

'No, Eminence. I want the kind of power you have, the kind of power that's listened to and that can influence others to make things happen in any part of the world. I want the kind of power that runs this place and—'

'And?'

'And that gets to kick some peasant's arse back to a piss-poor village in Italy.'

Maglione gazed at him for a long time.

'It comes at a price,' he said softly.

'I know—'

'No, you don't know,' Maglione interrupted. 'You think you know. You think the price is celibacy and being subject to authority. It's more, much more. It's the absence of friends because no one can have claims on your time or expectations of your favour. It's the commitment to ruthlessness in pursuit of an objective for the sake of the institution because it's the institution that's guaranteed to prevail against the gates of hell and people must become means to that end. It means making hard decisions, Father Steiger.'

He snatched a document from his desk.

'This is from a German diplomat who warns that the Jews of Rome are in Eichmann's gunsights. He begs that I inform the pope.'

He picked up another document with his left hand.

'This is from a French priest who reports that the French Vichy government is assisting with the deportation of Jews. He begs the pope to intervene.'

He thrust both documents at Max.

'Which request should I favour?'

'Neither.'

'Explain.'

'The Jews of Rome have been a thorn in Eichmann's side since Wannsee. It's common knowledge that von Kesselring doesn't favour any action against them because of the possibility of criticism from the pope and a Roman Catholic backlash throughout Europe. Let the Germans obstruct the Germans in this matter.'

'And if they move on the Jews?'

'The pope may instruct a Vatican diplomat to negotiate with his German counterpart. This shields the pope from directly confronting the Reich. It's also evidence that he didn't stand idly by.'

'And the report of Vichy's collaboration in the deportation of the Jews?'

'The ship should not alter course when it is so close to port, Eminence. If the Church allies itself with one side, it will alienate the other and fragment the universal Church along national lines. When the war is over, only the pope can claim to have shown neither fear nor favour, and the world will listen to his voice.'

Maglione slumped back as if exhausted. After a few moments, he took a sealed envelope from a desk drawer and slid it to Max. 'I am instructed by His Holiness to give you this,' he said formally. 'Read it and hand it back.'

Max slit the seal with his thumb and read the letter. He folded it inside the envelope and handed it back.

'Yes, Father Steiger,' the cardinal nodded, 'the pope grants you permission to prepare and present a formal case for the establishment of a new religious order in the Roman Catholic Church. He has appointed me as your mentor; for mentor, read watchdog, Father Steiger. My reputation now rides on your success. Get this wrong and I'll devour you – in the service of the Church, of course.'

★

'You don't seem concerned, Signor Foa,' Karl said as the car sped along the Lungotevere. 'Are you confident you can raise that amount of gold?'

'Maybe we will, maybe we won't,' Foa shrugged. 'If we don't, what can the SS do to us?'

'I think you know the answer to that question, Signor. There are precedents.'

'Let me ask you a question,' Foa said, suddenly serious. 'Why haven't they come for us already? And I will answer my own question. It's because we are Rome's Jews. Do you think the pope would allow them to take us from under his very window?'

Karl stood in the vestibule and waited. Through a glass panel in the synagogue door he could see the driver light a cigarette from the butt of the previous one and then flick the butt into a sparking arc. His eyes followed the flight of the tiny star and he saw two soldiers wrestling in the snow for an officer's discarded cigar. A polite cough brought him back to the present.

'Leave one Jew in a room and an argument will begin,' Foa said apologetically. 'There are twenty on the council and, so far, I've heard forty opinions. I'm sorry to have left you standing like this, Captain. The council has decided you may enter. Try not to sit too close to Rabbi Zolli.'

'You say von Kesselring is not in favour of this – ransom,' a young man with a pale face and long, black locks asked.

Karl gave them a brief account of the meeting in the field marshal's office.

'So von Kesselring loves the Jews,' the young man sneered.

'I don't know how he feels about the Jews,' Karl answered. 'I do know that his priority, as military commander, is to avoid alienating the Vatican.'

'How do you feel about the Jews, Captain?' an elderly man in the front row of chairs asked softly.

'The only Jew I ever really knew was my first teacher in Hallstatt. I admired him, not because he was a Jew but because he was such a fine teacher.'

'And I suppose he went on to become a lecturer at the University of Vienna?' the young man laughed.

'No. He filled his pockets with stones and walked into the lake.'

They were shocked as much by his pain as by his anger.

'Simon Tauber taught us that we were all Austrians – Christians and Jews,' he whispered into the sudden silence. 'He was wrong. When he discovered that, it killed him.' He shook himself free of his memories and looked up at the men arrayed before him. 'Signor Foa says you are Roman Jews. Put the Romans to the test: ask them for help with the ransom.'

He overrode the sudden hubbub.

'You can't be in and out at the same time, can't be a part of and apart from. Put them to the test: ask the Romans. And while you're at it, ask the pope. If you believe he'd never let them take you from under his very window, then ask what price he's willing to pay to keep you in Rome – not because you are Jews but because you are Romans.'

There were no more questions. Karl turned as Ugo Foa approached.

'Signor Foa,' he said, 'can you do something for me?'

'Yes – yes, of course, Captain.'

'Can you remove this ring from my finger?'

'What?'

'Please.' He gestured with his left hand. 'I can't do it myself.'

Carefully, Ugo Foa worked the ring from his finger.

'This is my mother's wedding ring,' he said. 'I give it to the Jews of Rome, to honour the memory of my teacher, Simon Tauber.'

THE SAN GIROLAMO, ROME

Max contained himself until he reached the sanctuary of his room and the door was locked behind him. He threw up his arms and gave a cry of exultation. The pope had filled his sails and Maglione, for all his bluster, would tack to the prevailing wind. His head reeled with possibilities. This wonderful news would inflame the committed and embolden the cautious among those he was recruiting to his cause. He could—

Abruptly, he dropped his arms and was still. Something was wrong; he could sense it in this Spartan room. Slowly he turned a complete circle, his eyes frisking the space for clues. Nothing seemed to be missing or out of place. Instead of soothing him, that fact twisted the knot of his anxiety even tighter. With an increasing sense of foreboding, he paced forward until a floorboard creaked. Feverishly, he tugged the floorboard free and plunged his hand into the recess. The cool kiss of the metal file-box spread, like a balm, from his hand to his arm and suffused his body. It proved a short-lived respite. His heart was drumming as he raised the lid and lifted the documents clear. He laid them on the floor and knelt over them, riffling through the pile with trembling fingers. Nothing was missing and they were all in order. As he straightened with relief, a single drop of sweat fell from his eyebrow and splattered on the top document. He bent again and began to peel them away, raising each document to the light. The sweat mark was on the document he prized more than any other. Illuminated from behind, it was oval-shaped, with ragged edges and totally dry. He raised his head and sniffed the air. The faint smell of sweat could be his own, he thought, but it was weak and acrid, like day-old incense in an empty church.

'Ah, Father Steiger. What can I—'

Father Dragonovic read the face of his visitor and reduced his question to a single word.

'What?'

Steiger's pallor accentuated the twin, livid weals that snaked from his eye to the corner of his bloodless lips. 'I need to find someone,' he said tonelessly.

'Who?'

'Someone who has taken something of mine,' he answered, and Dragonovic flinched from the cold anger in his eyes.

'A thief?' Dragonovic almost laughed with relief. The San Girolamo housed an assortment of professional thieves and—'

'I want to speak to your masters,' Steiger said.

'My … What the hell are you—?'

'I think he means me, Father Dragonovic,' the American woman said as she stepped through the door behind him. 'Why don't you go downstairs to the refectory,' she said, as if addressing a child. 'They'll be serving supper shortly.'

He opened his mouth to argue and closed it again. When the sound of the slammed door had subsided, she slid into his empty chair.

'How did you know?' she asked.

'If I provide that information, will you help me?'

'We may.'

He moved to a chair before the desk and sat.

'There is a Brother Anselmo, in the kitchens,' he began. 'Sometimes he brings trays to Dragonovic. Anselmo likes to gossip, especially when he's had lots of wine. I keep him supplied with drink and he feeds me information. He claimed he heard a woman's voice coming from this office the last time he brought a late supper to Dragonovic.'

'And you didn't conclude that the good Father was having an illicit relationship,' she said, with a faint smile.

'No. I know for a fact that the good Father's predilections are focused … elsewhere. The real purpose of the San Girolamo is known to too many to remain secret. I suspected that, sooner or later, Dragonovic would be compromised by some intelligence agency.'

'To what purpose?'

'The San Girolamo is being readied as a sanctuary for those who would prefer to avoid the consequences of their actions when the war is over. Some of those who arrive here will be murderous thugs; others will be murderous thugs who have secrets to sell or talents that can be redeployed. It will be like the post office in Hallstatt,' he continued, with a small, tired smile. 'Some of the parcels will be returned to sender and others will be re-addressed and forwarded, in this case to the United States.'

'And everyone in the village knew all about it?' she said softly.

'Yes, and the owners lived upstairs.'

'And Father Dragonovic, which category of – parcel does he come under?'

'Father Dragonovic was sent to prepare the way. I was given the money and the names.'

'I think we can do business, Father Steiger,' she said. 'Who is this person you're looking for?'

'I don't know.'

FIELD MARSHAL VON KESSELRING'S OFFICE, ROME

'What were you thinking of?'

'It seemed the right thing to do at the time, sir.'

'And now, in the cold light of day?'

'I still think it was the right thing to do. I'm sorry if I've embarrassed you, sir.'

'Embarrassed me? Karl, I am a Luftwaffe general who didn't learn to fly until I was forty years old. Also, I am commander of an army that's retreating before the Allies. No,' he chuckled grimly, 'it's Kappler and his ilk who were embarrassed when the Jews produced the gold. Where they got it is the mystery. No shortage of theories, of course. They ranged from Roman philanthropists to the Roman pontiff. My sources tell me that Kappler and his bully boys made them weigh it three times.' He laughed delightedly and then became serious again.

'The SS have long memories and a longer reach, Karl. If *I* know about your – little gesture, you can be sure *they* do. Better stay out of the way. Get yourself a set of civvies and see Rome. That's an order, Captain.'

★

Brother Anselmo's title was 'a flag of convenience'. He was a man of healthy appetites and wasn't about to let his title inconvenience him, not when a pretty lady presented herself and a bottle of brandy in his room. Any suspicions he might have harboured were allayed by her religious habit and her explanation that she was working as a spiritual advisor to those of the San Girolamo brethren who had 'special needs'. When she had energetically satisfied his 'special needs' and the brandy bottle sat empty between them, she'd ruined the evening by producing a pistol and his dossier.

'I think we can skip the formalities, Wilhelm,' she said in her flat American voice. Against all the conventions of the romantic novels he read so avidly, she proceeded to tell him his life story. He'd spoiled the recitation by throwing up, convulsively, when she'd mentioned Mengele and the medical experiments.

'Of course, you were just a junior doctor,' she'd said, passing him a clean handkerchief. 'But!'

He'd never appreciated how such a small word could carry so much menace.

'But,' she continued, 'you did manage to pay your way here. Now, a post-war tribunal might interpret your flight as an admission of guilt. My superiors, on the other hand, might interpret it otherwise and find suitable outlets for your talents. If—'

He'd discovered an even shorter word that promised salvation.

'If?' he prompted, hopefully.

Brother Anselmo waded through the noise of the San Girolamo refectory until he stood behind Brother Lazarus. 'It's not enough,' he whispered, as he bent to retrieve his plate. Brother Lazarus went to stand and Anselmo pressed him back into the chair.

'Don't be stupid,' he whispered fiercely. 'He said it's not enough. You must go back.'

★

Autumn was kind to Rome, Karl observed. The slanted, yellow sunlight gilded Bernini's tritons and dolphins in the Piazza Navona, turning the fountains molten. Following a tourist map, he found himself in the piazza. Della Rotonda, soothed by the solid façade of the Pantheon. The smell of strong coffee lured him under a café awning and he luxuriated in the anonymity of his brown pants and nondescript jacket. The coffee was delivered by a waiter who balanced it carefully on a small tray to compensate for a pronounced limp. Deftly, the young man slid the cup and saucer to the table. As he did so, his eyes fastened on Karl's gloved left hand, and when their eyes met, he smiled. Karl sat over his coffee, inhaling its rich aroma. Ever since Barbarossa, he'd struggled to enjoy the little pleasures others took for granted. 'It's no testament to the dead if the living withdraw from life,' Bertha had said one evening over supper when he'd toyed with the food on his plate.

'Marcus Agrippa,' a voice interrupted his musings. He hadn't noticed her take her place at the next table. She had raven hair and dark eyes that sparkled in a pale face.

'Pardon?'

'The inscription,' she said patiently. 'It reads Marcus Agrippa, son of Lucius, consul for the third time, built this. Not very modest, was he?'

He couldn't help smiling.

'No,' he conceded. 'Hadrian should get some credit for redesigning the bulk of it.'

'Hadrian,' she snapped. 'That bloody archaeological magpie couldn't keep his claws off any piece of antiquity. That's when he wasn't cluttering up his villa in Tivoli with recreations or brooding on his artificial island.'

'You're a historian?'

'I'm an archaeologist, Signor,' she said calmly. 'You are the historian.'

'How can you tell?'

'Ugo Foa told me. He also told me that he would meet you at the Santa Maria de Pescheria at one.'

'I see.'

'Not very much, I think,' she said, dipping her voice to a whisper. 'You have been followed from the Navona.'

'Why would someone follow me?'

'Why would a Wehrmacht captain give his mother's wedding ring to the Jews?' She smiled suddenly, and his chest tightened at the way it transformed her earnest face. 'There is a taxi rank at the other side of the Pantheon,' she said. 'Ask for Luigi – he can lose anyone.'

MAX'S ROOM, THE SAN GIROLAMO

He was on all fours, clutching the floorboard, when the lights snapped on and strong arms dragged him to a chair.

The priest sat at the other end of the room, his head bowed as if in prayer.

He rose and walked forward to stand before Caspar. 'Look at me, Caspar,' he commanded. Rough hands twisted his head until he was looking into the priest's eyes. At that moment, his 'gift' betrayed him. He could detect no trace of emotion in the fathomless eyes. He imagined he saw himself reflected in those dark irises as a subhuman, someone who might go left to the showers or right to the work detail, at a nod of the head. His fingernails had embedded themselves in the floorboard and he clung to it with the grip of a dying man.

'You are nothing to us,' the priest with the terrible twin scars intoned, as if confirming his own imaginings. Caspar knew from experience how this interview would progress and resolved to shorten his agony. He told the priest everything, running his words together in his eagerness to be rid of them, like a sinner granted the gift of confession before his death. The priest nodded and shifted his gaze to the men holding him. It was the first sign that Caspar interpreted correctly and he opened his mouth to scream.

★

'Isn't this a very public place to meet, Signor Foa?'

'This,' Foa said, with a broad gesture, 'is the church of Santa Maria de Pescheria. In the bad old days, the Jews were herded inside once a week, on the orders of Pope Paul IV, to hear Christian sermons. People around here give it a wide berth. Anyone else would be a stranger and a cause for suspicion. Come.'

He led Karl through a maze of alleyways, past high apartment buildings that sliced the sky into narrow blue ribbons. Lines of washing belled and flared overhead, the international flags of the poor. The restaurant had wood-panelled ceilings, polished to reflect the warm glow of table lamps.

'*Buona sera*, Signor Foa.'

The stocky man in the gleaming white shirt and black trousers pecked Foa enthusiastically on both cheeks before turning his attention to Karl.

'This is Captain Karl Hamner, Enrico,' Foa said.

Enrico took Karl's hand in his. 'So this is the captain,' he said. 'Please, sit.'

'He seems to know me,' Karl whispered as Enrico hurried to the kitchen.

'I have a confession to make,' Foa said, as he poured the wine. 'After you left the council, we argued late into the night. By eleven the following morning, the response to our request was pitiful. Someone had the brilliant idea of spreading the story of a Wehrmacht captain who had donated his mother's wedding ring. Actually,' he added modestly, 'it was my idea. The response was overwhelming.'

'Did you approach the pope?'

'Of course. Didn't the heroic Captain Hamner say we should? Someone knew someone who knew a religious superior who had contacts in the Vatican.' He waved a bread roll airily. 'You know how it works. The pope offered to pay the ransom – as a loan.'

He sipped his wine and held it on his tongue as if clearing his mouth of a bitter taste.

'At that stage, we had no need of it and declined the offer. The gold that flowed in from every level of Roman society came as a gift. It seems we are Romans after all.'

Their conversation was interrupted by a succession of dishes, presented by different members of Enrico's family. To Foa's amusement, they lavished attention on Karl, who was touched to see they had cut everything, even the artichokes, into bite-sized pieces. Coffee came with a familiar face.

'It seems you have made history, historian,' she smiled, before leaving them.

'I fear I may have done you a disfavour, Captain,' Foa said anxiously, 'by bringing you to the attention of the authorities.'

'Simon Tauber told us it was a Chinese curse,' Karl replied.

'The SS do not forget,' Foa said urgently. 'Should you need sanctuary, we will hide you in the Roman ghetto.'

'What would Rabbi Zolli say?' Karl asked, to lighten the mood, but Foa didn't laugh.

'Rabbi Zolli and his family have taken refuge with a Catholic family,' he said soberly.

'Do you really believe the pope will protect you from deportation?' Karl pressed.

'The pope stands between us and Auschwitz,' Foa replied. 'Not because he loves the Jews but because the Nazis fear him.'

He raised his cognac and touched glasses with Karl.

'*L'Chaim*,' he toasted. 'To life.'

CASTEL SANT'ANGELO, ROME

Tisserant's secretary stood before a fresco of *The Angel of Justice*. The SD officer took off his hat and shook drops from the brim as he entered.

'Do you admire Domenico de Zaga, Monsignor?' he enquired.

Without turning, Emil Dubois added, 'He was unfortunate enough to be born in the same century as Bernini, but he was a fine artist all the same.'

'I passed between guarding angels on the Pont Sant'Angelo,' the SD officer said. 'Even in the rain, they were quite wonderful.'

'Copies, I'm afraid,' Emil informed him. 'The Barberini Pope thought they were much too beautiful to be rained on. He brought the originals inside the Vatican.'

Satisfied that all the codes they'd agreed by letter had been included in their conversation, the SD man laid a sheaf of documents on the floor.

'I have placed a small donation to Justice on the floor behind you, Monsignor Dubois. Might I suggest that you take the Passeto back to the Vatican.'

'Why would I take the Vatican corridor?' Emil asked. 'A little rain won't harm me.'

'No, the rain won't.'

The SD officer saw the monsignor stiffen as the import of his words struck home.

'You could come with me, through the Passeto,' the monsignor urged.

'I could, but it would compromise the cardinal. Another time,' the SD man added and left.

The dripping angels standing on the balustrades of the Pont Sant'Angelo seemed oblivious to the rain as he passed from one pool of light to the next. He couldn't afford such insouciance, he was all too well aware of the footsteps that echoed his own. Two pursuers, he decided. The handbook would prescribe two others, at the far end of the bridge, who would wait for him to arrive before stepping out from their hiding places. The Lungotevere Tor di Nono was a busy street, even after dark, and they wouldn't want to attract attention. The handbook was quite explicit about that too, he thought, before he burst into a sprint.

The element of surprise gave him a headstart and wrong-footed his reception committee. He saw them peel away from the doorway on the other side of the street as he turned off the bridge and pounded down the pavement. He heard horns protesting their efforts at crossing the road and increased his pace. In his peripheral vision, a car glided up to keep pace with him. The back door swung open and a woman shouted at him to get in. On impulse, he ducked into the moving car, dragging the door behind him. Immediately, he was rocked back in the seat as the car accelerated.

'You drive like a Roman,' he said admiringly.

'And you run like an ageing SD officer,' she replied, without taking her eyes from the road. 'I hope Monsignor Dubois was grateful for the donation,' she added, as she twitched the car between two taxis that were travelling together, companionably, in the middle of the road. He waited until the twin blasts of horns had receded before replying.

'He was. Does that disappoint you?'

'Not at all. At least Tisserant will have something to hold over a very ambitious young priest. I can drop you off at the Vatican or at the American embassy,' she added, 'it's your call.'

'I think the American embassy might be to our mutual advantage.'

'I was hoping you'd say that,' she said, and dropped the pistol in the glove compartment.

The Razzia, Rome, Saturday, 16 October 1943

Bells rang in his dreams. Rome was a city of bells. They became part of the background sound and rarely bothered his sleep. He sat up and grabbed the telephone on his bedside locker.

'Hamner.'

'Captain Hamner, this is Field Marshal von Kesselring.'

The tinny sound quality didn't dilute the urgency in von Kesselring's voice and Karl swung his feet to the floor.

'The SS are rounding up the Jews,' von Kesselring barked.

'Kappler?'

'No. A superior breed of bastard called Theodor Dannecker. He's Eichmann's expert at Jew hunting and he's on his way to the ghetto with a pack of Waffen bloodhounds. I don't have the authority to call them off but I can dispatch an officer and troop to oversee the operation. See what you can do, Karl,' he added, and hung up.

The Wehrmacht troops were still asleep on their feet when the truck roared away from the barracks. The tyres threw sheets of water against the walls of the high houses as they slalomed through the alleyways. Karl wound down the window and stuck his head outside. Above the growl of the engine, he heard the sound of screaming, and an old rage welled up inside him. 'This way,' he shouted, and the driver hauled the truck in a slewing turn that brought them to the chaos at the heart of the ghetto.

'Out,' he roared, slapping the sides of the truck with his pistol. The soldiers tumbled from the rear, now wide awake and looking to their captain for orders. Fifty yards from where they stood, Karl saw rumbling, open trucks standing nose to tail beside the kerb. Men and women were being herded into the trucks and Waffen SS flung children to be caught by their parents. The sergeant hovered at his elbow. He was an old Wehrmacht man from Hamburg, the kind of man who opened his wallet at every opportunity to show pictures of his children. His face looked haunted in the light of the headlamps.

'What do we do, Captain?' he asked.

'You come with me, Sergeant,' Karl said. 'You men,' he said to the others, 'get among the Waffen and let them know we're watching.'

He led the sergeant at a hard trot through the alleyways, working from memory, until he came to Enrico's restaurant. Enrico and his family huddled in the doorway as two Waffen prodded them with rifle butts.

'Come on, Heine,' one of them shouted in Enrico's face, 'where's the fucking money?'

Karl felt relief surge through him. The Waffen pair had left the main group to do a little looting on the side. He eased up behind them and struck the soldier prodding Enrico behind the ear with the butt of his pistol. As he crumpled, his companion whirled around. 'What the f—?' he began, and gasped as the muzzle pressed into his throat.

'Looters are to be shot on sight,' Karl snapped. 'Are you a looter, Waffen?' he demanded, gouging the muzzle into the man's Adam's apple.

'Sir,' the sergeant said, coming up beside him. 'I think this soldier made a mistake – in the confusion, sir. He should be back where the trucks are. Isn't that right, soldier?'

The terrified Waffen tried to nod his head. The sergeant placed his hand on Karl's rigid arm and pressed firmly until Karl lowered the pistol.

'He killed Dieter,' the Waffen protested hoarsely.

'Idiot fell and hit his head,' the sergeant snapped. 'Drag him out of here double time or I'll kick your arse.' The Waffen picked up his comrade and dragged him into the darkness. Karl watched them go until they turned a corner.

'They're Waffen, Captain,' the sergeant said urgently, 'they'll be back. We need to get these people out of here.'

His voice shook Karl from his rage. He ran ahead of the group, with the sergeant bringing up the rear. At an intersection, he waved them to a halt and checked carefully, left and right. 'Enrico,' he called, and the man passed his wife to his daughter and joined him. 'I'm lost,' Karl whispered. 'I think if we can get to Tiber Island, they won't bother searching for us there.'

'Julio knows the streets, Captain,' Enrico said. 'Too well for his own good, sometimes,' he added, tapping the boy lightly on the ear. Karl was struck by the simple gesture of affection and had to wait a moment until he could trust his voice.

'At my shoulder, Julio,' he said, and the boy puffed with pride. They wove through the narrow streets until they came to the bridge that stretched from a small tower to the island. At the bridge, Karl changed places with the sergeant. He had a moment to notice that the sergeant was carrying a toddler.

'He came wandering out of a side road,' the sergeant said apologetically. 'I couldn't just leave him, sir.'

'I'll stay here until you're across,' Karl said. He scanned the streets they had come from as the footsteps receded behind him. He listened intently but the ghetto seemed eerily silent. A low whistle drew him across the bridge to the others.

'For the love of God,' the priest gasped as he opened his door to two armed soldiers and the exhausted family.

'*Per favore*, Padre,' Karl begged. 'Please.'

He saw the priest hesitate for a moment and then swing the door wide. When the family were safely inside, Enrico returned and lifted the toddler from the sergeant's arms.

'What are you called, Sergeant?' he asked.

'Paulus,' the Sergeant mumbled.

'He will be Paulo,' Enrico said, 'in your honour.' With the child already sleeping on his shoulder, he turned to Karl. 'I have no babies to name for you, Captain,' he said, 'but I would have been proud to be your father.'

They stepped over clothes and shoes strewn on the pavement, the only evidence that people had once lived in that place. Karl pocketed a tiny rag doll before the sergeant could see it. The troop leaned against the truck, smoking in silence.

'Dietrich!'

The corporal thumbed the head of his cigarette and shoved it in his pocket. 'I lost count, Captain,' he said. 'They just dragged them out and piled them into the trucks. Some of our lads tried to interfere and took a few lumps for their trouble. Fucking animals, with respect, sir.'

'We'll do a last sweep before we go,' Karl said.

The adrenaline had begun to burn away. He felt an aching emptiness inside and tasted bile at the back of his throat. The truck nosed slowly through the empty streets, like a lost dog whining for its owner. As they passed through a junction, Karl tapped the driver on the shoulder. 'Circle and come back, Dirk,' he whispered. At the other side of the junction, he opened the cab door and eased himself to the street, moving into the shadows under the houses. At the corner, he stopped and waited. He was certain he'd seen a movement as they'd traversed the junction. His patience was rewarded by the slap of bare feet on the pavement. He timed the steps and swung out his right arm to snare the fugitive. The boy wriggled in his grip but didn't cry out. Suddenly he went limp and Karl turned him around, keeping his good hand on the boy's shoulder.

'I'm Captain Karl Hamner,' he said slowly.

The boy's eyes flickered and settled on Karl's face.

'Captain Hamner?' he breathed.

'Yes,' Karl said.

'Ugo – Ugo Foa—'

That short sentence was longer than the breath he could muster. He stopped, and panic began to reclaim his eyes.

'Ugo Foa is a friend,' Karl said, holding the boy's eyes with his own. 'Where is he?'

'Gone,' the boy gasped, 'everyone's gone.' The tears came in a sudden, scalding rush. Karl crouched down to hold him around the shoulders, letting his chin rest lightly on the boy's head until the spasm had passed.

'What did Ugo Foa say?' he prompted gently.

'He said – if I found you – I should tell you tell Tiss – errant.'

'Tisserant?'

He hadn't sensed the sergeant come up behind him and clutched the boy protectively when the sergeant spoke.

'It's Cardinal Tisserant, sir,' the sergeant said. 'In the Vatican.'

For a moment longer, Karl held the boy close and then moved him gently towards the sergeant. The boy clung to him frantically and he placed the flat of his palm against his chest to soothe him, as he remembered Rudi had done for him. 'Paulus is my friend,' he said. 'He won't let any of the—'

'At the last moment, he closed his teeth on the word that would have panicked the boy all over again. He thought of another boy who had met the Waffen and he trembled with an echo of his old fear.

'Bloody right,' the sergeant said. 'We'll find a safe place for you, lad, until your parents come to—' He stumbled into silence and rallied again. 'You'll be safe with us,' he assured him. He stepped up close to Karl. 'Captain,' he whispered, 'if you go in there, you can never come out.'

'Yes. Yes, I know that, sergeant. I'm sorry if it seems like I'm deserting you.'

The sergeant shook his head. 'They know you now, Captain, and you know what they're like. Stay away, sir – until it's over. Come with us in the truck as far as the Ponte Vittoria Emmanuel,' he urged. 'They'll come back, sir, like dogs to their vomit.'

'Walked right in as His Holiness was praying.'

'Who?' Emil puffed, trying to keep up with the striding French priest from the Propaganda Department. They moved aside to let Cardinal Maglione barrel by. He passed them without a glance, his face reflecting the foreboding that had settled on the Vatican.

'Principessa Enza Pignatelli-Aragona,' the French priest said in the slow, patient tones people use to patronise the elderly. Emil considered taking umbrage but didn't dare risk alienating his news source.

'And?' he prompted.

'And she told him of the *razzia*.'

Seeing Emil's puzzlement, the priest explained.

'The roundup. The SS raided the ghetto early this morning and took the Jews to the Collegio Militare. The pope is furious. Lorenzo, from Protocol, said he ordered Maglione to contact the German ambassador immediately.'

He stopped as Emil placed a hand against the wall to steady himself.

'Monsignor Dubois, are you well?' he asked anxiously.

'No – yes,' Emil whispered. 'You'd better run along, Pierre,' he said more firmly. 'I'm sure you'll be needed.'

Pierre brightened visibly and walked on. Emil stood quietly for a few moments until his heart rate slowed. 'Bad news waits for no man,' he sighed.

'What?' Tisserant roared. He had been up from before dawn working on some documents which he swept from the desk in temper.

'It's as I said, Eugène,' Emil said calmly. 'The SS have taken the Jews to the Collegio Militare.'

'How many?'

'We don't know yet.'

'And Pius?'

'He knows. Some aristocratic lady dragged him from his morning prayers with the news.'

'We must contact the German ambassador. What's his name?'

'Weizsäcker. Maglione is meeting with him.'

'Meeting be damned,' Tisserant growled, slapping his skull cap on his head. 'The pope must speak out against this outrage.'

'Where are you going?'

'To tell him, of course.'

Emil placed himself between the cardinal and the door.

'You must calm yourself, Eugène,' he insisted. 'You are a Prince of the Church who should assess the situation calmly and not go roaring in like a—'

Tisserant loomed over his secretary.

'Like a bull in a china shop,' Emil snapped.

'You're shouting, Emil,' Tisserant said softly.

'I'm sorry. It's not as if it's a surprise. You remember the rumour that Montini and Tardini were supposed to have been informed that this would happen. But nothing happened – until now. It's a shock, Eugène.'

Tisserant placed a huge hand on his secretary's shoulder.

'Sit down and have a brandy, old friend,' he said, easing him gently to an armchair. 'When you get your breath back, do the tour of your contacts. Find out as much as you can.'

'But what will you—'

'I, Monsignor Emil Dubois, am a Prince of the Church. I will behave accordingly and not like a bull in a china shop.'

As soon as the door closed behind him, Tisserant's face hardened into stone.

The papal secretary half-rose from behind his desk and subsided again, averting his eyes as the cardinal stormed by. Maglione stopped mid-sentence when Tisserant entered.

'Please recap for His Eminence,' Pius whispered.

Maglione cleared his throat and began to speak in the inflectionless monotone favoured by Vatican diplomats.

'I asked Ambassador Weizsäcker to intervene on behalf of these unfortunate people for the sake of humanity and Christian charity.'

'When did we delegate a German ambassador as our spokesman?' Tisserant asked acidly, but Pius gestured at Maglione to continue.

'The ambassador asked what the Holy See will do if these things continue. I replied that the Holy See would not wish to be put in a situation where it is necessary to utter a word of disapproval.'

'We have already been put in that position,' Tisserant interrupted. 'If this is not the time to utter a word of disapproval, when, in God's name, is that time?'

The pope's eyes flickered to Tisserant for a moment and swung back to Maglione. 'Proceed,' he said.

'Ambassador Weizsäcker praised the Holy See for not rocking the boat throughout the previous four years of the war. He said the Holy See should consider whether it's worth putting everything in danger just as the ship is reaching port. I reminded the ambassador that the Holy See had shown the greatest prudence in not giving the German people the least impression of having done, or having wished to do, the least thing against the interests of Germany during this terrible war.'

'Did we protest or did we not?' Tisserant demanded.

'I think His Eminence has been quite clear on that matter,' Pius said firmly. He turned to Maglione. 'We encourage you to pursue the matter through diplomatic channels, Eminence, and report to us.'

Tisserant had forgotten how irritating it could be when the pope referred to himself in the royal plural. He managed to contain himself until the door closed behind Maglione.

'The Vatican has been silent in the face of the deportation of Jews from all over Europe, Holiness,' he said evenly. 'I accept that there was a reason for that – the Church did not want to express any criticism of any of the warring nations which might call our neutrality into question and risk persecution in those countries under Axis influence. I accept there was a reason for our inaction, even if I never accepted that reason as right. It was not right then; it is not right now. The Germans have finally come for the Jews of Rome. You are the Bishop of Rome. Silence is no longer an option.'

Tisserant read the distress in Pius' face and softened his tone.

'You don't even have to break your silence, Holiness. The Germans are terrified that you will speak out on this matter. Let Maglione carry that threat to Weizsäcker and through him to Berlin.'

'The war is nearly over, Eminence,' the pope said urgently. 'At this stage, we would risk everything we have protected since this terrible war began.'

'We seem willing enough to risk the Jews, Holiness, a small and voiceless people, while we speak with the strength of half a billion believers.'

'Be assured we will do everything in our power for the Jews of Rome.'

'Except break our silence?'

'We will keep you informed, Eminence,' the pope said and returned to the documents on his desk.

CARDINAL TISSERANT'S APARTMENTS, THE VATICAN

'Nothing?'

'Not a single word.'

'Maglione?'

'Dancing a diplomatic gavotte with the German ambassador. It's a farce, Emil. The ambassador asks what will the Vatican say and Maglione replies that we don't want to be put in the position of saying anything. It all boils down to saying nothing.'

'But the German consul, Stahel, telephoned Pius and asked him to object. Bishop Alois told me the entire German diplomatic corps is terrified of the repercussions if the pope speaks. He said they're even willing to negotiate the return of the Jews to the ghetto as a labour group. The implication was that it was a compromise solution to satisfy both parties.'

The telephone rang, shrilly, and Emil snatched it up.

'*Prego*! What? A moment, please,' he said and covered the mouthpiece with his hand. 'The Captain of the Swiss Guards says there is a Wehrmacht captain standing in the piazza. He says he wants to see you.'

'Me!'

'Yes. He says Ugo Foa sent him.'

Through the open door, Karl saw Cardinal Tisserant glowering at him from behind a desk. The elderly priest at the door wore a black cassock with a scarlet sash tied around his midriff.

'I am Monsignor Emil Dubois, the cardinal's secretary,' he said, extending his hand in welcome. The monsignor smiled at the Captain of the Swiss Guards. 'And thank you, Markus,' he said, 'especially for the all-concealing cloak. Under the circumstances, marching a Wehrmacht captain across Saint Peter's Square might have precipitated an international incident. Let's give the Swiss Guards their cloak back, Captain,' he said to Karl, 'and we can make you comfortable.'

Karl fumbled awkwardly with the clasp and the monsignor moved to help him. Karl felt a flash of irritation, but the monsignor's eyes were gentle and he relented. Again the monsignor showered the Swiss Guard with thanks, asked after his family, by name, and closed the door.

'Now,' he said, taking Karl by the elbow, 'let us approach the Gorgon.'

He sat Karl opposite Tisserant, spirited a glass of brandy into his hand and went to sit at the side.

'Who are you?' Tisserant asked.

'Karl Hamner, a captain in the Wehrmacht army, under the command of Field Marshal von Kesselring.'

Emil started and Tisserant shot him a glare.

'I beg your pardon, Eminence,' Emil said, 'but I believe I have already heard of this captain.'

'And?'

'And if my memory still serves me, this is the Wehrmacht captain who shamed the Romans into a ransom in September.'

'You say Ugo Foa sent you,' Tisserant said brusquely.

'Yes. He said tell Tisserant.'

'Tell me what?'

'What I've seen, Eminence,' Karl replied.

'Proceed.'

Karl told them his experiences of the *razza*. Although he didn't embellish, the historian in him didn't shy from the human details.

Both men flinched when he mentioned the clothes strewn in the street and sighed with relief when he recounted the hospitality of the priest on Tiber Island. Tisserant immediately turned to his secretary.

'He's most likely the parish priest of San Bartolomeo,' he said. 'Tell him we can give them sanctuary here, if they'll come. If not, see that food and clothes are sent. Very few Roman parish priests are accustomed to caring for a family,' he added, with a small smile.

Karl sensed that he was searching for some traces of human decency he could cling to in the face of the terrible things he'd heard, and he warmed to the irascible cardinal.

He resumed the narrative from where the sergeant had dropped him at the Ponte Vittorio Emmanuel. 'I hope she's worth it,' the sergeant had shouted when he'd alighted from the truck. He'd known it was for the sake of the men and appreciated it. He decided to skip that part of the story.

Getting from the bridge to the Vatican had been easy, he told them. He simply kept the huge dome of Saint Peter's in sight. Once, he'd hidden behind a fountain as a truckload of Waffen roared past. The sergeant had been right: they were going back to scavenge. Feverishly, he'd sluiced water from the fountain over his head and scrubbed himself with his hand until the skin of his face and neck felt raw. Again, at the mouth of Saint Peter's Square, he'd courted discovery, lured by the proximity of his goal. A child's cry had alerted him to the idling trucks that squatted just outside the embrace of the colonnade. He stopped and sipped his brandy. The two clerics seemed to sense his reluctance to go on and steeled themselves.

'The children were clutching at the sides of the trucks,' he said, as if reviewing the scene in his head. 'Their eyes – I could see their eyes from where I was hiding, they were huge and terrified. A woman called out for the pope to help them. Some of the Waffen were standing on the road, looking at the Vatican. From what I could hear, they'd taken a roundabout route so that they could see it. One soldier said his mother would never forgive him if he'd been to Rome and not seen Saint Peter's. After a while, they drove off and I presented myself to the Swiss Guards.'

In the ensuing silence, a clock ticked, like an old servant

performing the ordinary services, unobtrusively, when the house has been numbed by tragedy.

'Why have you come here?' Tisserant asked finally.

'Because Ugo—'

'No,' the cardinal interrupted. 'It wasn't because Ugo Foa sent you. I want to know why you agreed to come. You must have known that once you stepped into Saint Peter's Square you could never go back?'

'Yes, my sergeant said as much.'

'Why then?'

Karl raised his gloved hand and cradled it in his right hand. It was something he did instinctively, whenever his thoughts turned to Russia.

'During Operation Barbarossa,' he began, 'I was assigned to the horses – to protect me from the Waffen. Our troop had interfered with one of their actions in a village. The horse master took me under his wing. Later I discovered he was a priest.'

He was aware, at some level, of the two clerics leaning forward expectantly, but the tide of his memories pulled him on.

'He said he'd joined the army to get to Russia and find a Christian community he could serve. He said I could report him as a deserter if I felt that was my duty.' His voice trembled and he pressed his lips together and nodded until he could continue. 'I didn't. I – I felt that there were more important things than duty. Later, he left. He left without saying goodbye and without his identity card. Without that he could be shot by the Russians as an infiltrator or hanged by our side as a deserter. I've carried that card to Moscow and back.'

'Do you have it now, Captain?' Tisserant whispered.

Karl fished it, two-fingered, from his pocket and passed it over the desk. The cardinal cupped both hands to receive it, as if it was the sacrament. He read it carefully and passed it to his secretary, who did the same.

'Did he survive?' Tisserant asked.

'I don't know, Eminence. I never saw him again.'

Silently, the monsignor went to a cupboard and brought the brandy bottle and two glasses. He replenished Karl's glass and handed another to the cardinal. As he did so, he placed his hand, comfortingly, on the cardinal's shoulder.

'*L'Chaim*,' Tisserant toasted, as the tears ran down his cheeks to pearl in his beard. 'To life.'

★

'He's just a boy,' Emil said.

'Yes, a boy with an old face. We can't imagine what he's seen and suffered. Is he—'

'Sleeping. Have you read the documents from The Good Thief?'

'No, not yet. There's too much happening just now. What's the latest news?'

'They're talking about writing a letter.'

'A letter?'

'Pius liaises with the Germans through a Father Pfeiffer, a German priest. He does charity work in the city.'

'But, a priest!'

'I know. Others are saying they'll ask Bishop Hudal, the rector of the German Catholic Church in Rome, to write the letter. They say it might carry more weight coming from a bishop.'

'Letters,' Tisserant grunted. 'And what of the Jews?'

'Still in the Collegio Militaire. People began to gather outside with food and clothing but the soldiers ran them off. An Italian priest told me he saw a pregnant woman dragged into the courtyard to give birth and then locked up again with her baby. He said two hundred and fifty prisoners were released when their papers were examined. The rumour in the Vatican is that some mysterious cardinal intervened on their behalf. It's only a rumour. Can you imagine any of the ones we know doing that?'

'No. How many are still inside?'

'More than a thousand.'

★

THE NEXT DAY

'Are you bored, Karl?' Emil enquired.

'A little,' he admitted. 'Not by the company,' he added hastily.

'Of course you're bored,' Emil smiled. 'What are your interests?'

'I'm a historian.'

The monsignor choked on his croissant and Karl thumped his back.

'Oh,' Emil gasped, 'this is perfect. You are a historian who has taken refuge in the Vatican and you're bored.' He tweaked Karl's ear playfully. 'You are a child who has woken up in the biggest sweet shop in the world, my boy. Follow me.'

Karl trailed Emil into his private quarters and watched while he rummaged in a huge wardrobe.

'Try this,' he said, flinging a black cassock, a scarlet sash and a Roman collar on the bed.

'Ah, mon Dieu,' Emil crowed when Karl re-emerged in the clerical garb, 'it fits you like a glove.'

There was an awkward moment before Emil hurried on.

'If anyone asks, tell them you work in the Office of the Inquisition; nobody talks to them. As for the glove, you can say you killed a rival for a lady's hand in a duel. The glove and priesthood are your penance, very romantic. Here is a map of the Vatican. If you get lost, find a Swiss Guard and mention my name. *Au revoir.*'

'You did *what?*'

'Oh, don't fuss. He's quite safe. Who would ever suspect a monsignor is not what he appears to be?'

Tisserant stared.

'That's not funny, Eugène,' Emil said tartly 'Have there been any developments?'

'Yes. They're loading them into cattle cars at the Tiburtina Station, sixty prisoners to a car.'

'Maglione?'

'Corresponding,' Tisserant mumbled, 'while his staff play their silly war games.'

He stopped speaking and began to tug at his beard.

'What are you thinking?' Emil asked cautiously.

'You know that friend of yours in the Swiss Guards?'

'Markus.'

'Yes, Markus. You mentioned he had a family.'

'Yes, he has three little ones.'

'I want you to ask him for something.'

'Of course.'

'I also want you to research some monsignori for me.'

'Are you quite well, Eugène?'

'Never better.'

CARDINAL MAGLIONE'S OFFICE, THE VATICAN

It took a few moments for the first person to notice the visitor. Gradually, that awareness rippled through the monsignori gathered around Maglione's war table and the room fell silent.

'Who is in charge here?' Tisserant asked.

A young monsignor walked from a raised dais where he'd been overseeing the work of the others. 'I am, Eminence,' he said.

'Your name?'

'Jean Gaultier, Eminence.'

'Your father is a train driver.'

The monsignor rocked back on his heels before recovering.

'Y – yes,' he stammered.

Tisserant brushed by him to take a position at the map table. He took a toy steam engine from his pocket and placed it on the map.

'This is as near to the Tiburtina Station as makes no difference,' he said. 'I would like you to drive this train, Monsignor Gaultier.'

The monsignor looked puzzled.

'The Waffen SS have loaded over a thousand Jews into cattle cars at Tiburtina Station,' Tisserant said and a murmur of astonishment and revulsion rose in the room. 'I would like you to establish contact with your sources along the route so that we can track their progress. We're no longer playing with tin soldiers, gentlemen.'

'Cardinal Maglione has given us clear instructions to—'

The objector was cut off by the train driver's son.

'We will drive the train,' he said, and resumed his position on the dais. While the others took up their positions at the table and the bank of telephones, Tisserant joined Jean Gaultier on the dais.

'You know you risk Maglione's wrath?' he murmured.

'My father once drove a burning munitions train, Eminence,' Gaultier said calmly.

'Report from the Appenines,' someone called from the bank of telephones, 'freezing temperatures.'

'Padua,' a cry went up. 'The Bishop of Padua reports that the Jews are in a pitiable condition. He says they call out for water. The bishop begs the Holy Father to take urgent action.'

Some time later, when Tisserant left the room, the toy train was still moving, passed from hand to hand by sombre monsignori.

Throughout those fateful days, Tisserant railed against the stone-walling silence of the Vatican, but to no avail. He found himself excluded from meetings and avoided by his brother cardinals. On the fifth day, he went again to Maglione's war room.

He was struck by the silence. Some of the staff sat listlessly at the telephone bank, their headsets dangling around their shoulders. A hollow-eyed Polish priest looked up as Tisserant entered.

'We had reports all the way to Vienna, Eminence,' he said wearily, 'and then silence.'

'What does that mean?'

'We have few contacts along the particular route they've taken from there, Eminence. Perhaps they—'

The telephone buzzed and he pulled on his headphones and bent to his task. All around, his confrères rose and stood, listening. The telephone operator thanked the caller and clawed the headset from his ears.

'Our contact says that there are unconfirmed reports that over a thousand Jews have been gassed at Auschwitz–Birkenau,' he said.

Jean Gaultier descended wearily from the dais. He looked unshaven and rumpled and Tisserant wondered how much he'd slept over the five days. As he passed the map table, he picked up the toy steam engine and brought it to Tisserant.

'It would be better to buy a new one for the child who lent this to us,' he said hoarsely.

'Perhaps it would be better if you obeyed the orders of your superior.'

Tisserant hadn't seen Maglione enter. The diplomat had been involved in an exhausting series of meetings since the train had begun its journey. He looked haggard and angry and Tisserant almost felt sorry for him.

'This was my idea, Eminence,' he confessed.

'And those – sheep,' Maglione said furiously, 'were just unwilling actors in your charade.'

'No,' Jean Gaultier interrupted, 'it was a matter of conscience for us.'

'Conscience,' Maglione said contemptuously. 'Your first duty is obedience to the Church and to me as your ecclesiastical superior.'

'No, Eminence,' the young man said tiredly. 'Our first duty is to the people we serve in God's name – all the people. I fear I have become distracted from that truth. Please, Eminence, accept this.'

He took a small white envelope from his pocket and offered it to Maglione, who snatched it from his hand.

'And what is this?' he asked.

'It is a letter of resignation, Eminence.'

'Resignation? What of your career in the Church?'

'I didn't become a priest to have a career in the Church, Eminence,' Gaultier said. 'You will find that this letter of resignation contains fifteen signatures.'

He bowed formally to the cardinals and walked away. The others streamed after him until the two cardinals were left alone.

'I hope you're satisfied,' Maglione said savagely.

'Satisfied? No, Eminence, not satisfied,' Tisserant said softly. 'I am astonished – astonished to find that there are still priests in the Vatican.'

★

'This is good, Karl,' Emil said slowly. He placed the essay on the small table between them. 'In fact, it is very good,' he added. warmly. 'You hear that, Eugène,' he said, 'Karl has presented a most excellent essay on the anti-semitism of Paul IV.'

Tisserant had been sitting at his desk for the last two hours, gazing unseeing at the documents before him. He looked deflated, Karl thought, as if his normal vitality had been leached from him. He showed no sign that he'd heard his secretary.

'A forensic analysis of secondary source material,' Emil continued. 'Some of those articles were written by people here, people who will find their pomposity pricked if our young friend decides to publish.'

Tisserant turned his head away and transferred his gaze to the window.

'Of course,' Emil persisted, 'he needs to tidy his referencing and be careful with his footnotes.'

He stood up abruptly and approached the desk.

'He reminds me of a student I once had,' he said. 'He also had focus and intuition and courage – all the attributes of an exceptional historian – but he became a cardinal, a cardinal who thought he could play God.'

'What are you talking about?' Tisserant asked irritably.

'I'm talking about you, Eminence, a man who gives up when he falls short of omnipotence.'

'You don't know what you're talking about,' Tisserant growled.

'I know *who* I'm talking about. Who knows better than me? Did you harass the pope, to the point of distraction, to intercede for the Jews?'

'You know I did.'

'And in doing so were you careful in your analysis of primary and secondary sources and, to the point of obsession, with references and footnotes?'

'Yes, damn you,' Tisserant roared, like a wounded animal, 'and they threw it all back in my face. They said it was propaganda, that I had been duped and manipulated and—'

He seemed to run out of anger and his face sagged.

'And you felt that you had failed, Eugène?' Emil prompted gently.

'Yes,' Tisserant whispered. 'When a historian fails, he simply destroys his manuscript and starts again. My failure led to the deaths of innocents. The pope did not speak, Emil, despite everything I tried to do.'

Emil Dubois knelt before the desk and stretched across to grasp the cardinal's hands.

'Eugène, Eugène,' he crooned softly, 'did you do your best?'

'Yes.'

'That matters. No!' he held up a hand to forestall argument. 'I know it's not all that matters. You are a fine scholar, old friend, always have been. It is not in your nature to falsify evidence or present dubious data. The case you presented was worthy of respect and consideration and it received neither. To be disappointed is understandable, Eugène. To feel humiliated and a failure falls under the heading of self-pity. By focusing on your supposed failure, you also absolve the choices of others. Pope or not, Pius was wrong. Another pope, in another time, might have acted differently, perhaps his predecessor. No matter, that is wishful thinking. You are a Prince of the Church, Eugène. Have you forgotten what that means? It means you have the freedom to say exactly what you think and contest what others say – even the pope. Only cardinals have that privilege. Archbishops, bishops and priests are appointed by a higher authority and, to some extent, are beholden to that authority. You know how it works, you've seen it happen. How many courageous men have we known who were overlooked, sidelined or silenced? You can be a voice for them and for the Jews, the Muslims, the Roma and any people on the face of the earth who suffer at the hands of Church or state. Will you give up that right because you have been rejected? Because a fearful pope has chosen the well-being of the Church over the lives of thousands? Would you give up that privilege because brother cardinals have put their position and the favour of the pontiff before their duty to the Gospels and the people? Eugène Tisserant the student was not one to retreat before rejection, nor was Eugène

Tisserant the priest. Cardinal Tisserant is now faced with humiliation and rejection. Those of us who have learned to love him have confidence that he will do the right thing.'

He squeezed the cardinal's hands and released them.

'Come, Karl,' he said, 'the cardinal has papers he must study, documents a brave man has risked his life for.'

When they'd gone, Tisserant wiped his eyes and blew his nose in a capacious handkerchief. He hunched forward and scanned the top page of the file before him. Unconsciously, he drew a notepad and pen to him and began to scribble as he read. The file diminished rapidly under his intense scrutiny until he held the final page in his hand. He read it through three times and filled the pages of his notepad with his copper-plate writing. Finally, he dropped the document on his desk and slapped it with his palm.

'Oh, Father Steiger,' he murmured, 'like Icarus, you have flown too near the sun and become the author of your own fall.'

LATER

'Can I help?'

'What? Oh, I'm sorry, Karl. I've become quite immersed in this case the cardinal and I are investigating.' He set his pen aside and massaged the deep lines between his eyes.

'Perhaps I can help. If it doesn't involve too many footnotes and references,' Karl said wryly.

Emil laughed delightedly. 'No, nothing so exciting. I need some material from the archives.' He scribbled a note on the cardinal's headed notepaper and passed it to Karl. 'This should get you by whichever Cerberus guards the gate,' he said. 'You're looking for a file of correspondence between the Curia and Archbishop Stepinac of Zagreb. The curator should be able to retrieve it for you. Archbishop Stepinac has a reputation for holiness, Karl. I'm sure you'll find this assignment extremely dull.'

★

The priest sitting at the door seemed to have died some time ago and mouldered into the dark, mahogany background. Sparse, grey hair floated upwards from a mottled scalp and milky, white eyes haunted his mummy's face. Only the slow mastication of his jaws and the salami and garlic sandwich he held in his left hand gave him a semblance of life. With infinite slowness, he lifted the note to within an inch of his eyes. His other hand moved, seemingly of its own volition, to a metal stamp which he dragged to the note.

A newer model awaited Karl at the stacks. The bespectacled priest, with carefully parted hair and ruddy cheeks, read the note, conjured the documents sought and disappeared with a soft '*Scusi*'. After what seemed a long time, he reappeared and placed the file on the desk. He seemed distant and eager to be somewhere else. Karl thanked him and flipped the file cover.

The curator returned to his book-stacked office and pondered. After a few moments, he slid open a drawer and retrieved a sheet of paper. His finger trailed down the printed list until it stopped at Stepinac. The asterisk caused his finger to plummet to the bottom of the page, where it rested on a telephone number. He raised the telephone receiver and dialled.

Emil hadn't exaggerated. Archbishop Stepinac might be a very holy man but he was also a numbingly boring writer. A large number of his letters began with long and prayerful greetings. The subsequent paragraphs declared his delight and honour to have received a query from the relevant Vatican department. He then presented the information in a most ambiguous fashion. Karl could feel his attention slacken as one dull document segued into another. He was letting his eyes slide down the middle of the text; hoping to harvest the essential information, when they snagged on a name. Suddenly he felt as if the air had been sucked from the room, and concentrated on breathing deeply. He looked again. It was still there and his pulse raced. Perhaps it was someone else of the same name, the reasonable part of his brain protested. Anyway, how could Max be a priest?

He was wrestling with that question when a blow from behind pushed him into oblivion.

SANTA MARIA DELLA CONCEZIONE, ROME

In his dream, his father was standing in a meadow, stroking the mare's muzzle. He called out to him, 'Papa! Papa!' His father turned away and led the mare towards the forest. He was carrying a rifle in his left hand. Karl wasn't sure at what point his dream turned into a nightmare. He saw what seemed to be walls hung with human bones. Some were wired together to make shapes. In the dim light, he could identify a Sacred Heart and a Crown of Thorns. He was chilled to see full skeletons, robed in tattered brown habits. The skeleton of a child stood, forlorn and lost, in this bizarre ossuary. It was only when a face appeared between him and the *memento mori* that he knew he was awake. A spot behind his ear pulsed painfully and he tried to lift his hand. Both hands were tied securely to the chair he sat on.

'He's back,' someone grunted.

A figure detached itself from the macabre spectacle and approached. The man was cowled in the long Capuchin headgear and his face remained shadowed until he stepped into a pool of light.

Max thought the face before him was both familiar and strange. Instinctively he had thrown up his hand to ward his disfigurement from the light. Through the spaces between his splayed fingers he saw what remained of a face he'd loved. Karl's hair was still a ruddy brown, although lightly frosted at the temples. The high cheekbones stretched the skin under his eyes and the slopes of his cheeks receded into shadows. His mouth was set in that familiar stubborn line and the eyes – oh, Christ. The eyes, which had always been an innocent blue, carried the memories of sights no boy should ever see. Something seemed to break in his chest. He felt a bubble of emotion rise into his throat and force his lips apart.

'Karl,' he said.

Karl felt nothing. The face, sculpted by the light, was not Max's face but his death mask. Max had thrown up his hand against the light, but through the splayed fingers Karl saw slivers of familiar raven hair and the luminescence of snow-blued skin. It's Max, his brain prompted, and his gut concurred when he saw the eyes. Max had inward eyes, he reminded himself, his focus always on some inner space where he analysed the slights he imagined the outside world presented. He could remember rare times when those eyes were freed from suspicion and introspection. He remembered how they'd sat at the kitchen table, eating sticky strudel, their hunger making them oblivious to Rudi and Mutti. His mother had leaned over to fill their glasses and run her fingers fondly through Max's hair and Max's eyes had burned with warmth and longing. It had been like a single shaft of sunlight spearing the mountain on an overcast evening, brief and unforgettable. The eyes that peered at him through the raised hand seemed more alien and agonised than ever and his heart wailed for his lost friend.

'Max,' he whispered, at the precise moment his name burst from the other's bloodless lips. Their breath met and mingled and faded in the cold air.

They had bound him, trussed him like some criminal. 'Untie him,' Max ordered, and the brutes rushed to obey. He saw Karl wince and curl his left hand to his chest. The grey army-issue glove seemed like a rebuke and he averted his eyes. 'Leave us,' he said, and the brutes slunk back to the shadows.

'Your hand?'

'Russia.'

He parsed the word for any hint of recrimination and found none. Rage and bitterness he could have accepted but that single word left him wrong-footed. In the absence of accusation, he still felt a need to defend himself.

'It – it was my mother, Karl. She hated my father for what he couldn't be, and hated your father and mother and everyone in Hallstatt because – because that's the way she was. You know that, Karl, I know you did.'

'My father died in Russia,' Karl said tonelessly. 'The miner, Tomas, died too.'

'I'm sorry, Karl – sorry, sorry, sorry.' He knew that he was babbling and couldn't stop – daren't stop, because he feared the thread that bound Karl to him was so fragile it might never bear the weight of all he'd lost.

'Listen to me, Karl,' he begged, dropping to his knees before him. 'I – we have suffered. We were children and the war consumed our childhood. It's almost over, Karl. When it's over …' He spread his arms wide as if he was measuring the horizon of possibility, 'the pope will give me power, Karl.'

Max saw the look of incomprehension cloud Karl's face and hurried on. 'I'll explain everything later,' he promised, 'but for now, at this moment, I stand at the door to a future I can control. I want you to walk through that door with me, Karl. You've always had what I lacked; together we could do wonderful things. The pope will give me the power to create a new religious order within the Church. We'll be called "the Fratres", the Brothers. We'll have no history to slow us like a sea anchor, no hierarchies to tangle us in bureaucracy. The Fratres won't owe allegiance to any flag and won't be bound by any borders.'

Max knew his voice was rising and he let himself soar, consumed by his own vision.

The word 'Russia' hadn't given him pause, Karl thought. If anything, it seemed to have fuelled his passion to talk about the Fratres and his dreams for the future. There had been no acknowledgement of Rudi or Tomas. Nothing – nothing but Max's cold passion for his cold ambitions. He felt the anger ignite, deep in his bowels, and began to shake.

'You could be part of this—'

'No!'

The explosive rejection shattered the moment and Max clawed desperately to gather the pieces.

'Why?'

'Elsa.'

Max quailed before that name.

'Elsa,' Karl repeated.

'She was nothing,' Max whispered. 'Nothing. We were the friends, you and I.' He stretched forward until his face was just inches from Karl. 'We were the friends,' he insisted. 'She – she wormed her way between us, fawning over you, trying to prise us apart. And I ...'

His mouth moved but the words wouldn't come.

'You killed her, Max.'

'No,' he shouted. 'Don't say that, Karl. She – she made advances and—'

'No. You killed her, Max, and dumped her body somewhere in the mine.'

'Proof,' Max demanded, rising to his feet. 'Show me the proof, historian.'

Karl lifted the silver chain from inside his shirt. The tiny cross swung like a pendulum before Max's mesmerised gaze.

'Your father found it in the mine,' Karl said. 'He gave it to me.'

'It's mine,' Max hissed, 'give it back.'

'No, Max, it *was* yours, but you lost it.'

Max jerked back as if he'd been slapped.

'Keep it then,' he said viciously, 'a cross is what you've always wanted.'

He walked away to stand before the grotesque tangle of human bones.

'Pope Urban VIII, Karl,' he said, in a chilling parody of the way he'd spoken as a boy, a boy who'd hidden behind a lecturing tone. 'Urban had a vision of what Rome might become. It was Urban who commissioned Modena and Bernini and the others to make Rome a treasure house of art and sculpture. The Barberini Pope made a difference. His brother, on the other hand, chose to become a humble Capuchin friar, even after Urban had made him a cardinal. He could have shared the Vatican and his brother's dreams but instead he chose to live here. Fitting, don't you think, that the one who refused his share of power should accept to live above this monument to the dead? His lack of ambition soured into hopelessness, Karl. He's buried under the floor of the church above us. No marble sarcophagus, no Bernini angels, just a simple plaque with a simple inscription. Here lies dust, ashes, nothing. That's what becomes of men who reject possibility, Karl.'

He picked up a candle and passed before the display of the dead. Shadows of old bones stretched and webbed the wall behind him.

'This is what becomes of those who stand in the way of destiny,' he said, and raised the candle. The bloody face of the corpse in the friar's habit reflected the agony he'd suffered.

'Bind him,' he snapped, and his accomplices hurried to obey.

'Why not kill him?' one of them asked, with all the reasonableness of a man grown used to dealing death.

'And shorten his suffering?' Max mused. 'No, I think not.'

He pinched the flaming wick between thumb and forefinger and disappeared into the dark.

CARDINAL TISSERANT'S APARTMENTS, THE VATICAN

'And the doorkeeper?'

'Father Angelo believes Pio Nono is still on the throne,' Emil said, peevishly. 'I asked Markus to alert the Swiss Guards, but—'

His eyes rounded as the door swung open and Max Steiger stepped inside.

'What do you want?' Tisserant asked.

'To speak with you, alone,' Max replied.

'That is a privilege a cardinal grants to an equal, Father,' Tisserant said.

Max Steiger nodded. 'So be it,' he said. 'You have documents that were stolen from me. I want them back.'

Tisserant sat behind his desk and lifted a file.

'Tomorrow you will petition the pope to found a new religious order within the Church,' he said evenly. 'Pius will ask if there are any objections. I will argue, to the best of my ability, that your order would be detrimental to the Church. Not because of your … adventures in Croatia, Father Steiger, or because of the Ustashe gold, harvested from the corpses of Orthodox Serbs, Muslim and Roma Croats.'

He plucked a document from the file and brandished it before Max.

'Not even because you compromised a senior official of the Vatican Bank, a person not unknown to the Holy Father. But because you and your Fratres would mould the Church to your own image and likeness. We have had quite enough zealots in our unhappy history and too many opportunists, Father Steiger. If you thought you could beg me—'

'I did not come here to beg,' Max snapped, 'but to barter.'

'Barter?'

'The pope may be alarmed to learn that a Prince of the Church has given sanctuary to a Wehrmacht captain, one who has deserted his post and is sought by the German authorities. Rome is on a knife edge, Eminence. If the Germans learn of your actions, all protestations of neutrality will ring false. The pope would be presented with a dilemma.'

'Pacelli would never hand him over to the SS.'

Max stared at him in mock astonishment.

'How can a learned historian like your Eminence have learned so little from the gold ransom and the *razzia*? Do you really think that the pope who handed over a thousand Jews to protect the neutrality of the Church would hesitate to return a German officer? Captain Hamner is in my custody.'

When the two clerics started in surprise, he smiled self-deprecatingly.

'It was no more than my duty, as a priest of the Roman Catholic Church, to detain someone who has defied the legitimate authorities. That same duty obliges me to hand him over to the SS. The dilemma is yours, Eminence. You must choose between the Fratres and Captain Karl Hamner.'

*

Cardinal Tisserant entered the basilica through the Filarete Door and strode to the circle of chairs set before the High Altar. He bowed to the cardinals already assembled and sat. The ceremony was to be held in camera, and the vast basilica echoed emptily behind him. He tried to distract himself from his growing unease by reflecting on the provenance of the treasures around him. Bernini's Baldacchino, the great canopy of gilded bronze above the High Altar, seemed to hover over him like a bird of ill omen. Knowing that the Barberini Pope had filched the metal from the Pantheon didn't improve his humour. He started as the Sistine Choir trumpeted the opening of the hymn 'Sacerdos et Pontifex', 'Priest and Pontiff'. Julius Caesar had held both titles and the cardinal wondered if Pius appreciated the irony.

The pope was preceded by the superiors of the major religious orders and flanked by sword-bearing Swiss Guards. Tisserant thought that Pius looked frail and put aside their differences to bow as he passed to his throne on the High Altar. When the pope had prayed for God's blessing and the guidance of the Holy Ghost in his thin reedy voice, the assembly sat. Cardinal Maglione rose and invited the petitioner to present his case.

Tisserant watched with cold eyes as Max Steiger moved forward from a group of cowled Fratres to stand before the pope. He spoke in fluent Latin, thanking the pontiff and launching into a concise history of the major religious orders within the Church. Tisserant was relieved he hadn't begun with the Syrian eremites and taken the long trek to Saint Benedict. The old historian grudgingly admired his mastery of the material and the way he manipulated his audience.

As he'd anticipated, Steiger stressed the acute needs that had faced the Church in olden times and the courage of the popes who had supported the establishment of new orders. He saw the superiors nod their heads approvingly as he detailed the service they had and were giving to the Universal Church. He thought Steiger was vague when he outlined the work of the new order, tacking safely to the conservative views of the assembly and winning a nod from Pius when he mentioned a new crusade to post-war Europe. 'This,' he said, 'would bring the war-weary peoples of Europe back to the Roman Catholic Church and to its pontiff.'

He went on to pledge the Fratres' allegiance to the pope and suggested a fourth vow of obedience to the pontiff. Again, Tisserant noted the approving nods of the assembly, except for the Jesuit Superior, who sat stony-faced. The Jesuits were the only order who took this extra vow and he wondered if 'The Black Pope', as the Jesuit Superior was known, was feeling territorial. He was still mulling over that question when Steiger finished speaking and sat.

The moment he was dreading had arrived and he sat erect.

The master of ceremonies asked if there were any questions or objections and a young canon lawyer from the Congregation for Religious Orders asked if the Fratres would be subject to Archbishop Stepinac, as Father Steiger's diocesan bishop. Maglione heaved himself upright to state that Stepinac had waived his right and that the pope would accept personal responsibility for the new order. There were some murmurs at this precedent but they soon subsided. The silence stretched.

Tisserant rose slowly and was recognised by the master of ceremonies. He saw Maglione stiffen and the colour drain from Steiger's face. In a clear voice, he recommended a delay with granting the petition until the war was over. 'It would provide an opportunity for the new order to establish their structures and prove their seriousness of intent, as historical precedent required and as stated in canon law.'

He resumed his seat as various members of the assembly turned to their colleagues to debate his contribution.

The pope rose and was crowned with the tiara. He took the crozier in his right hand and leaned heavily on his Shepherd's Crook. He would grant the petition, he declared, and spontaneous applause echoed in the basilica. Tisserant watched with a jaundiced eye as Maglione relaxed in his chair. Max Steiger caught his eye and smiled triumphantly. However, the pope continued, canon law had to be observed and he would postpone the formal recognition of the Fratres until the war was ended.

'As suggested by our dear brother, Cardinal Tisserant,' he said. '*Procedamus in pace*,' he intoned. 'Let us go in peace.'

As soon as he'd departed, a buzz of conversation swept through the assembly. Tisserant sat apart, concentrating on displaying none of the small satisfaction he felt. He was powerfully aware that a young man's life hung in the balance and didn't want to tilt the scales.

The others drifted from the basilica and he waited until their footsteps faded before rising. As he'd anticipated, Max Steiger remained.

'I am granted my petition and you gain some petty vengeance, Eminence.'

'You got what you came for,' Tisserant said evenly. 'I have honoured our bargain.'

'Nevertheless,' Steiger said, 'you have placed yourself in the ranks of my enemies.'

'No,' Tisserant countered, 'I have placed myself on the side of the angels and their vengeance will not be petty.'

The master of ceremonies hovered at the door.

'His Holiness would like to see you, Eminence.'

Pius stood, like a tiny mannequin, in the middle of the Vatican sacristy. Augustinian friars moved about him like black wraiths, stripping him of his glorious vestments. Tisserant had a sudden vision of layer upon layer of cloth of gold peeling away to reveal nothing at the core, He felt relief when the white-clad figure emerged, like a butterfly from a chrysalis. The pope carried the equivalent weight of a soldier's pack every time he presided at a ceremony. Tisserant wondered how this, or any pope, could bear the burden of the papacy. When the last vestments had been spirited away to the massive wardrobes, the friars bowed in unison and disappeared.

Pius stood uncertainly for a time, his eyes huge and vulnerable behind the steel-rimmed spectacles. Slowly, his right hand rose to lift his skull cap and plant it more firmly on the crown of his head.

'You were opposed to the petition, Eminence,' he said.

'Yes, I was,' Tisserant admitted.

'And yet you counselled restraint and not refusal.'

'Sometimes,' Tisserant said slowly, 'it's necessary to be silent for the sake of a greater good. It isn't easy.'

'I know that, Eminence,' Pius said, with a sad smile.

Tisserant wasn't sure if the pope was referring to himself or to his irascible cardinal. Pius motioned him to join him at the vesting bench that stretched the length of the sacristy. He leaned his forearms on the bench and spoke so softly that Tisserant was obliged to move closer.

'Ambassador Titmann of the United States embassy came to see me late last night,' Pius confided. 'He told me that General Badoglio, the commander of the Italian armies, is negotiating with the Allies – in secret, of course.'

They both nodded, to acknowledge the oxymoron.

'The ambassador claims the war will be over soon.' He looked genuinely perplexed. 'Why are the Americans always so confident?' he murmured.

Tisserant leaned closer still, as if afraid of being overheard.

'They have a vast country and very little history,' he confided. 'Imagine never having to fight a war on your own soil or the luxury of having only two borders? From what I hear, the Mexicans want to be Americans and the Canadians consider themselves a more developed version of the species.'

Pius gave a startled laugh and quickly composed himself.

'The ambassador also delivered a document,' he said. His eyes became unfocused and he nodded a few times, as if carrying on some internal dialogue. He took a deep breath and continued. 'This document seems to suggest that a senior Vatican Bank official has been … indiscreet.' His right hand rose again and touched the cross he wore, as if for solace. 'The document would also seem to implicate Father Steiger.'

A shadow of disappointment crossed his face before he continued.

'I do not propose to take any action at this time,' he said. He looked directly at Tisserant, with haunted eyes. 'Am I wrong, Eugène?' he asked.

Tisserant was stunned by the question and by the naked pain of the man who asked it. Why ask me? he wondered. I didn't support your candidacy. I never deferred to you in council. We have never been friends. And yet, at that moment, he felt he'd heard the authentic voice of Eugenio Pacelli, the man, and his defences crumbled. Pius VII, Vicar of Christ on earth and Supreme Pontiff of the Universal Church, was utterly alone!

He was aware that the pope had an extended family in Rome. He knew they visited him once a year at Christmas, when they were carefully stage-managed by his domineering housekeeper. It was common knowledge among Vatican insiders that Mother Pascalina's influence extended to every part of his private life. He had two secretaries, an ambitious German Jesuit who carried more than a whiff of political scandal about him and another Jesuit who divided his time between lecturing at the Angelicum College and the pope's office. To anyone who bothered to listen,he complained that the parsimonious pope forbade him from using taxis.

Pius was a man who extended his arms in blessing over half a billion believers worldwide and hadn't a single friend he could embrace. Not for the first time, Tisserant thanked God for Emil, someone with whom he could be himself, warts and all. We raise a man up to the pedestal of the papacy, he thought bitterly. We imprison him in a role, distance him from reality and criticise him for being detached and aloof. Tisserant knew, in his heart, that he was looking at the loneliest man in the world, and in his heart he felt ashamed. He felt deeply ashamed that he, a Prince of the Church, had failed to befriend this most neglected of souls.

'I don't know,' he answered. 'We live in terrible times. None of us enjoys the luxury of being right all the time – even the pope. The best we can do is to act according to our conscience and do what we feel is right in our hearts. Time will tell, Eugenio,' he sighed. 'When this war is over, we'll have time to weigh The Fratres.'

'And Cardinal Maglione promises to keep a close watch on them in the meantime,' Pius said hopefully.

Tisserant wondered who would be keeping 'a close watch' on Cardinal Maglione but he kept that jaundiced thought to himself.

'I confess, I have always envied you, Eugène,' Pius said shyly. 'You have a wonderful facility with languages and such energy.

When I hear your voice outside my office, I know that you will come in like—'

'Like a bull in a china shop?' Tisserant offered.

'Pardon?'

'It's an expression my secretary uses. It means I lack the virtue of prudence. As for my facility with languages, I once boasted to Emil Dubois that I spoke seven languages. He was unimpressed. He said he'd had a student who spoke ten languages and didn't make sense in any one of them.'

'Did he?'

'What?'

'Speak ten languages?'

'It was a joke, Eugenio,' Tisserant said gently, 'at my expense.'

'Oh,' Pius said.

'As for my energy,' Tisserant continued, 'can I let you into a secret?'

'Yes, yes, of course.'

'Sometimes I take a siesta.'

'A siesta? You?'

'Yes, me. Every day I walk away from my desk and my diary and all the things I do that give me the illusion of achievement and I go to bed. When I wake up, I'm always a little annoyed to find that the Church seems to have managed without me.' He thought his heart would break at the slow smile that crept across the pope's face. 'We are no longer young, you and I, Eugenio,' he continued. 'Try to get some rest.' He reached out and patted the pope's hand. Pius took his hand and held it in a firm grip.

'Grazie, Eugène,' he said.

CARDINAL TISSERANT'S APARTMENTS, THE VATICAN

'Masterful, Eugène,' Emil declared.

'It was a sally rather than a rout, Emil,' Tisserant said tiredly.

'Max Steiger has suffered a setback, not a defeat. I've no doubt we'll cross swords again.'

They sat in silence until Tisserant felt ready to answer the unasked question. 'I couldn't sacrifice Captain Hamner,' he said, finally. 'As much as I dread the influence Steiger and his Fratres will exert on the pope and the Church, I felt that someone's life was not something I could ...' He lapsed into silence again, tugging his beard. 'I had to stay silent,' he said finally, 'and silence has never been my forte.'

'No, but you've never been one to put the institution before the person either, Eugène,' Emil said softly.

'How is he?'

'Sleeping. He walked in about an hour ago with a nasty bump behind the ear and rope burns on his wrists.' Emil sucked in a breath and continued. 'He was kept in the Santa Maria della Concezione – in the cellar.'

Tisserant stiffened and tugged his beard savagely.

'So,' he said, 'he was bound and condemned to spend the night with the bones of four thousand friars.'

'And a little Barberini Princess.'

'Did you ask—?'

'Of course. He just said he'd been to Russia. Can we keep him here?'

'Nothing stays secret here, Emil. We both know that. We must help Karl Hamner to disappear.'

THE CAPUCHIN INTERNATIONAL COLLEGE, ROME

The Swiss Guards at either side of the gate brought their halberds to the vertical in salute as the car sped from the Vatican. Karl sat in the back of the car with Emil and watched Rome go by. The monsignor attempted a half-hearted commentary on the churches and monuments that lined their route but lapsed into silence again before they'd crossed the Tiber.

Karl hadn't lost interest in the religious and historical treasures of Rome. He felt that recent events had shifted his focus from the past to the present. For him, the Ponte Vittoria Emmanuel would forever be associated with Sergeant Paulus and his troop of Wehrmacht veterans. He turned his head to track the passage of Tiber Island across the window and the memory that flashed before him was of a hospitable priest at an open door. The dome of the synagogue caught his eye for an instant and, instinctively, his hand moved to his pocket where a tiny rag doll had found sanctuary. Behind him, the dome of Saint Peter's loomed cold and remote over the Roman skyline. He did not look back.

They were crossing the quadrangle of the Capuchin International College when Karl stopped suddenly and cocked his head.

'What is it, Karl?' Emil asked anxiously.

'Someone's laughing,' Karl answered, and walked on.

The Capuchin priest hurried from behind his desk to greet them.

'Karl,' Emil began, 'I would like to introduce Père Marie-Benoît of—'

'Oh hush,' the Capuchin admonished him gently. 'You Vatican bureaucrats are so formal.' He stood close to Karl and looked at him intently. 'So this is the famous Captain Karl Hamner,' he smiled.

Karl blinked in surprise and opened his mouth to protest but the priest pressed on. 'I have friends among the Jews, Karl, who sing your praises. Enrico and his family wish to be remembered to you. Yes,' he added when he saw his look of concern, 'they are quite safe.'

He extended his hands. 'Welcome to the International College,' he said. Karl took his right hand and shook it. 'I should like to meet all of you, Karl Hamner,' the priest said softly.

Slowly, Karl drew his gloved hand from behind his back and placed it in the priest's hand.

'Where?' Père Marie-Benoît asked.

'Barbarossa.'

'My wound was at Verdun, in the last war,' he said. 'I was very young and I desperately wanted to recover – to get back the carefree boy I'd been. I didn't recover but I did heal – in time.

Come, sit!'

When they were seated, he leaned back in his chair. 'You are welcome to live here until this war is over, Karl.'

'You know that the Waffen SS are looking for me, Father?'

'Yes, I know that. The Waffen have hunted me from Marseille through Nice to Rome. They may actually catch me some day, but I refuse to hide in the meantime. You can regard the college as a sanctuary that will keep you safe within or as a doorway that will lead you out to all sorts of possibilities. The choice is yours. Emil tells me you are a historian.'

'Yes I am, Father.'

'Good. If you wish to study, it can be arranged. Our students go to the colleges in Rome while they live here. What would you like to study?'

'I'd like to study the Jews of Rome in the reign of Pope Pius XII,' he answered.

Père Marie-Benoît pursed his lips and looked at him thoughtfully. 'In Rome,' he said slowly, 'it is sometimes prudent to wait for a pope to die before examining his words and deeds.'

Karl nodded to acknowledge the warning. 'I can't unsee what I've seen, Father,' he said. 'I can't do that and be a historian – or a human being.'

'Very well,' the priest announced, 'we will make the arrangements tomorrow. Today, we must ensure the Waffen and any other wolves will have difficulty finding your scent.'

'How do you propose to do that, Father?'

'By turning you into somebody else, of course. Ah,' he continued, seeing Karl's puzzled face, 'I see that the Vatican bureaucrat has not told you everything. I am a Capuchin priest, Karl, you already know that. My doctorate in Theology was conferred on me for my study of Judaism. I am also a forger.'

'A forger?'

'Yes. I and my helpers in the college produce identity cards and travel documents for Jews and other refugees. If I say so myself, we have developed a certain competency.'

'Competent enough to spirit more than two thousand Jews out of Marseille,' Emil interjected.

'Please, Emil,' the priest protested before returning his attention to Karl. 'Like a good historian, you want to ask why, don't you?'

'Yes.'

'You see, Karl, I also found it difficult to believe the evidence of my own eyes. When I did, I was faced with a dilemma. I was a priest of the Roman Catholic Church, a Church that has never come to terms with the fact that Jews and Christians are sons of Abraham. I decided to champion the cause of the Jews. Naturally, that brought me into conflict with my own Church. What was the Church to do with this troublesome priest? What was the priest to do with a Church which preached love and practised blindness? We found a middle way. I don't hammer my opinions into Pacelli's door and he pretends not to know what I'm doing. We co-exist, Karl. One day, when all of this is over, we may reconcile. Enough!'

He opened a drawer and began to riffle through files.

'Some of our students return to their own countries on vacation and don't make it back.' He picked a file and opened it on his desk.

'This is a Polish student who was caught in Danzig. May the Lord be merciful to his soul. Oh I beg your pardon, this must sound very macabre. I haven't even asked if you would mind taking a dead man's name. I take it all for granted. Many families give a son his father's name. In religious life, a name is also passed to the next generation. Perhaps it's as close as we can come to having sons of our own.'

'What was his name, Father?'

'His name was Tomas. Would you be willing to be known as Tomas?'

He felt Emil's hand grip his arm and he clung to that anchor as waves of memories and emotions swept over him. He saw the smiling face, looming over an enormous snowball. He heard the steady drumming of the miner's heart when he'd held him close after his first terrifying taste of war at Smolensk. He felt again the power of those arms when the miner had carried him to the plane and freedom. When his tears had run their course, he raised his head and nodded.

'I would be honoured to be known as Tomas,' he said.

AUTHOR'S NOTE

Hitler invaded Yugoslavia in April 1940. Shortly afterwards, the Croat fascists were allowed to declare an independent Croatia under Ante Pavelič. Pavelič's group, the Ustashe (from 'ustati', to rise up) had resisted the Kingdom of Yugoslavia after the first World War and, under Mussolini's protection, Pavelič had planned the assassination of King Alexander of Yugoslavia.

The historical background to the setting up of the NDH (Nezavisna Drzava Hrvatska) or Independent State of Croatia was a combination of ancient loyalties to the papacy, going back thirteen hundred years, and the fact that both Serbs and Croats equated ethnicity and religious identity - Orthodox Serb versus Catholic Croat.

This was also the background to the campaign of terror the Ustashe carried out against Serb Orthodox Christians, Jews, gypsies and Communists between 1941 and 1945. It was an attempt to create a 'pure' Catholic Croatia by enforced conversion, deportation and extermination.

Pope Pius XII warmly endorsed Croat nationalism. When a national pilgrimage came to Rome, in 1939, the pope used a phrase first applied to the Croats by Pope Leo X, referring to them as 'the last outpost of Christianity'. 'The hope of a better future seems to be smiling on you,' Pius said. 'A future in which the relations between Church and State in your country will be regulated in harmonious action to the advantage of both.'

In April 1941, the first Jews were transported from Zagreb to a concentration camp at Danica.

Details of the the massacre of Serbs and the elimination of the Jews and gypsies were known by the Croatian Catholic priests and bishops. Indeed, as tribunals discovered, after the war, clergy often took a leading role in the atrocities.

By the most recent reliable reckoning, 487,000 Orthodox Serbs and 27,000 gypsies were massacred between 1941 and 1945 in the Independent State of Croatia. In addition, approximately 30,000 out of a population of 45,000 Jews were killed; 20,000 to 25,000 as a result of Ustashe death camps and another 7,000 deported to the gas chambers.

Historical Characters

Cardinal Eugène Tisserant (1884–1972)
A French cardinal of the Roman Catholic Church who participated in the conclave of 1939 that elected Eugenio Pacelli as Pope Pius XII.

Francis D'Arcy Osborne (1884–1964)
The British ambassador to the Vatican during the papacy of Pope Pius XII.

Doctor Carl-Ludwig Diego von Bergen (1872–1944)
Baron von Bergen was announced as German ambassador to the Vatican in 1920, however, he was not regarded as sufficiently pro-Nazi and was recalled to Berlin in 1943.

Ante Paveliç (1889–1959)
A Croatian fascist leader who ruled as Poglavnik, or head, of the independent state of Croatia, which was created as a puppet-state of Nazi Germany in occupied Yugoslavia. He was also the leader of the Croatian fascist militia, the Ustashe, who were responsible for atrocities against Orthodox Serbs, Jews and others during the war years. After the war, he fled to Rome and then Argentina. A Serb shot Paveliç near Buenos Aires in 1957 and he died of his injuries in 1959.

Father Ludwig Kaas (1881–1952)
A German Roman Catholic priest and politician during the Weimar Republic. Kaas was an advisor to Eugenio Pacelli when he served as a papal nuncio to Bavaria. During the war, he became the close confidant of Pope Pius XII.

Father Robert Leiber, SJ (1887–1967)
A German Jesuit who became the private secretary and close advisor of Pope Pius XII.

Cardinal Luigi Maglione (1877–1944)
An Italian cardinal who served as the Vatican Secretary of State under Pope Pius XII.

Pope Pius XII (1859-1958)

He was born Eugenio Pacelli, in Rome, and served as a papal nuncio and later as Cardinal Secretary of State under Pius XI. As Secretary of State, he signed a concordat between Germany and the Vatican in 1938. Elected Pope in 1939, he was leader of the Roman Catholic Church throughout the war and until his death in 1958. Pope Pius XII was criticised for failing to speak out against the Nazi extermination of the Jews in Europe, and the massacre of the Orthodox Serbs and others by the Independent State of Croatia under its leader Ante Paveliç. Immediately after his death, Pope Paul VI began the process for his canonisation. In 2009, Pope Pius XII was declared Venerable by Pope Benedict XVI.

Friedrich Werner von der Schulenburg (1875–1944)

A German diplomat and the last German ambassador to the Soviet Union before Operation Barbarossa. After the failed plot against Hitler in 1944, von der Schulenburg was hanged.

Vyacheslav Mikhailovich Molotov (1890–1986)

Molotov served as Minister for Foreign Affairs in the Soviet government from 1939 to 1947. He signed the Nazi–Soviet non-aggression pact with von Ribbentrop in 1939.

General Semyon Timoshenko (1895–1970)

A Soviet military commander of the Red Army at the beginning of Operation Barbarossa in 1941.

Lavrentiy Beria (1899–1953)

Chief of the Soviet security and police apparatus (NKVD) under Stalin.

General Georgy Zhukov (1896–1974)

A Soviet general who played a pivotal role in defending Moscow during Operation Barbarossa.

Joseph Stalin (Iosif Vissaryonovich) (1878–1953)

A Georgian-born Soviet politician and Bolshevik revolutionary. He was First General Secretary of the Communist Party of the Soviet Union from 1922 until his death. In August 1939, Stalin's USSR signed a non-aggression pact with Nazi Germany. In June 1941, Germany invaded the USSR under the codename Operation Barbarossa.

Lazar Kaganovich (1893–1991)
A Soviet politician and administrator. He was one of the main associates of Stalin. For his ruthlessness in carrying out Stalin's orders, he was known as 'Iron Lazar'.

Anastas Mikoyan (1895–1978)
A Soviet politician and close ally of Stalin. He served as Minister for Trade throughout the Second World War and was placed in charge of food and supplies when Germany invaded the Soviet Union in 1941.

Waffen SS
In the early days of Operation Barbarossa, the Waffen SS fought Soviet partisans behind the German lines. Later, they were removed from the control of the regular army and took part in the murder of Soviet prisoners and the liquidation of Jews in the Soviet Union.

General Gunther Adolf Ferdinand 'Hans' von Kluge (1892-1944)
Commander of the Fourth Army Central at the beginning of Operation Barbarossa, he was promoted later in the campaign after the dismissal of General Fedor von Bock. General von Kluge was implicated in the assassination attempt on Hitler and died by suicide in 1944.

General Franz Halder (1884-1972)
Chief of the General Staff. Halder's opposition to Operation Barbarossa and to Hitler's strategy led to his demotion in 1942. While he did not actively participate in the assassination attempt on Hitler, he was arrested and sent to a concentration camp where he remained until the war was over.

Bishop Alojzije Miscic (1859-1942)
The Catholic bishop of Mostar in Croatia. He was an enthusiastic supporter to Ante Paveliç and the Ustashe and advocated the mass conversion of Orthodox Serbs to Roman Catholicism.

Archbishop Aloysius Stepinac (1898-1960)
Became Archbishop of Zagreb in 1937. After the German invasion of Yugoslavia, Stepinac issued proclamations celebrating the new Croatian state and welcomed the Ustashe leadership of Ante Paveliç. In 1943, he objected to the Nazi laws, the persecution of Jews and was critical of Ustashe atrocities. Stepinac was convicted of collaboration by the Yugoslav communist government in 1946 and imprisoned. Later, he was released and

kept under house arrest. Pope Pius XII made him a cardinal in 1953 and he died, probably as a result of poisoning, in 1960. Aloysius Stepinac was declared a martyr and was beatified by Pope John Paul II in 1998.

Fra Miroslav Filipovic (1915–46)
A Croatian nationalist and Roman Catholic priest, he was convicted of war crimes by a German military court and a Yugoslav civil court and hanged in Belgrade.

Ustashe
A Croatian, fascist, anti-Yugoslav, separatist movement. The Ustashe promoted persecution and genocide against Serbs, Jews and Roma people during the war. It was responsible for atrocities against various communities and in concentration camps throughout Croatia. It is estimated that almost 300,000 people were murdered by the Ustashe before the German surrender in 1945.

General Fedor von Bock (1880–1945)
Von Bock is best known for commanding Operation Typhoon, the failed attempt to capture Moscow during the winter of 1941. After the Soviet counter-offensive, he recommended a withdrawal and was relieved of his command by Hitler. He personally despised Nazism but did not sympathise with plots to overthrow Hitler. Von Bock, along with his wife and daughter, were killed by a strafing British fighter-bomber on 4 May 1945 as they travelled by car to Hamburg.

General Erich von Manstein (1887–1993)
During Operation Barbarossa, von Manstein served under General Hoepner. In September 1941, von Manstein was appointed commander of the Eleventh Army tasked with invading the Crimea. He was dismissed by Hitler in 1944 because of their disagreements over military strategy. In 1949, he was tried in Hamburg for war crimes and sentenced to eighteen years in prison. He was released after four years and became a military advisor to the West German government.

General Maximilian von Weichs (1881–1954)
Von Weichs led the Second Army, as part of von Bock's Army Group Centre at the Battle of Smolensk and later at Bryansk.

General Erich Hoepner (1886–1944)
Commander of the Fourth Panzer Group during Operation Barbarossa,

Hoepner was arrested and executed for his part in the failed assassination attempt on Hitler in 1944.

General Konstantin Rokossovsky (1896-1968)
Rokossovsky played a key role in the defence of Moscow. He went on to even greater success during the counter-offensive and became a marshal of the Soviet Union.

General Leonid Govorov (1897-1955)
An artillery commander, Govorov commanded an army during the Battle of Moscow in November 1941. From 1942 to the end of the war, he commanded the Leningrad Front and reached the rank of Marshal of the Soviet Union in 1944.

Doctor Rusinovic
A Croatian medical doctor, Rusinovic represented the new Croatian state at the Vatican.

Father Krunoslav Dragonovic (1903-83)
A Croatian Roman Catholic priest, Dragonovic was accused of being one of the main organisers of the 'ratlines' which helped war criminals escape from Europe after the Second World War. His centre of operations for the Croat ratline was the monastery of San Girolamo in Rome, from where he is believed to have helped Ante Paveliç and Klaus Barbie escape to South America.

Albert von Kesselring (1885-1960)
A German Luftwaffe General during the Second World War, von Kesselring defended Italy against the Allied invasion until he was injured in an accident. He was tried for war crimes and sentenced to death, though his sentence was commuted to life imprisonment and he was released in 1952 on health grounds.

Pè re Marie-Benoît (1895-1990)
A Capuchin Franciscan friar, Marie-Benoît helped smuggle approximately 4,000 Jews to safety from Nazi-occupied southern France. While in Rome, he set up a unit in the International College to forge identity papers and travel documents for refugees. In 1966, he was honoured with the Medal of Righteousness among the Nations for his courage. His actions on behalf of Jews during the Holocaust earned him the epithet 'Father of the Jews'.